FLAMES OF REBELLION

"Lark, I know not what folly I bring upon myself with this," Christopher whispered hoarsely, touching her face. "Or upon you. But I care not . . . I care only for this, for you."

With tumultuous, breathless ardor then, sparing no more time for gentleness or wooing, the earl crossed a forbidden boundary and merged with the cotter's lass. He became part of her, and she a part of him. And neither would ever be the same again.

The Trysting Moon

≫ DEBORAH SATINWOOD ≪

HarperPaperbacks
A Division of HarperCollinsPublishers

HarperPaperbacks *A Division of* HarperCollins*Publishers*
10 East 53rd Street, New York, N.Y. 10022

Cover illustration by R.A. Maguire

First printing: November 1993

Printed in the United States of America

HarperPaperbacks, HarperMonogram, and colophon are
trademarks of HarperCollins*Publishers*

❖ 10 9 8 7 6 5 4 3 2 1

This one's for you, Beverly. . . .

Get up, our Anna dear, from the weary spinning wheel;
For your father's on the hill, and your mother is asleep:
Come up above the crags, and we'll dance a highland reel
Around the fairy thorn on the steep.

—from an Ulster ballad by Sir Samuel Ferguson

1

Ireland, 1796

A miserable night it was. Clouds galloped
like pale horses across the sky, racing from north to
south in some celestial contest of speed. Beneath
them the sea looked alive as well, leaping upward
and unwinding its silver waves in some ancient water
dance. Winter blew not far away, and as a grim
reminder she would leave her icy calling card this
night upon brittle branch and heather spray.

Lark Ballinter huddled more deeply into her
threadbare cloak, shoving her mittened hands inside
its pockets and bending her head against the gales of
freezing wind. No moon shone and no lantern swung
from her hand. At a time when other, more prudent
souls dreamed in their beds, she walked along a
crooked path of stone beside the sea.

At least her destination was only a little farther

now. A few more paces and the path would fork and climb steadily upward, away from the sea and toward a stony brae. God willing, she would not have to wait long. Then she could do what she had to do and hurry home again. Pushing down her dread, she searched for the eerie landmark that was the meeting place, that bleak, gnarled skeleton with its twisted trunk and knotted branches.

"'Tis only a tree," she chided herself through teeth clenched from the cold. "An ugly old misshapen thing not even fit to grace a boneyard."

But legend argued otherwise, and as Lark sighted its towering outline at her journey's end, she could not help but wonder at its spell.

The tree grew atop a hill's crown, its bark so pitted and black some said it had been born at the time of earth's creation. Its bony twigs turned upward as if supplicating the heavens, and its roots bored deeply into the ground. Leafless rowan bushes encircled its trunk, their branches bowing down like faithful worshipers kneeling before an idol. Oddly, not even the sea breezes dared fret about this mystical place but left it still, undisturbed, frozen in time.

The villagers said it was the tree of enchanted beings, who danced and sang and plotted their capricious deeds beneath its darkened shade. Shy young milkmaids made offerings here, pouring forth from their pails the froth of first milk. No mortal hand was ever to touch the woody, living shrine, not even its deadwood, and woe to the one who dared.

So grew the Faery Thorn. . . .

Slowly Lark approached it. Never had she entered its inner circle or touched its rough bark. Already she risked danger from men through her acts of folly; the faeries' ire she hardly needed.

She shivered. Soon *he* would come. Each Sabbath they met in this clandestine way, at midnight and with hoods drawn over their heads, for his identity must not be discovered, nor hers. With a cloak wrapped round his form and a dark-colored hood drawn to shadow his face, he would appear atop the hill and, after pausing to search for her own shrouded figure, saunter forward on his long booted legs, trespassing boldly across the Faery Thorn's sacred ground as if he felt no fear of its evil magic.

How he arrived in this place was a puzzle. Whether a boat rode the waves just out of sight or a horse was tethered over the rise, she never knew. At times she thought the man had no transportation at all but simply materialized in the frigid air like a spectral curl of smoke.

Even before he came into view tonight Lark felt his presence, a presence that was an inexplicable mixture of turbulence and calm, wildness and mastery. She sensed he was a young man, for the tilt of his head and the quickness of his stride suggested not only agility, but a certain recklessness found in men not yet past prime.

As for his manner, it was never warm in the way of a comrade, nor was it grateful for the information she passed. It was cool, disdainful, barely more than forbearing. But after all, this was no lover's tryst, it was the perilous business of the times.

Now she caught sight of him, a mere movement of black against the sapphire-gray sky. As he crested the hill only a fleeting glimpse of his covered head appeared, an eerie, disembodied image before his shoulders, torso, and legs joined it. She did not move as he halted and focused his eyes to sight her. As the wind lifted his cape, she thought he might have been one of the Faery Thorn's deities, some other-worldly king surveying his realm. For a moment Lark almost believed him inhuman.

As he neared, Lark's fingers curled more tightly in her pockets. The muscles of her neck grew taut with expectancy. As was customary when he approached, she pulled her hood more securely about her face to hide it.

One might have thought her cohort would raise a hand to signal greeting or call out a word, but that was never his habit. Indeed, he spoke little during these frequent, fugitive moments, and when he spoke, his voice blended with the sea's roar, just as his form melted into and out of the night in a strangely insubstantial way.

At last he stood before her, more tall than was natural, more ominous for his lack of visible features. His shoulders were wide beneath the cape, as wide as those of some mythical warrior of old. His very being seemed enlivened by some force of energy not possessed of ordinary men. It was strange how Lark felt intrigued by him, but perhaps, she thought with a thrill of danger, one is always intrigued by that which frightens the soul.

"So . . . the Faery Queen awaits me." He uttered the words in a voice low and chilling to match his dark aura.

Lark nodded mutely.

"And what will she offer me tonight?"

Taking a deep breath and staring up at his concealed face, Lark fought a strong sense of vulnerability.

But she would not let a man such as this see her weaknesses lest he take advantage of them. She felt proud of herself when her voice came strong and steady to deliver the critical dispatch.

"He said he could not yet make payment. You requested, of course, at least fifteen thousand pounds, but he has only five to give you. 'Twill take him two or three more months to collect the difference."

She watched her dark companion closely for some reaction. Rain had begun to fall, descending in erratic droplets so cold they might have been chips of ice. He tilted his head back to observe the roiling clouds for a moment.

Lark glanced at the sea and the clouds herself, then back at him, wondering now if it was her piece of information he pondered so intently or only the weather. The message she had given him was a coded one, of course, like all the ones before it, but through hours of study she had managed to decipher most of its meaning. Suddenly, for the first time, she wanted *him* to know that, wanted this phantomlike figure to know he did not deal with an ignorant messenger used only as a pawn by him and his co-conspirators.

"He speaks of men, of course," she announced boldly. "At the moment the French government has only five thousand soldiers outfitted to sail for our cause—ten thousand short of what you'll be needing."

Her companion's head snapped downward from its viewing of the sky, and she felt his gaze fasten upon her face. Mustering courage, she stared back just as fiercely, then suppressed a shiver as he took a step forward.

"Ye were in a precarious position before," he

said with contempt, as if knowing she had revealed her knowledge only out of pride. "Now ye are in a dangerous one."

"I *know* what position I am in," she answered with unshrinking courage, her tone as cold as his. "And I'll not be trading it for any other."

He raised a clenched fist and shook it at the sky, exclaiming, "God save me from the foolishness of women! Here we are, standin' on the very brink of revolution in Ireland, and through some cruel twist of fate, I must get the information crucial to my cause from a presumptuous *peasant* lass! I do not deserve this thorn in the side . . . no matter what my sins, I do not deserve *this.*"

He stopped speaking, then bent his head down as if reevaluating his problem and considering a change of tactics.

"Do ye know there are United Irishmen rotting in gaol?" he said at last, using a tone one would use with a dull-witted child. "And do ye know that there are even *more* rotting in coffins for the risk they have taken to win Ireland her independence? Have ye any idea of the danger involved in this plot?" He snorted. "Bloody hell! Of course ye don't."

Lark raised her chin a little higher, biting hard upon her lip, not only to stop its fearful quivering, but to squelch a hot retort. Gone was the phantom's usual cool dispassion. Tonight his temper seemed to be a furious one, and her impertinent remarks had only unleashed it. As for the fear she felt, *that*, she would never let him see.

As if taking her silence for admission of all he believed, her companion continued his dire warnings. "It doesn't take much to convict an Irish Catholic rebel, ye know. One slip o' the tongue, lassie, an' ye could find yerself in trouble. Have ye ever watched a gibbetin'?" He took another step forward until the hem of his cape touched her skirts. "Nay? How would it feel, do ye think, to have yer soft little gullet squeezed by a braided noose?"

To her horror, he swiftly put his hands to her throat and tightened his fingers until they pressured the vital pulse below her ear. The menace of the cold leather gloves, the nearness of his towering form, and the fear of his intent caused Lark's knees to wobble and her nerves to freeze. What if she were to faint and fall at his feet, be completely at this devil's mercy? At the very thought, she could not keep herself from swaying.

As if realizing her unsteadiness, the phantom removed his hands from her throat and clasped them about her waist, dragging her close against his chest. She could smell the earthy odor of horses and hear the strong beat of his heart. The sound disconcerted her, making her aware that he was not some cold apparition but a man, warm and breathing and alive.

Suddenly, struck by some perverse whimsy, she felt the urge to reach up and draw back his hood, behold the face of the one who both terrorized and fascinated, and uncover once and for all the mystery that bound her. More insanely still, just as one is tempted to stroke the head of an untamed beast despite its dangerous jaws, she yearned to put out a quivering hand and touch her cohort's flesh. She knew it would be young and vital.

When Lark would have pulled away, her captor increased his grip and bent so low that his breath brushed her cheek. It was warm, like the touch of summer's sun, and she could feel the gloved fingers move upon her arm, less roughly than she would have thought.

"Remember, colleen," he warned in a soft voice, "one slip o' the tongue—just one wee slip—and ye'll find yer bonnie neck bruised."

Speaking just as gravely as he, she replied, "Rest assured, I have good mastery over my tongue."

As if she had made some clever joke, he laughed out loud. The fact that he released her in the midst of his mirth was little consolation.

Lark was highly indignant. "I made no jest," she said, putting hands to her hips.

He chuckled and in an unlikely show of concern reached out to pull the hood more snugly about her face. "Nay? Then perhaps 'tis just my turn of mind tonight. Yet I wonder how far I can trust ye with the secrets of our cause. Do ye never gossip with the other maids, lass, or whisper confidences against yer lover's ear?"

She drew herself up. "I have no lover."

Instead of giving him reason to respect her independence, her declaration seemed only to arouse her cohort to amusement again. She could have sworn a broad grin brightened the darkness of his hood.

"I hardly thought ye did," he said, adding to her pique. Then, as if sharing a secret, he leaned close and whispered, "A man can tell, ye know. 'Tis obvious by the way a woman walks."

Unable to help herself, Lark shifted on the uneven ground, resisting the impulse to ask him the details of this peculiar male knowledge. Instead she said, "Shall we be getting on with our business now you've been entertained?"

"Very well," her companion conceded after a

moment, as if reluctant to relinquish the lighter mood. Never had he indulged in so much conversation with her. "But why don't ye save yerself a great deal of future trouble and get out of this game like a good lass. I'll correspond with yer contact directly from this night forward. Just give me his name and the way to reach him. There's no reason for yer bein' involved in this at all—I thought 'twas foolhardy from the first."

Unwilling to let her panic show at the mere mention of such an arrangement, Lark was silent for a moment. In times of revolution no one could be trusted, not even those who claimed to be comrades. This man she would not trust with the life of a flea, much less that of her contact. "Nay," she said simply.

The agent's hand jerked at his side as if he yearned to take some physical action against her. "Ye obviously pride yerself upon bein' uncooperative," he said, his voice sharp and humorless now. "But I warn ye, lass, 'twill only bring ye trouble before we see an end to it all."

Lark had had enough of his scorn. "Careful, or you'll find yourself alone here next Sabbath."

"Do not threaten me, lass."

"Then do not insult me."

Though their faces were invisible to each other, Lark felt their gazes meet in that moment, as if some instinct locked male and female eyes together much in the way two sun rays can merge into one bright beam. Seconds passed, during which her companion made no reply. But she thought he finally smiled, for a bit of white seemed to flash in the black recesses of his hood. Then he made a token bow, and the breeze ruffled his garments, giving Lark a brief hope that a glimpse of him might be possible. But, quickly, he put a gloved hand to the hood and shifted it back into place.

"My regrets, mistress. For the insult, of course. And for yer . . . tragic lack of a lover."

Bristling, Lark managed an answer through her teeth. "Until next Sabbath." With that, she pivoted on her heel and began to walk away. Knowing that the faceless man probably watched, she slowed her step with conscious effort and strolled along more leisurely, swinging her hips until she feared they would slip entirely from their sockets.

She smiled smugly. It was the first time *she* had ever dismissed *him,* the first time she had ever turned her back upon the formidable black form even while it faced her.

He made no retort. She did not know if he continued to stare after her or if he made his own unconcerned way back over the hill. Perhaps he did neither. Perhaps he only idled awhile, surveyed the wild landscape, and plotted sly designs while the rain pelted his back beneath the charmed branches of the Faery Thorn.

"Blasted devil!" Lark mumbled when she was well out of earshot. With difficulty she pushed herself up from a moss-coated rock that had just tripped her up. "He's surely one of Satan's own! Saints preserve me, and keep me from having to deal with him much longer!" She steadied herself against the gusting wind and raised her muddied skirts. "If only Virgil hadn't asked me to do this thing for him. If only . . ."

She closed her mouth upon the words. It was not

that she didn't believe fiercely in the cause she helped, whose aim it was to overthrow the English-appointed puppet government. She wanted to help win fair treatment and a say in Ireland's future for her fellow Catholics, but she had never intended to join in their fight for freedom quite so completely, quite so . . . dangerously.

Passing a hand across her brow to wipe away sea spray and rain, she stumbled on, clenching her teeth against their painful chattering. Doubts assailed her, evoked more by exhaustion than by any lapse in her dedication. Perhaps that hateful scoundrel she had just left was right. Perhaps she was not up to political intrigue, secrets of state, and midnight meetings. Perhaps she should be like other girls and stay home beside the hearth.

"Aagh! I'll not be letting that blackguard weaken my will and make me a coward! I'll not be giving up the cause no matter how often he threatens me with harm!"

Sniffing, she trudged on, then halted suddenly at an eerie sound. Was that a feeble cry riding upon the wind? She waited, but it did not come again, or if it did, the rumble of surging breakers drowned it. More uneasy than ever now, Lark continued along the path, watching the shadows alertly.

Turning in the direction of the cottage, she looked up, not yet expecting to see the outline of its welcome shape, for it was much too dark. But as she focused her gaze the tiniest flicker of light caught her eye. She quickened her pace until she could distinguish its source: a candle glowing faintly in the window—a candle she knew she had not left burning.

Immediately she surmised her uncle had been

unable to sleep and even now sat over a bottle of whiskey, hoping to ease his cares. Well, it would not be the first time he had caught her out, and though he would frown at her with concern and a little disappointment, he would never demand an explanation.

But what if the candle burned for another reason? Her breath caught. Perhaps her brother Jamie's cough had worsened, and he had awakened feverish. Suddenly anxious, Lark began to run across the turf as fast as the sodden hem of her gown would allow. She did not know why she approached the window of the cottage instead of bursting through the door, she did so without conscious thought, standing on tiptoe and peering through the hazy glass.

Simultaneously, horror froze her features.

Scattered papers, open books, and the sprawled body of her uncle Jerome lay together in a jumble upon the floor. The poor elderly man rested facedown, a candlestick without its candle lying within reach of his hand. His nightcap was displaced and his head was bare, bare except for its fringe of gray . . . and its gruesome stain of blood.

Above him, with a hand firm upon the body's wrinkled neck, crouched the figure of a dark-cloaked man. . . .

His face, Lark thought in that dizzying moment, was the most striking she had ever seen, an odd blend of classic line and hard masculine expression. His features were so well cut, his jaw so cleanly contoured, and his head so proudly set that he could have been some dashing hero from an ancient storybook. Nothing about his visage was displeasing to the eye . . . but his pose over her uncle's body told her he was a murderer.

In a sudden, violent gesture he threw back his

drenched black cape revealing a finely ruffled shirt, fawn-colored breeches, and expensive black boots. Lark noticed the boots were splattered with heavy mud.

She felt a sudden terrible suspicion. Could this golden-haired man and the fierce rebel agent she had just met be one and the same? Could that dark, unnamed spy have conjured up a flying black steed, one just as wild as he, and arrived here at the cottage ahead of her?

Nay, 'twas impossible, she reassured herself frantically. Every inch of this man's garb, every movement of his body, bespoke wealth, privilege, and power. He was no low-bred, coarse-spoken rebel, but some arrogant member of the aristocracy she so heartily despised.

He rose up now, unbending his long legs, and for a moment stood staring down at the body at his feet. By his expression he seemed to be at war with himself, fighting some inner battle, evidenced by the glimmer of indecision crossing his face. And then, suddenly, he was gone, leaving the room to its deadly stillness.

Lark longed to scream madly, to run for help. But she could ill afford to call attention to herself; she could not ensnare in her intricate web any neighbors whose consciences were clear. They were not to be involved in this twisted plot, not to be endangered.

Not, at least, until she had had a little time to think.

2

Autumn had settled fully upon the land, adding splashes of gold to the usual emerald hues, abandoning everywhere ragged leaves and withered stalks. Wildflowers bloomed no more, and tender creatures of the field busily stored up food. It was a season of dying.

In the lonely hour after Jerome Ballinter's roughly made coffin had been sunk forever into the Irish earth, Sebastian O'Keefe strolled with Lark upon the homeward road to her cottage, his impatient gait slowed to match her less hurried steps. For the duration of the two-mile journey the pair had trailed behind the other mourners, keeping their thoughts unspoken as they passed moldering stone walls and thatched huts where nothing stirred but a humid breeze. When a flock of sheep crossed the path, Sebastian stepped into their midst without a word and helped the shepherd prod his lagging charges off the lane.

He was a tinker by trade, and with his dark-visaged face and flashing eyes he resembled a Gypsy, a flamboyant wanderer of the road. Lark thought surely he had come from a place of camp fires and storytelling and fevered dances, but she had never heard him speak of it. On the subject of his origins he was strangely, almost guardedly, silent.

He had dined often at their table these past months, sharing with her uncle Jerome a passion for ships and sailing and anything connected with the sea. Upon reflection it was rather odd to Lark how the young man had entered their lives so precipitously, having met Uncle on the old man's usual Saturday night at the alehouse and afterward accepting every invitation to their cottage. With little waste of time, he had become her most persistent suitor. Still, Lark did not resent his presence, for he was pleasant enough, though his manner was often more intense than made for easy company.

"'Tis lonely here," Sebastian commented as they resumed their walk through a patch of fog. "And now you will be lonely, I suppose—you and wee Jamie."

Overwhelmed suddenly by a need to voice her fear and grief to a sympathetic ear, Lark reached out to him and allowed him to pull her against his chest, welcoming the feel of a human touch. With Uncle gone, and amidst her precarious circumstances, it felt good to have a place to lay her head, to shed tears upon a masculine shoulder.

For a few minutes she remained pressed against him, taking some comfort from the heat of his body even if the intimacy did nothing to stir her. Instead another male presence came to mind, one that both intrigued and frightened her. How could the tall black-garbed spy who had held her to his chest last eve—as if it were his prerogative to do so—evoke more feeling than this pleasant man who posed no threat? Quickly, as if to defy the phantom who had insinuated himself into her thoughts, she clasped her arms more tightly around Sebastian's slender waist.

Encouraged, he took her hands in his and laced their fingers together. Then he raised her hand to his lips and kissed it in a courtly fashion, showing as he often did a polish of manners that matched his refinement of speech—oddities, she thought, for one of low birth and simple tastes. When he lifted her chin a bit so that he might kiss her mouth, she was surprised, but in a sort of desperate need she could not explain she welcomed the kiss, her very first from any man. Would such an intimacy, the mere touching of mouths, help ease her sorrow, her fear, her loneliness? Would it increase her feelings for Sebastian? She closed her eyes and hoped.

After a moment he drew back his head and frowned as he searched her face for reaction. She knew he would find none there, for though she felt no disgust in his arms, neither did she feel any swell of passion.

"I'm deeply sorry about Jerome," he murmured after a few seconds, his obvious displeasure with her indifference deepening his voice. "I would not have thought such a gentle man would have an enemy in the world. . . ."

"'Twas a terrible shock."

"Aye. . . ." Sebastian took her hands again. "Have they any idea who . . . did the vile deed?"

She studied his thin face, noting the familiar jutting chin and downwardly curved mouth, and wished she could trust him with the secrets she shouldered. But she could hardly say that a finely dressed Loyalist had strolled into the humble cottage, strewn papers about looking for communiqués, and then throttled her uncle for political secrets the poor old man knew nothing at all about. She could hardly tell Sebastian O'Keefe that she was a rebel spy, a conspirator of the most traitorous kind against the Irish government.

At her hesitation he looked at her strangely.

"N-nay," she said. "Nay. They've not the faintest idea who killed Uncle."

"What did the magistrate say?"

"Och! Hardly a thing." Lark could not keep the bitterness from her voice. Her hatred for those titled lords who ruled the country ran too deeply. "Why should that pompous toff be caring one whit about a simple cotter?" she cried, tossing her mahogany hair in its black kerchief. "All Uncle's death means to him is one less mouth for Ireland to feed. Why, I've no doubt a'tall the man'd grieve more for the loss of one of his hunting hounds than for my own dear uncle."

The burst of anger combined with her already high emotional state put Lark near to tears again, and Sebastian tugged insistently upon her arm. "Let's walk along the sea. 'Tis a fine day for it."

They crossed over to the seaward path, their black leather shoes leaving faint tracks on the damp grass. Here the trees grew more stunted, crouching defensively to prepare for the winter winds that would soon shriek across the ocean.

"The villagers say rebels are roaming the country-side," Sebastian commented after they had reached the rise overlooking the sea. "They say they're robbing homes of weapons, even killing for guns and powder at times. They'll do anything to gather arms for the uprising they hope to incite. A ruthless bunch they are." He looked at Lark closely. "Perhaps your uncle was the victim of such wicked shenanigans?"

Lark lifted her shoulders, stared expressionless toward the sea. "'Tis possible, I suppose."

"Bloody devils!" Sebastian exclaimed. "The government should round up the lot and hang them."

"They say there's not enough proof to try the leaders."

"Rubbish!"

Glancing at the young man by her side, Lark wondered about him. She had heard him enter into political discussions such as this with her uncle before, prodding the apathetic old man to voice an opinion, growing frustrated when he would not comment either on the Loyalist viewpoint or on the cause of the underground United Irishmen.

"Of course," Sebastian continued in a more conciliatory tone, "the rebels do seem to have some legitimate grievances. . . ."

"I wouldn't be knowing. I'm hardly interested in politics."

Sebastian moved to stand before her, his action so abrupt and aggressive that it seemed to carry warning. "You should take an interest. If the rebels manage to bring the French over to their side and start a revolution against the government, we could all be involved in a bloody mess."

Lark had to hold her tongue to keep from lashing out at him. He seemed almost to be goading her. How could he not see the justness of the rebel cause? He was of the lower class, too, after all.

"Such serious thoughts cause my head to ache," she said, using the convenient feminine excuse. Wherever Sebastian's sentiments lay, it would not do to reveal the vehemence of her own, for he was a clever man whose suspicions she would be foolish to rouse.

"What will you do now your uncle's gone?" he asked, breaking the silence a moment later.

Tilting her head back, Lark stared at the oyster-colored clouds. "I hardly know. Uncle Jerome lost his lease on the property last week. That high-nosed buffoon of a landlord said 'twas more profitable to graze cattle than to let a cotter farm it. Blasted greedy gentry! We were to be turned out today, Jamie and me. But the priest went a-pleading to the landlord, and the old skinflint finally consented to let us stay on another few days. Big-hearted of him, wasn't it now?"

"Have you no money?" Sebastian asked.

She was reluctant to admit she hadn't even a penny to her name, as Sebastian would surely insist upon giving her silver, and she was too proud to accept.

"We have the pony Jerome used for plowing," she answered. "Jamie and I will go to Dublin tomorrow and sell him at the fair."

"Lark . . ." He paused, taking her hand in his and shifting his feet upon the stony ground. "I know 'tis not decent of me to speak so on the day of your uncle's funeral, but when your time of mourning has ended, would you . . . would you consider becoming my wife?"

Hiding her chagrin, Lark stared down at his hand, which gripped her fingertips. It was hard and brown and finely boned, much like his face. Wanting to judge his expression, she directed her scrutiny upward. His mysterious eyes, oval in shape, burned now with their usual intensity. She thought he had the most willful face she had ever seen, but most disturbing of all, it lacked tenderness, at least the kind of tenderness one would hope to find in a lover's look. There was not even the glint of common lust in the depths of his eyes, such as she found in those of the randy village lads.

"I . . ." She trailed off, not knowing quite how to respond. She did not love this man, a man of many inconsistencies, but she was fond of him, used to his sitting by her side at the table, accustomed to his presence by the fireside. And considering the vulnerable state in which she found herself now, a man's support was tempting. Yet she held back.

"'Tis a kind offer," she said, knowing that marriage to Sebastian would put an end to her involvement with the rebel cause. "But I cannot."

"And why not?" They had resumed walking side by side, and now Sebastian forced her to stop and pay closer attention to him. His expression was so fierce, his breathing so uneven, Lark feared his temper hovered upon the brink of explosion.

"You need a husband to support you, and Jamie needs a man about," he said. "'Tis a hard life for a woman alone, and you have no other suitors. At least you've told me that you don't."

"'Tis too soon," she replied. "I'm in mourning, after all. It would hardly be appropriate—"

"I fear you've not listened to a word I've said." Annoyance marked Sebastian's tone. "As I told you, we needn't marry until your mourning has ended."

Lark lowered her eyes, too weary to debate with him. "I should be getting home. The pony needs feeding."

In uncomfortable silence they entered the violet shade of the thatched, rectangular byre, and while Sebastian lounged sullenly against the door, Lark tramped through moldy straw and fondly caressed the neck of the sand-colored Connemara pony.

"Do you never hear from your brother in France, Lark?" her suitor asked suddenly, catching her off guard. "I've always wondered—what sort of business does he do there?"

Avoiding the tinker's probing eyes, Lark went to open the grain bin and scoop out a generous measure. "I've no idea," she said lightly. "France was in near turmoil when Virgil made arrangements for me and Jamie to leave there. My mother and father had just died in gaol—"

"Accused of being revolutionaries, as I recall."

"Aye," she admitted, assuming that Uncle Jerome had babbled in his ale. "After the death of my parents, Virgil went away to work in the vineyards. He was a man, after all, and wanted to make his own way in life. He hardly could bear the responsibility of raising Jamie and me, and so he sent us back here to Ireland, knowing Uncle Jerome could provide a more stable home for us. I did receive a few letters from him at first, for he was concerned that we had settled in, but since then there has been no word at all."

She dumped the mixture of oats and bran into the feed trough and watched the pony's muzzle sink deep into the pile of grain. All the while she held her breath, hoping that her lies had discouraged her curious suitor from pursuing the particulars of her brother's life.

Sebastian crossed the short space between them and grasped her arm, turning her around to face him. "That makes my point clear. You need me. I want to look after you, take care of you. We'd get on well together, I know it." He glanced down at her aproned black dress and her old ill-fitting shoes whose scuffed toes peeked out from beneath a too-short hem. "I could give you better, Lark. And Jamie, too. Won't you say yes?"

Before she could speak he bent his head and for the second time that day kissed her, chastely at first, then with near vehemence. She allowed it to go on, even tried to enjoy it, to capture the passion that he displayed. But when he finally drew back she raised her hand to her mouth and without consciously meaning to, wiped the sheen of dampness away.

"Why don't you just say you find me disgusting?" Sebastian demanded, his face darkening with anger. Without another word he swung around to leave.

"Sebastian!" Unable to let him go in such a temper, Lark ran after him and reached him just as he put a hand on his horse's harness to yank the reins around.

"Please, Sebastian . . ." Breathless with exertion and with a confusion of sentiments she could not begin to name or understand, Lark threw her arms around him, losing her shawl, and laid her smooth ivory cheek against the prickly tweed of his coat. "I don't want you to go like this, I don't want you to be angry with me. You're rushing me, that's all it is, rushing me into something I'm not ready to think about so soon after Uncle's death."

He stood stiffly, silently, within her embrace, and for a moment she feared he would disengage her arms and push them away. But, at last, she felt his chest rise and fall with a heavy sigh.

"Very well, then," he murmured. "Perhaps I am being too impatient."

She drew back and put her hand on his in a brief caress. "You'll be back tomorrow? You'll see me to Dublin?"

He hesitated, but only for a moment. "Aye. I'll see you to Dublin."

As he climbed onto his wagon and released the brake, Lark stood silently at the pony's head. Then with troubled eyes she followed the progress of the vehicle down the narrow lane, hearing the tinkle of its assorted pots and pans fade away.

Why do I cling so doggedly to Sebastian O'Keefe? she asked herself. He was moody, manipulating, and nearly violent at times. Although he'd proposed marriage, she found no gentleness in his eyes, only a sort of dark frenzied fire that she did not understand. Did she feel genuine affection for him, or did she allow his attentions because he was the only man left beside her in a time of danger?

She turned back to the cottage. She did not know the answers, but it occurred to her suddenly that perhaps she clung to him only in hope, as an awakening sleeper clings to a fleeting, not yet unraveled dream, hoping to find it delightful.

*   *   *

Later, as she sat alone eating the stringy leg of mutton and the round buttered oatcakes the mourners had brought that day, Lark stared morosely out the cottage window and watched eventide slowly but inevitably rob brightness from the garden. Jamie's cough had returned, and she had put him to bed early, noticing that he fell asleep almost as soon as his head touched the pillow.

Finding herself just as exhausted as he, though perhaps more from turbulent emotions than physical exertion, she had only washed her hands and face before supper, not bothering even to pull the black kerchief off her hair. She wished her view did not include a glimpse of the byre's roof, for it reminded her of the earlier, distressful scene with Sebastian. He obviously suspected her involvement in the currents now swirling below Irish soil, and that was a disquieting realization. She could not permit him to establish himself as her protector and stick his nose where it did not belong. Only if their relationship progressed toward marriage would she confide to him the nature of her activities, and if he did not agree to honor her independence in that regard, she would not go to the altar with him.

Realizing suddenly that she had only picked at her food and that the poorly cooked mutton had long ago grown cold and congealed, she pushed her plate aside. She rose and went to draw the frayed muslin curtain, wanting to shut out the depressing dimness of early eve.

Her hand stilled upon the window sash and her breath caught in her throat. Something was moving around outside, a silhouette of blackest black against the sapphire-colored sky. Was it a horse and rider prancing along the pebbled path that led upward from the sea?

Aye . . . the horse was long and sleek, its legs churning the earth like spinning windmills, its tail a trailing ribbon. Astride it rode a dashing shadow. Both were nothing more than a streak of black, a blurred etching in the night, but so dynamic they resembled a centaur carved upon an ancient frieze.

Lark put a hand to her throat. "Sainted Mary, preserve me. . . ." This was no vision, this was not even a nightmare like the ones that came to frighten her in her bed. This was a thing of substance, a living thing, moving, breathing in the darkness. . . .

What man hid beneath the concealing mantle of night? Was it the golden-haired assassin with his muddied boots and damp cape? Had the nobly bred fiend who had murdered her uncle realized his blunder? Had he since discovered that it was not Jerome Ballinter, but the young woman of the house who betrayed the Loyalist government with her meetings beneath the Faery Thorn? If so, then surely he had come for her now, his mission incomplete, and at any moment would fly into the room and strangle her to death.

Realizing her face would be framed in the candlelit window, Lark stepped back hastily, her limbs so frozen with dread she could scarcely make them move.

"I'll kill him," she whispered, thinking as much of Jamie's safety as her own. She snuffed the candle and seized the knife beside her plate.

Stealthily then, she crept back to the window and,

peering through a rent in the curtain, searched the darkness once more. Horse and rider had not moved from their place atop the ridge but commanded that piece of earth just as if it were their own. Though the horse tossed its wild-maned head, the man sat as still as stone upon its back, his shadowed face turned in the direction of the cottage.

Lark waited, clutching the knife, praying to every saint she knew that the fiend would ride on. Why did he sit so motionless, with nary a flinch of muscle or a shift of posture? Why did he stare so fixedly at her window when she knew he could see nothing? Was he plotting, patiently pondering the method of his murder?

At last, in a movement so slight Lark could barely discern it, the rider put a heel to the flank of his beast, caused it to rear up on its hind legs and plunge violently forward. A cry rose from her throat and she jumped even farther back from the window.

But he did not come toward the cottage. Wheeling the steed around, the ghostly rider turned in the direction of the sea again, his mount lunging through the air as if carried upon great feathered wings. Lark stared as the mysterious equestrian gave her window one last look before slowly, distinctly, nodding his head, as if he knew she watched him.

Then he and the horse were gone, disappearing in a swirl of black tail, dashing hooves, and furling cape.

For several seconds Lark stood in place, watching, holding her breath. But no flash of black legs or yellow eyes or spur-heeled boots appeared again. For a while she remained vigilant, standing in darkness with the knife in hand, listening to the silence. Then she began to doubt her own good sense. Had she been mistaken in her imaginings? Had the unknown rider been someone besides her uncle's murderer— someone who had another unfathomable purpose on his mind?

Visions of mysterious meetings and swirling black cloaks began to spin around inside her mind, until they dizzied her with their motion. At last, when eleven o'clock struck and no dark centaur materialized, she let her eyelids droop, sank into a chair, and dozed, though she fought against it.

But not half an hour later a sound startled her into wakefulness. Her eyes immediately went to the window. At first she thought the moon had risen and now brightened the night sky just above the roof of the byre. . . .

"Oh, Lord!" Lark gasped, saying a quick, half-formed prayer as she threw on her shawl and dashed out the door.

Before she stepped out onto the turf she could already smell the acrid pungency of burning thatch. Woolly billows of smoke whirled upward to form an evil cloud in the sky. Tiny sparks danced like fireflies above the byre, whose thatched roof was being quickly consumed by a blazing fire.

"Little Dun!" Stumbling down the hill, Lark screamed the name of the pony, knowing that he was tethered behind the door. Already she could feel the heat of fire, and she was not yet within forty paces of the flames. As she raced toward the building, she stumbled and fell to her knees, scraping the palms of her hands upon the ground before pushing herself up to continue. With arms outstretched she hurled herself at the double doors,

not even aware that their layers of chalky paint had already blistered.

When she released the bolt and flung wide the portals, the conflagration within knocked her backward with its furious heat. Prostrate on the ground, she put her hand over her eyes and felt the scorching of her cheek like the cruelest of sunburns. Even against the roar of a hundred flaring blazes, she could hear the pony's cries, shrill and wild. With no time to think, no time to return to the cottage for a quilt to throw around her, she used only her fringed, loosely knit shawl, covering her head as best she could to meet the hellish flames.

"Little Dun!" As she screamed and inhaled another breath, Lark felt her nose and lungs clog with smoke. It curled thickly, obscuring the paralyzed horse until it was nothing more than the faintest blur of tan. Flaming pieces of thatch fell, catching the hay afire, igniting the brittle straw. Lark felt it sear her flesh, felt the soles of her shoes grow hot. Still she darted forward through the furnace, barely able to see through the scorched black wool of her smoldering shawl.

She heard the animal shriek. Crawling through the straw, she went to him, searching desperately, thinking only of his terror. Something hard struck her hand . . . the pony's hoof? If so, she had only to raise up a little to pull the slip-knotted rope . . . just a little, and a little more . . .

Embers fell, showering her with their deadly brightness, and she screamed as her face was branded and her eyes burned. Then, with a force so mighty its flare resembled the very sun, an explosion roared.

*   *   *

Within the cottage a figure moved by the light of a single candle. Stealthily it went, casting a slender shadow upon wall and ceiling beam. One by one tattered books were slid out of their pockets, delved into with the swiftness of one accomplished at questing, then hastily shoved back again. Page by page letters were perused and then meticulously retied in ordered bundles. The old scarred clock chimed and chimed again. All the while, the searcher searched.

3

Though he had done all he could to prevent it, a child had died beneath his hands that day, and he did not intend that the girl who lay so still upon his mother's bed should do so as well.

Christopher Cavanaugh, the golden-haired Earl of Glassmeade, leaned over his patient to take up her white drooping wrist, put his fingers upon the pulse, and reassure himself yet again that she lived. As he counted the beats of her heart he was tender with his touch, for much of her fair, delicate skin was seared. Though she could not know it, Lark Ballinter's unconsciousness was a blessing, for when she awoke she would suffer pain such as she had never known before. The burns would torture her, the bruises would ache. Yet even those torments would not begin to compare with that other injury about which he had to prepare himself to tell her. . . .

Letting his patient's bandaged hand rest lightly within his own for a moment, Christopher studied it, his expression grim, his long-lashed eyes deepening to a cerulean color. His face was young and attractive but marked with that certain stamp of wisdom that stemmed from a close witnessing of tragic ills. In his eyes there were traces of disillusionment as well, the disillusionment found in men who had realized injustices could not be changed merely by the passion of youthful idealism. Yet this blending of natural good looks and harsh experience settled well upon his face, giving it maturity without the loss of boyish charm.

With a hand adept at mending bodies, he smoothed the girl's brow. Her head rested upon a pile of pillows, and with the bandage wrapped around her eyes she seemed as defenseless as a fledgling bird fallen out of its aerie, and just as tender. Gently, as if he were indeed handling a nestling, he put her hand back atop the covers and set his jaw, his pity slowly transforming into a sort of dangerous rage. A madman had tried to take Lark Ballinter's life, and though it grieved him to guess the name of that madman, he feared he could do so accurately.

He sighed. For now he had to keep his suspicions and his grief to himself, while making certain that the girl upon his bed was kept safe. Only by his fortunate timing and the grace of God did she breathe at all.

Glancing at his own bandaged hand, Christopher adjusted the gauze so that the rawness of his burn was protected. Then he turned from the bed and walked to the hearth to retrieve the cup of coffee he had placed upon the mantel. The brew was half-cooled but black and potent, and he drank it down, staring pensively into the glow of embers that warmed his feet.

Then he dropped wearily onto a chair, stretched his long legs, and let a sigh of exhaustion hiss through his teeth. He could not remember when last he had slept. There had been no time for sleep, only time to bring new lives into the world, splint legs, stitch wounds, and close the soft-lashed eyelids of a boy who had seen less than five years.

"God . . ." He groaned a prayer, remembering the tragedies of the day. When he had set out to become a surgeon he had never dreamed the world had held so much misery, so many tears. Nor had he ever dreamed that the course of his life would take such complicated turns.

Rubbing a hand over his bristly jaw, he laid his head back, feeling overwhelmed by the weight of his troubles. For a while he gazed at the objects of the room, letting them soothe him with their familiarity. This had been his mother's room, and since the earliest days of childhood Christopher had visited it often, touching with reverent fingers the objects she had loved. Though large, the room was cozy, made so by the heavy dark furniture glowing with an aged patina, the richly hued woven pillows, the glossy paintings of sad-eyed spaniels and rosy-cheeked children.

His eyes wandered to a tapestry firescreen folded beside the hearth. Patterned with mythical beasts and trailing vines, it had been fashioned by his mother's hands. He had never known her, for she had died giving him life, and he wished he had had even a few years in her company, had even the dimmest memories to bring forth and hold close like treasures from a chest. He knew she had possessed a fiercely independent nature much like his own—his father had told him so—and Christopher suspected she could have been a formidable ally, a kindred spirit to understand his heart in a way no other could.

His father thought him mad to do what he did, thought him mad to treat the dying and diseased, especially those wretched souls in the streets who had no ability to pay. After all, as the Earl of Glassmeade, and the future Marquess of Winterwoode, Christopher had one of the loftiest positions in the land. With great wealth, power, and popularity, why spend years studying medicine, and still more years in the gloomy halls of hospitals? Why waste time saving filthy beggars, most of whom would die before the age of thirty anyway?

"You labor night and day, throwing away your youth, neglecting your birthright," his father had scorned repeatedly. "'Tis ridiculous, 'tis bourgeois. You should be riding and hunting on the estate, drinking and enjoying the women like any other young man of your class."

But his rebellious son was driven by other passions, bright ideals that led him again and again into the drab, dirty streets of Dublin, into rat-infested tenements and malodorous hospitals, into lightless rooms where hope had never lived. Those same ideals compelled the young lord to risk his neck fighting for a freedom he did not need, fighting against injustices that did not affect him. They motivated him to become an elusive creature of the night who awaited messages beneath the branches of an old twisted tree.

What would his father say if he knew the whole truth? What would the bejeweled lords and powdered ladies who were his friends and peers say if they could read the secrets hidden beneath the folds of his midnight cloak, the deceit guarded in his heart? To them he was an eminent surgeon, a sought-after bachelor, a staunch Loyalist. None would dream that the Lord Glassmeade they knew by day was by night the most notorious rebel spy in Ireland. What would they say were they to happen upon such knowledge?

Christopher pondered their reaction. They would say nothing, of course. They would be too busy hanging him from the tallest, most public gibbet they could find in the country. Not one of them would have an iota of mercy for him, a traitor to their way of life, a danger to their selfishly secure lives.

So be it, he thought with a scowl. He held little affection for most of them anyway.

Rising from his comfortable chair, restless in spite of his weariness, Christopher paced before the fire, then wandered to the undraped window. Absently he watched a carriage lantern as it bobbled in the night, watched the glint of brass harness buckles and iron-rimmed wheels before they spun out of sight again. All at once he experienced a profound sense of isolation, an isolation that the sheer busyness of his life usually kept at bay. It was not that he minded the danger he courted with his treacherous activities, or the peril of his unpopular politics. But, more and more, he minded the loneliness brought on by the protection of his secrets.

Turning away from the window, he looked at the girl who lay upon the bed like a battered doll. He moved closer to her and sat down upon the mattress for a moment, gazing at her bandaged head and the slender form of her body where it scarcely raised the covers. The sight of her touched him somehow, made his belly knot in a strange way, until he felt . . . he didn't know what.

He had tried to dissuade this innocent, frighten her, coerce her into abandoning her dangerous involvement with his cause. He had used mockery, scorn, even cruelty in his efforts, but she had refused at every turn. He had called her foolish once, presumptuous and callow, but in truth he believed her courageous.

And for her courage she had paid a price tonight, a very heavy price.

As he looked at her ravaged face and fire-scorched hands and remembered her as she had been only last Sabbath, he thought that if he could, he would have paid the price for her . . . every pound and penny.

When she emerged from the depths of the netherworld that had harrowed her with its heat and left her wondering if its horror was real or imagined, she could only teeter momentarily on the edge of reason. Her brief awareness told her that her pain was not a dream, nor was the darkness an imagined thing, nor the disturbing odor of burnt hair. She opened her mouth to question whoever might be near, but she could coax no words from her tongue. So she allowed the swirl of senselessness to enfold her again and again, welcoming it only for the reprieve it offered from physical pain.

When finally she began her last, arduous climb upward from unconsciousness, she realized night still reigned. Would morning never come and touch her eyes, reflect itself off of sky or ceiling or heaven's dome so that she might make sense of her surroundings? Strangely, she thought she heard a merry whistle, a sweet chorus of birdsong. But it could not be, she told herself confusedly, for sparrows did not trill at night.

She lifted a hand. It was stiff, bound somehow, but the fingers were free and she put them to her eyes, feeling only a soft wrap of cloth where her lashes should have been. Upon further inspection, she found the side of her face covered in a sort of gauze, and agonizingly raw. It did not bear touching. Much of her flesh felt as if it were afire, as if its top layer had been peeled away to expose the nerves. Bewildered and in pain, seized by an unnameable anxiety, she made to rise, emitting a cry when agony tingled along her arms like a thousand flickering flames.

Something touched her hand. She closed her fingers about the thing, concentrating. It squeezed back lightly but very firmly . . . a human hand . . . warm, hard, much larger than her own, and surely masculine.

Again she tried to get up but through some misconnection between mind and nerve found herself unable. Who sat beside her in the dark, speaking no words and clasping her fingers? Had he harmed her in some brutal way? Visions of a swirling black cape and flashing hooves came to haunt her. Dazed and close to panic, she groped about, reaching out to establish her bearings, only to touch instead the person at her side.

"Can you hear my voice, lass? Can you speak at all? No, no . . . don't alarm yourself. You're safe, quite safe now."

The words were spoken softly and relayed considerable concern. They drifted to her ear as if from a great distance, and she concentrated, hoping to discern the speaker's identity. The deep voice seemed familiar, and yet it was much too eloquent, too well bred, to be anyone of her acquaintance. But its reassuring quality eased her fear of danger, and in appreciation for the way the speaker squeezed her hand so firmly, she squeezed his back. She tried to ask a question, but it emerged as no more than a wheeze from her raw, tightened throat.

"Speech is difficult for you, I know," her companion said, his voice as strong as hers was weak. "'Twill likely continue to be so for a while. I know you have many questions, not the least of which concerns my own identity, and I'll do my best to answer them."

Lark relaxed but tensed again when the person beside her shifted his weight, leaned close, and put his hands behind her shoulders. At her grimace he paused and moved his hold to the center of her back. Then, with little effort he pulled her forward and supported her with care. Though he was quite close, she could form no impression of his physical self, except that he seemed large of frame and steady of hand. Even his scent she could not detect, for the odor of ash and cinder clung too heavily to her nose and throat.

"Before I begin," he said, "I'd like you to drink some water and take a dose of laudanum to ease your pain. Here's the laudanum . . . now the cup."

She opened her mouth for the medicine reluctantly, for accepting any sort of drug in darkness and from a stranger's hand seemed imprudent. But pain prodded her, and when she felt the smooth curve of a china rim against her swollen lips she opened them, accepting a generous gulp of liquid before ignobly sputtering half of it out again. Dismayed, she realized swallowing was no less difficult than speaking. Streams of water dribbled from the corners of her mouth, and wherever it trailed, its coldness burned like the lick of a blaze. A soft cloth, perhaps her companion's handkerchief, was put without delay to her mouth and dabbed about very gently across the tender flesh.

"We'll try more water later. Just lie back for now."

He lowered her to a reclining position again and, from the sound of it, set the cup aside. Then he took up her hand once more, cradling it within his palm. "My name is Christopher Cavanaugh. I'm a surgeon, and you're in my Dublin home, which adjoins my medical offices. You were brought here last evening by a . . . passerby."

"Wh-who . . .?" At last, breathily and with great triumph, she managed the word.

"I don't seem to recall his name at the moment," Christopher hedged. "Perhaps it will come to me later. But I'm certain we shall have occasion to talk about the fellow all in good time."

"F-f-fire . . .?" Lark rasped.

The surgeon gave her hand another press. "From what I understand, the passerby noticed sparks in the sky, and when he rode in their direction saw the roof of your byre collapsing. He discovered you inside the burning structure, lying unconscious, and pulled you to safety."

"W-was . . . he hurt?"

"Nay. Got his clothes scorched, but other than that I could see little damage done to him. He seemed a hardy fellow. But I'm certain," Christopher added softly, "he'd appreciate your asking after him."

When Lark moved her mouth again and jerked her hands in agitation, he added quickly, "Your brother is safe and sound in my kitchen, eating breakfast with the cook's son like he's never seen food ere now. And don't fret over the pony, either, for he is well, and if you'll pardon me for my bluntness, fared much better than yourself."

In relief Lark's hand went limp in his. Now it was time to inquire of her own injuries. She touched the wrap of cloth about her eyes, then moved her hand down to indicate the layer of gauze on her face.

Christopher's answer was not immediate, for he felt a need to assemble his words carefully. One or two of Lark Ballinter's injuries he did not intend to address at this point, yet he did not want to give her a false sense of hope, so he made his tone sober and to the point. "You've been badly burned, lass. Most of the burns are minor, a few are moderate, and . . . one or two are quite serious."

Mentally she began to take inventory of the wounds, beginning with her blistered toes and moving upward across her arms, down her fingertips, and finally to her face. There was no doubt that this last had suffered the most seriously.

"You have no burns that won't heal," Christopher explained, sensing her anxiety. "But the burnt skin must be kept as clean as possible to prevent infection, so you'll have to endure my ministrations in that regard for a while. Much of your flesh will remain sore for quite some time—I have salve for that and, of course, the laudanum. Certainly you may not leave here until the more serious injuries have healed."

"H-hospital?"

"I've decided not to send you to Queens. You'll simply stay here, remain as my special patient for as long as I believe necessary. You'll have a chambermaid, and I want you to feel at home, ask for anything you need."

"Jamie . . .?"

"Jamie is welcome here for as long as you stay. I will allow him to visit you tomorrow, perhaps, if I feel you're up to it."

Much relieved to hear it, Lark relaxed, only to be plagued by other unresolved questions. "The fire"—she coughed with rawness in her throat—"how . . . did it start?"

"You don't know?"

Lark shook her head.

"I am dismayed, then, for I had hoped you had some knowledge of it. 'Tis my guess that 'twas started deliberately. Did you see no one?"

Recalling her wild dash to the byre, Lark moved her head back and forth upon the pillow. "Nay. . . ."

Even as she made the denial, an eerie image of a wild black beast and its shadowy rider flashed to mind. She tensed, and the surgeon tightened his hand about hers. She was glad of it. This holding of hands was an intimate thing, warm and personal, that gave her no thought of impropriety but much security. She wished she could fling the bandage from her eyes and see this stranger who comforted her in utter darkness.

"You have had a troubling thought?" he asked, perhaps sensing her disquiet.

She found she liked the deep richness of his voice as much as she liked the strength of his presence. "There *was* . . . someone . . . a man."

"Yes?" the surgeon prompted sharply.

"'Twas just an hour or so before the fire. He came riding a black horse, halting it some distance from the cottage. Then he seemed to stare at my window for an age, just as if he could see me through the darkness. I believed he would come and kill me, he looked so terrifying . . . but he never made a move to enter the cottage. After a while, he rode on, down toward the sea."

"You found him frightening?"

"Aye. There was a moment when I thought he could have been Death itself."

"You don't say?" Christopher was hardly flattered by her description of himself. He had forgone supper with friends to make that journey to her cottage, see that all was quiet there. Little good it had done. If his intuition had not provoked him into turning back a quarter hour later . . .

"No one else?" he persisted.

Lark frowned, not understanding his easy dismissal of the spectral nighttime visitor. If the fire had indeed been set purposefully, it seemed natural to assume the black-draped rider was the culprit. "Nay," she replied. "I saw no one else."

For a moment they sat in silence, and Lark sensed her companion had fallen deep into thought.

"Why did the . . . passerby bring me here to you?" she asked. "There's a surgeon in my village."

Christopher smiled with humor only he could appreciate. "He knew of me and seemed to think me better qualified to tend you than anyone else."

"And are you?"

"Eminently," he declared with all the certainty and none of the conceit of a naturally confident man. "But that, you shall decide for yourself over the next days."

"I—I would like to thank the . . . the passerby. Will he return to see me?"

Christopher put his other hand atop hers, his eyes brightening with the barest gleam of mischief. "He struck me as being a rather unsociable sort—one of those solitary, reclusive types. Yet I feel rather certain he and I shall be crossing paths in the near future, and when we do, I shall be sure to pass on your gratitude."

With that, the surgeon slid his hand from hers and rose from the bed. Feeling bereft in her darkened world, she put her fingers upon the spot where he had sat, touching its dwindling warmth. Then in a spontaneous gesture she reached out for him again, fumbling about, mortified when she accidentally touched another part of his anatomy—most probably his thigh.

Clasping her foundering fingers, he drew them back to her chest.

"Do not feel embarrassed," he said in a slightly teasing tone. "'Tis not an easy thing to be graceful in the dark, though I've heard it can be learned with a bit of patience."

"I—I feel I should thank you," Lark said, realizing suddenly that the hand she held was bandaged just as neatly as her own.

"My pleasure," he replied.

"Your hand . . . the bandage?"

"Ah, that—'tis nothing. I injured it—er, helping a friend out of a rather precarious predicament, you might say. Nothing more dramatic than that. Now," he continued. "There's a glass of water here upon the table beside you." He directed her fingers to it. "Drink as much of it as you can. Also, there is a bell here which you may ring should you need anything."

She nodded. The laudanum was slowly enclosing her in a murky cloud that blunted thought and eased her pain. Only dimly did she hear a tap upon the door and the inquiring male voice that followed it.

"My lord?"

"Yes?" the surgeon answered.

"A messenger downstairs bids you come to the hospital at once."

Christopher's sigh was quite audible, and Lark was conscious enough to discern the heavy note of weariness in it.

"Very well. Tell him I shall be there shortly." He turned to Lark and touched her shoulder. "I must leave you now. Rest and do not worry yourself over anything. I shall see you again when I can."

Lark felt for his sleeve and grasped it. "You . . . you are titled?"

"I am the Earl of Glassmeade," he said casually, with no trace of self-importance. "But you needn't address me so formally—we have already become fast friends, have we not?"

Something in his half-serious, half-jesting tone sparked a disturbing memory in Lark's brain, but the unformed thought was quickly lost at the sound of the surgeon's heels thudding upon carpet, then ringing against hardwood. His tread was the measured stride of a man with little time to waste, Lark noted even as she drifted toward a ponderous, drug-induced slumber. As if struck by a premonition, she suspected that the cadence of his step would become a familiar sound in the days to come, a sound for which she would listen attentively, even too eagerly.

But what title had he used? Lark struggled against her befuddlement, holding on to a thought she knew to be important. He had declared himself as the Earl of Glassmeade, had he not? Aye, he had, and that would make him the son of her uncle's landlord, the one who had evicted them all, who was one of the most powerful, most corrupt men in all of Ireland!

Oblivion beckoned. Though Lark yearned to remain alert, to grasp the significance of the information she had gleaned, she found herself unable. But just as unconsciousness descended upon her, she managed to mouth a most desperate sort of prayer.

Sainted Mary, preserve me . . . give me strength. I lie in the house of my enemy. . . .

4

"Dia dhuit."

A new voice entered Lark's darkened world. It was a coarse female one, and elderly in its Gaelic greeting.

"Are ye awake yet, mistress? I dearly hope ye are, because I brought ye a cup of broth and some water for washin' up." A clatter sounded against the bed-side table. "And yer hair, we must do somethin' about yer hair," the servant muttered as if to herself. "I swear 'tis as tangled as a bird's nest."

Lark struggled to clear her brain of grogginess, turning her head toward the screechy voice, making sense of only a portion of its prattle. Her hair . . . was there something the matter with it? Holding a feeble hand to her head, she felt only the clean coolness of linen.

"I helped Lord Glassmeade change yer kerchief last evenin' when ye were brought in," the woman explained from somewhere across the room.

"Scorched, it was, and vile smellin' like yer poor withered clothes. But ye were lucky to be wearin' it, for it saved most of yer pretty locks, it did."

Relieved for that mercy, Lark let her hand drop back to her side. Her hair was her private vanity, bequeathed to her by her mother and indulged nightly with one hundred vigorous strokes of a boar's-hair brush. But what had the servant said about Lord Glassmeade?

With a gasp Lark struggled to sit upright, reaching out her arms as if expecting to find something threatening in the very air surrounding her. The wrap of bandages completely obscured her vision. She remembered suddenly where she was, she remembered that she lay beneath the roof of one of the most bitter enemies to her cause. The thought left her not only sick with hostility, but weak with fear. Visions of her poor strangled uncle came vividly to mind. No mercy had been shown a man suspected of treachery to the Loyalist government, and she had no doubt that her own fate would be much the same were her identity discovered. The words of the Faery Thorn agent echoed eerily in Lark's ears:

Remember, lass, one slip o' the tongue—just one wee slip—and ye'll find yer bonnie neck bruised.

"Here, and what are ye doin' now, mistress?" demanded the flustered servant as Lark threw off the coverlet and made to rise. "Ye can't get out of bed."

Laying her hands upon Lark's shoulders, the woman pushed her firmly back against the pillows. Lark attempted to wrench free, but her poor seared flesh hurt so badly with the effort that she cried out.

"See there!" the old woman admonished. "Ye're too weak and injured to be goin' anywhere. Lord Glassmeade says he's keepin' ye here for weeks."

Weeks! Lark despaired at the very thought. Tomorrow, just as soon as she had regained sufficient strength to drag herself from bed, she and Jamie would flee this Loyalist house, beg for temporary lodging with a cotter's family until she could secure some kind of work. She would not stay beneath the roof of the enemy a moment longer than necessary.

"I guess ye'll be wonderin' who I am," the servant offered belatedly, tucking Lark's legs back beneath the covers. "Me name's Grindle."

A rough, strangely clawlike hand touched Lark's fingers briefly before removing itself and leaving the smell of onions lingering behind. "Lord Glassmeade said I was to serve ye while ye're here—just like a real lady's maid, I'm to be."

"Wh-what time is it?" Due either to her few hours' rest or to the laudanum's dulling of pain, words came easier from Lark's raw throat than before.

"About seven in the evenin', mistress. Past time for ye supper. Aren't ye starvin'?"

Lark refrained from replying that she lived often on the fringes of starvation, that a gnawing in her belly was no strange companion. But she would eat every morsel offered in this earl's lavish house and with every mouthful remember all the cotters who went unfed.

"Aye, Grindle," she said. "I'm starving."

Over the next hour Grindle proved a forbearing attendant. She did not seem to mind at all that Lark's blistered lips and thickened tongue made for an inelegant diner but simply mopped up the dribbles of broth while chattering on about the poor beggars the butler had had to disperse from the gates an hour past.

"Somethin' should be done about 'em," she said. "Scores of starvin' people in the streets, there are. Floodin' in from the farms, wantin' work when there's none to be had. Why, a body can scarcely step out from a decent household without bein' pestered for coins."

Lark lay back pensively against the pillows while Grindle set the dishes aside. If the servant's comments were indeed true, it did not bode well for her quest for employment in Dublin. She wondered if she and Jamie were in for great hardships during the days ahead. Perhaps she would have to permit Sebastian to aid her after all. . . .

"Now, do ye think we can manage to brush out yer hair, mistress? I brought a pair of scissors with me to trim off the singed parts, and His Lordship gave me a bottle of perfume to take the scorched smell away. He said 'twould be a day or two before I could wash it for ye."

The brushing out was uncomfortable, for Lark's scalp was tender from a raised lump upon the crown, but she found herself relieved to hear not more than three short snips of the scissors. The odor of the snarled strands was repellent, however, and both women lauded the surgeon's gift of perfume as a thoughtful gesture.

"Grindle," Lark began, "about the household . . . is it large or small, in the center of town or on the edges?"

"Oh, 'tis quite large, mistress," came the lofty reply. "And 'tis in Henrietta Street, at the end. We have a fine garden, lovely in season."

Putting the brush aside, Grindle lowered her voice, whispering low as if to share a secret. "There's a holy well down there, mistress . . . in the heart of the garden. Bubblin' 'neath a wild rose bush. Springs up straight from the ground, it does, pure and sacred."

When Lark made no comment, but only leaned farther back into the pillows, the servant moved closer and went on. "The holy water has healin' powers. Me mother and her mother before her knew how to make a special draught from it. Folks from far and near has always come askin' us for cures. Even the fishermen keep bottles of it strung upon a line in their curraghs. Keeps evil away, it does."

Grindle paused for effect, then spoke in a slow, deep tone as if savoring her knowledge. "The healin' draught must be mixed with live moss scraped from a skull bone—" She giggled. "I find bits of skulls round the old battlefields, ye know. Gruesome things. But when the draught is drunk, the one who needs healin' must say a special prayer. Most of all . . . she must believe."

Coming nearer the bed now, the servant leaned upon its edge, then put her face so close to Lark's that a breath of onion tarried. "'Course, Lord Glassmeade don't believe in it, bein' a man of science an' all. But, if ye'd like, Mistress Ballinter, I could get ye some."

Suppressing a strong shudder of disgust, Lark drew back, shaking her head. Though holy wells and miraculous cures were very much a part of her religion, the servant's odd intentness and ghastly details repulsed her.

"Don't believe me, do ye?" The servant snorted. "Well, ye may change ye mind afore ye leave this house. If ye do, just put a word in me ear."

The maid took up the brush once more. At one point she grew careless and raked a length of Lark's delicate scalp, but Lark neither winced nor uttered a cry. When another dab of expensive tea rose fragrance was applied and combed through her knotted locks, she asked, "Is . . . is there a mistress in this house?"

"Ouch! None a'tall. Lord Glassmeade doesn't have a wife, and his poor, sainted mother died bearin' him, God rest her soul. A most dreadful bad labor 'twas, with her pushin' and screamin' for three days before dyin' just as the babe slipped from between her legs. She died right here in the very bed ye're lyin' in."

"And his father?"

"Still livin', the old marquess is, though he's not in the best of health, or so I'm told. He stays at the auld country estate. Used to be an important man in Parliament before he fell so ill." She snorted. "Some say he deserves his illness—all that money and fine livin'."

Even here, Lark thought, the dissatisfaction of the poor over the sumptuous excesses of the rich was apparent. The mention of the man who had evicted her uncle fueled her anger, and she began to recall all the marquess's many injustices. Three years past he had doubled the rents when Uncle made improvements to the cottage, so that Jerome had to grow most of his grain just to pay rent, leaving only a small plot of potatoes to feed his own family. Last winter when the potato crop was inadequate, the three of them had nearly starved to death, resorting to a loan from the despised "gombeen man" who charged a high rate of usury. Repaying him had taken nearly six months of forgoing the meal of beef they usually enjoyed on Sundays.

She wondered about Lord Glassmeade's relationship with his detestable father. Indeed, if the marquess had fallen ill, were orders regarding the vast and powerful estate issued by his son?

"Does Lord Glassmeade see his father often?" she asked.

"Oh, aye. As often as his schedule allows. He gets on right well with the old man, dotes on him. And the old man believes the sun rises and sets on our Lord Glassmeade." Grindle laid the brush aside, fluffed the cloud of hair falling newly untangled over Lark's shoulders, and tied it back with a ribbon. "'Course, the two of 'em argue a deal. The old man's never quite satisfied with what the younger one's about. 'Tis no secret the marquess is pushin' to get his son wed before another year passes—heirs and all that, ye know."

"And is there a . . . lady?"

"Dozens of 'em," Grindle supplied, eager to gossip. "But he'll not be an easy catch, that one."

"Why do you say that?"

"How can he be? He won't take time to court the ladies. Overworks himself, he does. Has patients queued up outside the door before dawn—he sees the poor as well as them that can pay, ye know." The pride in Grindle's voice made it clear that her disdain for the marquess did not spill over to his son. "And every day he spends a few hours over at the Foundlin' Hospital, sewin' up little childer, an' all."

She crossed the room in an uneven shuffle, and a moment later Lark heard the sound of draperies being drawn, followed by the easily distinguished clank of a poker as it was withdrawn from its stand.

"Can't let the fire go out, ye know," Grindle said with a knowing cackle. "Disgruntles the faeries. If they come to warm themselves by yer fire at night, and 'tis cold in the grate"—she paused for emphasis—"they take the souls out of the people livin' in the house."

Though Lark did not consider herself fanciful, she found these morbid snippets of country folklore oddly depressing. And Grindle's descriptive recipes for spiritual cures had strained her already taut nerves.

She shivered. "When . . . when will Lord Glassmeade return?"

"I can't say, mistress. We never know when to expect him home. Comes in late more often than not, sometimes well after the midnight hour." She gathered up the dinner tray and hairbrush. "Now, ye have the bell. Ring for me if ye need anythin'."

"Could you bring my brother to me?" Lark asked.

Grindle seemed to consider. "Well, His Lordship said not till tomorrow, but I suppose a wee visit wouldn't hurt. I'll bring him up after a spell. In the meantime, ye rest yerself."

"Lark?"

The tentative little voice startled her from a doze, but Lark welcomed the sound of it and stretched out her hands instinctively.

Six-year-old Jamie made a whistling sound through his gapped front teeth, not moving immediately to touch his sister. "You look like a ghostie wrapped up in all them rags."

"Would a ghostie be talkin' to you, now?" Lark teased. "Come, take my hands. I can't see you, you know."

Still a bit reticent, Jamie eased down upon his sister's bed and clasped her bandaged fingers. "Why do you have a wrap around your eyes? And why is your face all red? Are you goin' to be all right?"

"Aye," she reassured him. "'Twill take some time, but the surgeon tells me I'll be right as rain. Now, tell me how you're faring. Have you had plenty to eat?"

"Oh, aye!" As if a dam of excitement had been suddenly released by her question, Jamie squirmed on his seat. "'Tis the grandest place, Lark! They had six different tarts for me to pick from at dinner, and big bowls of fruit, and punch the color of those berries in the market we never have enough pennies to buy. 'Not a single spooleen in sight, either," he added, referring to the thick lumps of salt beef and cabbage they ate at home sometimes.

"And then . . ." He sounded sheepish. "I almost got sick on the sweetmeats."

Lark could imagine his wide green eyes beholding the sugary treats he had previously viewed only through the windows of expensive confectioneries.

"And, Lark, this house is like . . . like a *castle*. There's angels painted on the ceilings and big rock statues of naked people all round. And, there's even gold chairs and silver pots, and lamps hangin' from the ceiling made of giant white diamonds."

Lark could sense her brother's utter awe of his surroundings, and instead of amusing her it only roused contempt. Much of Ireland starved while men such as the earl wallowed in their ill-gotten wealth. It was an abomination!

"Jamie," she said crossly, attempting to push down her umbrage, "the surgeon . . . have you met him?"

"Oh, aye," her brother replied, affection clear in his tone. "He's a right fine gentleman, he is. You know what he did? He fetched a crate of toys for me,

said they were his when he was a wee lad. I've never
seen the likes of 'em before. Why, there's a little spotted horse that goes on wheels, and a wooden puppet—I couldn't pull the strings proper, but Lord
Glassmeade could ever so well. He—"

"Jamie," Lark interrupted, experiencing sharp
resentment over his esteem for the wealthy aristocrat,
"you know we're only here for a short while. And
when we leave, we'll be going back to our old life."

Jamie grew silent, obviously failing to understand
why he had been admonished for simply having fun.

Lark knew she should apologize, but she did not.
She hoped her young brother would indeed enjoy
himself here, be indulged in every form of excess, and
never forget the taste of luxury. Perhaps then, when
he was a man laboring hard just to keep hunger at
bay, he would remember the sinful lavishness of the
nobles and feel the fire of injustice burn in his breast
just as strongly as it did in hers. If the common man
did not win independence in the days to come, Ireland would need passionate young leaders to carry on
the cause.

Tenderly she stroked her brother's arm. "And
what are Lord Glassmeade's looks?" she asked in
spite of herself, recalling steadying hands in the dark.

Without hesitation Jamie answered, "He looks just
like the picture of Icarus in that old mythology book
the priest lent us, the one about the fellow with the
waxen wings. Real tall, he is, with gold hair. He
smiled at me a deal, and laughed and laughed when I
wiggled the puppet, but . . ." He trailed off.

"But, what?"

"Well, I don't *really* think he was merry."

"What do you mean?"

"Well . . . his eyes were sad." The observation was made with all the unself-conscious perception usual to young children.

"Humph! They shouldn't be sad," Lark snapped. "After all, he has everything he could ever want—including a dozen cotter's homes his father just emptied of decent families."

Jamie grew silent beneath her heated tirade.

"Ah, forgive me, wee one," she said, her hand moving clumsily to pat the top of his head. "You can't know what it is that makes your poor foolish sister so vexed today."

Mollified, Jamie squeezed her fingers.

"Tell me about last night, sweeting—about the fire," she prompted with a serious frown. "Were you awfully frightened by it?"

"Nay, I didn't know anything about the fire till the stranger who brought us here woke me. My head was all fuzzy from the cough potion you gave me, but I remember he picked me up and carried me outside. Little Dun was harnessed to the wheel-car, and you were lyin' in the back of it. The man laid me beside you and covered me up, I think. I don't recall much after that—only wakin' in a great big bed with feathers in the pillows."

Lark felt an enormous debt of gratitude to the stranger who had saved her life and hoped to discover his identity in order to thank him properly. "What were the stranger's looks, Jamie?" she asked. "Are you certain you didn't know him from the village?"

Her brother pondered the question. "I dunno. 'Twas awful dark, and I could hardly keep my eyes open. But . . ."

"What?" she pressed.

"He had a black horse—a great big beastie. He was tied to the back of the wheel-car, and kept snortin' and snufflin' the whole way. I thought he was part of a dream at first, but I remember him clearly now."

"Hmm . . . I wonder how the man came to be travelin' the road so late at night."

Jamie seemed tired of the subject, wriggling about on the bed and humming to himself. As the pain of her burns was beginning to weary her, Lark said, "Is there anyone to watch after you in this house, sweeting?"

"Aye. Lord Glassmeade asked a kitchen maid to tend me. Her name's Meg."

"Good. Can you go and find her now? I need a bit of rest."

When he had skipped from the room, Lark settled more comfortably against the pillows. She was vaguely disturbed over Jamie's description of the passerby or, rather, over the description of his mount. That forbidding rider she had seen just before the fire had ridden an ebony horse. Had the man set the byre aflame and then returned to rescue her?

Rolling onto her side and grimacing with the raw pain of her cheek, Lark sighed, unable to solve the riddle. There was nothing to do except press the surgeon again for the name of her mysterious rescuer, in spite of the fact that he seemed reluctant to provide it.

She wanted very much to speak with the owner of that spirited black horse.

It seemed as if she had closed her eyes for only a moment when a noise alerted her, the jangle of fire tools blending incongruously with the sound of a clock chiming eleven times. A few seconds later a quilt was settled gently across her shoulders.

"Who is it? she asked anxiously, sitting up. She hated having the bandage around her eyes.

A hand touched hers where it lay atop the covers. It was of a familiar shape and size and smooth in the way a surgeon's hand would tend to be, yet not soft. Lark thought she would remember the feel of it always, just as it was tonight, warming and encircling her chilled fingers like a glove in winter.

"It's your foot-weary surgeon," Christopher announced, "who apologizes for putting you at the end of his roster today . . . but you have the unfortunate privilege of being conveniently on the path to his bedchamber."

His voice was warm and throaty, his hand firm upon hers, and in her mind's eye Lark envisioned Jamie's Icarus, that faded etching of a character in a tattered children's book.

At the same time, she heard an inner warning, a call for self-preservation.

He is the son of the Marquess of Winterwoode, a member of the very nobility you so despise, an enemy to you and your cause.

In spite of this, she could not seem to summon anger. "You've had a long, strenuous day?" she asked softly.

Her companion leaned close, sagging the feather tick as he eased his weight down. "Of late, they are all long."

Great weariness marked his words. Guessing him to be of an enduring nature, Lark did not think he intended to reveal his fatigue to such a degree, but it had come out. Perhaps, with the wrap about her eyes, her ears had grown more discerning than usual and could pick out nuances of feeling that would otherwise go undetected.

Now she sensed he studied her in the way a physician studies a patient, searching for symptoms and signs of distress. At their first meeting she realized this man had a great gift for compassion. With a mere touch of hand or lowering of voice he could make her feel as if his attentions were solely upon her, interested and undivided. She wondered what power and appeal lay in his eyes if she could but see them.

She could not know that Christopher was scrutinizing far more in the capacity of a young man assessing a female than that of a surgeon appraising a patient. He had never seen her hair before, since her head had always been covered with a hood or kerchief. Now its umber-red length fell down to her waist, the curls thick and shining in the firelight.

Shifting a bit, he shrugged out of his black cutaway coat and rolled up the cuffs of his ruffle-edged sleeves, forcing his thoughts to a more professional level. "Tell me, how do you feel tonight? Any better than when last I saw you?"

In truth, she felt considerably improved for his mere presence, but she could hardly admit that, even to herself. "Aye," she said, "the agony is not so great as it was. 'Tis mostly the place on my cheek that pains me—that, and the fingers of my left hand."

"Do you need more of the drug?"

"I believe I can endure without it, thank you."

"But I don't want you to endure. I want you to have a restful night, and if that means another dose of the drug, I'll administer it. Its long-term continuance would be ill advised, of course—I never risk addiction with my patients."

"What of the bandage on my eyes?" she asked, touching the wrap with a finger.

His answer was firm. "I think it best to keep it on for a while."

She found a dose of laudanum pressed to her lips after that, a few bitter drops in a spoon, then a cup of sweetened tea. As she swallowed, she heard the surgeon handling some other object.

"This is a mixture of tannin and other emollients," he explained as he began lightly to stroke her brow and temple with an oily balm. "'Tis a healing salve. We'll apply it twice each day to the burns. While you were unconscious I applied ice and wet compresses every few hours. One of my apprentices will continue to do the same for a while, whenever I'm unavailable."

Finished with the task, Christopher withdrew his hand and reached for a handkerchief to wipe the excess from his fingertips, his eyes tarrying again upon his patient's lovely hair. From there his regard moved to her face with its patch of gauze, then on to her full bowed mouth. The time had come to broach a subject he did not relish in the least.

"Coincidentally," he imparted in an offhand manner, putting off the task, "I had another burn victim today, a small boy who'd tipped a kettle of boiling water onto himself and scalded his arms."

"Poor soul. Was he in great pain?"

"No greater than that which you are in, I suspect."

"Still . . . pain must be far crueler when it attacks a young and innocent person."

"You speak as if you consider yourself something other than young and innocent," he teased.

"If you consider eighteen young," she replied, "then young I am. But I am not innocent."

Christopher grinned, realizing it was the first time he had done so all day. "You've tempted me to make an indecorous remark, but I shall be a gentleman and refrain from it—at least until I know you better."

Lark regretted her phrasing of the comment and even more resented his amusement. She started to inform him that he would not have the opportunity to know her better, as she would be leaving on the morrow. But she held her tongue, knowing that her departure would have to be a stealthy one. She feared that Lord Glassmeade, with his cursed inborn tendency for command, would not allow any patient to leave until he granted permission to do so.

With shrewd eyes Christopher watched Lark's mouth open and close as if upon a thought, and he wondered at it. She was plotting something, to be sure. But what? He would have to be careful not to bully her and cause her to dig in her heels in that mulish way of hers. A more subtle handling would be required for this red-haired rebel.

"Do you have something to say to me, Lord Glassmeade?" she asked now, interrupting his thoughts.

With a sort of bland amusement, he fancied she had put the slightest emphasis of mockery upon his title. "Aye," he answered. "I had hoped to wait until tomorrow to have this discussion, but since you're awake and seem to have your wits about you, I'll speak about your injuries now."

She waited. The pressure of his hand increased, and his voice lowered to one of a sober concern. "I told you this morning that you had one or two serious burns—you remember our conversation?"

She nodded.

"As I said, they'll all heal. Most are only superficial. There'll be tenderness for a while, naturally, and we must take pains to keep the most serious wound free from infection. But I don't expect any complications. The injury to your hand—it wouldn't be from the pony's hoof, would it?"

She frowned and focused her thoughts. "Why, I believe I do recall him striking me . . . aye, that's how I knew I'd found him in the smoke. But how did you know?"

He laughed softly. "Because you were wearing a very distinct horseshoe design just below your left wrist."

She smiled a little and tried flexing her hand, finding it tender but quite functional.

"It's not serious," Christopher assured her. "But . . ." He paused. "I'm afraid the injury to your cheek is a quite different matter."

Lark felt him rise up from her bed then. She guessed that he walked in the direction of the fireplace but could not be sure, for the carpet muffled his steps. She had the impression that he found himself unsure as to how to proceed with the conversation.

"What is it?" she asked, her voice rising, betraying distress. "Tell me."

The fire popped, followed by the hollow clip-clopping sound of hooves on wet pavement outside. Beside the mantel Christopher ran a hand through his fair hair in indecision and glanced at his young patient. It was imperative that he detain her for as long as necessary. To have a valuable member of the underground wandering around in such a vulnerable condition would be folly. Not only did she carry secrets of the

underground, but more important, he feared someone had uncovered her identity and meant to use it
against her. He knew it must rankle her temper to
stay in the house of a man she believed to be a Loyalist,
but he could hardly reveal the truth about himself.
Nor could he allow his faery queen to walk out his
door and into the arms of peril. He quickly pushed
aside the notion that a more personal, even selfish,
motivation influenced his keeping her there.

Without a doubt, the excuse of her burn would
have to be employed to its fullest extent—perhaps
even exaggerated a bit. As for the other injury . . . he
feared she was not strong enough yet to be told about
it. The worst would simply have to wait.

From his stance beside the hearth he glided a hand
over the surface of his mother's thimble box, idly
opened its silver lid, and then fastened his eyes upon
Lark's face.

"There are some recently improved techniques for
treating burns, Mistress Ballinter," he began carefully.
"I'd like to speak with you about them. Since I have
considerable interest in this area of medicine, I've
spent years studying with various European surgeons
who claim expertise in the field. As a matter of fact,
the salve on your cheek is from a germicide formulated
by a Hindu surgeon I heard lecture in Rome last
year."

He closed the lid on the thimble box and added,
"I've had success in preventing serious scarring in a
number of cases like yours."

"What are you saying?" she demanded, shifting
against the pillows in agitation. Her inability to see
Lord Glassmeade frustrated her. She sensed he was
leading up to something frightening, and she yearned

to see the expression upon his face, as if by doing so she could discern his true meaning.

Preparing to deal with a hysterical reaction, Christopher moved nearer the bed. "Though a surgeon always wishes to spare his patients unpleasantries," he said gently, "'tis only fair that I be honest. You've had damage to your cheek . . . considerable damage. I believe with proper treatment I can prevent undue scarring. But I must have your assurances that you'll stay here until I deem it prudent for you to leave."

His words struck Lark forcibly. Feeling self-conscious all at once, she bent her head low, appalled that her appearance must be a hideous one, far worse than she had ever imagined. Was she now some poor wreck with a ravaged face, some freak who should fear the light of day?

Several moments passed. She swallowed against the threat of tears and shuddered. She wanted to jerk the bandage from her eyes, demand a mirror, and see for herself what had become of her face, but just as fiercely, she did not want to see.

She steadied her voice, deepened it to hide the trembling, and instead of demanding a mirror, asked him, "Are my looks . . . quite spoiled, then?"

Immediately Lord Glassmeade returned to her side, sat down upon the bed, and put both hands upon her shoulders. He grasped her just above the arms and on the borrowed gown, his fingers strong, insistent, as if he were drawing all her attention toward what he had to say. She caught the pleasant scent of him—soap, and the brandy he had likely drunk after dinner.

"I can assure you to the contrary," he said. "Your looks are not spoiled. I only thought to . . ."

He was leaning so close she could hear him breathe, she could almost hear the sentence suspended upon his lips. "Thought to what, Lord Glassmeade?"

Christopher sighed, knowing he had stepped onto ground so precarious that no amount of tact could save him. He removed his hands from her shoulders, rubbed his jaw, and pressed forward. "Well, since 'tis natural for a comely young woman to be vain about her appearance—especially if she is as yet . . . unattached—"

"In search of a husband, you mean," Lark snapped.

Christopher was unable to suppress a smile at her honest phraseology. He was inordinately glad, however, that she could not see it. "Aye," he conceded. "In search of a husband."

"And this treatment . . . it will make me marriageable once more?"

"I did not say, or even imply, that you were not now marriageable—as you put it."

"Oh, but you did, Lord Glassmeade, whether you intended to or not."

"Don't judge me unfairly, Mistress Ballinter. I also implied that you were comely."

"A compliment for which it seems I should be thanking you," she returned sourly. "Unless I misunderstand, it's a poor scarred spinster I'll end up being if I choose not to have this—this treatment you speak about."

Christopher wondered at exactly what point he had gone wrong in his approach. He had expected tears from her, or shrieking at mention of a scarred face, not a personally directed indignation.

"My apologies," he said. "I hardly intended for this conversation to lead us down such a prickly path. I fear I've led you to jump to conclusions concerning the extent of your disfigurement—'tis not really so dreadful as you seem to imagine."

Disfigurement. That he had used such a word confirmed Lark's fears. His belated claim that the injury was not so dreadful as she imagined seemed to her no more than a token platitude.

She resisted an impulse to put a hand to her cheek. All at once, for the first time, she was fully aware of Lord Glassmeade not as a hated aristocrat or a skilled surgeon, but as a man. A young man who she sensed was attractive. Was he staring at her face, finding it unsightly to look upon? Did he feel pity for her? She turned her head a little, as if to hide the injured cheek from his view.

"Why are you offering to do this for me?" she asked. "You surely know that I am naught but a country maid with little money. I cannot pay you for the services you'll be providing. Indeed, I thought to leave here on the morrow."

"You will not leave here on the morrow! You will not leave here until I say. You cannot go back to some filthy mud cottage without risking infection."

His imperiousness immediately sparked Lark's antagonism. She started to say she no longer had a filthy mud cottage to return to, but she held her tongue. She sensed that now was not the time to put forth complaints.

"I'll go whenever I please," she announced, "and no fancy surgeon with a high opinion of himself is going to tell me nay!"

Christopher longed to reply that he could very well lock her in this chamber if he chose to do so, but he was in no mood to suffer the fit of feminine histrionics such a comment would likely prompt. Besides, if he lost his temper, she might suspect an underlying motive to his vehemence.

"We'll speak of it later," he said with forced calmness even while he glowered. "And I do not expect payment for my services. The fact is, I have taken a special interest in your case, though the reasons for that interest I shall not go into at present. Now, will you consider the treatment?"

"I'll consider all you've said," she told him stiffly. "And, if you don't mind, I'd prefer to speak no more about it tonight."

"Mistress Ballinter—"

"Please," she interrupted. "I'll give you my answer in a day or so. In the meantime, I'd appreciate it if you'd stop feeling pity for me—" She raised her chin, wanting to disconcert him. "Aye, my lord. Just because I cannot see your face doesn't mean I cannot sense your thoughts."

Christopher unbent his long legs and rose. For a moment he stood above his intrepid little patient with crossed arms and knitted brow, puzzling over her stoic front.

Lark felt his eyes upon her, felt him staring at the face he termed disfigured, and could not bear the scrutiny. In a pointed gesture of dismissal, she jerked the quilt up over one shoulder and turned her head away.

Christopher sighed, exasperated. It had been a hellish day, and this was hardly a satisfactory conclusion. But he put a gentle hand upon Lark's hair and stroked it once. "Sleep well."

After a moment Lark heard him walk from the room. She did not stir an inch, did not move a muscle, just listened until the very last of her enemy's measured footsteps had faded away.

5

She had learned to count the clock chimes, for with her eyes wrapped as they were, she had no other means of determining the hours around which life evolved. One, two, three, four, five knells, she numbered now as they floated dimly down the corridor. The grand house would be astir soon, she guessed, bustling with an army of servants doing their sweeping, bed changing, and dusting. Accustomed to toiling from sunrise to dusk in the keeping of a humble cottage, she could well imagine the number of hands required to keep a pampered earl well fed and comfortably housed.

Lying in a bed far softer than any she had ever slept in before, Lark waited in the darkness, recalling again the dreadful shock of the surgeon's news last eve. Instinctively she raised an exploring finger to the still stinging wound upon her cheek, hoping as if by some miracle to find it smooth again. But it was not smooth, of course, not vanished in the night.

She despaired that she would have to stay beneath this roof awhile, tarry here and allow the surgeon's treatment of the injury or else suffer some hideous form of scarring. She reassured herself that Lord Glassmeade could know nothing of her involvement in the underground. No one knew of it except the trusted messenger who delivered the dispatches to her directly from Virgil each week . . . and the hooded figure to whom she passed them along under the trysting moon that glowed above the Faery Thorn.

Did the evil-hearted monster who had so ruthlessly murdered Uncle Jerome seek to find her now? Had he realized that he had killed the wrong Ballinter? He was certainly a member of the aristocracy and likely moved in the same elite circles in which Lord Glassmeade traveled. Were the two acquainted? Through casual conversation with the surgeon, would the golden-haired assassin discover the whereabouts of Jerome Ballinter's niece and attempt to smother her in the night or have her arrested for sedition?

She shuddered, thinking of the rider of the huge black steed. How did he fit into the whole of this ever-spreading puzzle? Had he indeed been her rescuer, and if so, who had set the fire?

Her dilemma remained unresolved. And between the wound upon her cheek and the bandage over her eyes, she could formulate no plan to advise the messenger how to reach her with Virgil's communiqués. Nor could she devise a way to tell that phantom beneath the Faery Thorn that, for a while at least, his thirst for secrets must go unquenched.

"Brrrr!"

Grindle's whispery exclamation of cold and her hurried footsteps caused Lark to start in nervousness.

"Och! The fire's nearly gone out. Look at it now! I should've braved the cold and got meself out of bed an hour ago, instead of coddlin' me bones like some fine earl's lady." All this the servant spoke to herself in undertones while poking fiercely at the fire. Before long, if the warmth in the room could be used as an indication, she had coaxed it strongly back to life.

"Good morning to you, Grindle."

"Oh, mistress . . . I didn't wake ye, did I now?"

"Nay. I've been awake awhile."

The maid clucked her tongue in sympathy. "Couldn't sleep, could ye? And who can blame ye? All scorched as ye are, it must be hard to lie abed, much less rest with any comfort."

"I'd like to try to get up today." As Lark announced this she began slowly, and with the greatest of care, to push away the layers of sheet and coverlet.

"Oh, no, mistress!" Grindle protested, throwing down the bellows and rushing to the patient's side. "Ye'd best wait 'til Lord Glassmeade says ye may. 'Tis nearly six, ye know, and he'll be about—always breakfasts at half-past the hour, he does. Pray wait for him—there's no tellin' what damage ye might do."

"Come. Help me, Grindle." Not easy to dissuade once her mind had been set to a purpose, Lark inched her legs over the side of the bed and, holding out her arms, waited patiently for assistance.

"Well, if ye insist upon it," the maid muttered in clear displeasure. "But here, let me help ye with a robe. 'Tis the old mistress's, and a bit large, but 'twill do to keep out the cold."

Lark allowed the maid to take hold of her arms and slip them through long silken sleeves. Then, when the sash was tied securely about her waist, she put her arm around Grindle's shoulders. "Now, guide me to a chair, if you please. I'd like to sit awhile before my breakfast."

Only a few steps were required, then a turnabout, before Grindle had positioned her in front of a seat. Lark sank down, feeling for the chair arms and settling herself gingerly.

"I'll just go and get yer tea, now, mistress, and here's a quilt—put it round yeself—can't have ye gettin' chilled, ye know. Freezin' out, it is today. I'll wager frost is thick on the lawn and the old sycamores."

Grindle went to pull back the draperies, and Lark heard their heavy swish as their round brass rings scraped discordantly against the rods.

"A lovely sunrise, it is," Grindle went on, "the colors all pink and lavender. There's snow on the mountaintops, too, and ice crustin' the birdbath. Mark me words, we're in for a harsh, cold winter this year."

When she had gone, Lark sat on the fireside chair, bowing her head pensively, wishing she could see the lovely rise of dawn herself. Surely its shine would cheer her, lift her spirits like nothing else could on this depressing morn.

Did she dare get up and wobble to the window on her blistered feet? Did she dare to unwind the yards of bandage from her eyes?

Aye! She would do it! If only for a moment, she would stand and admire the sunrise to cheer herself.

Or was cheering herself only a feeble excuse? Did she not really yearn with both cold dread and fevered curiosity to find a looking glass, gaze at her reflection, and see for herself how disfigured the fire had left her face?

Of course! And she *would* see!

The surgeon need never know. She would rebind her eyes after she had stolen this little liberty and never tell him of it.

Her steps were slow and tentative. She walked upon the sides of her feet, as the heels were too sore for a normal tread, and crouched down with her hands spread out before her. Fortunately she encountered no obstacles in her awkward walk toward the window, and before long her hand touched the cool, thick velvet drapes she had heard Grindle draw aside. Behind them a slight draft wafted from beneath the sash, and Lark felt for the panes, pressing her palms squarely against their leaded, icy diamonds. Fumbling, she put her hands behind her head, searched for the end of her bandage. She found it, began to pull it round and round . . .

The chill of air brushed her brow, her matted lashes, her teary eyes. She opened the lids and prepared to see the sun, but no soft gleam appeared, no ray of morning color shone.

Frantically, impatiently, she put a finger to her lashes, finding them sparse, withered, and agonizing to touch. Were the lids not fully opened—what was wrong, what was wrong? Wildly, and with trembling hands, she touched the moist, round curve of her eyeballs, exploring them, feeling them opening wide, wider.

But no faint glimmer met their depths, no reflection registered as shape or color or shadow. All was dark, everything, *everything!*

Whirling around, Lark turned and turned again, attempting to locate the fire, a candle, anything ablaze. But nothing took form, everything around her was a dead, lightless void . . . she had no sight. None at all.

Blind! *She was blind!*

The world became an unbalanced place, a place of terror and fear and confusion. She stumbled, spinning round and round, her arms stretched full length, her mouth agape with shock. Suddenly the objects in the room became a maze of obstacles, and she staggered around them, grasping them with clutching fingers to keep herself from falling. In a mindless panic she stumbled in the direction of the door, where she gasped and cried out before whirling back around to find the window. Surely she would be able to see the sun if she searched for its shine again!

Suddenly, in her disoriented staggerings she stepped upon the trailing hem of the wrapper and fell hard, joltingly, to the carpet. She groaned, crawling on her hands and knees, feeling as if she were lost within the darkest, most horrifying tunnel. When her wildly searching fingers at last discovered the surface of a wall, then the length of velvet drape again, she seized upon it, clutching it like a long slender lifeline to pull herself aright.

Her balance was so disturbed, she could only dangle from the drape, gripping it as if for life, wailing, weeping, and—though she hardly realized it—screaming with mad abandon for the lord of the house.

That gentleman sat at his table finishing an excellent breakfast. Garbed in a gray cutaway frockcoat with square tails, brocaded waistcoat, and nankeen breeches, he made a debonair figure, epitomizing the elegance of his station in society. Even his hair was cut in the now fashionable shorter style instead of heavily powdered or bewigged.

Behind him, an unobtrusive footman stood at the mahogany sideboard, tending an array of dishes steaming on silver platters. Attired in resplendent gold-and-azure livery, the servant complemented the splendorous dining room, which was painted powder blue and decorated with rococo plasterwork of intricate design. He stepped forward to refill the master's china coffee cup, but Lord Glassmeade absently waved him away.

"Shall I dispose of the scraps in the usual manner, my lord?" the footman asked then, referring to the leftovers that Christopher routinely ordered scraped into bowls and given to the poor queued up at the gate.

"Aye, Connor," the young earl murmured, folding his newspaper and frowning. The headlines were disquieting. The previous day a mob of Catholic Defenders had been arrested in Phoenix Park, some of them bayoneted by the militia before they could even be put into irons. And along the border of Ulster and Leinster fierce clashes raged between the Defenders and Protestant terrorists. Everywhere trees of liberty were being planted openly by the rebels and bonfires lit to celebrate French victories across the Channel.

The news hardly improved Christopher's already irascible mood. All night he had mulled over a particularly vexatious problem, paced the red-and-gold Turkey carpet in his bedchamber, until, finally, half-dead from fatigue, he had slumped onto a chair and dozed. Had a milk cart and its braying donkey not awakened him an hour past, he would have missed his breakfast hour, which he never did.

Pulling the gold pocket watch from his breeches waistband to check the time, he wondered if the mahogany-haired problem that had kept him up all night had yet awakened. He hoped that a night's sleep had made her a little less bullheaded and a deal meeker. Finding a way to both protect Lark Ballinter and obtain her source of information without risking his own neck would require skill on his part and cooperation on hers.

He realized suddenly that he was drumming his spoon upon the damask table linen and set it aside with a scowl. Hearing a disturbance outside the paneled door, he rose irritably and crossed the black-and-white marble tiles into the grandiose hall.

"What the devil is it?" he called as two of the upstairs maids came running down the steps, the ribbons on their white caps flying.

"'Tis that cotter's lass, my lord!" one answered in a scornful rush. "Gone stark mad, she has!"

Not bothering to ask for details, Christopher dashed up the stairs two at a time, the heels of his polished top boots clicking on the marble. When he entered his mother's room he found Lark clutching at the window drapes, the bandage gone from her eyes. "Good God!" he exclaimed, rushing forward.

Hearing Lord Glassmeade's voice, Lark turned her head and cried out his name. Then, still clenching the drape with one hand, she reached out for him with the other, hurling her weight forward when she felt his arms go round her.

She flung her arms around his neck, anchoring herself against both the terror and the spinning in her head. Her balance was so disturbed that she could not keep from swaying, and shock had weakened her legs to such a degree, they threatened to buckle and make her fall again.

"For God's sake, Lark!" Christopher said, moving to break her viselike grip from his neck. "What have you done? Let me get you back to bed where—"

"Nay!" she shrieked. "Don't let go of me! I beg you, don't let go!" Like a madwoman she clawed at his coat, fastening on to it with her fingers as if fearing he would escape. "My eyes!" she screamed at him in total horror. "I cannot see! I cannot see!"

His resulting silence was so ominous, so doomful, all the air seemed to fly from Lark's lungs at once. "Did you not hear me?" she repeated, grasping his collar. "I said I cannot see. I have gone stone blind!"

Christopher's fingers tightened around the curve of her waist, and he drew her close as if to protect her from his answer. Then, shutting his eyes in anguish, touched by infinite sadness, he delivered the brutal truth. "Aye, Lark. You are blind."

His confirmation of her nightmare caused a convulsive shudder to rack Lark's body. Her throat constricted, her limbs froze in shock. She had expected him to counter her words, soothe her fears, tell her all would be well.

"Tell me 'tis only temporary!" she implored him. "Tell me that tomorrow, or the day after, I will be healed, able to see again!"

He took her head in his hands, holding her firmly, and spoke low and honestly. "I swear, Lark, if I could move heaven and earth to tell you what you wish to hear, I would do it. There was an explosion during the fire—I believe the intensity of the light may have done damage to your eyes. God knows I wish I could assure you that you would wake on the morrow with your vision returned. But I dare not. I cannot say that you will ever see again."

Her voice rose high in panic. "Are you telling me there's no hope a'tall?"

"It would be unkind of me to give you false expectations," Christopher answered quietly, tightening his grip about her waist when she swayed. "But I should like to think, in your case, there is most certainly a good measure of hope."

Inhaling a ragged breath, Lark struggled to digest the surgeon's words. When the staggering truth began to penetrate her consciousness, she groaned and cried out, "Nay, *nay!*"

Then, in devastation, she wept against the surgeon's waistcoat, clutching him as if he were the only safe harbor in a furious black storm.

Christopher simply held her close, raging inwardly that he had not the power to redeem her sight for her.

Finally, after a long while, Lark's tears spent themselves, and with their end, the trauma of her newly discovered condition receded from wild disbelief to nothing more than numbness. She sagged in his arms and felt him catch her lest she fall to the floor.

He put an arm behind her knees and another across her shoulders, tilted her back against his chest. In spite of the fact that she was held so securely, she flung her hands around his neck again and held on as if no force on earth could prize her free.

When he had lowered her carefully onto a seat and

then began to ease himself out from beneath her locked embrace, she cried out.

"Steady on," he reassured her. "I'm only going a few steps away to retrieve a footstool. . . . There, now I'll sit at your feet and hold your hand. Don't be afraid. I'll not leave you."

She felt her hand cradled within his and leaned toward him, listening for his voice, striving to hear his breathing. The air around them was quiet. Only the rattle of coach wheels, the scratch of a brittle twig upon a pane of glass, and the shrill yap of a dog reminded Lark that life continued in its usual rhythm in the world outside.

After a moment she spoke. "Y-you said you . . . *knew.*"

A slight pause ensued. "I feared that I knew."

"And yet you said nothing to me 'til now."

Christopher bent his head. "I had hoped to let a little time pass, time during which you would have become stronger, better able to endure the shock of it."

Lark knew the hearth blazed just behind his shoulders, and in a sudden desperate effort, she leaned forward and strained her eyes until she felt them bulge. But not one flame could she see, not one pinprick penetrated the cloak across her eyes. Her body grew taut and her breathing sped up as another surge of panic seized her.

"Grindle!" Christopher bellowed, his large hand grabbing both of Lark's fluttering wrists to pinion them together. *"Grindle!"*

A few seconds later a flurry of footsteps pounded the carpet, then the breathless question of the summoned servant followed. "M'lord?"

"Bring some brandy. Quickly!"

Lark hardly heard the exchange. She had slipped beyond reason momentarily, imagining a life spent in total darkness, a life where she would be helpless and without the ability to care for Jamie. All the while, she was only distantly aware of the low, urgent words Christopher said to her, to console her, to bring her back to reason.

At last her jaws were grasped and a cool, fiery liquid forced between her teeth. She sputtered, gasped, then allowed more drink to trickle down her throat, vaguely understanding it would help to numb her frenzied mind.

When she had taken all she wanted to take, she tilted her head away from the glass. With dismay, she realized her fingers gripped the surgeon's hands so savagely that her nails surely cut his flesh. The thought caused her to struggle to regain her wits.

Loosening her hold just a bit, she murmured in a small voice, "Would that your skill was one of restoring eyes rather than faces, my lord. . . . I would readily chose my sight over my appearance."

He said nothing, nor did she for a while. She merely fixed her useless gaze to some point upon the ceiling while her body remained deceptively serene within the chair, its stillness a contrast to the thoughts that churned about her head.

"What are you thinking, lass?" Christopher asked. He shifted his tall frame on the tapestried stool and reached out to touch her sleeve.

Her eyes blinked, then opened wide, seeing pictures as they passed across her mind. "I am thinking of the things I can no longer do. No more will I see the rise of morning, will I? Nor will I walk the paths along the fields, or pluck berries from the woods. I'll never see sun sparkling on water again, or a bird in flight. I'll not be able to distinguish a red flower from a yellow, or see springtime come again. I'll not be able to read a book or . . . oh, Lord Glassmeade! The list goes on and on."

"'Tis natural to dwell upon such things at first. Indeed, 'tis all a part of acceptance and healing. But I believe you have a most resilient nature, Lark Ballinter, and over time you'll find yourself able to cope better than you now believe you can. And," he added softly, "I'll be here to help you, of course. You've only to ask for what you need."

Tears began to slide from beneath her lids then, and she marveled that her eyes could manage that sorrowful function so well when they could perform the other, more crucial one not at all. One by one clear drops of brine rolled downward in a trail, burning her cheek beneath its pad of gauze.

Though she did not bother to wipe them away, another did, and his hand was inutterably gentle.

Every day Christopher witnessed anguish in all its dreadful forms, watched young and old alike groan in pain and die in torment. Though he had never become immune to it, he had at least learned to detach his emotions tolerably well. Now, however, to witness the suffering of the brave little rebel who had stood beside him in the moonlight touched him deeply. He felt connected with her, and he had never felt connected with anyone in his life ere now, not even his father.

Using the best form of consolation he knew, the most instinctive kind, he lifted her from the chair, eased her down upon his lap so that her head rested against his shoulder.

Lark knew by intuition that he held her as a man held a woman when giving comfort. Inexplicably reassured by it, she lay back within his arms securely.

For a brief, unreasoned second, she even thought that the forfeiture of light was a fair exchange for this.

6

With a thoughtful frown Christopher made for the stables, shrugging into his blue redingote and settling his bicorn atop his head while he walked. He had left strict instructions for Grindle to remain at Mistress Ballinter's side throughout the day and send a messenger promptly should the patient require him. Though the initial trauma over the discovery of her blindness was now behind her, he knew there would follow many harrowing days of adjustment. Occasional fits of hysteria or rage over her fate would not be unlikely. Being well acquainted with her backbone, however, Christopher had no doubt she would soon learn to cope.

The stable he approached was a large one, clean and cobbled, steepled and crowned by a copper weather vane turned to verdigris. Already the groom had made ready the master's horse. Its gray coat was sleekly brushed, its hooves blacked with tar, and its silky tail squared neatly at the end.

Not for the first time, Christopher realized with a pang of both compunction and disquiet that his horse was better fed than half the population of Dublin, and though he enjoyed luxuries as naturally as any man, he was not without guilt over enjoying them when so many others suffered. He felt his title far more a burden than a blessing and was ever torn between loyalty toward his father and a sense of justice. Though he used his money and influence to their best benefit, he would have chosen a simpler life had he been given the option.

Settling his medical bag before the pommel, Christopher gathered the well-oiled reins and swung up into the saddle, turning his horse onto a strip of drive lined with autumn-colored sycamores. The day was crisp, brilliant with flashes of sunshine escaping through a galloping flock of clouds, and tangy with the pungent aromas of falling brown leaves and damp black earth. Here the streets were clean swept and in good repair, the houses tall and imposing.

From their conservatory window next door, the viscount and his lady waved a greeting to Christopher from their satinwood tea table. As his horse carried him away, he imagined them shaking their bemused heads and commenting that their eccentric surgeon was off yet again to wade through the slums and tend the rabble.

Soon the dappled gray left behind the stately streets of privilege and crossed into less ordered avenues, tossing its head at the traffic noise and the smoke of glassworks and countless coal fires. Bootblacks juggled for positions along the walks, stopping well-dressed gentlemen who only shoved them aside with the tips of their gold-headed walking sticks. All around, the loud cries of the street vendors battled to be heard with such offerings as "Herring! Cockles and mussels! Buy the dry turf! Here's the dry bog-o-wood!"

Upon one auspicious corner workmen hastily erected a gallows where some unfortunate soul would meet his end before the sun set. Already the hangman in his grotesque black mask paced around the unfinished structure as if eager to earn his wage. A sedan chair passed him, and its richly gowned passenger put a handkerchief to her powdered nose and bade her footmen run faster.

Beggars loitered everywhere, huddling in shop doorways and upon corners, imploring every passerby for coins while thrusting malnourished infants out for view. Some had grown weary of their efforts and merely sat upon the muddy curbs in listlessness, drawing their bare feet beneath the hems of their ragged garments while tantalizing odors from the coffeehouses wended about their heads.

With a sudden clattering of iron shoes, the gray sidestepped two industrious waifs holding out their hands in the midst of trundling coaches, post chaises, noddies, jaunting cars, and landaus. Christopher tossed guineas to them and bade them stand out of the danger of traffic, thinking the Foundling Hospital hardly in need of two additional cases to treat in its inadequate wards.

He was on his way to pay that institution a call, as he did every few days, in order to follow up on various cases and argue with the governors over badly needed reforms. After turning onto James Street, he entrusted his horse to an enterprising urchin and entered the hospital, trying his best to ignore the ever-present stench.

Though the feeble patients eagerly awaited visits from Lord Glassmeade, Christopher knew the staff skirted him with ill-concealed care, fearful of being on the receiving end of one of his vociferous lectures concerning hygiene. On more than one occasion he had flung trays of filthy basins and soiled linen to the floor with a few choice curses and bellowed for just one blessed pair of clean hands to assist him in surgery.

The patient he had come to see today was the small boy scalded by boiling water he had earlier spoken to Lark about. Having walked through ward after ward of rickety wooden cots, where children lay coughing, crying with fever, or swathed in bandages, Christopher halted midway between two double rows of beds.

"How are you faring today, Sean?" he asked cheerfully, leaning down to inspect his patient.

The child shifted on his thin mattress, his hands anxiously clenching the broadcloth sheet. "'Me arm is hurtin' me awfully, sir," he complained, obviously dreading to have the dressing changed. "Has me mum come yet?"

"Do you like cinnamon?" Christopher asked, avoiding the question while he unwrapped the bun he had earlier put in his pocket.

Sean reached for the bread, bit into it greedily, and between huge mouthfuls managed to say, "Aye!"

"Then I'll bring you two tomorrow."

Before long Christopher had completed his snipping and replacing of gauze, tossed the soiled dressing in a basin, and praised Sean for his stiff upper lip.

Then, drawing up the sheet again, he growled in disgust at the sight of vermin. Patting Sean upon the hand, he promptly located the nurse and summarily lectured her yet again on the need for regular bathing of the patients and the changing of their beds.

After completing his rounds, Christopher quitted the institution with half the chastised staff gaping at his back, his boots ringing against the grimy tiles with more force than when he had entered.

At a brisk clip he proceeded to his next appointment at the fashionable club called Daly's in College Green. A footman in powdered wig and livery took his hat and redingote in the vestibule, and Christopher entered the once simple chocolate shop that had become the most sumptuous gaming house in all Dublin. Along with half the members of the nearby House of Commons, every rakehell buck in the city frequented the tables, carousing day and night while wagering for high stakes.

Christopher focused his eyes in the dim light, for during the afternoon the blinds were drawn and the chandeliers lit to simulate evening. All around, the shining surfaces of polished marble, mahogany, and beveled glass reflected lounging gentlemen—some sober, most half-foxed, and a few snoring raucously in their high white stocks. Only the clink of glasses and the occasional burst of triumph from a winner interrupted the low hum of masculine conversation.

Upon seeing the latest patron enter, the proprietor detached himself from a hazard table, strolled forward, and bowed respectfully. "Do you require your usual table, my lord?"

Christopher scanned with shrewd eyes the various velvet- and brocade-clad groups of gentlemen pinching snuff and tossing down claret. "Aye," he said. "The usual."

"And will you be playing a game? Or just drinking?"

"Just drinking."

"Very well, my lord."

Escorting Christopher through a pair of paneled doors, the proprietor unlocked a private room and invited his guest to sit down while he fetched refreshments. A moment later he returned with a decanter of brandy and watched mutely while Christopher withdrew a coin from his waistcoat pocket and, in an uncharacteristically clumsy move, dropped it to the floor.

Only the keenest eye would have noted it was not an ordinary guinea, but a very ancient coin stamped with a snarling lion.

As Christopher leaned to retrieve the piece from the floor, the proprietor bowed in answer to the signal and exited without saying a word.

Not three minutes later there came a discreet rap upon the door, followed by the entrance of an unimposing figure with a sharp chin and homely face ravaged by smallpox scars.

"Beauchamp!" Christopher greeted him, rising and holding out a hand.

"'Tis grand to see you, Christopher," the visitor replied, leaning to pour himself a brandy before sitting down. "Is all well in your medical practice these days?"

"As well as can be."

"Good, good. I've been wanting to seek your advice on a matter myself."

"You're not going to badger me about finding a cure for balding again, are you?" Christopher asked with a twinkle in his eye.

Beauchamp chuckled, touching his scanty straight hair. "You are too astute. I suppose I shall have to live with it or take to wearing my wigs again, eh? Always fancied I looked deuced attractive with a paste curl or two above my ears."

He grew silent then. Recently Beauchamp Harvey had emerged as one of the chief leaders in the United Irish underground. Like most of the upper echelon of rebel leaders, he was Protestant, vastly wealthy, and quite influential. A member of the bar, he was known for both his wit and his numerous skillfully fought duels. It was said this man of diminutive stature feared nothing.

"Do you have news for me?" he finally asked.

Christopher cleared his throat, running a hand over the strong edge of his shaven jaw. "Not of the sort you would like to hear, I'm afraid. Indeed, I don't know when I shall receive another dispatch. Our line of communication has been . . . interrupted."

"Oh?"

"Christopher nodded, swirling the brandy in his glass. "As luck would have it, my contact has become indisposed."

"Can you not replace him?"

A pained expression crossed Christopher's face. "Unfortunately, you have got the gender wrong—'tis a young woman to whom I refer."

"A young woman?"

"Aye. A very contrary young woman."

Beauchamp shifted his thin frame upon the plushly upholstered chair and drew his brows together. "Well, what the deuce is the matter with her? Why is she indisposed? On second thought, don't tell me. You're surely to launch into a graphic description of some frivolous female complaint."

Christopher raised his glass to his lips and drained the last of the brandy. "Truth is," he said, his voice low from the fiery draft, "she's suffered an accident. Short of a miracle, she's simply not capable of receiving and delivering any more messages."

"Replace her, then!" Beauchamp exclaimed as if the solution were a simple one.

"Believe me, I am endeavoring to find a way to do just that." Leaning back in his chair, Christopher gave an exasperated sigh. "Unfortunately, however, she is far from malleable."

"Ah, come now, Chris!" the older man cajoled, putting a teasing hand upon his cohort's shoulder. "You cannot but stroll down the street without having every curly-lashed eye within a hundred yards fixed in your direction. Indeed, I have heard it said that there are peeresses as well as doxies who invent maladies just to contrive a few moments of your charming attention. Surely you can manage just one indisposed little rebel."

Christopher was silent, recalling a mulishly set chin and stubborn mouth.

"I shall be waiting to hear from you, then," Beauchamp said with good-natured confidence, pushing back his chair. "Things are progressing well in my arena. Our military forces are drilling regularly by unit and should be in good fighting form by Christmas. But take care," he warned. "There are informants in every circle. And I needn't remind you that the lofty Lord Glassmeade would be quite a sensational catch for the government."

Her surgeon came to dine with her very late that evening. When his footsteps rang upon the hardwood just outside her door, Lark was seated on a chair at the window, her bandaged eyes gazing out into the darkness as if she could actually perceive the cold beads of rain sliding down the pane. For an hour she had been listening to the storm and the clatter of hurrying coaches and whip-wielding drivers, waiting foolishly for the sound of a familiar step. Though she loathed the notion of it, Lord Glassmeade seemed her only source of light in a dark and frightening world.

She knew he pushed the tea trolley before him. Grindle had rolled it in earlier, and her now sensitive ear had noted the creak of its one ungreased wheel. Though the servant had uncovered delicious-smelling foods at breakfast, noontime, and tea, Lark had refused everything but a few sips of cold coffee. Undoubtedly her stubborn behavior had been related to that esteemed personage who ruled the house, and momentarily she expected his endeavor to modify it.

She knew he stood behind her now—her nerves seemed to have a special sense of him—but she did not turn around on the chair, merely waited for him to speak.

"'Tis a miserable night," Christopher said to break the silence. He regarded her through narrowed blue eyes and, taking in her rigid posture and high-held head, decided she was feigning a stoic front rather than show him weakness. He was glad she was proud, as her pride would be a resource in the days to come. He did not intend to permit her to sit on a chair and brood day after day, and he would jolt her out of her melancholia if need be in order to turn her mind away from self-pity.

And if there was a way, ere long he would have her back beneath the branches of the Faery Thorn.

"Have you been out in the midst of the storm?" she asked.

What a shame he could not share with her the irony of her question, he thought. She would appreciate the news, that he had just come from a turbulent meeting of the United Irish in the back room of a tavern.

"Aye. And quite a riotous storm it is."

"Did a surgery keep you late? A broken limb, perhaps?"

"Nay. 'Twas a break of a different sort that needed mending. But enough of talk. I'm famished, and it just so happens I've brought along supper."

"Have you not eaten?" she asked, surprised, for she had just heard the watchman cry out the hour of eleven.

As intended, Lark had played directly into his hands, and Christopher availed the opportunity with a slightly brooding response. "Nay." He sighed. "I had hoped to share my supper tonight with a lively companion. I find my appetite is never a healthy one when I'm forced to eat alone."

Lark let out a breath in an exaggerated fashion, going along with his ploy but taking care to put plenty of resignation in her tone. "Very well, then. I wouldn't want you to be going without a hearty meal on my account. What has the cook prepared?"

He wheeled the trolley close and removed the dish covers. "Overdone leg of lamb, underdone beef, pickled salmon, potatoes with parsley, fruit, strangely wilted vegetables, and buns that have sat too long in butter. Ah, and I save the best for last—pudding with a skin upon it."

Lark almost smiled. Cooked well or not, the menu sounded like a feast to her. But she would not give

Lord Glassmeade the satisfaction of knowing that. "You have hardly tempted my appetite," she replied.

"I engaged a new cook this morning," Christopher admitted. "And now haven't the heart to dismiss her. She's one of my charity cases, as Father so scornfully terms them. We'll hope her culinary talents improve soon." Uncovering one last dish, he muttered, "Odd-looking thing. Wonder what it is. . . ."

Lark could not stifle a laugh.

"Sorry," he said, suspending a handful of cutlery and giving her a sidelong look. "Perhaps I should keep my ill-mannered remarks to myself and deceive you about what I am shortly to serve."

"Are you good at deceit, Lord Glassmeade?"

"Very."

Lark suspected he had spoken with some underlying meaning and frowned a bit over it. "I believe I'd like to have honesty from my surgeon, if you please," she said slowly.

"Then your surgeon shall endeavor to give it to you. Beginning with the admission that I detest pickled salmon."

"Then have the beef."

"I shall." She heard him clattering plates and jangling cutlery again. "And to you, I'll give a little portion of everything, starting with a goblet of wine."

He put it to her hand, and after catching its tempting bouquet, Lark sipped it enthusiastically, having tasted nothing so delicious since her time in France.

A moment later she realized Lord Glassmeade had settled a table before her chair, and atop that, her dinner. After draping a napkin across her lap, he took hold of her hand to place within it a piece of cutlery, presumably a fork. She clenched it tightly and hesitated, dreading the awkwardness of what was to come. Did he not realize that poking randomly at bits of food on a plate was an intimidating experience to a person newly blind?

Across from her, Christopher seated himself. A long silence fell. "Are you accustomed to saying grace?" he asked finally, as if suddenly realizing a blunder.

"Aye," she murmured, as much to procrastinate as to reply with honesty. "But . . . you offer it."

He did so with no delay, and then she felt him pause expectantly, waiting for her to begin her meal so he might begin his. She lowered her eyes toward the plate, attempting to focus them upon the food, though of course in vain. *How was she to eat?*

Frustration beset her, and she feared she would fall into a fit of panic at any moment.

When she heard Lord Glassmeade put down his fork, she tensed, knowing he was about to rush to her rescue. No, she told herself. I will not have some high-nosed lord of the realm feeding me like a helpless infant.

Hastily, and with recklessness, she began stabbing with her fork, hearing first the thud of tines on wood, then the scrape of silver against china, all with no knowledge of what scrap she had managed to snag. She raised the fork to her lips and clumsily got it into her mouth, only to find it devoid of any crumb of food.

Lark sat frozen with embarrassment, her hand suspended in midair. She, who had been so proud of her independence only days ago, had just humiliated herself in the simple act of eating. After lowering her hand to set the fork aside, she squeezed her eyes shut against the galling prick of tears.

Across the table she heard the sound of chair legs being dragged across the plush carpet. A second later two firm hands placed themselves beneath her arms and lifted her up. Lord Glassmeade drew her close even as the flood of rage burst forth.

"What a helpless wretch I am! I cannot even feed myself!"

"'Tis my fault," Christopher insisted. "At first I was stupidly unaware. Then I thought to let you try alone, so that you might learn to conquer the blasted task. I should not have. 'Twas too soon—"

"Nay!" she cried, pulling away. "I don't want help! I want to manage alone. Sainted Mary! How idiotic of me not to be able to do even such a simple thing as eat!"

"Sit down," he said calmly, "and let me give you just the briefest direction. Then I'm certain you can proceed quite well by yourself."

Hardly in a frame of mind to favor healthy digestion, but wanting to show Lord Glassmeade a spirited front, Lark mustered her natural stoicism and complied, lowering herself back onto the chair. She felt his hand close over hers and wondered suddenly at what point he had ceased to touch her as a surgeon touched his patient. His contact now lingered just the briefest moment, and though it was perhaps not intentional, it was distinctly delivered as male to female.

"Here," he said, guiding her hand around the table. "This is the butter dish and knife—feel them? And over here . . . your bun withering in its puddle

of butter. Perhaps you could start with that—
unattractive as it is."

Through dwindling tears she smiled, showing her
pretty teeth, and with an adeptness that was certainly
respectable in a first endeavor, she managed to break,
lightly butter, and eat her bread. Though her host had
disparaged the food, she had never in her life eaten
bread so tasty, nor certainly worked so hard just to
get it into her mouth.

Feeling she deserved it after her accomplishment,
she downed the remainder of her wine. It slid down
her throat smoothly, not at all like the bitter poteen
she had drunk behind her uncle's back. She decided
she rather liked the earl's vintage and was gratified to
hear him fill her goblet again when she had barely set
it down.

"When did you decide to become a surgeon?" she
asked a moment later, her composure quite restored
by the claret. "I mean to say, 'tis not as if a man needs
employment when he enjoys a position such as
yours."

Observing her with amusement, Christopher took
a bite of beef and chewed it. "And what 'position'
might that be, Mistress Ballinter?" he asked.

"Well, Lord Glassmeade, since you're bein' contrary, I'll spell it out for you. P-r-i-v-i-l-e-g-e."

"Ah. *That* position."

"Aye. That position."

"Do I detect a note of resentment in your voice,
Citizeness?" he asked with good-natured sarcasm and
an affected French inflection. "Have you been
inspired by our new republic across the Channel?
Don't tell me you're one of those hotheaded, trouble-
making rebels I've been hearing so much about, who

run around taking oaths and calling for the 'Triumph of the Gael.'"

Lark barely managed to prevent her jaw from dropping at the remark. Attempting to gather her wits about her, she felt for her refilled goblet, located it, and fortified herself with a hearty swallow. How could she have forgotten she dined across the table from the enemy? He was clever, and she must remember to beware his ruses.

"If I were, I would hardly be admitting it to an illustrious member of the aristocracy such as your-self, would I now?" she countered.

"A corrupt aristocracy who does the bidding of London for special favors, you would like to add, no doubt," Christopher said to incite her, smiling at the way she tossed her head. He leaned forward with the wine decanter and, chasing her goblet with it, filled it to the brim once more.

"I'm certain you would be knowing more of corruption than I," she said with a pert raise of the chin.

"Would I now?"

"Don't you?"

"If that's your considered opinion of me, Mistress Ballinter, then I'm certain I should be hard pressed to convince you otherwise."

She took another sip of wine, and another, grow-ing more bold with each swallow, her sense of wari-ness dwindling. She had all but forgotten her despair of a moment ago. Nothing spurred her to liveliness so much as a round of political debate, though she had not the least notion that this tendency was being duly noted and encouraged by the other member of the room.

"Someone must clean out the government," she asserted. "'Tis wickedly unfair of you and your high-flown friends to deny the vote and seats in Parliament to honest men simply because they weren't born Protestant—or should I say, with strings attached to their limbs which can be pulled by King George the puppet master."

Throughout the meal Christopher had discreetly attempted to rearrange the food upon Lark's plate, putting it in piles between each stab of her fork so that she might better spear it. Now, however, she punctuated her heated tirade with an especially energetic thrust and caught him in the knuckles.

"With your vast wealth of knowledge, Mistress Ballinter," he answered through teeth gritted in pain, "I can see you know exactly the measure of every Irish nobleman."

"Everyone knows that any decent Irish nobleman spends his time gambling, drinking, and wenching." The words were a taunting condemnation. "Feel at liberty to correct me, my lord," she added impertinently, "if my information is wrong, or if I have gotten these priorities out of proper sequence."

"I would put the last one first. Personal preference, of course."

Initially Lark felt inclined to scowl in disgust and mutter some disparagement against the male gender in general. But as she sat there sensing the earl's gaze upon her face, she burst into a fit of laughter. After all, she had sermonized him quite ruthlessly, and although he had answered with sarcasm, he had managed to keep his good humor quite intact.

His deep, easy laughter joined hers a second later, and it struck her she had not heard it before. Its vibration, its tone, and its very character were rather pleasant, and she set them to memory.

Christopher could not remember when he had had such an enjoyable dinner. His little rebel's company certainly outweighed the simpering chatter of the powdered and perfumed females he usually squired about town. He decided she should stay away from drink, however, as she could not hold her liquor above half. A glass or two, and the highest secret of the rebel cause would be in jeopardy of being loosed from her seditious little tongue. God forbid she should ever wander downstairs and stumble into one of the bacchanalian routs his peers so enjoyed.

Eager to test his theory, he said smoothly, "You seem quite well instructed for having been raised in a cotter's home. Surely no simple hedge master could have provided such an education."

"I—" Lark shut her mouth abruptly. She set aside the goblet with a frown. Warning bells were suddenly ringing in her fuzzy brain with such shrillness that her temples ached. She would hardly be wise to say she had been educated in France by revolutionist parents. Better to pretend that a sympathetic teacher had broken the once strict law against the formal education of Catholics.

Straightening on her seat, she replied, "He was quite a good hedge master."

Christopher grinned. Even with a decanter of wine flowing through her veins, she had caught herself in time. But he was not yet finished.

When she put a hand to her mouth to smother a hiccough, he reached across the table to steady the wine goblet, which was in her other hand and threatened to slosh over its brim onto her lap.

"*Desirez-vous du café?*" he asked casually.

""*Non. Merci.*"

One glass too many, he thought. She had slipped. Not that he hadn't already known she was a native of France. He knew a great many details about her, except, of course, the name of her French contact.

Across from him, Lark frowned, feeling rather giddy and wondering if she had said anything she should not have. She had the strangest notion she had just spoken French. Or was it Gaelic?

She began to wield her fork again, hoping that more food would help to clear her mind. She was amazed at how much more adroit she had already become with her cutlery; her fork never once came up empty.

After she had taken a bite of spice cake—the tastiest item on the evening's menu—she opened another conversation, wanting at all costs to draw discussion away from politics.

"I—I want to thank you for seeing after Jamie."

Christopher leaned back in his chair and stretched his long legs. "You're quite welcome. He's been enjoying himself. I had a pony saddled this morning for his use and sent him to the confectioner's with a groomsman. Tomorrow I promised to take him on a ride to Phoenix Park. The races are on in the morning."

"Thank you for your generosity," Lark responded, though experiencing a sudden spark of annoyance. "But I'd rather you not carry it too far. We'll be back to our old life soon, and I wouldn't want Jamie to be growing too . . . soft."

Silently, and with the utmost care of her fork, Christopher slid another piece of cake onto her plate. "Ah. Softness. Another of those vile character flaws we Irish noblemen possess. Perhaps, as a remedy, I should try to eat more potatoes and a little less cake, eh?"

Lark almost choked upon her own bite of sweet and hastily put a napkin to her lips. Unaccountably, then, she fell into a ridiculous episode of giggling.

Deciding it was time to get her to bed before she fell face forward into her plate, Christopher rose from his chair. When he put an arm around her waist, she protested in a slurred voice, then gave up and rested her head on his shoulder.

"I—I've decided t' stay, you know," she said when he had deposited her upon the coverlet. "But just until my cheek heals, of course . . . not a min-minute longer." Closing her eyes, she concentrated, so drowsy she could barely get the words out. "Somethin' I have to do. Important. What was it? Ah, I 'member—" She held up an unsteady finger. "An assig-assignation. I have an assignation with a thoroughly . . . vile and vulgar *polisson*. . . ."

Christopher frowned. Really, she used the most unflattering descriptions of his character. Tossing a quilt over her small body and noting the sleepy smile curving her lips, he muttered, "Aye. Well, see you meet him soon. I've an idea he's a most impatient vile and vulgar reprobate."

7

For several days Lark went without a visit
from the surgeon, having been told by Grindle that
some matter of business had called him to his father's
country estate in Kildare. In his absence his apprentice came daily to tend her burn and on the third day
allowed her to remove the wrap from her head. As
soon as he had unwound the bandage, examined her
eyes, and departed, Lark rushed to the window, compelled as before to test her eyesight. Throwing aside
the drapes, feeling a circle of weak sunshine beam
down upon her face, she leaned forward, trying to
perceive even the faintest halo of light. All in vain.

At the cruelty of her plight she could not help but
feel both rage and self-pity, and she wondered what
unconscionable and unwitting sin she had committed
to deserve such a merciless punishment from fate.

Upon the street below came the stirring sounds of
morning. A vendor's cry, the rolling of a wheel upon
cobbles, and the exuberant shriek of a child gone out

to play proclaimed that life in its very normalcy abounded. But instead of comforting Lark, it only gave her reason to feel a greater alienation from the rest of the world. When a bird trilled from the tree branches just outside, it enraged her that she could not see it, or the garden, or the sky. Blackness! Only suffocating blackness made up her life.

Language seemed to have no description of her desolation, and in helpless fury she pounded a fist against the window frame. She punctuated the thud with a curse muttered under her breath. Then, with more volume, she repeated every oath she had ever heard the cotter's sons hurl in the heat of their drunken brawls.

In between these choice invectives, a sound caught her ear and she stilled, tilting her head to one side and suspending her fist in midair. The faintest creak of a floorboard came from the corridor. She swung around. The step was not that of Grindle, nor that of either of the upstairs maids or the apprentice who had just departed. And certainly it was not the confident rap of Lord Glassmeade's boots. It was a tentative approach she did not know.

"Mistress Ballinter?"

The soft voice floated from the direction of the threshold, its volume not much louder than the plush rustle of voluminous skirts accompanying it.

"Who are you?" Lark asked.

Venturing a few steps closer, the visitor answered, "I'm Lady Helen. Lord Glassmeade's cousin. I—I've come to see you. But, if this is not a convenient time . . ."

Lark realized the lady must have heard her passionate swearing and probably had her ears scorched. Feeling a bit ashamed, she said, "Er . . . please, come in."

She heard the sigh of the lady's petticoats brushing the carpet and smelled a cloud of sweet perfume drifting up from her person. "My cousin asked me to call upon you, thinking perhaps you might need some . . . personal items. If you do, I'll be happy to get them."

Already Lark had learned to form a first impression by sound rather than sight, gleaning insight into character not by physical appearance, but by tone of voice and step. She judged Lady Helen to be younger than herself, not above seventeen, and rather timid in nature, though how anyone born into privilege and luxury could be less than self-assured, she could not fathom.

"'Tis kind of you," Lark replied awkwardly. Accustomed only to contempt—or indifference—from the fine ladies she had chanced to encounter in the country, she was a bit nonplussed by this one's solicitude. "Actually," she said, "I would like to have my clothes and Jamie's fetched from the cottage. Those, and the furnishings we had there." She wondered if the Marquess of Winterwoode had had the meager pieces thrown out onto the lane now that the eviction date had passed. "They aren't much," she added, "but if they just could be stored somewhere for a wee bit—"

"Lord Glassmeade has seen to them already," Lady Helen cut in. "Everything is in the carriage house. All but your . . ." She paused. "Clothes. I have those here in my hands."

Lark could well imagine the lady's look of disdain, for she possessed only two very humble garments. The best one the fire had apparently destroyed, and the remaining skirt and jacket had been for her daily labors about the cottage, the garden, and the fields. They were worn, frayed at the hem, and many times mended.

"Th-they've been laundered," Lady Helen added politely, perhaps trying to atone for her initial reaction.

Suddenly Lark wanted nothing so much as to get out of the borrowed robe and nightshift and into her own familiar attire. In spite of Lady Helen's opinion, she would wear her peasant's garb proudly and refuse to apologize for it in any way.

"Would you help me to dress?" she asked.

Lady Helen hesitated. "Why, I believe Chris—my cousin meant for you to wear new clothes. I brought three gowns with me which are just being pressed belowstairs. I've already seen to it that your brother is properly attired. He was quite delighted with the things I selected for him."

"I've no doubt he was," Lark commented stiffly, "but I prefer to wear my own clothes. If you'll just help me put them on?"

During the ensuing second or two of silence, Lark received the distinct impression that one did not ask a nobly bred woman to do anything for which a servant had been hired. Perversely, however, she did not relieve Lady Helen of the request, but merely unsashed her robe and made to slip out of it, thinking it would be a good exercise in humility for the spoiled aristocrat to put her soft white hands to good use.

"Er . . ." Lady Helen moved closer, her tone somewhat disconcerted. "There's a screen just over there—in the corner. Sh-should I . . . lead you to it?"

At first mention, Lark had envisioned the type of screen that protected a hearth, only belatedly realizing that grand houses must have screens for dressing. At Uncle Jerome's cottage she had strung up an old curtain for privacy, of course, but it had not occurred to her to shield herself from the eyes of another woman.

Feeling Lady Helen's velvet-smooth hand upon her wrist and not wanting to offend her sense of delicacy any further, Lark obediently allowed herself to be led a few steps forward.

"Now," Lord Glassmeade's cousin pronounced, "I shall turn my back. When you have disrobed, simply say so, and I shall hand you one garment at a time over the top of the screen. Just reach up and feel about for it. Are you ready?"

Lark was amazed at such prudishness. "Really, Lady Helen, you needn't be so particular about turning your back. I'm not nearly so modest as all that. And besides," she added, "being blind, I'd hardly know it even if you were fair staring a hole through me, now would I?"

The next silence stretched so long, she feared she had shocked her companion. Then she heard the beginnings of a giggle, a tinkling melodious sound that was quite delightful.

"Oh, Mistress Ballinter," Lady Helen said, "you are indeed blunt, are you not? I must confess, Christopher warned me of it."

"Did he? And what else did he have to say about me?"

"Oh, nothing ungentlemanly," Lady Helen put in hastily. "He simply said you were outspoken and direct—and he didn't use those adjectives in a disparaging way. Of course," she continued in a bashful tone, "he *did* have that cross look upon his face when he spoke of you. But then, whenever Christopher feels thwarted, he looks cross."

When Lark handed up the nightdress, Lady Helen said, "Oh, just leave it on the floor. The maid will find it."

Mindful of the work of the maids, who were up before dawn and did not retire until after the residents of the house were abed—be that nine of the clock or midnight—Lark declined to follow Lady Helen's directive and folded the nightdress neatly before draping it atop the screen. All the while she listened with interest as Lady Helen continued to chat. Apparently, though class widely separated the two girls, the noblewoman felt it no barrier to the sharing of feminine gossip.

"Truth to tell, I fear my cousin is put out with me. Papa purchased a new mare for my pleasure, and I begged Christopher to teach me to ride—no one has more skill with horses than he. But when it came to actually mounting the beast, I found myself positively petrified. Its teeth were so large and its hooves so menacing, I didn't want to go within a yard of it. Chris attempted to cajole me at first, then persuade me to mount, but I was simply too fearful to do his bidding. At last he sighed in exasperation and called me the biggest ninny he had ever known. Though he said it with a smile, I could tell he was quite cross. His jaw throbs, you know."

Reaching out for her well-worn undergarments, Lark muttered, "Sounds like an unattractive trait."

"Oh, there's nothing in the least unattractive about Christopher, I assure you. Actually, he is so handsome I would be unnerved in his presence were he not my cousin. All my friends implore me to use my influence to arrange an introduction, but I tell them they're wasting their time. Christopher is too preoccupied with his work to embroil himself in a serious romantic relationship. And anyway, Mama says 'twould take a most exceptional woman to handle him in marriage."

Lark stretched out her hand toward the screen to locate her skirt. "Why is that?"

Lady Helen seemed to fall into thought. "I don't know, exactly. Except that Chris is . . . complex. One never quite knows what's going on in that head of his. He's rather tormented, I think, driven by passions the rest of us can't understand. He suffered a most dreadful tragedy when he was a boy, you know . . . but I mustn't be indiscreet." Handing over the last garment, she concluded, "He's really quite a delightfully charming man, when he wants to be, with a smile that can cause one's heart to turn over."

Lark experienced a curiously intense desire to see that smile, then reprimanded herself for the sentiment. She hardly need to be further endeared to the high-hatted earl. "Do you have a suitor, Lady Helen?" she asked, changing the subject.

"Nay," came the answer. "I am the plain one of the family. A sparrow amongst peacocks, as my sisters jestingly say. My dowry will likely be the attribute that catches a husband for me. And Papa will arrange that."

"Humph. Then I wouldn't marry at all." Lark completed her changing of clothes and turned her back to allow Lady Helen to fasten the buttons of her blouse. When the young woman clumsily complied, Lark shrugged into her old black jacket and laced it up. After pulling her unbound hair over one shoulder, she began to plait it in the traditional way of an Irish peasant maid, her hands, sore as they were, still adept at the task she had done every morning since the age of five. She finished by withdrawing from her skirt pocket a worsted emerald tassel to bind up the end of the braid.

Her feet remained bare, for she had owned only one pair of shoes and stockings, and those had presumably been lost to the ravages of fire. But like most impoverished country maids, she was not accustomed to wearing them often, for their cost was so dear that only Sundays, funerals, weddings, and the cold days of winter warranted the wearing out of good leather.

"Now," she said, feeling cheered by the familiarity of her clothes. She stepped back a bit from Lady Helen and held out her arms. "How do I look? Nothing's askew, is it? Or on wrong side out? My hair is not standing on end, I hope?"

Her companion remained mute for several seconds, during which time Lark guessed the girl struggled to find words. Perhaps she had never seen a humbly dressed cotter's lass before. Perhaps she did not know that men and women lived and died so that she and her kind could live idle lives of luxury. Perhaps she had never noticed them trudging down the lanes with pinched faces and starving children.

"Er . . ." the lady finally stammered. "You look quite . . . comfortable."

"She does indeed."

Lark froze in place. It seemed ages since she had heard the deeply pleasant voice.

Still wearing the fawn breeches and brown boots stained with water from boggy paths, Christopher tarried upon the threshold of his mother's chambers for a moment, regarding with an intense gaze the woman who stood in the center of it, assuring himself she was really substance. He had nearly ruined his horse getting back to Dublin, beset with plaguesome concern that his faery queen had flown the house during his absence and disappeared into the streets. The sight of her gave him an unreasoned relief.

He almost smiled. How defiantly out of place she appeared in her own garb, standing next to the elaborately dressed and coiffed Helen, her tall figure framed against a backdrop of Flemish paintings worth a king's ransom. Her long slender feet, peeking out from beneath her hems, were bare upon the Turkey carpet. She wore a white blouse that was clean but patched, a black skirt hiked up on either side, tucked beneath the waistband to reveal petticoats dyed brightest emerald. He was not surprised at the choice of hue. Most country lasses selected crimson, but leave it to Lark to flaunt the color symbol of Irish liberty.

Contrasted with her elegant setting, she should have appeared plain and coarse, but she did not. Quite the opposite, he thought, feeling not for the first time a masculine rush of strong fascination for her.

"Christopher!" Rushing forward, Helen stretched out her arms to him and smiled nervously, her discomfiture over her failed mission obvious.

Before he had left the city, Christopher had requested that she come here specifically to attire Lark in suitable clothes. It would hardly aid his already unorthodox reputation to have a cotter's girl in ragged peasant garb wandering about the fashionable Henrietta Street address when members of Parliament were so often dropping in and out. They would whisper about it for months and pose blunt questions that would require careful explanations.

"Helen," he muttered under his breath, squeezing her hand a bit more forcefully than necessary, "why is Mistress Ballinter dressed like that?"

"Sshh! She'll hear you!" Lady Helen admonished, glancing over her shoulder. "The truth is, she wanted no part of the new gowns, was quite adamant in her desire to wear her own clothes. I couldn't persuade her to change her mind, Chris, 'tis all there is to it."

Christopher rolled his eyes. No one was more meek than Helen. He supposed he would have to deal with the situation himself.

"You're looking well, Mistress Ballinter," he said. "How do you feel?" He strolled forward and took hold of her hand. He had thought a great deal about touching her while he was away, a very great deal. The preoccupation puzzled him, and he looked deeply into her eyes as if seeking to find answer there. They were clear and wide, the greenish hue of the sea on a stormy day.

Unable to fathom why she felt a sudden awkwardness in the surgeon's presence, Lark removed her hand from his firm grasp and said crisply, "I'm feeling fine. Thank you."

"My apprentice has taken good care of you?"

"Aye."

"Good. And my cousin—she has been helpful?"

"Most helpful. She would make an able lady's maid."

At Helen's expression of horror, Christopher smiled, giving her a wicked wink to annoy her further. Turning back to Lark, he continued in a smooth voice, "Then I'm certain she will be most proficient at helping you into one of the new gowns she's ordered made up."

"She's quite generous, I'm sure," Lark replied, "but I won't be wearing any new gowns. My own clothes suit me fine."

Christopher glanced at his cousin, then, seeing her smug countenance, contemplated the rebel in green petticoats again. Her chin was set in an all-too-familiar way, and he ran an impatient hand through his hair, wondering how best to proceed. After due consideration, he decided groveling stood the best chance of success.

"Mistress Ballinter," he said, "I would deem it a personal favor if you would wear the new gowns and the appropriate accessories while staying in my house."

Determined not to emulate the class of nobles she so despised, nor relinquish her own identity and heritage just to save the conceited earl a twinge of embarrassment, Lark shook her head. "Forgive me, Lord Glassmeade, I am beholden for your consideration of my needs, of course, but I feel more comfortable wearing my own clothes. And surely you want your patients to be comfortable."

Behind him, Helen had the audacity to giggle. Christopher glowered at her and regarded Lark again, wondering what his contrary rebel would do were she to find her clothes vanished upon waking tomorrow.

"Cousin," Lady Helen said hastily, obviously noting his gathering frustration and wanting to break the impasse, "how was your visit to Kildare? Papa said there was violence at the estate again."

Lark listened attentively for Lord Glassmeade's reply, not failing to mark the slight lapse of time before it came. Clearly, he was reluctant to speak on the subject.

"There was a bit of violence, Helen," he said, as if careful of his response. "But 'tis quelled now."

"Did they slash the poor cattle again?" Helen asked anxiously, referring to the Catholic terrorists' vengeful act of cutting the hamstrings of their landlords' livestock.

"Aye. A few," he replied.

"Oh, 'tis just terrible to think of the suffering of the beasts! And how frightening for your father to be at the mercy of the deranged insurgents roaming the countryside. Why, Papa said they are not above murder. When will this madness end?"

Unable to keep herself out of the discussion, Lark took a step forward and addressed the earl. "Aye, Lord Glassmeade. Tell us . . . when will the madness end?"

"My talents do not include those of a soothsayer, Mistress Ballinter. Most things beyond the realm of wenching, drinking, and gambling confound me. Remember?"

"My lord?" A footman appealed to the earl from the doorway before Lark could sputter a response.

"What is it?"

"A . . . person is here to see you. You have . . . er, been expecting him, I believe."

Christopher's face darkened at the words, and he glanced first at Lark, then at his cousin, before saying, "Excuse me, ladies, I fear I have business to attend. Thank you, Helen, for coming today—if I hear of any openings for lady's maid, I'll be certain to mention your name. And Mistress Ballinter," he added, grinding out the words as pleasantly as possible, "if you could force yourself to wear the new gowns, you would earn my undying gratitude."

After his abrupt departure, Lady Helen stammered her own excuses, graciously inviting Lark to send for her should she need any feminine shopping done.

Suddenly left alone, with no place to go and no occupation to claim her, Lark experienced a niggling restlessness. She had been in the bedchamber for days, and other than the burn upon her cheek and a few other unhealed spots, her injuries gave her no particular trouble. Her young woman's body, used to much activity, begged for exercise.

She determined to assuage her boredom by familiarizing herself with the room. With hands outstretched and body slightly bent, she went from one piece of furniture to another, running fingers up and down, back and forth, until she knew well their shapes and placement. Each object, whether functional or decorative, she immediately and without surprise discerned to be costly, for no one, not even one sightless, could mistake the feel of fine workmanship and rich fabric. There were ornate curved-legged tables, a desk with parchment and ink pots and quills. Two chairs angled beside the hearth were plushly tapestried, their pillows tasseled and edged in heavy braid.

Lark moved on, touching the marble mantel and, upon its shelf, porcelain figurines so exquisitely wrought that she had no trouble identifying five distinct breeds of dogs. The value of such things she could not begin to imagine. In France she had lived in a modest country farmhouse, then in cramped city quarters before being sent to Uncle Jerome's cabin. The richness here both awed and repulsed her.

Continuing around the room, she trailed her hands over many large paintings, their canvases sporting intricate frames and nameplates, their surfaces of brushwork so smooth that no inkling of subject matter could be gleaned. She discovered a workbasket full of silken threads, a clothes press stuffed with satin gowns and fur-lined cloaks. Beside it, hanging on the paneled wall, she touched the slick surface of a looking glass and could not help but smile bitterly at the reflection she could not see.

Having finally gone the circumference of the room, she plopped down upon the bed again. The house was quiet in its afternoon leisure, for all tidying had been done earlier, and the staff had likely sat down to sip their tea. Feeling curious to know the mansion better, she took advantage of the temporary afternoon lull and carefully ventured forth to the corridor.

Each day she seemed to discover some new disadvantage to her blindness. A terrifying state, it left one vulnerable to all those unseen things that gave no warning to the senses. She felt as if she must beware the rugs, the furniture, the very walls, just as if they were sly beasts ready to trip her up. She could never know if curious eyes stared at her from unknown vantage points, or if her exploration would end with her blundering into a roomful of people. And the stairs of this grand house, did they descend to her right or to her left, or did they curve with a deadly, serpentine grace straight before her path?

Staying close to the heavily molded walls, her bare feet treading upon fringed carpets, Lark employed both her hands and feet to search for obstacles, encountering in her bungling journey smoothly waxed tables, hanging tapestries, and cool stone statues. Once, she accidentally thrust her hands into a huge arrangement of flowers and fern and nearly upset the bowl. At last she found her fingers upon a polished bannister rail and, gripping it securely, descended, pausing occasionally to turn her head this way and that in a hunt for sounds. There were many steps, thirty-three in all, she counted. Their long cascade seemed to end its graceful plunge in some magnificent foyer, for at the bottom step she could sense about her a great height and space. From Jamie's description, she knew a wondrous crystal chandelier shimmered on a chain here, and above it rose a dome of painted angels.

Just as she entered the vast foyer, she heard footsteps in some distant part of the house and, hoping to conceal herself, darted through the first doorway she found on her left.

She was startled to hear a pair of low voices emanating from a chamber not a stone's throw away. By the muffled tones the conversants seemed to be behind closed doors, but wanting at all costs to avoid them should they decide to exit, she turned to retrace her steps. A sudden heated outburst from one of the speakers arrested her in midstride.

"Don't think to bully me!"

Lark gasped. The angry masculine voice was one she knew well; there was no mistaking its stormy tones. *But why was Sebastian O'Keefe in Lord Glassmeade's house?*

"Under my roof I shall bully you as I please," she heard the surgeon reply in a barely controlled tone of fury.

"Damn your interference!" Sebastian shot back. "You have meddled again where you should not!"

"And if I hadn't, where the hell would you be now? Floating offshore in a convict ship? Rotting in gaol? Aye, Sebastian, 'tis a great disservice I've done you these last few years."

"I never asked for a damned jot of your pretended concern!"

As Lark stood as still as death, listening to the conversation, she heard one of the speakers approach the door. The sound startled her into action. Unwilling to be caught in such a compromising position, she desperately felt along the wainscoted wall until she discovered an alcove furnished with a potted palm and a heavily draped window. Crouching down and ducking under the fringed velvet, she continued her eavesdropping quite shamelessly, incredulous that Sebastian O'Keefe seemed to be on intimate terms with Lord Glassmeade. With interest she listened as the former walked toward the closed door and put a hand upon the latch.

"You have no right to deny me a visit, Christopher," he said, his tone both threatening and sullen. "If *she* were asked, I know she would consent to see me."

"But she will not be asked," came the calm, unyielding reply.

"You have no right—"

"I have every right, and well you know it!" replied the lord of the house.

"The devil take you!"

The door latch clicked suddenly then, causing Lark to start. Footsteps rang dangerously close to her hiding place, thudding against the marble in an irate retreat to the foyer. Then the outside door was flung open with such force, it reverberated against the wall before being slammed shut again.

It seemed Sebastian had let himself out.

Lark heard Lord Glassmeade mumble an oath then, short and to the point. Although he remained in the room where the argument had occurred, the doors now stood open. Still pressing back into her little refuge like a wary dormouse in its hole, Lark waited, not daring to move a muscle. For whatever time necessary she would merely crouch there, she told herself, until the earl took himself somewhere else and left clear her way upstairs.

In the meantime, a new set of footfalls, ones she did not recognize, beat rhythmically upon the tiles, approaching the chamber where Lord Glassmeade tarried.

"My lord?" a male voice inquired.

"What is it, O'Neal?"

"A messenger has just arrived from the country estate. He has a most distressing tale—"

"Well, what is it?" Great impatience, no doubt spawned by the earlier argument, sharpened the surgeon's usually calm voice.

"It seems, my lord, that there's been another uprising involving the peasants. Apparently, some of the tenantry your father evicted from his land attempted to torch the outbuildings shortly after your departure today. The marquess intervened and in the process was struck down. He's injured, and though his valet would have called in the local surgeon, the marquess refused, insisting upon being brought here. The messenger informed me that the Winterwoode coach is traveling quite slowly and will likely not arrive in Dublin until well after dark."

"Did the messenger indicate the seriousness of my father's injuries?"

"He said they do not seem to be life-threatening, and that the marquess is well enough to argue spiritedly for himself."

"He could argue spiritedly for himself even were he lingering at death's door. What news is there of the uprising?"

"I'm told 'twas put down, my lord."

"Very well, O'Neal. You may go."

With the dialogue ended, both men made their way together down the long hallway. Breathing a sigh of relief, Lark waited until their voices could be heard no more, then made her way upstairs as quickly as her blindness would allow.

Once there, she sank down upon the bed and fell into a long interim of troubled thought.

Sebastian O'Keefe and Lord Glassmeade knew each other, and seemingly quite well. Indeed, by the earl's words, they had been acquainted for years, though their relationship hardly gave the suggestion of friendliness.

She wondered how Sebastian had known where to find her, and why Lord Glassmeade had flatly refused him the visit. More puzzling yet, why did there exist such an obviously bitter contentiousness between the two men?

She recalled their conversation again and again, frowning with concentration, trying to make sense of the connection between a humble country tinker and one of the most powerful lords in Ireland.

Lying back and closing her eyes, she felt as if she stood among a thousand shattered shards of tile that had once made up a intricate mosaic. The more she attempted to fit the pieces back together, the more numerous and splintery they grew.

She longed to sweep them all away and forget their existence but sensed that, somehow, it was vital to her survival that she persevere and make the picture whole again.

One thing was certain: no one was who he seemed to be.

8

Christopher had barely gotten his father settled that evening when a small tattered lad pounded
persistently upon the green enameled door leading to
the surgeon's office. It was not unusual for the
impoverished of the lower classes to be queued up on
the stoop at night as well as day; but unless the matter were dire, an apprentice asked the patients to
return during daylight hours, which undoubtedly
they would, for Lord Glassmeade's charitable reputation was renowned among the destitute. However,
this particular caller raised such a ruckus, speaking
vociferously in a garbled mix of English and Gaelic,
that the London apprentice had finally thrown up his
hands in frustration and summoned the earl.

After only a few moments of lending his ear to the
frantic boy, Christopher was on his way to a destination in the country, his black surtout flying out
behind him, his gray steed a blur in the waning light.
The lad rode pillion, explaining in more intelligible

tones that his father was in dreadful pain, having been "pitch-capped" on suspicion of being a United Irishman. It was a deplorable practice Christopher had treated more than once, where the victim's head was covered in brown paper dipped in hot tar. Most surgeons and physicians refused to treat those openly branded as rebels for fear of being themselves accused of sympathetic leanings toward the insurgents' cause. However, it was a well-known fact in and around Dublin that the brash young Earl of Glassmeade had no such reservations.

Once at his destination, it took Christopher hours to clean and treat the wretched patient, and when at last he snapped closed his bag and remounted, he could think of nothing but a hot bath and warm bed—those, and the company of a certain young woman who had come to fascinate him.

He journeyed fast through the night, its darkness crisscrossed with shreds of drifting mist driven inland by sea winds. Beads of moisture clung to the steed's mane and to Christopher's glossy boots, and trembled delicately from every barren twig and dry gorse bloom. The scent of the sea hung strong in the air, its salt accentuating the softer smells of wet foliage and flooded soil, while blending not unpleasantly with peat smoke released from distant cottage chimneys.

In the foggy stillness no sounds touched Christopher's ear, save the steady cantering hooves of his horse as they squelched upon muddy lanes. Yet he sensed a presence in the sapphire gloom and with an abrupt tug on the reins halted his horse in order to listen.

Somewhere behind him the faint jingle of a bit disturbed the sullen air, then the stamp of an impatient hoof. Withdrawing his pistol, Christopher nudged his horse to proceed again, keeping its pace slower, his senses alert. He had been trailed before on his rounds, and though the episodes had grown more frequent of late, his follower had never revealed his cowardly face.

Nevertheless, Christopher exercised particular caution when going about his political work, exchanging horses and clothing at different designated sights before traveling swiftly and circuitously to his destinations. Using such elaborate evasions, he knew his rendezvous at the Faery Thorn had never been detected.

Thinking again of his little rebel cohort, he urged the horse into a slightly speedier stride, hoping to speak with her before she slept tonight. All afternoon he had been troubled by a piece of information gleaned from Sebastian O'Keefe, and his jealousy had been sorely pricked by the tinker's words. To the self-mastered earl such an emotion was an unaccustomed companion, a consuming one, and it rankled him to the point of ill humor. Reflexively tightening his grip upon the reins, he resolved to take steps to rid himself of it soon.

Christopher had come to within a dozen miles of Dublin when a circle of lights penetrated the floating veils of mist and caught his attention. Pulling his horse up short, he narrowed his eyes, just making out the glow of torches before the sound of angry shouts filled his ears. Spurring his mount, he approached the confusion, which seemed to revolve around the perimeters of a humble mud cottage.

Half a dozen mounted Yeomanry—the military corps loyal to the government and, in effect, the pri-

vate army of the landowners—surrounded the mean
dwelling. Several of the soldiers waved flaming torches
while their red-coated officer yelled commands at a
huddle of women standing upon the threshold.

"Get ye out! 'Tis my last warning afore I order the
men to torch the place!"

Christopher had slipped within their midst unno-
ticed; halting his horse just to the rear of the officer's
bay, he demanded loudly, "What have these women
done that you would burn their residence?"

In his voice rang the tones of authority and noble
breeding, and lit by the golden flares, his face bore the
unmistakable princely stamp of a patrician lineage.

The heavyset officer straightened in his saddle,
immediately prepared to curry favor. "Their men
were rebels, sir," he said. "They were recognized running with a mob that tore down Lord Beresworth's
fences last eve. Troublemakers all! 'Twas our duty to
shoot 'em, ye know, which we've done. Their cottage
will be fired, as well. Just as soon as these caterwaul-
ing women remove their ignorant arses from the
premises. O' course, if ye say I shouldn't be so
lenient, I'll just burn 'em in their miserable hut."

Giving the officer a wrathful look, Christopher
dismounted and asked, "Where are the slain men?"

With the tip of his riding crop the soldier indicated three dark forms lying motionless beside a turf
stack. "They be over there. A Papist father and his
two young whelps."

After removing his gloves, Christopher examined
the men, confirmed that they were dead, and with an
oath stood up. He had to duck his head to enter the
low-framed door of the cottage, and glanced first at
the keening widow and her three young daughters,

then at their pitiful abode. Lit by rushlights, it was a typical one-room cabin, built of mud kneaded with straw, its ceilings seven feet high with exposed beams of bogwood. Above, he noted the thatched roof was in such a bad state of repair that weeds sprouted down from it. An old scarred deal table and a few crude stools completed the furnishings, with piles of rushes laid down upon the earthen floor to serve as beds. The peat fire smoked, laying fresh soot upon the blackened walls, and the smell of potatoes and cabbage lingered faintly.

He suspected the tenants had habitually existed upon the edge of starvation. With the menfolk dead, these women would not be able to survive a fortnight.

Turning his attention to them, seeing their frightened faces and red-rimmed eyes as they cowered across the room, Christopher addressed them in Gaelic. "Have you any kin to go to?"

Mutely, the widow shook her head, her eyes sliding from Lord Glassmeade to the Yeomanry officer, who stood impatiently at the half door, watching the exchange.

Without sparing the soldier a glance, Christopher removed coins from his waistcoat pocket, handed them to the woman, and named a charity institution in Dublin.

"Go there and tell them Lord Glassmeade sent you." Drawing on his gloves, he made to depart then, finding the broad-faced officer eyeing him with much speculation.

"Lord Glassmeade, is it, eh?" the soldier said. "I've heard of ye afore." He looked as if he would have liked to say more but, pricked by some caution, checked himself.

Christopher came to stand within inches of the officer, his tall height an impressive contrast to the other's, his classic features cool. "I daresay you have. Now, leave these women be. And their house. 'Tis enough their men are dead."

In response, the soldier drew himself up, his infuriation over the interference obvious. He moved his bulk aside to permit Christopher to exit, but his slowness suggested insolence.

"Hear ye, men!" he announced to his torch-bearing command as Christopher went to mount his horse. "'Tis Lord Glassmeade we have here in our midst. He has ordered us to leave this rebel house standing. Doesn't want the women touched, neither. Seems what's said about him is truth."

Unhurriedly Christopher swung his leg over the cantle and, gathering up the reins, gave the officer a warning look from beneath the brim of his bicorn. "If 'tis said I'm particularly tolerant these days, you'd better hope rumor is accurate. In years past, I've run through pompous tin soldiers, then sewn them up again."

His white teeth flashing in the circle of torchlight, he grinned, reined his horse around, and said, "Good eve to you now, gentlemen."

Earlier Jamie had fallen asleep in Lark's bed, drowsy from a long evening of storytelling, secure in the circle of her arms. Lark could have roused him and sent him to his own bedchamber, but she, too, welcomed the closeness and kept him with her for a while. Yet, as she hugged her brother's wee, skinny form to hers and felt his springy red hair crisp against her chin, she shed tears, wondering how she would find a way to provide for him once they left the shelter of Lord Glassmeade's manse. Given his situation, she feared Virgil could not be relied upon to house them permanently, even if she were to beg him to do so. Sebastian, who had at least come there to seek her out, would be willing to help, of course. But as far as she was concerned, accepting his aid would mean marriage, and she had grave doubts that his offer would still stand once he saw her blinded eyes and scarred cheek.

Grindle entered the room to tend the fire one last time and, at Lark's whispered request, gently removed the sleeping Jamie from her arms. The mantel clock chimed midnight, and just afterward, from the street, Lark heard the watchman call out, "Past twelve of the clock and a foggy night!"

Though she had listened intently all eve, she had yet to hear the surgeon's footfalls and could not help but wonder what kept him so late this night. Did he treat an ailing patient, or was some perfumed partner dancing with him across a festooned, candlelit ballroom? She found herself intrigued by the man Lady Helen had termed complex, thinking he did indeed possess at least two sides—that of the compassionate healer and that of the arrogant earl.

And, sometimes, she sensed there lurked beneath his polish yet another self, one he strove hard to hide.

"You are not asleep?" a low voice asked softly.

Lost in thoughts of him, she had failed to hear Lord Glassmeade's entry into the room.

"N-nay," she faltered, surprised yet pleased that he would pay her a call so late. Suddenly wondering if he had been detained by the old marquess, she asked,

"Your father . . . I heard he was injured at Winter-woode. How does he fare?"

Hours before, she had heard the coach arrive, then a commotion downstairs, and finally the ancient, queru-lous voice of an elderly man whose very tone suggested an accustomedness to giving orders. She asked not out of concern for the greedy, callous marquess, of course—the evictor of her uncle could rot, for all she cared—but out of concern for his son, the surgeon.

Sighing, Christopher walked to a chair beside the hearth and pulled it slightly closer to the flame. He sat down upon its cushioned seat and stretched his long legs forward, positioning himself so that he might have the advantage of looking his fill at Lark Ballinter.

With appreciative eyes he regarded her night-gowned form, the soft cloud of mahogany hair touched by firelight where it spilled over her slender shoulders. He decided to make no pretense that his visit was as surgeon to patient. She would see through it, and he was ready to change their relation-ship to one of a quite different variety.

Strange, he thought, how it seemed so natural to sit there beside the fire in her company and speak softly with her. He needed this interlude for a reason he could not explain, except that it seemed a tranquil end to a very trying day. And yet, just beneath the surface of tranquillity, his passion churned, a passion that would not go much longer without being released to follow its natural course.

"Father took a blow to the chest," he answered her finally, concern over his sire still keen, "and one to his head, but his life is in no danger. Indeed, he's as spirited as ever, as you shall likely determine for yourself in the days to come."

Pausing, Christopher grew introspective, then absently voiced his worry. "Never was there a sharper mind than Father's. Although admittedly a bit blustery, he has always been hailed for his shrewdness, his calculating judgment. But . . . his faculties seem to be deteriorating with gradual stealth, for each time we're together his periods of forgetfulness grow longer and more complete. Soon I fear he'll be lucid no more."

"Will you keep him here?" Lark asked quietly, touched by the depth of sorrow in the son's tone.

"Aye. Though he does not yet know it, he won't be allowed to return to the country again without my escort."

"And do you go often to the country?"

"Alas, nay. I've been neither to my own estate nor to Winterwoode, on a pleasure trip since Christmas last."

For a moment they sat in silence, yet the silence was not a burdensome one to either, but companionable. Lark guessed Lord Glassmeade dwelled upon thoughts of his grand rural home, and using her bright imagination, she envisioned its grandeur, with babbling fountains and gold-painted ceilings. Suddenly she wished she could see it, in spite of the fact that she was blind, and that the estate was the seat of power that had enslaved her uncle and so many like him for generations.

Pushing aside the fact that its very heir sat near, exciting her with his nocturnal presence, she let her thoughts take her back to the harsh memories of cottage life and, finally, to the fire.

"Lord Glassmeade," she said impulsively, "I've been thinking much about the passerby who saved me from the fire. There is a deal about him that puzzles me. Will you tell me his name and how to reach him? I'd like to send round a message."

Christopher glanced up. He had hoped she had forgotten about his other, shadow self. "Ah," he began, his lip curling into a trace of a smile. "Truthfully, your rescuer prefers to remain unnamed and unlauded. As I've said, besides being a most chivalrous fellow, he's rather shy. Of course, I've already passed along your gratitude, but beyond that, he expects no—"

"But—"

"Lark," Christopher said firmly. "There are circumstances under which I would consider revealing his name to you, but . . ." he lowered his voice. "The time is not yet right."

Lark's eyes grew stormy and her mouth petulant as she crossed her arms in an attitude of pique. Christopher liked her in this posture and grinned, giving full rein to his masculine imaginings, were her rebellious energy channeled into an amorous bent.

Simultaneously, with an unpleasant jolt, his jealousy returned to goad him.

"Mistress Ballinter," he said, agitatedly rubbing a hand over the edge of his bristled jaw, "what is Sebastian O'Keefe to you? Is he your lover?"

The bluntly intimate question caught Lark entirely unawares. All day, of course, she had contemplated that heated, puzzling conversation between her surgeon and her suitor, but she had not intended to broach the subject tonight, even had she been able to invent an excuse to do so. She had no particular wish to admit her eavesdropping. Yet she was abashed now, not only by the earl's audacity, but by the note of imperiousness in his tone—an imitation of his father's, she imagined.

In retaliation, she asked, "What is he to *you*, Lord Glassmeade?"

"If we continue to answer question with question," Christopher said tightly, "we will go nowhere with this conversation. So, I will concede and answer first. Mister O'Keefe is a thorn in my side, that's what he is to me. Now, I ask you again, what is he to you?"

Lark smiled, and though the smile was prompted by private musing, she did not conceal it upon her lips. "At times, he is the very same to me."

Her smile, with its effrontery and loveliness, only roused Christopher further. "And at other times?"

"A suitor," she said smugly.

"Ah, and how far has the suitor . . . got?"

Lark was astounded that he would venture to ask such a private question. This was not the sensitive, gallant surgeon at all. Nay, this man who prodded so personally and with such insolent purpose was definitely the haughty aristocrat.

"I think you have stepped beyond your boundaries, *Surgeon*," she chided, reminding him of their relationship. "Sebastian O'Keefe is my suitor, and I'll not be discussing what's private between us. And since we are asking such personal questions of each other," she went on, "I'll ask my own. Why did you refuse to let him see me today?"

Again silence reigned a full moment before the answer came from the fireside chair. Then the reply was delivered with another smooth feint in this sudden contest of evasion, though its note of chagrin could not be concealed. "It seems I am not the only one to have overstepped boundaries today, eh, Mistress Ballinter?"

She had revealed herself, exposed her little excursion and its spell of eavesdropping. So be it. Lark regretted only that she had not arrived at that closed door a few moments earlier, so she could have learned more of the association between her suitor and her surgeon. But she would let the earl wonder how long she had stood beside the portal, let him wonder how much she knew.

"Do you like bargains, Mistress Ballinter?" he asked with a sudden casual and amiable air.

She noticed that the subtlest bit of amusement now warmed his tone and relaxed that harder edge it had held before, and she sensed this man greatly enjoyed contests and relished now this round with her.

"If they are fairly made . . . aye," she replied.

"Then this one will be quite fairly made. 'Tis this—I'll answer your question as to why I forbade O'Keefe his visit, if you will answer a question of mine."

He paused briefly, and she heard him rise and cross to a corner cabinet she knew to be locked. Before long, the clink of crystal against crystal sounded, then the gurgle of liquid as it tumbled into a waiting vessel.

"By the by," the earl said genially, "this is quite a good bottle of brandy—would you care for a snifter?"

She accepted, hoping it was a potent draft, for her nerves were tightly stretched. She was quickly losing confidence in her ability to handle this opponent, and her poise was not aided one bit when she felt his weight upon her bed. She wished he had not seated himself so close, but stayed in his place beside the fire, because he now had an advantage over her, that of scrutinizing her face closely while she could not enjoy a like opportunity.

He placed the snifter in her hands, were she could smell its heady fumes. Then she raised the rim to her lips and took a sip.

"Now," Lord Glassmeade said, "there is but one condition to this bargain: you must answer my question before I answer yours."

While she pondered the rule, he removed the snifter from her grasp and swallowed a draft himself before returning it.

Lark felt sudden discomposure, for the sharing of a cup seemed quite an intimate gesture, one usually made between two lovers. Why, then, did she so eagerly put her lips to the glass and let them linger there to find the warmth of his mouth still tarrying upon the crystal?

"Agreed?" he asked, as if she had somehow, with her partaking of the cup, sealed the bargain.

"Agreed," she replied.

"Very well. Explain this. Before the fire destroyed it, why did you house within your cow byre a very large store of gunpowder?"

Her hand faltered, and the brandy sloshed from its snifter and ran over her fingertips, wetting a spot on the linen between herself and the earl. A slow, telling tide of color rose upward to her neck, cheeks, and brow as she felt the impact of his knowledge.

A month before, Virgil's messenger had brought the stores by boat from France and asked her to hide them for the rebel army.

But the kegs had been well concealed—even Uncle Jerome had never found them. And then, by the earl's own statement, the fire had annihilated the evidence.

So how could he possibly know of their existence?

Oh, what a quick and perilous turn this play had taken! She had to test the earl's wit with hers and in doing so take care to reveal nothing by her answer.

"I'm astounded that you'd ask me such a ridiculous question," she said lightly. "'Tis so unlikely I cannot think what prompted you to pose it."

For a moment he did not reply. Then he stroked the straight line of her nose with a fingertip.

Two conflicting reactions battled within Lark at the touch. One insisted that in indignation she push his hand away; the other begged her to raise his knuckles to her lips and kiss them. But neither did she do.

Watching her changing expressions, Christopher leaned closer, wanting to catch the scent of tea rose in her hair. In spite of caution, in spite of reason, a devil prompted him to play with her this way. Perhaps he had gone a little mad with wanting her, but he yearned to bring her under his control, make her entrust her secrets to him. And only then would he entrust his to her. It was an honesty he fiercely desired to share. He wanted to end the charade they perpetuated, even knowing that in unmasking himself, he would place his very life in the tender young hands of a Papist rebel lass.

"When you were brought half-dead to my house the other evening, colleen," he whispered close to her ear, "the powder upon your nose was not of the usual variety found upon feminine faces. There was an explosion in the byre, remember? I believe I need say no more, for you are a clever woman and surely understand my meaning."

He had outwitted her, and she could think of no words with which to defend herself. Her political connection was conspiratorial, treacherous, and now it seemed Lord Glassmeade held it like a captured prize between his palms. If he chose to release it, share it with his lofty peers, little would her life be worth.

But he would not. Surely he would not. Or would he?

"I await your answer, Mistress Ballinter."

"I . . ."

"Go on." Relentless was he in this match.

Lark swallowed. "I have no answer."

A lengthy pause ensued, and she sensed her response had greatly disappointed him.

"You forfeit the game?" he asked at last.

She bent her head. "Aye . . . I forfeit the game."

"Ah, well." He sighed and then added, "Don't feel disheartened. Perhaps you'll win some other time. I assure you, I too have my vulnerabilities in strategy. Indeed . . ." His fingers traveled the length of her nose again in a lingering, sensuous slide. "A very crafty player *could,* with just the right moves, manage to outmaneuver me."

To what vulnerabilities did he allude? Lark wondered, still deeply unsettled by this late night encounter. And where was her solicitous surgeon, that tender man whose consoling arms had so comfortingly embraced her in recent days? She despaired for him, yearned for his kind, undesigning nature. This other provoked her, made her as skittish as a fine-bred mare, and though his hand was just as gentle as that of her courtly counterpart, its mastery upon the reins seemed bent upon testing her mettle.

"More brandy, Mistress Ballinter?"

She accepted it gratefully, took too large a mouthful, and gritted her teeth as it made its burning way down. Then she suddenly smelled the odor of tannin and knew her companion had uncorked the bottle for her daily application.

Had the surgeon returned? She was not sure, as she could no longer distinguish one presence from the other.

His fingers dallied as they spread the salve upon her face, made leisurely paths that they retraced several times. Then, taking an entirely unnecessary route, they moved downward to embrace the soft curve of her throat.

The touch both titillated and relaxed her senses to such a degree that she slowly shut her eyes. When she went limp against the pillows, he leaned closer still. She thought perhaps he had drunk a great measure of the brandy, for he smelled strongly of its expensive fire. It reached her nostrils in gentle wafts, and because she knew it came to her from the breaths he breathed, she was stirred.

All at once she felt her lips touched, and they were touched not by stroking fingers, but by a mouth firm and sure and daring. She became unaware of anything but the intimacy, of anything but the man. For a moment she simply existed in thoughts of him, in the feel of his flesh.

His mouth bestowed its astonishing caress for only the barest moment, leaving almost before Lark's spinning brain had time to register fully the shape and feel and wonder of it. In amazement her lips remained parted, and though she wanted to utter either outrage at his bold liberty or a protest of his quick departure, she seemed unable. Confusion beset her, and she opened her eyes wide with an instinctive need to see the face whose lips had caused such havoc.

Touching the tip of her nose one last time, Christopher said with the warmest laughter in his voice, "I think you are a good sport, after all, rebel. Good night to you."

Rising from her side, he drew the coverlet over her shoulders, then headed to whatever chamber housed him, leaving her alone.

Lark put a hand to her lips. She had been roused, tantalized, then abandoned to an unsettling state by a man who was a beguiling mixture of both chivalry and devilment. What an unpredictable nature he possessed, she thought, one that swung from pole to pole with the ease of a pendulum. In one moment he could cause her to feel the greatest serenity and security; in the next he could disrupt her composure with the ease of a stone skipped across still water.

What was his aim? What was to be her fate there beneath the rafters of this house? Would the surgeon restore her health, patch her flesh, and see her strong, only to relinquish to the earl a United Irish rebel?

She must watch herself. She must be wary. Like any good soldier in the hands of a formidable foe, she must be on guard.

But just for the moment, as night enfolded her in its soft silent wings, she did not want to be a soldier. She wanted to be a more tender creature, a woman who, until dawn's arrival, at least, could languish in thoughts of a forbidden and a most hazardous kind of love.

9

The Sabbath arrived, the third Lark had spent beneath Lord Glassmeade's roof, and though she knew it was the height of folly, she determined to venture out into the frightening night and meet the phantom agent. At ten of the clock on Sundays, Virgil's French messenger met her at a site upon the coastline, handed his message to her, and rowed wordlessly out to sea again. After reading the dispatch and destroying it, Lark then passed on the information to the agent beneath the Faery Thorn.

Tonight would be no different, except she would have to take Jamie out and involve him in this dangerous intrigue. She wondered in truth if her brother were more endangered outside these sumptuous Loyalist walls . . . or *inside* them.

All day she had pondered the reason behind Lord Glassmeade's kiss. She knew enough of men to be wary of their attentions and realized that he might press his ardor, use his knowledge of her rebel involvement to make her a willing partner to his desire. His interest could scarcely have been motivated by any feeling other than the baser variety, she decided. No genuine fondness for a cotter's girl could have breached his pride or overcome the hurdles of both class and principle.

And her own feelings for him . . . those, she smothered resolutely.

In any event, she had to leave his mansion soon, leave the shelter, the comfort, the bountiful meals Christopher provided so generously to her and her brother, and search out a way to survive. True, her cheek had not yet healed, but of what significance was her appearance now? No man would ever want a blinded wife, regardless of her looks.

She shifted her feet impatiently and from her stance beside the door counted the chimes of the clock, marking eight.

Where was Jamie?

She began to wonder why she had ever dared to think a lad of six could carry such responsibilities as she had placed upon his youthful shoulders tonight. This plot she'd devised was too outrageous, too intricate and fraught with danger. What if he had been caught in his theft of the household key and was even now receiving chastisement from some stern, unrelenting butler who would report the transgression to the master of the house?

Clenching her fists, Lark began to pace before the velvet-hung window, stepping every few moments to the door, where she leaned her temple against the smooth, waxed frame and listened. Each time all was quiet. No maids lugging coal buckets clattered down the hall, no gentleman's measured tread fell on fine woven carpet, no voices drifted upward from the vestibule.

And then, suddenly, she discerned the faintest pitter patter upon the marble stairs, and she opened the portal and thrust out her head. Reaching out a hand, she felt another, quite smaller one take hold of her fingers. She dragged him inside and shut the door.

"Did you get the key, my darling boy?" she asked with both dread and excitement.

"Aye! I got a whole bunch of keys—seven or eight," he answered triumphantly, pride ringing in his piping voice. "'Twas a bit of a sticky job, though. Meg *would* want to hang about the pantry and kiss the gardener's son. I thought surely she'd get caught at it, and she almost did. The butler came lookin' for a coat brush and near ran into her. Fast lot of talkin' *she* had to do. But that's when I filched the keys."

"What a clever dear you are!" Lark said as he slid the long metal prizes into her hand. "Now we shall be able to slip in and out of the house tonight with no one the wiser. Are you warmly dressed?"

"Aye," he said, placing her hand upon his bony shoulder. "'Tis the new coat Lady Helen gave me. Feel how soft the wool is?"

"'Tis as soft as a lamb's belly," she replied distractedly, bent upon her purpose now. Her tactile sense having grown quite keen, she had earlier discovered her old black cloak hanging amidst the gowns in the clothes press, and she donned it now. Then she laced up the pair of soft leather shoes Lady Helen had left.

Motioning Jamie to the door, she bade him check the corridor. "Do you see anyone?"

"Nay."

"Good! Now we have only to get Little Dun out of the stable without anyone noticing," she said, knowing this to be one of the most difficult parts of her precarious plan. "Are you sure you know exactly where the pony is, and that you can lead him out without alerting the grooms?"

"Aye." Jamie sighed with childish impatience. "Like I told you, Little Dun is at the end of the stable, near the back doors. After supper all the grooms play cards and drink 'til they're in their cups. They'll never hear us."

Lark nodded, pushing down the impulse to abandon her mad venture and send her brother to his warm feather bed. "Take my hand. You must lead me, sweeting. Every step of the way, I fear. But if along our journey we meet with danger, you must run, leave me. I'll cope alone."

Jamie's bravado and sense of adventure obviously waned in the face of her dose of hard reality, and his fingers gripped hers with more determination.

"But I couldn't leave you—"

"You must." Her voice was firm. "Now, lead the way like a brave soldier."

As nimbly as a cat, he guided her down the stairs and through a side door. Immediately the cold air whipped her skirts, and she breathed deep of the autumn night's sharp fragrance. Before her blindness she had not realized there were so many varied sounds and smells to life, nor had she imagined they could be used so well to orient oneself to any surroundings.

Nevertheless it was a terrifying, frustrating thing to walk always as if in blackest night, and she clutched Jamie's small hand as he directed her down a seldom used path where twigs and vines snagged her sleeves. At last, by the odor of fresh-cut straw and sweet hay and horses, she knew they neared the stable. Shortly after Jamie left her standing beside the garden gate she discerned the approaching stride of the Connemara pony.

"Good work, Jamie!" Lark whispered. "Now," she said, reaching out her hands to locate the pony's reins, "I'll mount first, then pull you up in front."

"Can you do it, Lark?" he asked her doubtfully as she groped to feel the line of the horse's back.

"Papa taught me to ride before I was even out of nappies, didn't he now?" Grabbing a wad of coarse, reddish-black mane, she swung her leg up gracefully. Then, she bunched up her petticoats, reached down, and hoisted Jamie up in front of her.

"Can you handle him now, pet? And are you sure you know how to get us back to the cottage?"

"Aye, Lark. How many times do I have to keep tellin' you? Didn't I just come to Dublin with Uncle Jerome last month? I remember the road like it was the back of me own hand."

"Shhh! Lower your voice, you clever boy, and just get us home."

Their journey proved one of the most harrowing ordeals Lark had ever endured, mostly because in her blindness the sounds of night seemed unnaturally amplified and difficult to identify. She could not tell if the rustle in the hedge was some thieving wanderer poised to jump out and wrest the pony from their hands, or if the muffled clip-clop on the lane behind was a desperate highwayman ready to pounce upon easy prey. Once, before taking her fears firmly in hand, she even imagined that Uncle

Jerome's high-born murderer stalked them slyly and would leave them dead upon the road before the eve was out.

Apparently sensing her nervousness, Jamie tried to reassure her by describing in aimless detail everything he spied.

"'Tis only a Johnny-the-bog flyin' up from a puddle, Lark," he said the third time she started. "And behind us there's an old man traipsin' to town with a lamb in his arms. And that whinin' beside the lane, 'tis only an old dog sniffin' for hares in the rowan." Completely at ease in his capacity of guide, Jamie added, "You fret too much. Wasn't Uncle allus sayin' so?"

Lark playfully pulled his cap over his eyes and bade him watch where he was going. Yet in spite of the lightened mood, she could not quite dispel the notion that somewhere behind, a horseman followed.

At last, after what seemed an interminable trek, Jamie exclaimed, "I see it! I see the cabin yonder! 'Tis all dark and boarded up."

Lark craned her neck in an automatic effort to focus her eyes. "Do you see anyone about the place?"

"Nay. But what a sad thing is our old home now. And the byre's mostly burned up."

Hearing a nostalgia in her brother's voice that wrenched her own heart, and remembering with a shiver that Jerome had been murdered here, Lark speedily changed the subject. "No need to go closer, pet. Swing Little Dun down toward the sea. And pray to the Holy Virgin that there's someone there to meet us."

She had earlier fabricated a ridiculous story for Jamie's benefit that her meetings tonight were for the

purpose of possible domestic employment. Fortunately
her sibling was young enough to accept almost any
explanation. She would ensure that he stood well out
of earshot of both conversations, of course, so as not
to glean the true nature of her business.

"I think we should be gettin' off the pony now,"
Jamie said presently. "'Tis too rocky and steep for
him to get down to the shore."

Having been about to utter the same suggestion
since Little Dun was stumbling over the slick, moss-
coated earth, Lark dismounted. Then she drew her
brother down and bade him find a tree to which to
tether the horse.

Breathing deeply, she hugged herself with her
arms, thinking the sound of the sea especially eerie
now that she was unable to see starlight glittering
upon its endless waves. Alone in her darkness, terrified to move lest she misstep and tumble down the
cliff, she realized with dismay the dreadful extent of
her defenselessness here. Even the wind, whistling
around her and spattering cold flecks of sea foam
upon her face, unnerved her.

Relieved to hear Jamie scrambling over the rocks
again, she stretched out her arms and drew him
close. Then, wanting only to finish what had to be
done, she instructed him urgently, "Lead me down
the path to the shore now, sweeting, and look for a
man waiting there. Take me to him, then stand aside.
He will be giving me a slip of paper which is most
important. You must read it aloud to me, carefully—
I've flint and candle in my pocket."

She bent down and pressed his small hand to her
lips. "I know 'tis a large order to ask of a wee one,
but do you think you can manage it?"

"Aye, except for the part about readin'. Sometimes I have trouble with the big words, you know."

"Then you shall simply spell them out to me," she replied. *Thank God she had insisted he learn his letters!*

Being deeply rutted, the path down was fairly easy to find even in darkness, and in a matter of minutes brother and sister stood along the crescent-shaped shore, their shoes sinking into sand, their hair tossed wildly by wind. Lark felt her cheek throb, and she wondered what damage she did exposing it to the elements. She would probably hear about it in no uncertain terms tomorrow when the surgeon visited. At least he would not intrude into her room tonight and find her gone, for she had overheard him mention to his valet that a rout would keep him late.

"Do you see anyone, Jamie?" she asked, the back of her neck prickling with anxiety. She could not rid herself of the notion that they were not alone in this place, yet no one came forward to greet them. "A man should be waiting at the water's edge, or at least approaching the beach in a curraugh. I know 'tis dark, but look close all around."

"I am. But I don't see anyone." His teeth chattered. "'Tis a bit skeery, isn't it? Do you think the little people are about?"

Dispelling his fears as best she could, she bade him patrol the shoreline with her, up and back, up and back, but with nary a sighting to report. Finally the two of them went to sit down upon a boulder to wait. Plagued by apprehension, Lark shuddered in the moist cold air and pulled the shivering Jamie under the protection of her arm. Then she fumbled in her pocket and withdrew an object, which she transferred to her brother's hand.

"'Tis a watch, sweeting. Can you possibly see to tell the time?"

"Gor, Lark!" he exclaimed, taking in an astonished breath. "Where'd you filch *this*? 'Tis fine, real fine. Gold, it is, and heavy."

Beside him, Lark stiffened. "I didn't filch it, and I'll thank you never to accuse me of such a terrible sin. I only borrowed it. 'Twas in one of the drawers in the bedchamber where Lord Glassmeade has me staying. I believe 'tis a lady's watch—the type a woman would pin to her bodice. 'Tis probably his dead mother's, but I'll wager the man has so many watches and gewgaws about his house, he's forgotten this one. Anyway, just tell me the time."

She could sense her brother's concentration, feel the slight movement of his hand as he turned the piece this way and that either to catch some stray moonbeam or to study the position of the pointing hands and calculate the time, a feat at which he was not yet proficient.

"'Tis after eleven," he finally announced, handing it back.

"Good Lord! 'Tis as I feared. When I didn't meet him last Sabbath, the messenger likely assumed something had gone awry in our connection, and now won't come again out of caution." She did not voice aloud the fact that tragedies often befell those suspected of linkage with the United Irishmen, nor did she say that Virgil would likely assume her in gaol or murdered. She had no way of reaching him, had not even been able to inform him of Uncle Jerome's death, but now he would surely be alarmed and come sailing over to Ireland to search for her and Jamie.

"Oh! What a fine kettle of fish I've put us in now!"

Jamie said nothing but huddled close to her for warmth.

Lark gritted her teeth against cold and dread. "I must go to that fiendish brute beneath yonder tree with nothing to report, and likely receive the lash of his tongue for all my trouble this eve!" Fear squeezed her chest when she thought of what the agent might say or do in his wrath, and she felt a scathing sense of shame as well, for she had secretly been proud of her part in the underground espionage. Now she would be verifying the phantom's opinion of her inability to carry out her part.

She wondered with chagrin what effect her failure to deliver a dispatch would have on the cause. Had she seriously jeopardized the revolutionary plan? She knew by her own messages that intense efforts were being made to coordinate the impending landing of French forces, but surely Virgil would find another to carry his reports from across the channel. After all, trustworthy spies as well as informants and turncoats could be found in any Catholic village.

Still, she had yearned to be a vital cog in the wheels of insurrection, to stand amongst her cohorts waving green ribbons in the sign of victory when triumph came. And she also yearned to snub her nose at that ebony-clad phantom who had so candidly doubted her will.

A noise startled her from her thoughts and she straightened, listening for long, tense moments. But nothing more threatening than nature's eternal sounds of wind and surf met her ear. No footsteps rang on pebbles, no voice broke the air, yet Lark could swear a presence lingered near, watching.

"Jamie. Jamie, lad," she said nervously, fear freezing her limbs. After nudging him awake and pulling his hood more snugly over his wind-pinched ears, she gathered him closer and came to her feet.

"Now, Jamie," she whispered urgently, as if someone would hear. She shook him to rid him of his grogginess. "You must direct me down the sea path. Do you recall the high cliffs, the ones where that ugly old Faery Thorn grows?"

"Uh-huh." He yawned, shuddering with a sudden chill. "I remember. 'Tis where the little people dance. 'Tis where everyone's afraid to go."

"Aye. So it is. Now you must be very brave and take me there."

10

From his vantage point Christopher watched the two small, vulnerable figures negotiating the treacherous path along the cliffs. He could just discern their shapes in the capricious light of the moon. The pair resembled lost lambs crawling over the fierce and tameless landscape, their bent forms buffeted by the strength of the howling gusts. Indeed, it seemed as if the very night itself would swallow them up.

He could not believe she had done it, so soon after her injury. In spite of the fact that he desperately needed the information only she could pass to his ear, he was furious with her daring. To think that she had ventured out into the cold, traveled along remote and dangerous lanes, and now trod beside a steep and perilous trail with only the guidance of a lad barely breeched!

"She's mad," he muttered, checking the restive, sideways movement of his stallion. "Witless. Bereft of reason. Too independent by half. 'Twill be a miracle if she doesn't get herself killed one of these days, dabbling in politics and traipsing about carrying sensitive secrets. I'd like to know whose harebrained notion 'twas to include her in this scheme. I'd wring his foolish neck for it with no remorse."

Seeing that the intrepid pair climbed higher, nearly to the point of their destination, he wheeled his black steed around and made for a sheltered, well-hidden cavern tucked beneath a jutting slab of rock.

Only an hour past, he had been gaming in the company of two dozen opulently attired nobles among tables aglitter with silver coin. While he had conversed with Ireland's highest official, the Viceroy himself, the notion that his faery queen might attempt to make her Sabbath meeting struck him like a blow.

He had laid down his cards, excused himself hastily—murmuring some half-baked lie regarding a patient in need of his attention—and left the gathering with twenty-four astonished pairs of eyes staring at his back.

After confirming, indeed, that Lark was not in her bed, he had ridden at a rapid clip directly to the ramshackle inn where his black mount was discreetly stabled. There he had exchanged horses and borrowed a dark cloak to envelop his evening clothes. Then, pushing the steed into the breakneck pace it relished well, he had made for the country, not halting once until he was at the base of the Faery Thorn.

Now he grumbled a private curse, angry at Lark's foolhardiness, angry with himself for not suspecting that the little hellion would venture out tonight. No doubt she had met someone earlier in the night—the contact whose identity he yearned to know. Damn! What a fool he had been to lose such a chance!

Christopher yanked the hood up over his hair in case Jamie's eyes proved sharp and reminded himself to use the coarse country accent he usually affected. As he strode forward, intending to castigate the girl for her folly, some inner consciousness warned him to curb his temper.

He needed the information she could give, and she had risked much to bring it to him for the cause. This association he had with her was for the business of liberty, not pleasure, and he could not discourage her participation in it.

Taking a breath to calm himself, Christopher sauntered toward that eerie place whose mysterious connection with faery folk so awed the natives. Even he, unfanciful by nature, had to confess the tree claimed some inexplicably dark and otherworldly charm.

Fixing his eyes on the magnificent profile of the tree ahead, he sighted his cohort's form, held proud and straight even though the vicious wind flapped her skirts and hair. She progressed across the craggy earth, using mincing, uncertain steps, shuffling forward rather than walking, so as not to trip. Christopher could only assume she had left her brother hidden behind a sheltering shrub or rock nearby, for no trace of the boy could he glimpse.

He approached, deliberately trodding hard upon the frozen ground so as not to startle her. He saw her turn slightly at the sound and instinctively put out her hands before hastily clasping them behind her back again. Though his natural reaction was to be brusque with her over such courting of danger, he found he could not. How dignified and determined she was, a blind cotter's lass facing not only hostile elements, but a man who was scarcely less hostile, a man who had threatened her at their last encounter. He recognized that the same loyalty, the same idealism, the same faith that drove him, drove her. She risked her life no less bravely than he did. More than ever he felt an affinity with her, a respect, a lessening of the emotional isolation that had plagued him all his life.

He reached out and touched her frozen hand.

She started violently, and he put gentleness in his tone, speaking in his lowest accent, glad that the sound of the crashing sea was raucous. "*Failte,* Faery Queen. What do ye have for me this Sabbath night?"

Lark took her hand from his gloved one and reached up to draw her fluttering hood over the gauze upon her cheek. She did not have to see him to imagine him clearly, his tall, dark form a mingled outline with the twisted, talonlike branches of the ageless tree. How would he react to her lack of news? Even as she experienced a thrill of cold fear, the usual strong fascination he commanded warmed her in a rush.

Gathering her bravery, she said forthrightly, "I've naught to report to you this eve. Naught a'tall."

Wondering if he had heard her correctly, thinking the wind had snatched a part of her words, Christopher demanded, "What did ye say?"

At the sharpness of his tone, Lark's defiance surfaced. She raised her chin. "I said, I have naught to report to you tonight. My contact failed to come, probably because I couldn't meet with him last Sabbath. I came to inform you of it, at least, rather than let you pace about here all night, waiting."

Because his disappointment was keen, and because she would expect some outburst from the hot-tempered agent, Christopher sneered, "Like ye did last week. O' course, I'm hardly surprised, for as I've said ere now, the frailty of yer gender does not lend itself to this work."

"Deal with me or deal with no one," she snapped. "I, too, have no liking for the one I'm forced to meet in this place, but my cause is more important than my preference for cohorts."

"Ye are sharp-tongued tonight," he observed in his heavy brogue.

"'Tis the company."

"Ye assured me ye were up to this task, lass. Much depends upon yer part. Now, ye surely see that ye must relinquish to me the name of yer contact. Pray God I can locate him meself and reopen communications."

Inhaling a deep breath, Lark summoned the will to speak in a steady voice that would belie her trepidation. "I will not give it to you. I'll be finding my own way to resume contact soon—after all, I, too, yearn to see Ireland free. But the name of my connection I will protect. To my death."

Christopher knew he had lost in this battle of wills, and though his impulse was to lash out in frustration, he would not. His usual equanimity would be thoroughly out of character, of course. But looking down upon Lark's shivering young frame, surely frozen in this weather, and seeing how she fixed her eyes upon his face in order that he should not guess her blindness, defeated him in some way. He recognized courage, and hers was extraordinary. It deserved his respect.

Lark held herself rigidly, fearing his response. When no explosion came, when no mocking or cruel words were flung in her direction, she was a bit bewildered. She even thought she heard the ghost of a resigned sigh issue from the phantom's lips.

Thrusting gloved fingers through his layers of clothing, Christopher felt for a coin in his waistcoat pocket. He pulled one of Lark's bare hands from the pleats of her cloak and pressed it firmly in her palm. "Dangerous days are upon us, colleen, and they will grow more dangerous as we near the end. Though ye scoff at the notion, ye may have need of me some hour. Should there be dire reason, see that this coin reaches an apothecary by the name of Alabar in James Street. He will find me and send me to meet ye here without delay."

Although unable to imagine a reason to summon him, and loath to make such a promise, Lark nodded mutely.

"And," he continued, "when ye have a communiqué for me again—and I hope for yer sake as well as mine 'tis soon—break off a forked twig from a thorn tree and take it to Alabar. 'Twill be a signal for me to meet ye here the following Sabbath."

Even as he uttered the words, the ancient tree rising up upon its spearlike hill groaned, as if the violent sea gales had somehow penetrated its frigid inner circle. Lark fancied it owned a soul, an animation possessed by no other mere tree, and she wondered if it was giving them warning against severing a thorn twig. Perhaps the faeries had materialized suddenly amongst its branches, even now perched upon the boughs with sharp pixy faces aglower and silver wings twitching in ire at such mortal mention of stealing a piece of any of their shrines.

Instinctively Lark stepped back. The agent still held her hand in his gloved, iron grip. "I—I shall do as you say," she stammered through chapped, numbed lips, finally withdrawing her hand from his. "And now, as we have nothing further to say to each other, I bid you good night."

She prayed he would simply turn and depart, go his way without looking back at her, for she did not want him to see her stumbling ignobly over the earth or hear her crying for Jamie to leave his hidey-hole and help her.

"Good eve, Faery Queen," he said, the whirling wind nearly carrying away his words. "I commend ye for yer courage, if nothing else. May God be with ye."

He left her then to the clamor of the sea, the crunch of his boots just audible as he found purchase on the steep descent. When at last his retreat could be distinguished no more, when the wind's howl came high and alone across the scattered rocks, Lark turned around.

Then, belatedly, with an inexplicable little sigh, she murmured, "Godspeed."

Christopher followed the pair all the way to the city, keeping well behind on the shadowy, water-logged roads so as not to alarm them with the splash and clop of hoofbeats. As they entered the outskirts of Dublin, however, he closed the distance, for cut-throats and desperate men abounded along the rotting quays and crouching warehouses, lounging ominously in doorways, awaiting opportunity.

Ironically, though, no trouble met the unlikely trio until they had crossed into the smarter section of town, only blocks from Henrietta Street, where oil lamps lit the avenues and watchmen patrolled.

Not that the "charleys" were much of a formidable force.

Dressed in long frieze coats, capes, and crowned hats, they toted lanterns and carried poles to light the lamps; as weapons, these poles were woefully inadequate, the crooked ends a mere token threat. Often old and feeble, organized by local charitable efforts, the watchmen were not only ineffectual against crime, but not averse to taking bribes.

When one of the old men crossed Lord Glassmeade's path, Christopher raised his riding crop in mock salute and went on, passing through quiet, empty streets lined with shuttered houses. Just as he breathed a sign of relief that the vulnerable pair he surreptitiously escorted had nearly arrived home without a single incident requiring his interference, the sudden sound of shattering glass pierced the tranquil night. Then, in an ear-splitting series of pops, the glass tops of the street lamps began to explode, one after another, all the way down the block. Both the sound and the sight resembled a fireworks display and sent splintery, oily shards flying everywhere.

The gleeful hoots and snickers of a group of young men punctuated the show, echoing between the tall brick houses, from which a few residents began to poke their nightcapped heads out windows. In a flurry of black tailcoats and ruffled shirts, the miscreants fled the neighborhood, jeering all the while.

"Trinity students again," Christopher muttered, working to bring the high-mettled black stallion under control while scanning ahead for a glimpse of his charges. As he sighted them and spurred the stallion forward, he slid out of his voluminous black cape and draped it behind the saddle, for Jamie was a perceptive lad.

Lark had nearly taken a tumble, her balance upset when Little Dun started violently at the disturbance. Rearing, the farm-bred pony spun round and round in panicked confusion, while Jamie clutched its flying mane for dear life.

Thinking musket fire had erupted all about them, Lark was leaning over her brother in a frantic attempt to shield him, while extending her hands forward to find the reins.

"Holy Mother of God! Hang on, Jamie!" she cried. "We're about to be murdered in the streets!"

Just as the wild-eyed pony had plunged forward and nearly unseated them again, Lark heard the thunderous clattering of another set of hooves. She felt the brush of a hard leg against her own as a rider reined close, then the abrupt, bone-jarring halt of her horse as it was brought firmly under control.

"Out for an early morning ride, Mistress Ballinter?" Lord Glassmeade inquired before she had even got her breath. "'Tis really not the best time for it, you know. I could recommend more favorable hours—and I always advise an escort."

Immediately recognizing the cool, unruffled voice, and feeling a prick of annoyance at its tone, but mostly a huge measure of relief, Lark demanded, "What in the name of heaven is happening? Are we under attack? Are there murderers in the streets?"

Christopher threw back his head and laughed. "Oh, without a doubt, there are murderers in the streets. But they are not the cause of tonight's entertainment. 'Tis a prank often played by the university lads. They put gunpowder squibs in the lamps so the things explode and throw the streets in darkness. They seem to find it quite amusing. And indeed it is, when one is eighteen, irresponsible, and full of drink."

"Well, blast them!" Lark swore in response. "They like to have sent Jamie and me to an early grave, they did! I hope every last one of the wicked little toffee-noses gets sent down!"

"Wicked little toffee-noses with noble sires don't get sent down," Christopher responded with a grin, not even blinking when his fiery cohort's temper exploded over this new tidbit. In no uncertain terms she proceeded to consign every one of the pranksters and his paternity to a permanent stay in a very warm place.

Suddenly Christopher wanted to laugh affectionately and draw her close, kiss her mouth, and feel her grow inflamed not by the heat of politics, but by the kindling of his own body. But Jamie interrupted the direction of his thoughts.

"I'm gettin' tired, Your Lordship. When are we goin' home?"

Nudging his horse forward and pulling the pony over the glass-strewn cobbles, Christopher answered with a fond pat to the boy's shoulder. "Now, Jamie lad. We're going home now."

At his front door, he left Lark and the boy in the hands of the sleepy-eyed butler, then led the horses around back, where he tethered the stallion behind the garden in a place the stable crew would not notice. Before dawn's light he would have to return the horse to its usual stall, but first he wanted to bid a certain red-haired United Irishwoman good night.

Inside the house, after tucking Jamie beneath his quilts, Lark accepted the butler's escort only as far as the stairs, wanting perversely to cling to the shreds of her beleaguered independence and make her own way to her chamber. She was tired to the bone, shaking from reaction to the frightful scare in the street. No matter how she tried to calm herself, her knees trembled and her hands shook as she grasped the bannister and mounted the steps. Had Lord Glassmeade not rescued her from the streets when he had, he might have found her at dawn, cowering in some darkened alley with Jamie.

She had come to depend upon the surgeon's aid, his compassion—and, yes, even his provoking charm—far too much.

As she neared her chamber, thoughts of the phantom agent beset her, and she remembered his dire warnings, his unexpected forbearance, his instructions on how to summon him. She found the coin in her pocket and clenched it tight, running her fingertips over its worn ridges and indecipherable imprints. Would she ever use it? Would circumstances ever give her reason to trust in his assistance?

Suddenly a hand seized her arm and she gasped, whirling around. The coin fell from her clutches, landing with a thud upon the carpet runner before bouncing noisily onto the hardwood floor.

Releasing her, her captor bent down to retrieve it. "I believe you've misplaced something."

The voice was low and deep-timbered to her ear, causing her nearly to cry out in fright. Preoccupied with thoughts of the phantom agent, she fancied it to be his voice before reason returned and she recognized the smooth intonations of her host.

"A-aye . . . 'tis mine," she stammered, reaching out to snatch at the token. But it was not immediately returned to her.

"Hmm . . . 'tis an interesting piece. Where did you get it?"

Alarmed, her wits too overtaxed to give quick answer, Lark hesitated.

"Ah . . . a secret, is it?" Christopher asked with maddening perception. "I swear, all in the space of a second your expression turned from sweet and vulnerable to sphinxlike." He dropped the coin into her rigid fingers and closed her fist. "Here. You needn't tell me where you got it. And I apologize for startling you."

His tone was quiet now, genuine. She felt him put a hand to her brow, gently smooth back her damp, twining mass of hair. The intimacy caused her to grip the coin in her hand more tightly rather than yield to impulse and throw her arms around him. In spite of herself, she yearned for his comfort after her harrowing ordeal in the night, yearned to be held in strong arms. She could smell the familiar scent of his garments, feel the heat of his hard-knit body, and sense his piercing regard.

No doubt he was about to inspect her cheek for signs of damage and berate her for her foolish outing. No doubt he would demand an explanation for her presence in the streets tonight, and she had none to give. But until he did, she would simply delight in his nearness.

When he took her chin in hand she leaned forward, wanting madly, foolishly, to feel again the wonder of his mouth.

He obliged. His lips were warm and firm, his breath hot against her own. She had never guessed kissing could be done so artfully. The couplings of others she had glimpsed behind byres and peat stacks had been crude, frantic unitings to be gotten over quickly. Sliding her arms around his neck and pressing close, she relinquished herself entirely for the moment, wondering whimsically as he pulled her hips to his if class and wealth and education somehow made a man more adroit at lovemaking.

And with that thought came remembrance of who he was. What had she become to desire this man? Had she let his polish, his power, his flattering charm, dash away all the principles that gave meaning to her life? Were her ideals so fragile, her anarchist blood so thin, to allow her flesh to hunger for the craven breed she had been raised to hate? With this intimacy, did she not betray her lineage, her family, Jamie's future, and every starving and forgotten soul her cause sought to aid? And most of all, did she not betray *herself*?

Suddenly, as if tainted by his very hands, Lark shoved him away. "I despise myself for this! I despise myself for what I've become in this house!" Though she hurled the cries in his direction, they were spoken for herself.

Having been lost within a net of his own tenderness and yearning, Christopher was caught off guard by her sudden, bitter condemnation. By his gentleness he had hoped to make her gentle, make her simply a woman, not an enemy to wrestle against. His temper snapped, and once he began to speak his mind, he could not stop.

"You are a coward, Lark Ballinter, a dyed-in-the-wool coward. For all your self-righteous defense of the lowly masses, for all your own conceit, in your very heart you do not feel yourself my equal. That's what really eats at you. You're intimidated by me, by my wealth, my education, my privileged place in life. You tremble at the thought of having any feelings for me, because you fear I might look upon your ragged clothes and bare feet and see you as nothing more than a common drudge born to serve me." He seized her arms, his face twisting now with both hurt and wrath. "You do, don't you? Admit it! By God! You feel *inferior!*"

Giving no thought that her hand would miss its mark, Lark lashed out at him. With sickening dismay and a shuddering heart, she heard and felt her flesh render pain to his. But her reaction was eminently justifiable, she told herself, for already, in his brutal attack, he had struck her and felled her pride.

Several seconds passed, as if he stood on the brink of retaliation. She held her ground, remained defiant, daring him to respond.

"I shall leave you to your bitterness," he said at last in a voice cold and brittle enough to freeze the very air. "After all, 'tis a friend whose company you seem to enjoy above all others."

He strode away then. And she let him, listening with an aching heart to the beloved footsteps that did not proceed in the direction of his chamber, but rapped furiously down the stairs again.

Away, and out into the night.

11

During what remained of that night, Lark suffered a ghastly nightmare. She had visions of a groaning tree, from whose boughs sizzled bolts of whitest lightning and from whose knotted, earth-bound roots sprung an elfin clan. Worst of all, there hung from the loftiest branch the cape-clad figure of a faceless phantom. His towering form swayed in the wind, and silver mist dripped from the heels of his burnished boots. Kneeling upon the stony ground beneath, Lark wept for him.

Her own tears awoke her from the dreadful dream, and she wept a while longer for many reasons—her blindness, her future prospects, her failed mission.

But, most of all, she wept because she was in love with Christopher Cavanaugh. Aye, she loved the compassionate surgeon, and—God help her—she loved the earl.

But what did he feel for her? Did he feel passion or a challenge? Or did he seek to use her somehow?

She did not know. Perhaps he felt only contempt now. His blunt and scorching words last eve would seem to say so. She wished she could ask him outright what he really thought of her, but if he were to answer, she would only doubt the reply. Along with the barrier of his nobility and all it signified, there was about him an indefinable mystery that kept her from trusting him.

Beset by troubles, not the least of which was her anxiety over Virgil, she fumbled about the writing desk, awkwardly and painstakingly penning a note to her parish priest, informing him of her whereabouts. If her brother arrived in Ireland to search for her, he would surely inquire of Father Peabody, for it was fact that priests knew more than anyone else in the parish about the private lives of their flock. Using subtle overtones only Virgil would be able to catch, she included a warning in the missive that her brother should not call openly at the house on Henrietta Street but contact her in a discreet way.

After asking Grindle to see it delivered, she begged the maid to escort her down to the garden. Though uncertain that her master would approve, Grindle at last relented, declaring him already on his rounds at the Foundling Hospital that morning.

The air outside was brisk, the temperature cold enough to turn breath to vapor, but with the sun's intermittent peeking through the cloud, Lark needed only a light wrap over her dress. She trod with care over the unpredictable paths of rounded stepping-stones that wended through the garden, keeping her hand lightly upon Grindle's guiding arm, though such dependence nettled her.

"There be a bench in the center of the garden," the slow-footed maid said. "Placed right before the holy well, 'tis. I'll seat ye there, but take care that ye do not fall into its pool."

Shortly, the sound of tinkling water met Lark's ears, making her eager to sit for a while and enjoy the natural tranquillity. Perhaps, as the maid had claimed, it was indeed a sacred brew, some angel's chiming fountain pouring forth from a holy spout.

"Are ye certain ye don't want me to make ye up a draught of the healin' potion, lassie?" Grindle asked in her creaky voice. "'Tis been known to open eyes that have been darkened even since birth, sealed shut from the light o' day for fifty years or more." She cackled. "Might give ye back yer sight, let ye get a glimpse o' things that'll both shock and delight ye."

Disconcerted, Lark shook her head, rubbing the length of both arms as if a chill had taken her. "Nay, Grindle. And you may leave me for a spell. I'll be fine sitting alone."

Seeming disappointed, the maid departed, muttering to herself in Gaelic, and Lark leaned back her head to let the peace of the morning overtake her.

Unfortunately she was not to enjoy it long.

"I cannot think where I put my walnut cane. . . ." The cracked, complaining voice drifted along the path to reach Lark's ears. "You know the one, the cane with the gold dragon head atop it—it came all the way from the Orient, it did."

"You left it at Winterwoode, my lord. I'll get you another—"

"I don't want another! I want that one. Send someone back to the country immediately to fetch it. And see that tea is ready in an hour. I shall return to the house then and take it."

The command made in such despotic tones could have come from no other, Lark decided, than the Marquess of Winterwoode himself. She formed an immediate impression of Christopher's father: aged, self-indulgent, indifferent to the feelings of anyone on a social plane beneath his own, and, as his son had said, a bit full of bluster.

At last she would face the landowner who had tyrannized, evicted, starved, and made beggars of so many. When she recalled the wrongs the man had initiated against Uncle Jerome and so many like him, her wrath began to simmer. She yearned to stand up and curse him for his cruelty and greed, to revile him for a devil. He deserved to be made aware of the suffering he had caused, he deserved the abuse of her tongue, and, to her mind, he deserved the harshest judgment from heaven.

Even as she burned inwardly, Christopher's brutal words came back to sting her. Was she bitter?

If I am, the evils of his class have made me so! her heart responded.

She heard the old nobleman shuffle toward her secluded site and stop abruptly.

"Who the devil are you?"

She fixed her sightless eyes straight ahead, struggling to control her hatred. Finally, affecting her coarsest country accent, she replied, "Me name's Lark Ballinter. *Mistress* Lark Ballinter."

"Are you from that rabble queued up on the street, young woman? Because if you are—"

"I have leave to be here," she announced.

"Given by whom?"

"Given by your son. As a matter of fact, I'm livin' here as his guest."

"By God!" the old man exploded, sitting down on the other end of her bench. "The lad's getting more bold every day! Why, Lord Barrington called upon me this very morning to complain that Christopher openly criticized Viscount Pilkington last night, admonishing him for the treatment of his own tenantry. If he doesn't watch himself, my fool of a son will be ostracized before the year is out!"

"Your son is a good man," Lark countered, experiencing a trace of astonishment that the defense of Lord Glassmeade came so readily to her lips, especially after his unsparing words last night. She realized upon saying it that it was a most sincere defense.

"A good man?" the marquess repeated, as if considering the notion for the first time. "I suppose he is. But I discouraged him strongly against the medical profession. 'Tis really beneath him. Of course, I'm told he's brilliant with the scalpel, respected throughout the realm and Europe. Nevertheless, though he will argue heatedly to the contrary, he did not *have* to do it, there was no need."

The elderly one thumped a hand upon his thigh. "I've told him I wouldn't mind so much if he confined his practice to the nobility, but instead he would soil his hands on the filthiest of the riff-raff."

"But he is compassionate," Lark said.

"Bah! Compassion for the rabble weakens the structure of the aristocracy. And these days we cannot afford to be anything but iron-fisted and stern lest we lose our power."

Lark jumped to her feet, her temper gone beyond its bounds. "Then you *should* lose your power! Those who work to make you wealthy will die without your compassion. They *are* dying even now—"

"Sit down, young woman!" The marquess stamped his foot. "For heaven's sake, you needn't stand over me. And why do you not look me in the eye when you speak? 'Tis a most irritating habit. You may rant and rave about your radical notions all you want, but I shall not listen. Christopher will hear of my displeasure as well. If he does not cease mingling with his inferiors, he will rue the day!"

Seized by a spell of coughing then, the man grew silent for a moment, then continued in a petulant tone. "I had hoped he would have given me grandchildren by now. He can't even seem to oblige me in that. All he'd have to do is settle upon a lady and—"

"Father, perhaps you should go in and rest."

Lark started at the sound of Lord Glassmeade's low, solemn voice. Absorbed in her argument with his father, she had failed to hear his approach. His nearness made her nerves prickle and her breath grow shallow. She wondered how long he had stood behind them, how much he had heard.

"Ah, Christopher!" the marquess greeted him. "But, where is my other son? He is a rascal for taunting me so! And look what he's done to you. Doing mischief, engineering one devilish prank after another, expecting you to take responsibility, to extract him from the trouble he's made for himself. Why, many are the times I threaten to administer a cane across his back, but you, my dear Chris, will never hear of it. 'Tis disgraceful, I say, how undisciplined the ruffian's grown."

Lark frowned, realizing the old man must have fallen into one of the befuddled states Lord Glassmeade had mentioned, for she knew Christopher to be his only offspring.

She heard the son come around the bench and speak firmly to his sire. "Father, I'll escort you inside now—"

"I do not want to take a blasted nap! Why must you bully me so? Do you think I am an idiot?"

"Of course not," Christopher said as he took his father's arm. He glanced at Lark. The sunlight shone on the richness of her braided hair, and he noted her complexion was flushed. No doubt she had been arguing heatedly with his sire . . . as always, she had to play the rebel.

He addressed her stiffly. "Mistress Ballinter, will you come in, too?"

Lark kept her face averted at the cool, impersonal tone. "Nay. I'll find my own way back."

"See that you don't tarry too long, then," he said curtly, angry that she never relented. "There's a storm brewing."

Favoring him with a caustic little smile, she said, "Aye, my lord. There is indeed a storm brewing."

Lark did not heed the earl's warning soon enough. Barely a half hour after he left her the heavens opened up at once, not with a few gentle drops, but with an earnest deluge. She stumbled around the gardens alone, slipping, taking a wrong turn somewhere on the confusing paths before finally, thankfully, feeling flagstone instead of pebbles beneath her feet. By the time she staggered through the servants' entrance, she was soaked to the bone and shivering.

Meeting no one along the corridors, and knowing that finding her way to her chamber without assistance would be nearly impossible, she began to hunt for any room warmed by a fire. Her clothes stuck unpleasantly to her flesh, tendrils of hair trailed over her damp face, and her teeth chattered.

Feeling her way along a wall, she discovered double doors that opened wide into a room where crackling sounds suggested a blazing hearth. She ventured in after hesitating a moment on the threshold. No sounds of stirring, no voices, alerted her to the presence of anyone else. Indeed, all was so quiet, she could even discern that two hearths were in use, one at each end of the room. With her pale, half-frozen fingers she groped along a stretch of rich wood paneling, finding shelf after shelf of leather-bound books so finely engraved that she fancied she could have gleaned their titles by touch, had she the time.

At last she arrived at a high-backed chair angled beside the far hearth. She huddled down onto the cushions and hugged her arms to herself, wondering morosely what kept Jamie occupied on such a dreary day. The household staff seemed to keep him well entertained, a kindness she selfishly resented from time to time in the face of her own isolation.

Suddenly the swish of skirts and the taps of slippered heels roused her from her musing. At the other end of the room she heard the jingling of a delicate bracelet and a feminine sigh.

"The warmth feels good, doesn't it, Helen?" a lady murmured. "But where is your cousin?"

"He will be here shortly, Isobella. And you needn't make your interest in him quite so obvious. After all, you've been chasing him now for nearly a year with no results."

"Well, I can assure you," the lady replied, "I

don't intend to sit by meekly, as you do, and let all the best catches go." She took in a quick breath. "Lord Glassmeade!"

Lark tensed as she heard the earl enter the room, and she inched down farther onto her seat, hoping he would not linger in the room.

"Good morning, Lady Isobella, Helen. Father wishes to sit with us a while, if you ladies have no objection."

"Of course not," Helen said.

But doubt marked Isobella's tone. "Are you certain the marquess wouldn't be more comfortable lying down? He looks a bit peaked today."

Christopher paid no attention to her. His eye had just caught the edge of a green-hued petticoat, a petticoat not quite concealed by the arm of a tall, wing-backed chair across the room.

He frowned, and then, though he was feeling thoroughly put out with Lark Ballinter, he could not prevent the corners of his mouth from lifting with the trace of a smile. So she had gotten herself trapped. He wondered what she would do now: stand up or stay for another round of eavesdropping.

"Here, Father," he said, keeping a covert gaze upon the scrap of petticoat while he handed the marquess a glass of wine. "Sip it slowly."

For a few moments Lark listened uneasily to the polite social exchange between Lord Glassmeade and the ladies, wondering if she should stand up and speak out. Did anyone know she sat in the corner of the room, or did her chair and the darkness of the storm outside conceal her from the others' eyes?

"How relieved I am that you decided to quit that dreary hospital and join us for a while," Lady Isobella said. "It has been so long since you've been at home for calls. Of course, we were all quite pleased to see you last night at Lord Pilkington's. I'm only sorry you found it necessary to leave so . . . abruptly."

"That is his usual habit, I believe," Lady Helen commented in a cousinly taunt.

"You were quite the center of attention, Lord Glassmeade," Isobella continued. "Discussed long after your departure."

Christopher lifted a brow and smiled wryly, noticing the petticoat being tucked out of sight by a stealthy, slender hand. "No doubt."

"You should have been there, Helen," Isobella went on. "You would have been green with envy over the gown I wore. 'Twas as white as a snowdrop and studded with seed pearls. Oh, and Papa finally agreed to remove Grandmother's tiara from the vault so I could wear it—that, and the matching necklace."

Lark scowled. Trapped in her corner, she gave herself up to the pastime of imagining the looks of the vain Isobella, deciding upon a fair, piquant face framed with shining gold ringlets. Surely such a frivolous creature would possess a pouty mouth as well, one practiced at provocative moues. Did she glance flirtatiously from beneath her lashes in Christopher's direction, and if so, did his keen gaze encourage or ignore her?

"You made a most fetching picture, Isobella," he responded as any gallant should, but Lark smiled, her sharp ear recognizing just the faintest touch of mockery in his tone. "Er . . . the tea has been brought in. Would you care to pour, Helen?"

Lark heard the rustle of luxurious fabric, the clink of bracelets, the clatter of china cups upon saucers, and then her nose distinguished the delicious fragrance of sweetened tea and coffee.

She made a face, thinking the group would likely idle here for hours, sipping tea and chatting while her rain-drenched skirts slowly soaked the cushion. Just as she shifted slightly to prepare for the long wait, Lord Glassmeade strolled in her direction. With trepidation she listened as he took up a stance at the shelves just behind her chair. She could hear him slide a volume out of place, riffle the pages, and replace it, all with maddening clarity.

Hardly daring to breathe, Lark sank lower onto the cushions, bending her chin down to her chest and biting her lip even as she said a silent but most fervent prayer.

Suddenly she heard what she imagined to be a silver spoon jangled clumsily against a delicate china saucer, then a breathy feminine gasp.

"My heavens, Lord Glassmeade!" Lady Isobella exclaimed. "Who or what's *that* lurking in the corner there?"

Lark froze.

"That is Mistress Ballinter," came the calm reply. "One of my patients."

"Why is she in *here?* Good heavens! She is not one of those wretched people who is weak of mind and has wandered in by mistake?"

Christopher craned his neck just a bit and eyed the top of Lark's damp head. "Weak of mind?" he repeated, seeing the subject's fists close tighter in her lap at his hesitation. "Nay. I don't believe she lacks for anything in that department. It does appear, however, as if she has wandered in to escape the weather—despite a warning from a very astute and solicitous gentleman, I might add."

"What do you mean?" Isobella demanded. "How could she gain access to this house?"

"She has a room here." Now that the cat was out of the bag, so to speak, Christopher decided to have fun with it.

"You mean she *lives* with you?" The lady's tone revealed utter outrage, and he decided her pale green eyes could grow no wider. "But she is dressed like a—a *peasant,* for heaven's sake! What ails her that you would give her shelter in your house?"

Regarding Lark's small huddled form and judging she had endured enough, Christopher decided to give her opportunity to retaliate. "Mistress Ballinter?" he said, unable to keep amusement from his tone. "Are you inclined to satisfy Lady Isobella's curiosity now you have been discovered in your corner?"

Lark stiffened. Did he believe she had crept into this room and hidden herself purposefully in order to eavesdrop upon him and his guests? Had he forgotten she could not possibly know if her presence was seen? And that pretentious bumbleheaded lady beside him . . . how dare she act so affronted, as if the very air she breathed were fouled by the company of anyone not of her own inbred class!

Feeling humiliated and defensive, Lark lost control. She stood up to her full, slender height, lifted her chin, and let go the force of her resentment.

"I am wearing peasant clothes because I happen to *be* a peasant. And I'm staying here because it just so happens one of the greedy, high-hatted slave drivers of your cursed Ascendancy has had me and mine evicted to feed his stinking cattle. As for what ails me, why, 'tis mostly the company of a titled, over-bred *ânesse* like you!"

Such silence ensued that the drip of a raindrop upon the windowpane could be heard clearly.

To hide his smile, Christopher quickly raised his coffee cup to his lips, noting over the rim Helen's white face and Isobella's open mouth. Thank God the latter did not have the wits to know what name she had just been called, else he was certain he would have had to fetch a vial of hartshorn to revive her.

"Well!" she managed to sputter at last, obviously unsure exactly how insulted she should be. With hands on her hips she directed her wrath toward her host. "I hope you will not be so indiscreet to spread too far this tale of your indecorous associations, Lord Glassmeade. There are those who would frown upon it most mightily. Already I hear whispers of scorn over your visits to the filthy hovels that are breeders of not only the most despicable humanity, but of dreadful diseases. 'Tis our constant fear that you yourself will be stricken down one day as a result of your ill-advised associations and spread the blight into these streets."

Unhurriedly, Christopher slid a volume of poetry back into its niche, then rested his forearm against a mahogany shelf and eyed her through narrowed eyes. "Do not distress yourself, Lady Isobella," he said, barely disguising his ill humor. "Or think too hard upon it, for you will surely bring on another of your headaches."

Failing to catch the sarcasm, she took him seriously, dismissing her concerns with a toss of her ringleted head. "You are right, of course. It would never do for me to languish in bed with a damp cloth to my eyes. But—*you!*" she addressed Lark, her words accompanied by the furious tinkle of jeweled bracelets. "Sit yourself down again, or go to whatever place usually keeps you. Only do not hover there like some skinny shadow."

Lark opened her mouth to deliver a scathing retort. But she knew it would be far more dignified to sail haughtily from the room than to continue to hurl derogatory imprecations that the little fool would not even understand.

Without thinking, she marched forward to exit, only to be tripped up by the leg of a heavy easel. Amidst a jumble of charts and maps, she crashed to the carpet, landing upon her face like the most graceless of imbeciles.

Though momentarily confused and stunned, she remained acutely conscious of the eyes of her witnesses, so conscious she imagined she could feel them staring at her back. Closing her eyes tight against tears and clamping her lips together to smother a cry, she clenched the edge of the carpet and wished her heart would fail and allow her to die to end the humiliation.

But a firm and familiar hand, infinitely gentle, pulled her up.

"Are you injured?" Christopher whispered in her ear as she came to her feet. "Or only as mortified as hell?"

"What a clumsy thing," Lady Isobella said viciously.

"She is not clumsy, for God's sake!" Christopher shouted contemptuously. "She is blind."

Isobella hesitated. "Oh . . . well, you never said. We had a blind groomsman once. Remarkable what he could do with horses—I never *could* understand how he managed so well. My brother often teased him, though, naughty boy. Always went about tickling the old man's nose with a feather, then running

away before the wretched fool could seize him. Sometimes—"

"Perhaps we should be on our way, Isobella,"
Helen cut in after Christopher threw her a sharp
glance. "Remember that new dressmaker you wanted
to visit?"

"Oh, of course. And I must see about hiring a new
lady's maid as well. Siobhan can be such a slovenly
girl if not closely watched. I've become quite disen-
chanted with her."

"I'd like to quit this infernal room as well!" The
quavery but still magisterial voice of the marquess
interrupted them all. "Can't even find peace in the
damned library, for God's sake."

On his way out he passed by Lark and leaned close
to her ear to say, "Don't mind that silly slut, my dear.
I'll wager that you—Papist peasant stock or not—are
worth ten of her!"

Still smarting from both insult and her humbling
fall, Lark turned and left the room as quickly as she
could. She was painfully aware of how gauche and
vulgar she must appear, especially in comparison
with the elegant ladies. It hardly mattered they were
shallow in personality. They would be beautifully
garbed, graceful, eminent members of Lord Glassmeade's world, while at every turn she was reminded
of her handicap, her low station, her unacceptable
religion, her dependence upon charity. *Her inferiority,*
she added silently.

She knew Christopher followed behind her, no doubt
watching to make certain she did not stumble again like
a dolt and injure herself. But she did not heed him.

Breathlessly she ran, stretching out her arms to
find her way down endless corridors, having no

notion of where she went. She wanted only to find a secluded hole somewhere and hide there, indulge herself in a long, racking bout of self-pity.

She fled until she came to the end of a hallway, from which she could turn neither right nor left. Her path simply ended, and putting out her hands, she discovered only a recessed window, its cool panes keeping out the cold afternoon gale.

As she pressed her back against the window she heard the steady clicking boot heels of the surgeon. Giving her time to compose herself, perhaps, he had continued to follow her wild wanderings around his house with patience.

She thought she would forever love the sound of those footsteps, of their particular cadence as they approached, and she experienced a wrenching hopelessness she had never felt before. It had become an agonizing thing, this love and yearning she had for Lord Glassmeade, but she did not want to give it rein. To do so would be pointless.

There was nothing for her to do but leave, get away from him and the turmoil he brought her. Even begging upon the streets would be simpler. The pain of hunger in her belly was a familiar sort of pain, at least.

Though she could not see him, Lark directed her eyes in Christopher's direction. She knew many things about his appearance. She knew him to be tall, knew his body was hard and vital, his shoulders wide, his hands strong and skillful. He was handsome as well. Even had she never been told that fact, she would have guessed it, for he exuded the easy, confident charm of an attractive man.

He stopped a foot or so away from her, and she waited for him to speak. But he did not. Instead she felt his concern and his regret over her sorrow reaching out to her like tangible things.

Able to bear the poignancy of the moment no longer, she blurted, "I'm leaving. God knows where I'll go, but Jamie and I will depart on the morrow."

The words, uttered with such finality, struck Christopher with force. For a moment he only stared at her with stricken eyes, noticing how the rain-dotted window framed her lovely face, how the brooding light from outside put violet tints in her hair. She was so young and yet so very much like him.

With a sudden, fierce need of her, a desolate need, he knew he could not bear to let her go. And his reason for this had nothing at all to do with politics or causes or meetings beneath the moon. It had only to do with an elemental emptiness he had somewhere inside him.

"Lark . . ." His voice came unsteadily. Wincing at his own vulnerability, he cleared his throat. "If this is because of Isobella—"

"It has nothing to do with Isobella!" she cried. "It has to do with the world you live in—all of it. This house, the people in it, what it represents. It has to do with *you,* and what you represent!"

She felt tears start in her eyes, and clenched her fists to gain control. Swallowing, she closed her eyes and added, "You are a very intelligent man, Christopher. You know precisely what it is I'm speaking about."

He reached out and put his hands upon her arms. "Don't go, Lark. . . ." The words were a hoarse sound, barely above a whisper. "Don't go."

A little sob escaped her at the catch in his voice. She lifted her hand and, finding his jaw, ran her shaking fingers gently over his mouth and eyelids, desperate to read the expression there. "Why do you want me to stay with you?" she asked. "'Tis not really because of my cheek, and has never been, so don't say it is. Just . . . tell me the truth."

He looked into her eyes, so remarkably clear, so earnest, and wished she could see into his own. Perhaps then she could understand what he felt, for he was loath to put the emotion into words. In fairness to Lark, it was better that he not bare his heart, for he could offer her little to accompany such honesty. Not now, when his life was so entangled and hanging by slender threads. Not now, when he himself could see nothing but an uncertain future stretching ahead. Honesty would only lead them both closer than ever to folly.

Yet he was on the verge of losing her, and he had to follow the prompting of his heart rather than the advice of his intellect. Bending his head to a fractional inch away from hers, he whispered, "I want you to stay, Lark, because I love you."

He kissed her then, hard and urgently, releasing at last that which he had kept contained, sliding his arms around her waist, pulling her close until her body fit with his. And he realized, now that he had her in his arms, that he had to find a way to keep her there.

Knowing this might be the last time she would ever be held against him, and unable to help herself, Lark returned his kiss feverishly. She took from him all the rapture she could steal, like Eve, clutching at the gates of a departing paradise. When he grew ardent, more aggressive in response to her excitement, she let his kiss grow deeper.

Then his lips moved away and with no less passion explored her ears, her throat, and the pulsing hollow just beneath it. Their breaths turned to gasps, their pulses to twin thumping beats. His hands stroked the arch of her waist and the curve of her back and in the act of courtship moved even more sensitively, more tenderly, than they had in the act of healing.

Lark took the liberty to touch his face, explore its sculpted planes, discover its lines of temple, brow, and jaw. She put her fingers to his mouth, traced its molded shape, the well-cut underlip and deep corners. His hair beneath her hands was thick and fine-textured and surely shone with soft luster. When she moved her fingertips over his brow and lashes, she pictured his eyes, in a vivid azure hue she found from her imagination's brilliant palette, and impressed it in her memory.

Her hands wandered downward to the rough, warm column of his throat, and she met a vibration there, his groan of pleasure at her caress. He moved her backward, positioned her until her spine pressed against the wall, until their bodies met flush, and she instinctively guessed to what end his advances would lead.

Putting his lips to her ear and letting his hand wander over her yielding breast, he murmured, "I'll get you a house nearby—you and Jamie. You'll have everything you want, everything . . . and I'll come to you whenever I can, spend my nights with you—"

Abruptly Lark drew back from him. "What are you saying?" she demanded. "Are you meaning to set me up as your *doxy,* for heaven's sake?"

Christopher smiled at her stormy countenance and tried to draw her gently back into his arms. "You needn't term it so coarsely, Lark, 'tis—"

She put his hands away from her. "Then tell me what I should be terming it. Should I say you're setting me up as a *courtesan, a paramour?* Which is more genteel, Lord Glassmeade? Neither? Then perhaps we should simply call it *wenching.*"

"Lark, you go too far—"

But she grasped his sleeves and asked, "Do you believe that I am worthy of no more than *that?* Do you believe that just because you come from a long line of libertines with titles, you must seek to own everything and everybody in the whole of Ireland? Good Lord!" she exclaimed. "You have every blessed thing this life can offer, Christopher! You say you love me, but what could you possibly want with a blinded cotter's girl who hasn't even the sense to accept your offer and take you for all your worth?"

"For God's sake, Lark, stop it!" Christopher cried through his teeth, backing her against the wall again with the strength of his body. "Do you think so little of yourself? Of *me?* Have I ever harmed you, have I ever been anything but generous to you?" He took hold of her arms and shook her when she refused answer. "Have I?"

As if defeated, she let her head fall back and her eyes close, hating the tears that slid down her cheeks. "Nay," she replied at last.

His hands cupped her face and held it still, his fingers almost bruising her. "Then tell me what it is you feel for me, Lark . . . *tell* me. Give me that, at least."

She swallowed and opened her eyes, straining to behold his face through the veils of tears and blindness. "I love you."

Christopher gathered her in his arms again, breathing deeply with relief and with torment. "Then let me be with you. Call the arrangement whatever the hell you like, but—"

"Nay," she said, though with the simple rejection of him came agony. "*Nay*."

"Damn it!" he bellowed. "What do you want? What else is there for us?"

She smiled at him through her tears, and the smile held a dreadful sadness. "There is nothing, is there?" she responded. "There is nothing. Just think on it, Christopher. Have you ever spent one day of your life hungry? Have you ever lived a day in dread that you would not survive the winter? Have you ever grubbed in the dirt just to find enough fuel to keep from freezing to death? No, of course, you haven't. And as for myself—what place have I in fancy gowns and gold-buckled shoes, riding about in sedan chairs and having my hair powdered? Who would be my friends? Well-bred courtesans have a place in society, but I am not of their ranks. Where could you escort me without the wag of vicious tongues cutting you behind your back? Where would I belong? Even though you may valiantly try, mine is a world you can never understand. And yours—yours is a world I cannot stomach."

"I don't care about either of our damned worlds!" Christopher snapped. "This has only to do with us, with what we feel for each other. Why should we deny ourselves the pleasure of it?"

Lark pushed her hair back from her brow, knowing she must not waver. "Remember when I spoke about the softness of the aristocracy, Christopher?" she asked, her tone not condemning but quiet and grave. "'Tis just that you've been raised to believe you can have whatever you desire with a snap of your fingers—for no other reason than that you desire it. But 'tis not that simple . . . not for me."

"I'll not let you leave!" he warned, gripping her arms tightly. "Even if you don't know what's best for you, I do. And I'll not allow you to walk away from me and my protection."

"Aye, you will," she said. "For you'll find no pleasure in having me beside you if it isn't my own desire to be there."

Christopher flinched at the hurtful words, and his eyes grew dark and bleak. With the knowledge full upon him now that he was losing her, he bent down and kissed her roughly, possessively, using passion where words had failed.

Lark allowed it but did not respond. "Now, go!" she cried when at last, breathing hard with fury, he released her. "Go and leave me to stumble about this cursed palace alone. I'd rather crawl back to my chamber on hands and knees than have you lead me there like some pitiable, chained *dog!*"

She had done what had to be done, said what had to be said. But she had felt the most savage kind of anguish in it, one that left her on the verge of collapse.

For a long, torturous moment the surgeon stood before her so silently that she feared he would not go. She feared he would take hold of her again, tenderly this time, and if he did, she would surely crumple in his arms.

But he did not. He simply turned and left her alone.

12

That evening Christopher undertook his usual transformation from peer of the realm to traitor to his country's government.

After dismissing his valet at eleven of the clock, he wearily removed his velvet jacket with its rich braid and donned his plain dark apparel, comprised of close-fitting breeches and top boots, jacket, and black cape. As he passed before the gilt-framed looking glass, he caught a glimpse of his shadowy reflection. Sometimes he wondered who he really was, where he belonged, why he dwelled between two worlds—a true part of neither, deceiving both.

Recently, during long solitary nights when he lay staring up at the embroidered canopy of a centuries-old bed, he had allowed himself the fantasy of sharing his onerous secrets with another—one he knew was like himself in spirit. He had imagined unburdening his heart, confessing his deceits, and freeing himself within a pair of slender, sympathetic arms . . .

and, if he were fortunate, finding his identity somewhere within the act of loving.

But that, it seemed, was not to be. And she had known it was not to be, had realized the barriers between them were too substantial to cross.

Nevertheless, Lark's firm opposition to their being together galled him. Christopher's nature was a commanding one, his leadership so natural that even apathetic men eventually found themselves bending to his will. And now a mere slip of a girl had defied him and bruised his pride.

He set his bicorn upon his head with an ill-tempered jerk and cursed himself for a fool. Even with his reason so clouded by anger, he loved Lark Ballinter far too much to allow her to fall into the hands of either hardship or the enemy; so he had decided to have her followed, watched, and stealthily guarded from the moment she left his door.

From the bottom drawer of the clothes press he removed a pair of gloves, slid them over his hands. Then he flexed his fingers and made fists, before looking up and staring at his reflection again with challenging eyes.

He would not easily accept defeat, damn it—not even upon that treacherous battlefield of the heart.

With her heart in turmoil since the earlier scene with Lord Glassmeade, and beset by worry over where to go now that she had committed herself to leaving, Lark spent the evening moving restlessly around her chamber. Sleep was out of the question.

For a while she settled near the window, sat before it as she was wont to do, listened to the ping of rain upon the roof while agonizing over her precipitous decision to leave Henrietta Street. It had been a foolish impulse, for she had nowhere to go, no way of surviving, and certainly no means of supporting Jamie. Of course, there was always the House of Industry, the dreadful workhouse that even the beggars shunned rather than be stripped of their pride and freedom. She could scarcely imagine being subjected to the misery of that life, much less raising Jamie in it, and its rigid structure would mean the end of her involvement in the underground.

Twisting her handkerchief in her hand, she sighed. Her problems seemed endless, with nary a one solvable. But the most torturous one of all remained her relationship with Christopher. Irrationally, their falling-out oppressed her to a far greater degree than did the more elemental problems of the underground and survival. Her love for the surgeon consumed her with such unreasoning intensity that she could scarcely think clearly.

He seemed to desire her as well. But why? The reason remained a mystery she had pondered long and failed to fathom. She was blind, with a face no longer fair, dressed coarsely, and unrefined by his standards; what charm did she have to tempt a handsome noble?

Whatever spurred his interest, she knew his passion had been genuine today and his disappointment deep. Most startling of all, she did not doubt he loved her in his own way. But that way was the way of a lord seeking his pleasures with a concubine, and she would not succumb to that.

She knew she was a fool to spurn his attentions, reject the lavish gifts he would bestow upon her. Light o' love or not, if she accepted his proposal, she and Jamie would be well housed, well fed, and well protected . . . for a time, at least.

Yet as she sat staring blankly at the darkness before her eyes, hearing the drum of a sudden hard rain, she knew she would refuse Lord Glassmeade's offer again, if it were ever to be repeated.

A sudden thudding sound shook the door to her chambers. She froze. Then the latch rattled gently, once, twice, holding firm against its bolt. She held her breath, for surely it was Christopher's hand that tested her lock. Had he come to press her again, repeat his offer, use an even more persuasive manner to try to sway her?

Balling her hands in her lap and biting her lip, she sat still, knowing it best to keep him out.

"Lark . . ."

His voice was odd, she thought, unnaturally strained.

"Lark . . . open the door."

She stood up. His words had been nothing more than sharp gasps, and knowing him to be above trickery, she ran to the portal, unbolted it, and inched it open.

Immediately she discerned the sound of the surgeon's breathing, harsh and labored. With a mix of great concern and bewilderment, she reached out to find him. He was leaning heavily against the door-jamb, his clothes soaking wet, his hat dripping rain, his broad chest heaving beneath her palms.

"Christopher!" she cried, sensing danger, sensing some tragedy had befallen him. "What is it? What's the matter?"

"Help me," he said. "My . . . chamber . . ."

Terrified, with blindness making her fear more acute, Lark frantically moved her hands up to touch his face, only to feel his cheek clammy with perspiration. "What is it?" she cried. "What is it?"

"*Lark*," he gasped, and doubled over, pressing his hand harder against his wound. "If you don't . . . stop talking and help me lie down . . . I'll bleed to death at your feet. . . ."

"*Mother of God!*" In a frenzy she ran her hands over his torso and then wrapped an arm round his waist and did her best to support a portion of his weight. "Where is your chamber? I don't know what direction to take!"

"Left . . . at the end."

Struggling, she helped him move forward, her legs nearly giving way in the effort to keep him upright. He leaned upon her almost as if drunk, barely dragging himself on, and she repositioned her arm, moving it up from his lean hip to just under his rib cage. When the warm stickiness of blood met her fingers she started and gasped, "You're injured—badly injured! Let me call for a servant—"

"*Nay!*" he ordered her, the effort costing him strength. Faltering in his step and squeezing his eyes shut in pain, he whispered, "Not yet . . . not until I've gotten myself behind locked doors."

Failing to understand his logic, but trusting he had good reason for it, Lark managed to get him down the corridor. Both of them staggered, he from weakness and she from the unwieldiness of his weight.

"Here . . . help me inside."

As he hobbled across the threshold with Lark's aid, Christopher was only vaguely aware that a fire had been kept burning for his return. His wavering attention was fastened only upon the tall four-poster bed with its green velvet canopy and tasseled bolsters.

With his arm draped over Lark's shoulders, he stumbled forward until he was near enough to the bedpost to grab hold of it. Letting go of her then, he collapsed upon the mattress with a groan, holding on to his side and dragging up his knees. Only through dint of will did he cling to consciousness, wanting to feel just for a moment the cool dry hand that stroked his forehead, wanting to hear the sweet, anxious words of care.

"Go . . . now," he managed to say. "Close the door behind you . . . call my valet, O'Neal. Tell him to go to Chancery Lane. There's a surgeon there . . . MacTavish. Bring him—no other. And, Lark . . ."

He struggled against a rise of dizziness, then convulsed as a stab of pain seized his side again. "Keep everyone out . . . say nothing about the wound. Tell them I have . . . slum fever. And pray God I've . . . not left . . . blood all over the house."

"Christopher!" Lark exclaimed, almost paralyzed with fear over his condition, over the direness of his words. She found his hand and held it between her own, squeezing his cold fingers.

"Go," he said. "And if you have blood on your hands . . . wash it quickly."

"Can I do nothing to help you, nothing to ease the suffering?" she asked, loath to leave him.

He attempted to shake his head but found the effort too much. "Lark?"

She moved toward him again and bent low to hear him.

"Swear to me," he whispered, knowing he must stay aware long enough to secure her promise. "Swear to me you won't depart here on the morrow. . . ." He paused as dark oblivion swirled about in his brain and threatened to envelop him, then he narrowed his gaze, attempting to focus upon Lark's indistinct face. But rainwater rolled from the ends of his hair and stung his eyes. He shut them, and finished the vital sentence in a hoarse whisper. "Your life's . . . in danger, you know. . . ."

When he said no more, Lark made the promise repeatedly, moving her trembling hands over his face only to discover him still and unresponsive to her touch.

She slid her fingers down to his waist where she had earlier felt the blood. The warm wetness still trickled sluggishly from his wound.

Panicked at the thought that he lay dying, she stumbled from the room, shutting the door as he had instructed before running to her chamber. Fumbling about, she located the washstand and ewer and hastily plunged her hands into the cool water and rinsed them clean before screaming for O'Neal at the top of her lungs.

Within a matter of minutes several sleepy-voiced servants came rushing down the hallway, demanding to know the reason for her shrieking. At Lark's mention of the surgeon's fever, the lot of them hastily drew back from her, as if she herself were contaminated with the infection.

But at her frantic bidding, O'Neal immediately ran to fetch the surgeon MacTavish. As the sound of his clattering footsteps faded, she sat in her room tensely, hoping none of the servants would be so staunchly loyal as to charge into the master's room with the brave notion of tending him. None did, or, fortunately, did anyone remark upon traces of his blood, which Lark feared either stained the floor or spotted her clothes.

A half hour later, when a commotion in the vestibule announced the arrival of MacTavish, Lark hovered beside her threshold with a stricken face. When she heard the surgeon stride past, she stepped out and, unable to help herself, trailed behind him. Not hesitating, he entered Lord Glassmeade's chamber and closed the door in her face without a word.

Overcome with anxiety, she returned to her room to wait. Never, in all the years of her life, had she cared one whit if a nobleman suffered the pangs of death and went on to meet his judgment. Never had she cared one jot if a nobleman spent an eternity in Hades. Until now.

As luck would have it, Christopher regained consciousness just before the nimble-fingered MacTavish had finished stitching up his flesh. With a ragged cry of pain the young earl flinched, only to hear an admonishing string of oaths from the one inflicting the necessary torture.

"Blast ye, lad . . . hold still! I swear ye're bound and determined to wreck my fine handiwork! Ye couldna cooperate and stay insensible a few minutes more, now could ye? Well, don't worry, I'll give ye a swig or two of whiskey when I'm done. But for now, ye'll simply have to bear it."

Gritting his teeth against the tormenting manipulation of his wound, Christopher struggled to place the familiar Scottish accent, finally identifying it as MacTavish's. At the same time, with a low, frustrated moan, he recalled the circumstances that had prompted the man's presence.

"Ah!" the Scotsman exclaimed, still holding his

needle in place. "I see ye recognize me now. Though ye're as pale as a ghost, 'tis nae delirium in yer eyes, at least! Bleedin' like a stuck pig ye were when I arrived. Confused me at first when I saw nae signs of fever, but then I realized immediately why ye called me here. But, blast, man, what a dither ye've put the servants in. They wouldna even escort me up the stairs for fear of catching something."

MacTavish talked on while he finished his stitching, ignoring Christopher's sharp, indrawn breaths and hissed curses. "Ye look a bit green about the gills, of course. But, if I know ye, ye'll be up and about again in a week or two. Few men have such a hardy, well-conditioned frame as yers, damn ye, and fewer still yer stubbornness."

Christopher sucked in his breath and clutched the edge of the bed as his friend put in another exacting stitch. "God, MacTavish . . . must you be so . . . slow?"

The Scotsman laughed. "And who taught me to be so precise and slow? By the looks of this hole, seems as if ye were a bit leisurely yerself tonight. Becoming a mite too reckless, I'd say," he said, snipping the end of the thread. "What was it nicked ye, the end of an English bayonet?"

Able to relax some now that MacTavish had removed his hands from the wound, Christopher leaned back against the pillows, sweat rolling from his brow. "Aye . . . but I fear 'twas worse for some of my fellows . . . much worse."

MacTavish eyed the fine-looking, though ashen-faced, nobleman ensconced in his bed, and he leaned down to bundle up bloodied linens and ruined clothes. "An inch to the left, my fine friend, and ye yerself would even now be standing at heaven's gate."

Pausing for significance, he asked, "Are ye sure 'tis worth it, lad?"

Gingerly, Christopher drew a sheet up over his naked, bandaged torso and rubbed his hands over his chilled shoulders. "You need ask me that, Mac?"

The Scotsman poured a glass of whiskey and handed it over. "I'm of a different breed than ye. Those who grow up with nothing burn for their fair share, and they're fueled by a hatred for those who hoard life's riches and never contribute to the welfare of the lowborn. But I've always wondered, what fuels a man like ye?"

With a weak, unsteady hand, Christopher raised the glass to his lips, took a swallow, and eyed his friend. "Many things fuel me, and were I not in such a cross mood from your heavy hands, I might even say men like you fuel me."

MacTavish grumbled good-naturedly and shook his head. "Well, whatever it is that fires ye, I needn't tell ye to smother it for a few days. And don't be tampering with my embroidery or I'll skin ye alive."

As he picked up his hat and bag and shrugged into a greatcoat, he added, "Would ye have me instruct the servants to leave yer meals outside the door?"

"Aye. And if you could take the bloodstained linens out with you—tell the servants the things are infected or some such falderol—"

"My pleasure," MacTavish answered. "Anything for the Cause." He halted at the door. "By the by, who's the fetching young lady down the corridor? I thought she would follow me in. Looked more than a little concerned over ye."

Christopher lowered his eyes and focused upon his

hands where they lay spread atop the coverlet. "Lark
. . . her name is Lark."

The Scotsman lifted a speculative brow. "Ah, so
that's the way of it. Ye've been struck down at last,
have ye, ye big, ruddy stud? About time." He opened
the door and turned to bid the earl farewell with a
facetious grin. "Bless me! I don't ken whether to
shake yer hand or pity ye."

Lark heard the clicking of a latch at the end of the
corridor, then MacTavish's footsteps. Not wanting to
appear conspicuously curious, she hid behind her
door with a thumping, fearful heart, listening to the
surgeon as he spoke quietly with O'Neal and the
butler. It seemed the latter two hovered near the
stairway, unwilling to venture a step closer to the
infected room.

"His Lordship's sleeping now, at last," MacTavish
told them. "He'll recover, but he'll be in a bad way
for the next several days—I wouldna go in, if I were
ye. Just leave his meals outside the door. Dreadfully
contagious he is right now. The clothing and bedding
I've got here are fair crawling with the fever. I shall
do ye the favor of burning them, if ye like."

The servants accepted the offer only too eagerly,
and the three descended the stairs together.

Unutterably grateful that Christopher would
recover from his wound, Lark climbed into bed, too
tired and distracted even to unbraid her hair. Sleep,
however, would not come easily, its forgetfulness
fended off by plaguing questions. Lark tossed about
under the clinging sheets in agitation.

Why had Lord Glassmeade engineered such an

elaborate charade tonight? Why the need to conceal from his own servants the nature of his terrible injury? And why had he made her swear to stay in Henrietta Street, muttering cryptically that her life was in danger? Did he know something about the golden-haired assassin?

The mystery of the masterful Earl of Glassmeade, the tender surgeon, seemed to grow ever darker, and pondering it until she was beyond exhaustion, Lark at last succumbed to slumber. But just after dawn she awoke to the sound of the faint but familiar creak of her door being opened.

Alarmed but groggy with sleep, Lark called out in a quavering voice, "Who's there?"

"A most harmless intruder, believe me," came the hoarse reply. "One who came to reassure himself you hadn't flown away."

"Christopher!" she gasped at the sound of his weakened voice, and scrambled out of bed. She put out her arms and rushed forward until a warm, familiar hand took hers. Impulsively she pressed herself against him, careful of his wound.

For a moment they stood clasped together—she with her head upon the ridge of his shoulder, relieved to have him alive; he, with his cheek against her hair, relieved she had not left him. They whispered no words for the other's ear, as the time for tender, loving, hopeless words had come and gone.

"Surely you shouldn't be up," Lark murmured with her mouth against his soft dressing gown. "I mean, with such a roaring case of slum fever, I'm surprised you can walk a'tall."

"Amazing, isn't it?" he answered.

"I find everything about you amazing."

"I'm flattered."

"'Twas not meant as flattery."

"Oh. Then, in that case . . . help me to a chair, would you—unless, of course"—he inhaled suddenly through his teeth—"you'd like to try to catch me when I fall."

Lark clasped him around the hips and, quite experienced at it now, managed to amble with him toward a seat.

Using the utmost care, Christopher eased himself down. He knew he should not be out of bed. His injury throbbed relentlessly, and he had not regained more than a small measure of strength from the blood loss. But he had been unable to rest until he could reassure himself that Lark was still safely in his house. "I'm grateful, Lark, for your help last eve."

She put her fists upon her hips and cocked her head to one side. "If you're so grateful, perhaps you'll explain to me why you felt it necessary to deceive the entire household."

She stood over him, waiting for his reply as if she knew she had cornered him into honesty. When he did not speak immediately, she keenly felt the heat of his masculine scrutiny and scurried to the bed to retrieve a loose white wrapper. She slipped into it and sank down on the adjacent chair, tucking one leg beneath her in a childlike posture. "Well, Lord Glassmeade . . . why the deceit?"

He took a breath and asked, "Shall we play another game of questions and answers, my dear Lark? You know, like the one we played over dinner the other evening?"

Christopher was gratified to see her blush. Thank God she would be unable to read the papers tomorrow. The front page would surely be splashed with accounts of last night's incident, describing the escape of a tall, suspected United Irish rebel stabbed in the side by a bayonet-wielding dragoon on a tenement roof in the Liberties. She would put two and two together and in a flash know his secret.

Since it seemed as if their relationship was not going to progress into an intimate one, as he had hoped, he wanted at all costs to maintain the anonymity of the Faery Thorn agent. To do otherwise would be a danger to them both. In truth, he had been mad earlier to consider confiding in her under any circumstances.

"I don't like that game," Lark replied. "I have the most peculiar notion you already know the answers to questions you might pose to me. 'Tis decidedly unfair."

Christopher laughed, then winced and put a hand to his bandaged waist.

"If laughing pains you, 'tis only as you deserve."

He sighed. There were things that needed to be laid to rest between them—serious and wrenching things, and he would have to clear the air. "Lark," he began quietly, "yesterday, when I . . . offered a way that we could be together, I never meant to dishonor you."

Bending her head, Lark fingered the folds of fabric bunched across her lap. "Yet 'twas not really an honorable proposal, was it, Christopher? According to my church, 'tis a sin for a woman to live unmarried with a man. What does your religion say about it? Does it say a man is exonerated from fornication if he has a title and wealth?"

"Good Lord!" Christopher groaned in exasperation, thumping his palms upon the arms of his chair. "I had hoped you'd feel a bit of sympathy for me in my debilitated state. But it seems as if you are as unmerciful as ever in your blackening of my character, just because I had the misfortune of being born an aristocrat." He shifted again, the flesh around his waist fiery with pain. Glancing down, he noted small dots of blood seeping through the bandage. "And now, having said that," he added, "I must ask your assistance one last time. I fear I've overextended my stay and should get back in bed."

The strain was clear in his voice, and Lark jumped up from her chair in alarm. "Y-your wound," she stammered, overcome by remorse. Hastily she felt about for his hands, and when she heard him heave himself up, she slid an arm around his hips to help support his weight. "Does it pain you a great deal?"

Taking an unsteady step forward, Christopher regarded the pucker of concern between her pretty arched brows and almost smiled. Beneath the hard edges of her nature there dwelled a soft center, one that seldom appeared but stirred him when it did.

"'Tis nothing a bout with John Barleycorn can't cure," he reassured her.

She took a step with him, her leg moving in tandem with his. "I know those lily-livered servants of yours won't come near your chamber except to leave a meal tray. Is there anything I can do . . . anything you need?"

"Aye," he said, transferring his weight to the walking stick he had left by the door. "But I daresay you would be averse to providing it, and would tell me so in the most abusive terms."

"Christopher?" she asked uncertainly, ignoring his innuendo.

"Aye?"

"You said . . . you said my life was in danger. Is it true, or only some ruse to keep me here?"

Halting abruptly, Christopher put both palms atop the head of his cane and leaned hard upon it. For a second or two he observed the desperate expression upon her face and felt injured at her suspicions. Then, reaching out one hand, he touched her nose with a forefinger, slid it down from brow to tip in the significant way he had done many nights before.

"What do *you* think, Lark?" he asked gently, a note of sadness strong in his voice. "What do you think?"

13

Standing tensely over a hazard table in Smock Alley, wearing fine but understated clothes, Sebastian O'Keefe shifted his gaze around the cramped, smoke-clogged room. While his dark visage scowled with disappointment, he impatiently drummed his fingers upon the edge of the table and laid down yet another wager. As usual, the man he had come to meet was tardy.

An hour ticked by, and then a new group of patrons entered the gaming establishment. Sebastian's hands stilled upon the dice while his eyes narrowed. By their dandyish clothes and elaborate hairstyles, the new arrivals were obvious members of that bizarre class of gentry called "Bucks," whose pursuits revolved around acts of eccentricity and violence. Their clubs abounded all over town, claiming such savage names as the Hawkabites and the Cherokees.

Yet, since many of their members were either lords or high-ranking military officers, their criminal peccadilloes, no matter how malicious, often went unprosecuted. Sebastian noted that these particular specimens wore their scabbards with the tips cut out so the sword points protruded, a sign of their affiliation with the club known as the Pinkindindies.

Without making his interest seem more than nominally curious, he examined their faces more closely.

Laughing at some joke and handing their gold-frogged redingotes to their barbers—who trailed in their wake at almost every social gathering—the men swaggered forward. Suddenly Sebastian's black eyes locked with the pale gray ones of the leader. After a fraction of time, both men looked away again with no change in expression. The buck crossed the room to lounge about with friends, and for a quarter of an hour the tinker continued in his play.

After losing the entire contents of his purse, Sebastian strolled outside as if to take the air. He stood upon the dark street corner, waiting, chewing the stem of an unlit pipe, sullenly watching a trio of partygoers alight from a coach across the way.

"What news have you?"

Though he had expected to hear it, the cold, arrogant voice just behind Sebastian's shoulder made him start. He hated the disdain in it, hated dealing with the man who, in keeping with the Pinkindindies' tradition of nicknames, called himself Buck Infamy.

Suppressing his distaste, O'Keefe reminded himself that this self-proclaimed gentleman was an aide to the Viceroy himself, and through him, if Sebastian were calculating enough, any number of tempting favors could be earned: gold, land, perhaps even knighthood.

Of course, the price for this largesse was high—very high—bestowed only after the successful engineering of a certain delicate venture.

"Obtaining the information you want has proved more difficult than I expected," Sebastian answered as the nauseating smell of the other's pomade and powder drifted to his nostrils.

"You told me you knew the identity of the agent," the buck said, affecting a bored tone. "Are you so ineffectual that you cannot now put a bit of pressure on the subject, force a few confessions?"

Sebastian closed his lips upon an oath and replied, "The agent is a female. Through a . . . complicated series of events she's under the protection of the Earl of Glassmeade." The last three words he uttered with undisguised hatred.

"The surgeon?" Buck Infamy said with mild surprise. "Well, I'll be damned. I've heard his sympathies lie in the wrong direction." He shrugged. "Not that anyone could ever prove it. He's too crafty by half."

Sebastian's face hardened, and he shoved his hands in his pockets. "I need more time. If you give it to me, I'm certain I can get you what you want."

Buck Infamy watched a prostitute as she ambled along the rubbish-strewn curb. "The date of the French landing?" he said in a low voice, nonchalantly rubbing his thumb across the facets of a ruby ring he wore.

"I believe so," Sebastian answered. "I'm almost certain the female agent I'm following is one of several who will be entrusted with the information when it comes across the Channel—if it does."

"Hmm. If so, the Viceroy will be most grateful to have it passed on to the militia."

"And the favors you have promised to procure for me?" Sebastian prodded.

The buck idly removed a snuff box from his waist-coat and, after indulging, gave a sigh. "When last we spoke, I told you there was a rather . . . disturbing rumor flying about Dublin."

Sebastian bit hard upon his pipe stem and, rather than glance in the other's direction, fixed his eyes on the candlelit window across the way.

"Since then," Buck Infamy continued in a slow, malicious drawl, "it seems your former commanding officer has got wind of the gossip. To put it mildly, he is not pleased."

Already on the verge of explosion, Sebastian's temper snapped. Seizing the silk-clad arm of the buck, he growled an accusatory oath, only to feel, in a flash, the prick of metal through his breeches. Looking down, he saw the sword tip gleaming from the end of the buck's scabbard, poised just inches from his knee. With his hand upon the sheathed hilt, Buck Infamy bared his teeth in a vicious grin, daring Sebastian to make another threatening move. Quivering with hatred but unwilling to be run through and left for dead on the streets, the tinker released the other's arm.

"Listen, O'Keefe," the buck said, "I know very well that you're playing both ends against the other. I know you're selling British naval secrets to the United Irishmen for a little profit on the side, even while you're accepting gold from the navy to infiltrate the rebels and learn their plans. At this very moment, I possess enough evidence to have you arrested and hanged for a traitor."

He paused to toy with the expensive lace at his throat. "But, to your great good fortune, I am a reasonable man, with no loyalty to any cause on earth except that of greed. For an ounce of gold, I'd just as easily sell my soul to the devil as keep it. Besides . . . I know your value."

Sebastian leaned away, but the buck stepped so that the toes of his silver-buckled shoes touched the tinker's instep. "I want the date of the French landing, you brown-skinned little cur. And if I don't receive it, not only will you lose your chance for that paltry title you so enviously drool over, you'll experience the gruesome delights of the hangman's cord ere the year is out."

Sebastian was silent.

"Now," added the buck, "if you've a mind to spend the rest of the evening gambling, go somewhere else to do it. I cannot stand the sight of you."

Lark listened to the clamor dwindling beyond her window, measuring without the clock's assistance the waning of the day. As afternoon faded, she noticed that even the high-stepping hooves of the gentry's steeds pranced less spiritedly, that the thud of feet grew slower and the shouts of neighborhood nannies more shrill as they gathered together their frolicking charges.

She still lay abed, having slept exhaustedly after Christopher's exit, dreaming again of the phantom Faery Thorn agent. Now, staring unseeing at the opposite walls, her uninjured cheek resting against the feathered pillow, she felt disinterest even in getting up. Just as if a great pyramid of stone had been placed square upon her chest, her troubles, her loneliness, her tragic love, pressed her down.

She thought of Christopher lying in another bed, so close and yet so distant, and imagined him as he must look, with his strong brown arms and shoulders bare above the sheets. Rolling over, she let her fingers dangle above the cold drafty floor and dreamed of running into his chamber and sliding into bed beside him.

Suddenly Jamie burst into her room like an invigorating breeze and tugged her arm insistently. "Wake up, sleepyhead! Wake up! I got somethin' for you. A man brought it to the servants' entrance, and Meg said I could deliver it to you."

Lark pushed herself up, struggling to shake off the clinging shreds of listlessness. "What is it, sweeting?"

"'Tis a letter," he replied, thrusting a slip of crackling parchment against her hand. "Open it. See who 'tis from."

"Jamie," she said patiently, "you know I cannot see. How do you expect me to be reading a letter, now?"

"Oh . . . I forgot," came the sheepish reply. "Can I read it to you, then?"

She smiled. "Please do."

Jamie plopped down upon the edge of the bed and, unfolding the missive, began to relate its contents in a halting but most important voice. "It says, 'Dearest Lark, I am in the city and shall attempt to see you soon. The priest has informed me of your present diff—diff—'"

"Difficulties?" Lark put in breathlessly, realizing the message came from Virgil.

"Aye. Difficulties." He read on. "'Be assured I shall do whatever is necessary to cir-circum-vent them. Take care of yourself. V.'" Jamie raised his head, bafflement in his voice. "Who is V?"

"Never mind." Though Lark regretted not sharing with Jamie the fact that his older brother was near, she knew that the best course for the moment was discretion. At all costs she wanted to protect Virgil's identity from a certain mysterious Irish lord recuperating from an equally mysterious wound in his side.

To meet Virgil while she resided on Henrietta Street would be a delicate task at best. With his heavy French accent, questions might arise, and she did not want Virgil to be linked with her in any way. Lord Glassmeade already knew of her involvement with the underground; heaven forbid that clever mind of his should discover the name of her French alliance as well.

Redirecting Jamie's attention to other topics, she chatted with him a bit before embracing him affectionately and sending him off to play. After his departure, she concealed the letter in the pocket of her cloak and, nearly mad with restlessness now, ventured with tentative steps into the garden.

For half an hour she rambled about on the gravel paths, congratulating herself when she heard the babble of the holy well she had set out deliberately to find. For a moment she simply stood there, listening to its melody, letting it soothe her jangled nerves. She could feel sunbeams dancing all around like yellow sprites, spreading their warmth before winter's frostbite could come and nip their rays. This tranquil fold in the garden's center seemed a special place, and Lark explored it, using her fingertips in the way a butterfly employs the silken black threads of its antennae. She felt the scratchy coats of lichen covering the smooth stone, the soft spongy mosses whose pleats retained cold beads of water. She touched the hard,

still green, stalks of a rosebush and received the prick
of its thorns.

Crouching down, she stretched out her fingers to
discover a hollow of cool mud overlaid with vines.
The holy well trilled close to her ear now, so close
she could feel droplets as fine as dew clinging to her
nose. She reached toward the sound until the tips of
her fingers penetrated the pure column of water, the
hallowed jet rising up from the center of the garden.
Its energy startled her, and she felt sensations of both
heat and cold, as if liquid ice and molten silver had
somehow merged together.

Gasping, she closed her eyes and ran her tongue
slowly over her lip, letting the shivering, pulsating
angel's brew cascade between her fingers. The flow
relaxed her, charmed her, and she seemed caught in a
delight both sensual and spiritual.

Mesmerized, she knelt in that damp, bewitching
place for an unmeasured time, until the atmosphere
of peace was disturbed by the strident yowl of a
stable cat.

She pulled her dripping hands back from the holy
well and rose up. Feeling vaguely discomposed, she
stepped away from the enchanted wellspring, wondering what powers she had violated with her clumsy
touch. Strangely, she fancied she could see shapes
before her eyes, obscure things, darkest gray against
black that shifted and wavered before her eyes. She
tingled with hope. Was her sight struggling to restore
itself?

Much to her disappointment, the shapes faded and
disappeared after a few moments, but in the future,
she decided, she would have more respect for
Grindle's wisdom.

Venturing forth again, following a path away from the house, she tested her sense of direction; but that traitorous sense soon proved woefully inadequate, for the garden paths seemed to crisscross like the lines in some ill-woven plaid. Before long she realized she was wandering in circles.

"What a fool I am," she muttered, groping desperately for an exit from the maze. "Jamie!. . . Grindle!. . . Someone help me!"

When no one came, the familiar panic she so often experienced in her blindness began to rise. She put out her hands and walked faster, only to encounter dense, thorny shrubs at every turn. Soon her palms were scratched and bleeding, her hair straggling from its braid and her head dizzied with confusion.

"Lark!"

A hand clenched her arms and she cried out, startled by both the touch and the unexpected voice.

"Sebastian!" she exclaimed in astonishment.

"I hoped to find you here. I've been watching the house and have glimpsed you in the garden once or twice before."

The tinker spoke in the lowest undertones while gently pushing her a few steps backward in what she judged to be a shelter of high hedges. Recalling the recent confrontation he had had with the master of the house, it was not difficult to understand his precaution against discovery.

"I've missed you sorely, Lark," he said, encircling her in a brief embrace. "I've been so concerned, so keen to see you, so aggrieved at the news of your blindness. And your—"

She knew by his uncertain tone that he struggled to politely describe her scarred appearance. Though she still wore a light veil of gauze upon her cheek, she supposed her blighted looks were quite apparent.

"How did you learn of my accident, Sebastian?" she asked. "How did you know I'd been brought here? Did Father Peabody tell you?"

"Aye. I was stunned to hear the news of your tragedy. Knowing how alone you are, I naturally wanted to lend my help."

He snapped a twig between his hands, and his tone turned sore and angered. "I rushed here to see you, only to be denied the visit. And now I can't even get past the door. This morning the footman threatened to have me arrested when I refused to leave. 'Master's orders,' he said."

"Lord Glassmeade is . . . presently indisposed," Lark said.

"Is he, now?"

"Aye, he contracted a fever in the slums, I believe."

"Serves him right, the bastard. Did he even bother to tell you I called?"

"I knew."

"And what reason did the high-hatted master give for his refusal to let me see you?" Sebastian asked her sharply.

Lark recalled clearly the game she had played with the earl for that very piece of information. "He gave no reason at all."

Sebastian laughed bitterly. "He's an arrogant and selfish hypocrite—just like all of his class. I detest him."

Lark took offense at his disparagement. It was one thing for her to slander Christopher with an uncivil tongue, she decided, but quite another for someone else to do it. "As the Earl of Glassmeade he may be all you say," she said. "But as a surgeon, I have found him nothing but compassionate and charitable."

Sebastian captured both her arms, his fingers biting even through the heavy sleeves. "You have not been taken in by him?" Leaning toward her, he peered more closely at her face, so close that his breath brushed her hair. "My God, you have! Lark, you must be careful of yourself! The earl is a womanizer, well known for his illicit escapades. Even tilted, well-bred young women have fallen prey to his smooth-tongued manner, and you are but a simple country maid without wealth or family to protect you!"

He released her abruptly as his tone grew harder. "I feared 'twould come to this. I feared he would try to use you once he got you beneath his roof. By God, I would like to *kill* him!"

Stunned by the savagery of his words and by his hatred, Lark laid a hand on his arm. "Sebastian, calm yourself! Lord Glassmeade is not the villain you seem to believe he is. I know him to be a—"

"Oh, Lark, Lark, you have been misled. The earl only plays at being the benevolent surgeon. True, he is skillful with the scalpel, but his greatest skill is at deceit. My God, have you forgotten that you and your uncle were evicted from the very lands that the earl is due to inherit, that you were thrown out to starve? That was Lord Glassmeade's doing—he has his father's ear. To those of the lower classes he pretends a charitable sympathy, aye—but only when it suits his whimsy. You are a beguiling maid, and if he has determined to make a conquest, he will say anything to bend you to his purpose."

He took her chin in his hard fingers and tilted it up as if to read her face. She felt his breath hot upon her brow, imagined his eyes glowering in their fiercest way.

"The bastard has touched you already, hasn't he?" he asked. "He has begun to take some liberties, sought to woo you. Blast him! You are not even yet healed from your accident, you are blind, and still he paws your flesh!"

Despite this scorching onslaught, doubts assailed Lark. Could Sebastian's denouncement of Christopher be credible, even in part? Did the earl indeed use lightly and then discard the favors of many women? He had asked *her* to be his paramour, whispered seductively that he would give her everything she desired and lie with her at night. Did he also mercilessly unhouse starving tenants, adhere to the hedonistic practices of so many of his class, fabricate completely his compassion for the ailing poor? If so, her initial distrust of him had been well founded and now, her woman's tender instinct disastrously misguided.

Her misery must have been evident upon her face, though Sebastian obviously misread its cause. "Ah, Lark, I've been a thoughtless fool. After all, your accident must have been a horrifying ordeal, and now . . . the blindness. Rather than give you gentle sympathy, I've done nothing but curse Lord Glassmeade. Please, forgive me."

Relieved to hear a degree of calm return to his voice, she said, "We'll speak of it no more. Now, perhaps you can direct me toward the house. I fear I'm quite hopelessly lost."

"I'll return you safely to the door."

"Nay, you mustn't. Lord Glassmeade will be informed of your trespassing when he returns and—"

"I'm not afraid of his wrath or of the tales of his truckling servants. I will escort you back. But before I do . . ."

He placed a hand on hers, then, hesitating only briefly, encircled her waist in a more intimate caress. "I want you to know my proposal of marriage still stands, Lark, and that my feelings toward you are unchanged by your . . . tragedy. You must know I'm not good at making elegant speeches, but—"

He halted, obviously finding words hard-earned. "I'm mad for you, Lark. *Mad* for you! I've never wanted to offer my name, my life, to a woman ere now." He took a ragged breath. "Truthfully, I've never had anyone to love before."

This last was spoken with a strange plaintiveness, as if Sebastian believed that life's system of justice, rather than his own shortcomings, must be blamed for this sad omission.

"There must have been someone," Lark said gently.

"Nay," he insisted, and in his voice she heard the evasive key that had thwarted her before when she'd tried to learn his past. "I was orphaned at an early age. My father I never knew, and my mother . . . my mother was *taken* from me."

He turned away from her all at once and spoke harshly, as if some past anger had resurfaced without warning. "I've never recovered from her loss. I'm haunted by her still. In fact . . . she comes to me in strange, vivid dreams at night. I always see her face so clearly in them—the black and shining eyes, the wealth of blacker hair. And sometimes . . . she even speaks to me."

The tinker seemed to have fallen into a spell of deepest brooding all at once, and Lark thought that if she could see his eyes, they would be staring trance-like at some inner vision. In his voice there was a strange note of disturbance, as if he both dreaded and held dear these eerie dreams. Not knowing what to say, she remained silent, waiting for him to go on.

"I didn't mean to fall in love with you, you know," he continued, and, oddly, his confession seemed to hold chagrin. "And I certainly didn't intend to say anything about my mother. Now you'll likely think me a lunatic."

"Nay," she said, putting her hands on his shoulders. "Not at all."

"Then, leave with me!" Sebastian spoke with sudden urgency and pulled her close. "Now! Let me go and fetch Jamie, then the three of us can simply walk away from this place. I'll post banns immediately, and we'll be married before the year is out."

His voice lowered with emphasis as his grip increased. "You need a protector, now more than ever. And I need *you,* Lark. I need you."

How could any woman feel untouched by his offer? Were she in love with Sebastian O'Keefe, Lark would have thrown her arms around his neck and accepted the proposal joyfully. Her reason told her she was a fool not to agree, for after all, had he not just proved his earnestness, his willingness to be shackled with a blinded wife? It was an honorable offer, and painfully, like a dart pricking her heart, it reminded her of another proposition . . . one not so respectable.

For a moment she simply stood in the warmth of the autumn afternoon, feeling the length of Sebastian's slim, wiry body pressed against her own, breathing in the odors of wool and tobacco where her face lay against his coat.

It was strange, she thought, how love offered but not returned was an uncomfortable thing, even a frightening gift. It was as if the beleaguered tinker had wrapped his heart in silver paper bound with ribbon and laid it into her hands. Now she stood uncertainly, holding the gift, loath to accept it but loath to give it back.

She removed his hands from her waist and, without seeming to reject his affection, held them in her own. "I'm honored by your proposal, Sebastian," she said. "In time, we can speak of it more. But . . . I cannot yet leave here. There are reasons."

She sensed his disappointment or, more than that, his helpless anger over her response to his offer. Strong, violent emotion seemed to surge through his hands, causing them to clench and unclench where he held her arm.

"I'll take you back now," he said, his voice so tightly controlled that the words came out muffled. "But I must ask you to let me know when you leave here. Do that for me, at least, save me from having to search for you, Lark—'twould be cruel. I can be reached at the inn called O'Reilly's."

She touched the side of his face, caressed it tenderly, the gesture a sort of olive branch. In reaction he clasped her close, fastened his mouth on hers, and kissed her so hard that she was sure her lips would be bruised. Wordlessly then, he led her back to the door of the earl's mansion and bade her a stilted good-bye, promising to see her soon again.

Lark listened to his retreat, wondering if she should call him back and say she'd be his wife. She raised a finger to trace her mouth. After the touch of Lord Glassmeade's lips upon her own, no other's seemed appropriate there . . . no other's seemed so dear.

14

Sunlight slanted across Christopher's hand-embroidered coverlet, designed with the Cavanaugh coat of arms, and shone in through tall leaded casements unobscured by draperies. The beam sparked off the toe knuckles and claws of an Irish Chippendale chair, and through eyes half-closed against its brilliance, Christopher stared at it with a pensive, brooding gaze, his thoughts lonely ones.

The warmth, feeble though it was, penetrated the sheets and touched his legs, and he rolled onto his back and threw off the sheets. He cursed the man who had wounded him. The injury was on the mend but still far from well, and he had difficulty bending or twisting his torso without suffering pain harrowing enough to make him wince. He hauled himself to a sitting position, swinging his bare legs over the edge of the bed before running a hand through his tousled hair.

On the carpet at his feet, yesterday's *Evening Post* lay half-unfolded, and with a wry grin he noted again

the article written so unflatteringly about himself—
not that his name was mentioned, of course, as the
authorities had not been clever enough to discover
the identity of the wounded rebel. He supposed he
shouldn't be so cavalier about his narrow escape from
arrest, but as he moved to the mahogany washstand
with its rich brass fittings, a jaunty tune came to mind
and ended up as a whistle upon his lips. He had gotten his strength back—most of it, anyway—and could
walk without doubling over every few steps. The
improvement cheered him immensely.

Though he knew it was precipitous, he had decided
to end his recuperative rest and emerge today from
his chamber. Wounded or not, he was restive with
inactivity, and the demands upon his time were cease-
less. Every hour, messages from his apprentices were
hastily shot beneath his door by the cowardly hand of
some servant—most probably the one who had
drawn lots and lost—asking if he would be well
enough to attend this or that desperate patient. The
queue outside his medical office had no doubt grown
out of control.

He grinned and took a razor to his jaw with a
quick and steady hand. Social invitations had been
conspicuously absent from the lot of messages. Word
of his "fever" had apparently spread like the prover-
bial plague, and he guessed that contact with Lord
Glassmeade, persona non grata, would be avoided
with scrupulous care in days to come.

When he exited his chamber, freshly washed and
dressed, though moving stiffly, he hesitated at the
paneled door closest to the stair. It was slightly ajar,
and he stood beside it for a moment, strongly tempted to ignore his resolve and step inside.

Since the early morning hours after his encounter with the dragoon, he had not seen Lark but had purposely kept himself away. To desire her and not be able to assuage that desire, to see her and know that she could never be his, racked him like a physical pain. The sense of incompleteness stayed with him always, a thing that would not go away, not heal like the jagged, fleshy hole mending slowly in his side. But perhaps he was a glutton for punishment.

After nudging open the door, he stepped inside, the beloved objects of his mother's room giving him a rush of soft comfort. In the middle of the velvet-hung bed where Catherine had slept, had loved, and had died giving Christopher life, Lark lay relaxed and breathing deep, curled upon her side.

He moved nearer, his tread silent. The sunlight that had touched him earlier now touched her, streaming in like straight gold ribbons to illuminate the curves and hollows of her youthful face. Yesterday he had issued instructions to his apprentice to remove the gauze from her cheek, and now, in the light's honesty, a circular patch just below her cheekbone was pink and unsmooth. The scar would always mark the pearl luster of her skin, never disappear, but its presence certainly did not make her ugly. She did not possess classical beauty but claimed a lack of artifice that appealed to Christopher far more than the overblown daintiness that tempted other men. The lovely eyes that would likely never see again were closed, and the long lashes looked like twin fans spread open. But her real glory was her hair—thick, wild with curls that twined like a wreath around her face and shoulders.

He wished he could touch it, bury his fingers deep in its warmth, come to know its texture intimately. He wished he had the right to lie beside this woman who obsessed him, stay there until day had turned to night and revolved full circle into dawn again. At this moment he believed there was nothing he wanted more.

But, with one last look at that treasure some trick of birth had forbidden him, he turned and went out, leaving her to the sun.

When he returned home that afternoon from his rounds rain was falling, and after washing up in his office, he wearily made his way to the library. His wound pained him, his spirits were dampened, and he hadn't eaten since early morning. But he was not hungry. He could not shake off the oppression of the tenement he had visited earlier and yearned to sit down beside the fire, and rest in solitude.

But when he entered the book-lined room he found it already occupied. Upon the hearth his wolfhound, Bacchus, lay stretched, his great rough paws twitching in some dream of high adventure. On a wine-colored leather chair the marquess dozed with an open tome in his lap, his mouth sagging, the white hair on his head as fine as cobwebs. And set apart, dressed as always in her simple clothes, Lark sat fingering a piece of needlework. Obviously she had heard his step, for her hands had stilled upon the linen while her head was turned with expectancy in his direction.

How pretty she looked, he thought, how fresh and young . . . and welcome. Her hair fell across one shoulder in a long, thick braid, and the watery gray light of the window framed her head, emphasizing the gentle curve of her long neck and delicate chin. He glanced away guiltily, as if somehow, just through

feeling his gaze, she would know he had stood staring at her this morning with his heart in his eyes
while she had slept.

"I—I hope you don't mind my working this bit of
cloth," she stammered, disturbed by his silence. "I
found it in your mother's workbasket, along with
these embroidery silks. I—I know it sounds impossibly
optimistic, but I'm trying to create patterns on the
fabric . . . by touch."

"Let me see." He walked across the room and took
the sample from her reluctant fingers. "Why, Lark!
You have made a flower."

Her smile could have lit the room. He handed
back the piece and retrieved an emerald strand of
floss that had fallen to the floor, which he draped
gently across her palm. "Take anything in the work
basket you want. I'll purchase more if you need it."

Lark noted that his voice was dull with exhaustion.
She heard him sink onto the chair next to hers, stretch
out his legs, and lay his head back against the deeply
cushioned leather. She imagined his mouth and brow
marked with lines of fatigue and his hair in disarray.

"You lost a patient today, didn't you?" Her words
came softly, almost in a whisper.

Christopher turned his head, astonished. "How
did you know?"

She lowered her lashes, and her hands fidgeted
with the square of cloth in her lap. "S-sometimes
I . . ." She hesitated, as the intimate words were hard.
"Sometimes I feel so close to you . . . it's as if I can
read your thoughts."

Christopher bowed his head at the candid statement, deeply affected. He found he could say nothing.
He struggled with some emotion not yet sufficiently

controlled for speech, but he felt a sudden great need to share the thoughts that lay so heavily upon his mind.

"Today," he said after a moment, "all the suffering I've ever witnessed seemed to have condensed itself into one sickening experience. God, I can scarce describe it."

He paused, and Lark waited, hoping he would go on. She had hardly been able to endure these last few days, all the empty hours without his visits. She wondered if, now that she had rejected sharing a life with him, he was done with her company and would seek to spend time with her no more. Though she had willfully made the decision to spurn him, she found herself devastated by the possibility of his neglect.

After a moment she heard the monstrous wolfhound heave itself up from the hearth, pad to its master's side, and whine. By the jingle of its collar, she could tell Christopher moved his hand to stroke the dog's neck. Lark presumed the surgeon fell into deep reflection then, as he was silent for long moments. Finally he continued his dismal tale in a voice more slow and labored than before.

"I went to tend a woman in childbirth this morning. For two days she had suffered, struggled unceasingly to yield the child. No surgeon would come to aid her—most won't venture a step into the Liberties for fear of their lives—or," he added dryly, "for fear of not receiving their fees. When I arrived the woman was hemorrhaging, lying in a pool of blood, and though I worked over her all day, I could do nothing to staunch the flow. The baby I finally delivered—a puny, silent thing I hardly expect to live three days."

Christopher stopped speaking for a moment, staring into the fire, idly caressing the dog's bristly ears. "While I knelt holding the woman," he said quietly, "I wondered why the hell I was doing it—why I implored her to have courage, why I encouraged her to live. What hope did she have? Her existence was deplorable, squalid, degrading, an endless struggle. I should have helped rather than delay her passage into the next world, shouldn't I? I should have let the baby go as well."

A bitter sort of sound came from Christopher's throat, and he rubbed the burnished leather beneath his hand in a pensive way. "Sometimes I think I've got it all turned around. Sometimes I think I should send them all away from the door, leave them to try their faith cures and *Viper's Drops.* Don't you see, in saving the starving wretches from death, I'm committing them to . . ."

He turned to look at Lark, bewilderment in his voice. "To what, Lark? To *what?*"

Frustration marked his question, a kind of baffled frustration she had no words to lessen, no wisdom to allay. Reaching out, she found his hand, felt the hard ridge of his knuckles, the firmness of his palms, and thought of the skill that dwelled in the sinew and bone beneath the flesh.

In response he clenched her fingers hard, and together, while rain beat against the cold window-panes, the two unlikely companions shared a strange and profound sort of affinity.

Lark would have liked to rise and sit upon Christopher's knee, rest her head against his wide, weary shoulder. She would have liked to listen, even for a brief spell, to the drumming of his heart. But she dared not. Their spirits were too perfectly attuned in this moment. With the touching of their bodies, their flesh would only demand the same and be denied it.

"'Twould be best to let them all die."

Startled, Christopher glanced up. On the other side of the hearth, his father's gray eyes were open, staring at him gravely.

Lark's hand disengaged itself from his and fell away.

"'Tis the way of things, after all, Christopher," the Marquess of Winterwoode continued, his ancient voice quiet and lucid. "It always has been, and it always will be so. No matter how many idealist notions for reform you design, my dear boy, no matter how hard you slave to save it, the poor class will never be eliminated. There is a segment of every society born to shiftlessness and squalor. In their ignorance, they do naught but procreate, despite the fact they don't even have means of feeding their offspring. Why ever would we want to waste resources and money attempting to elevate them, when heaven has ordained their state of poverty? At least, by the sound of it, you are beginning to realize what your ancestors have always known."

Christopher stared at his father, his expression hard with resentment. He loved his sire, but they had never seen eye to eye, never understood each other's minds. He wished he could please this patriarch of the Cavanaughs, gain his approval, but if that approval meant abandoning his life's work, espousing the self-serving principles of the aristocracy, he would not do it. Ever.

"Father—"

"Spare me the rhetoric," the old man cut in. "I've heard it all before. And I'm disappointed in you, Christopher. You have carried your philanthropy too far, caused gossip, become an embarrassment to me before my peers. You have not lived up to your heritage. I have no quarrel with your practice of medicine, but this mingling with the rabble, this palaver that borders on sedition—I will no longer tolerate it."

With effort he rose, leaning upon his walking stick, his papery-skinned face choleric with emotion. "I ask little of you. You have made it plain you have no interest in the running of the estates. I accepted that long ago. However, do not think I will passively accept your abandoning one of the noblest lines in Ireland, letting it die out after four hundred years of existence. I shouldn't think it would be asking too much, after all, for you to pick from the ample supply of eager peeresses, force yourself to pizzle her, and get a child or two in her belly. Surely you can do *that* much. Otherwise, you have one or two cousins who would be all too glad to oblige—in return for your inheritance, of course."

The hollow sound of his faltering, three-pronged passage down the corridor echoed in the silence that followed his exit. Lark thought even the ticking of the mantel clock seemed extraordinarily loud. She did not dare to speak and, indeed, wished herself anywhere but there. For Christopher she felt immeasurable sorrow. It could not be an easy thing to live with a sire's disparagement. And for the first time she began to see that privilege could have its shackles.

"Well," Christopher said with quiet bitterness. "Now you have heard me properly chastised—"

"I—I'm sorry. So sorry to have been in the room. It should have been a private conversation."

"You needn't feel pity for me, you know. I've never pleased him."

"And yet," she said softly, "had I a guinea in my

pocket, I'd wager he loves you very much. Grindle even said as much. She said he dotes upon you."

"I used to believe he did. But my father is hard and unforgiving, and our differences over the last year have spread wide the gap in our relationship. Nothing means more to him than duty to one's status . . . not even love. And certainly not my own happiness."

"Would it devastate you to lose your inheritance, your lands?" Lark asked. "Do they mean so much to you?" It suddenly occurred to her that if she were ever to own a piece of the earth, she would do anything to keep it in her hands.

"Though I wish I could say the lands in Kildare mean nothing to me," Christopher answered with a sober thoughtfulness, "they are a part of my very being—the part inherited from my father and his father, no doubt," he added cynically. "But, aye, Lark. It would grieve me sorely to see my birthright passed on to any other."

"Your Lordship?"

Christopher glanced up, suddenly irritated that his life held so many interruptions. "What is it, Timms?"

"You have a—a guest, my lord."

"A guest? Who is it? I'm hardly up to company this afternoon."

"Er . . . perhaps you'd better come and see who it is for yourself, my lord. I've put him in the drawing room."

Checking a burst of annoyance, Christopher stood up and regretfully bade Lark good afternoon.

Bereft of his presence, she remained behind, disinclined to go to her chamber and distressed by the surgeon's troubles. After bundling up the contents of the workbasket, she set it aside and leaned her head back in the chair, having much to ponder. She thought perhaps she fell into a sort of doze after that, because she only gradually became aware of voices floating upon the air, contentious voices that soon dashed the grogginess from her head.

Was that Sebastian O'Keefe's voice reverberating through the corridors of Lord Glassmeade's house?

Hastily she made her way to the library door and paused there to listen.

"You cannot keep her from me forever," O'Keefe said. "I have proposed marriage to her."

"My God! You have not!" came the disbelieving reply from Christopher's lips.

"I have!"

"She has not accepted?"

"She has not declined."

"After what you've done, are you mad enough to think I would allow the marriage—even the continuance of your courtship? The hell I would! You'll not so much as see her again. And if I catch you lurking about my gardens for such a purpose, I'll personally come out and break your skull!"

"You can hardly prevent Lark Ballinter from wedding me if she chooses to," O'Keefe challenged him. "Now she is blind, she will need a husband in the most desperate way, and I have offered for her hand. She is free to make her own decisions, and even you, with all your money, can do nothing to stop her."

"Damn you if you think I cannot! Do you doubt for a moment my power? Do you doubt my influence, my ability to ruin you, Sebastian?"

Lark heard a fist pound against a wooden surface. "Blast your bloody power and influence, *Lord* Glassmeade! You have always been my nemesis, my curse! You robbed me of my birthright, stole everything meaningful in my life."

"Aye! And held myself accountable for it all these years. I've done everything that is humanly possible to atone for my mistake, and under my father's roof you were granted every privilege I was granted. But you could never speak even one blessed word of gratitude or forgiveness, never attempt to put aside your bitterness and come to terms with your fate. You couldn't use the resources given you to good purpose. Damnation, when I think of the disastrous course you've chosen to take, I could choke upon my disgust."

"'Twould please me if you did," the tinker snapped. "Then I would be rid of the obstacle you have made of yourself."

"Oh, for God's sake, Sebastian, if I hadn't followed you about, mopped up your trail of catastrophes, you would even now be rotting in goal."

"And who asked you to follow me, pray tell!" O'Keefe exploded. "Certainly not I. And I warn you now, stay out of my affairs. Lark Ballinter is *mine!*"

"Not for your abusive purposes!"

"Ah!" Sebastian countered. "And what of your own intentions? How honorable are *they*, you son of a bitch!"

Here some sort of violent struggle ensued. Lark could discern only the scrape of a chair, low, wrathful profanities, and the shattering of a few fragile pieces of bric-a-brac. Then the thud of flesh upon flesh and a groan of pain were clear signs that blows had been exchanged.

Horrified, Lark began to run, heedless of her stumblings and collisions with various obstacles in the hallway. She knew the direction of the drawing room and quickly discovered the door, bursting through it only to hear little more than harsh, labored breathing.

"What is it! What has happened?" she demanded, cursing her inability to see. "Christopher! Sebastian! Someone answer me!"

"Don't worry. Your suitor will come round with a little water dashed in his face," came Christopher's snide reply. "And I have received no more than I ever get from him."

Aghast that the dispute had erupted into a physical clash, and apprehensive still over the injuries suffered and the significance of the conflict, Lark made her way toward Christopher, finding him leaning against the wall. As if to assure herself of his wellbeing, she put her hands upon him, fervently touching first his chest and then his face.

Quickly he removed her fingers, but not before a film of blood had stained them. "Do you have a handkerchief?" he asked tersely. "I seem to have misplaced mine."

She pulled a lacy scrap from her pocket and handed it to him. "'Tis not your wound?" she asked alarmed.

"Nay. Only my lip."

Somewhere upon the carpet, several feet behind Lark's skirts, Sebastian moaned and rolled about.

"Timms!" Christopher bellowed, moving to yank the bell cord.

Seconds later the butler appeared and, uttering no word of surprise, obediently proceeded to heed his master's request for hartshorn and water.

"Now, carry him into my offices," Christopher instructed the servant, "and use the hartshorn. If that fails to bring him round, try a bucket of water. When he's fully roused, see him home. With the eye I've just given him, he may have trouble finding his own way."

With some grunting and obvious effort, the butler managed to lift his charge and drag him out.

"May I do something to help you?" Lark asked, standing uncertainly beside the earl.

"Nay," he responded after a moment. His tone was short, as if all reserves of forbearance had been spent by the trials of his day. "'Twould be best if you just retired to your chamber now and left me alone."

Lark hesitated, greatly troubled over the mysterious relationship between Christopher and Sebastian, and desperate to understand the heated and disturbing references made to herself. Keenly, she sensed Christopher's ill temper, knew anger flowed through his veins at the moment. Likely he would only snap at her were she to prod him for information. There would come a better time for discussion, a time when his ire had cooled and his mood returned to equanimity.

Congratulating herself on her own constraint, she turned to go, bidding him a soft and tremulous good night, hoping that he would come to her later, talk with her as intimately as he had done earlier in the library, and reclaim that singular bond they had shared there.

"Do you intend to take Sebastian O'Keefe as your husband?"

Lark froze. Christopher's question had been so belligerent, so coldly put, it stung her.

She took a breath and determined to make her answer haughty, knowing her defiance would provoke him more than her anger. "I have not yet decided, if you must know." Stepping forward, she put out a groping hand to find the open door. But her toe caught upon an iron doorstop, and she had to clutch the latch to save herself from a clumsy fall. The earl, standing only a few steps away, declined even to reach out and offer his assistance.

Lark suddenly grew indignant with his surly insolence. She whirled around and poured out her rancor. "I resent being a topic of discussion between you and Sebastian O'Keefe! I resent being spoken about behind my back!"

"You seem perfectly able to get all the information you need by listening at doors," he countered in a maddening drawl.

"Then perhaps you should invite me in, since it's my future the two of you are discussing. What right have you to decide my fate, Christopher? What right to deny Sebastian O'Keefe a visit to me, to forbid our marriage if we both desire it? He is a good man, of my class, and has generously offered me an honorable place at his side. Who are you to forbid it, I ask?"

For a moment he made no reply. In that space of silence between them, she could hear the unnerving gong of the huge clock in the vestibule, she could hear an iron gate scrape shut somewhere across the street and the galloping, uneven beat of her own heart.

At last the earl stepped forward, his swift movement stirring her hair as he passed her at the threshold. Over his shoulder he flung out a shocking answer.

"I am Sebastian O'Keefe's brother. That's who I am."

15

For two days Christopher did not come to her door. On the third day of his desertion, Lark sat alone, taking tea, listening to the wildness of nature as it cavorted beyond her chamber walls. The wind whistled round the recessed window, then swooped down to rattle a pair of shutters not firmly fastened below, and mischievous sprites of air puffed behind the velvet drapes. Even though her chair fronted the hearth, Lark shuddered and tucked her legs more snugly beneath a quilt. Her tea sat upon a tray at her side, and absently she stirred it, falling deep into thought.

Christopher's hostility at their last encounter had bitterly wrung her heart. During his absence over the next days, she had felt the breach between them painfully. She mourned the loss of his companionship and wondered if he would ever arrive to repair it. At the same time, she knew it was better that a distance be kept between them, for inevitably the time would come for her to leave, and they would be friends no more.

She thought much about that time, and she also thought about Christopher's relationship with Sebastian O'Keefe . . . his brother! She was stunned by the news, disturbed by unending riddles about such an unlikely kinship. Why had neither man mentioned it before? Why did Christopher live the comfortable life of an earl and Sebastian that of a tinker?

She had many questions to ask her host . . . if and when he deigned to appear upon her doorstep again. In the meantime, she would continue to nurse her resentment over his belligerence at their last meeting.

"Do you mind if I come in?"

She had failed to hear his footfalls, but he obviously stood now poised upon her threshold. At the swift surge of gladness his presence brought her, she let the quilt slip down from her knees and, forgetting her annoyance, stammered a breathless greeting.

Without answering, the earl strolled to the hearth and took up a position before the fire. Lark heard him toy with the display of porcelain dogs on the mantelpiece, then take up a poker and fuss with the dying coals.

"Does the afternoon find you well?" he said at last. His question seemed posed as a mere formality, and there was stiffness in it, too, the sort of stiffness that resulted from an argument between two lovers.

"Aye," Lark replied, picking up his stilted manner. "The afternoon finds me well enough."

"Lark?" he asked suddenly. "Will you walk with me? Will you walk with me across the fields for an hour or so?"

She would have agreed to walk with him to the

ends of the earth, had he asked. But she answered crisply, lest he think she was too eager. "Of course. Just let me get my cloak."

He retrieved it himself and settled it around her shoulders, then stood facing her to fasten the clasp. So close to the surface were her feelings for him that she flushed at his touch and felt her color mount as his fingers brushed her throat.

"Now, here is a muff," he said after rummaging about in the clothes press. "You'll need it, for the wind is harsh today."

As he put it in her hand, Christopher gave her a moody glance, wondering, as he had for the last two days, how in heaven's name she could consider wedding O'Keefe, how she could take his name, live with him, and bear his children. The thought of it fed his anger, and he scowled, wearing his sullenness like an armor. Rigidly he held out his elbow as an offer of escort, nudging Lark's arm mutely rather than murmur a solicitous word.

She accepted it, and like two strangers, they stalked out of the house together.

They traversed the lawn, passed the shelter of the garden walls, the tall privets and spiraling yews, and exited through the iron gate whose seldom used hinges grumbled with rust. Without speaking, Christopher took her through the elegant streets and onward, until they reached fields barren of tree and shrub, whose grass-shrouded lengths were scored with narrow, directionless paths.

Here, the wind was free to taunt them. It whipped Lark's skirts, loosened her hair, and made her sway a bit on her feet. But Christopher noted she relied upon his guiding arm as little as possible, stiffening when their shoulders or hips touched inadvertently. All too aware of her petulance, he grew more aloof himself, unsure as to how to heal this most recent rift, unsure even if healing were even the wisest course to take. Perhaps disharmony was better, all things considered.

He sighed. Regardless of their discord, he had many concerns to speak with her about today, and he resolved to plunge ahead. "The clouds are threatening, rolling like boiling water. They'll give us more rain ere the day is out, I'll wager."

She said nothing to his mundane remark, and he led her over pebbly ground, through stretches of dry heather whose waving, feathery tops brushed nearly to their knees. When the ground grew uneven, pitted with holes and strewn with rocks, Christopher held her elbow more securely, then put an arm around her poker-stiff back to aid her in the climb.

"I'd like to talk to you about Jamie," he said after a long while of silent walking. He halted so that she could catch her breath and he could ease the discomfort in his side.

At mention of her brother, immediate alarm showed upon Lark's face, an expression of fierce protectiveness as strong as that of a lioness for its cub. Christopher thought how fitting she appeared standing amidst the gorse, whipped by the wild breezes and backlit by the madder clouds.

"I'd like Jamie to go to school," he went on in a firm voice, determined to defeat any stubbornness she might affect. "He's a bright lad, Lark. With an education in a Protestant school, he could go far. There's quite a good academy here in Dublin—he'd have to live there, of course. I attended myself, as a matter of fact. Naturally, payment for his tuition would be guaranteed until he completed all his studies, regardless of our . . ."

Christopher paused, let the thought go unfinished, then proceeded more quietly. "I took the liberty of asking Jamie myself if he'd like to go to school, and he quite eagerly said he would. I think he deserves the chance." He touched her arm and added, "I'd like to give him the chance."

"'Tis impossible," she snapped. "For one thing, he's Catholic—"

"That can be gotten round. Money, you know."

"If this is a way for you to make amends or something," she answered stonily, "you needn't bother."

"It has nothing to do with that." He had been prepared for her suspicion but found himself a little stung by it nonetheless. "'Tis an offer made purely for Jamie's benefit. I've been thinking about it for some time."

"I could never repay you, of course."

"Of course."

"What do you mean, 'of course'?"

"I mean, I don't expect you to repay me, naturally."

"Ah, naturally." She turned away from him, contrite and overwhelmed at once. Despite the fact that she would like to assign ulterior motives to his offer, she understood him well enough to know he had made the gesture simply out of generosity. And because he liked Jamie. And . . . because he loved her.

Unaccountably, tears welled up in her eyes. Bending her head so he couldn't see, she wiped them away, using the edge of the fur muff that must have warmed his mother's delicate hands decades ago.

"So 'tis settled, then?" he asked, coming around to stand before her again.

She sniffled and let her hair blow across her eyes in order to hide their moisture. For long moments she considered his offer, battling with her pride and her need to attend to Jamie's future by herself, regardless of the fact that she had no means now that she was blind.

For Jamie, the academic opportunity of Lord Glassmeade's proposal was priceless. It would change the boy's life forever, give him the knowledge, the resources, he would need to climb out of poverty and strife. Could she, under any circumstances, allow her pride to stand in his way? Besides, didn't the selfish, hard-hearted aristocracy *owe* an education to the oppressed children of Ireland?

She bowed her head. Over recent days she had found it more difficult than ever to describe the Earl of Glassmeade as either selfish or hard-hearted. Feeling as if she were surrendering some part of herself, another piece of her independence, she murmured, "'Tis settled, then."

"Good."

He tightened his hold on her arm, and they walked on, the bitter wind stinging their eyes, the sounds of the undulating grasses as loud as sea waves in their ears.

Christopher tilted his head back to watch the sky, breathing deeply changing one subject for another; this one more unpleasant. "I owe you an apology, Lark," he said. "The other day, I left you abruptly— too abruptly . . . I think."

She said nothing, merely averted her face to show him she had not forgotten her indignation.

"To your misfortune," he continued as they walked, "you've become involved with two men of rather passionate natures—though our passions, you might say, greatly differ. The outcome of this involvement with us, you'll have to determine for yourself as time passes. But, at any rate, you're entitled to know of Sebastian O'Keefe's connection with my family. I'll give you some details, those that explain my relationship with him, and those that shed light on his character. But others, for reasons best kept secret, I must leave unsaid—save one. Stay away from him."

Lark heard the implacability in his tone and wondered at the mystery he felt bound to protect.

"I told you he was my brother," he went on, "but ours is not a blood relationship. Sebastian came to us as an orphaned child under . . . tragic circumstances. He's my foster brother, taken into my father's home at the age of five, when I was but a few years older."

He halted their progress then, and while Lark turned her body away from the wind, he stood facing it, as if challenging its strength with his own. She could imagine his hair blown into tousled strands, imagine his cheeks ruddy with cold and his eyes bright with the air's sting.

"When I was ten," he continued, "my uncle returned to Ireland from a trip to the Americas. With him he brought a gift for me, a very fascinating gift. 'Twas a snake—not venomous, but three feet in length and beautifully striped." He laughed softly. "I became the most popular boy in the county, as you might imagine, for deprived as we are of snakes in Ireland, the thing was an intriguing oddity. One day my cousin Jerrold and a few other lads challenged me to do mischief with it—just in the way most boys do. They dared me to hide in the hedge and throw the snake out into the lane when the next horseman or coach team rounded the bend."

Christopher scoffed. "Shameful prank, it was, startling an unwary horse, but not intended to harm anybody. I resisted at first, rarely one to be swayed by taunts, but we were idle that day, and spotting a distant horseman upon the road at that moment, we concealed ourselves behind a blackberry hedge to await him. Just as the horse cantered round the curve, I flung the snake in front of it."

"I'll wager the horse bolted like lightning."

Christopher pulled the collar of his greatcoat higher upon his neck against the chill. "I'm afraid you're right. The animal reared and plunged to the side of the lane, where it stumbled to its knees in a ditch. The riders—there were two of them—lost their seats. The lady fell against the rocky embankment flanking the road, and the boy tumbled atop her. As you might expect, my companions abandoned me posthaste. But I ran to see what calamity I had caused."

He sighed, and Lark could hear painful remembrance in the soft, heavy sound. "I found the woman lying with her skull smashed. The boy knelt beside her, screaming that I had killed his mother."

"Oh! How horrible!" Lark shook her head. "What a tragic tale. Such terrible grief and guilt for children to bear, and all because of an innocent joke."

Christopher seemed not to have heard her. "The lad knew only that he was called Sebastian, and that he had traveled to Ireland from England. He and his mother were quite richly dressed, and she wore a valuable ruby. Father thought with only a little investigation we could find the name of their home. We assumed, of course, that some family member anxiously sought them. But in spite of public notices and the work of agents, no address could ever be learned. To this day, Sebastian's origins remain a mystery."

"How did he come by the name O'Keefe?" Lark asked.

"Father asked him what he would like to be called, and O'Keefe was his choice—picked, I think, when a passing harper introduced himself by that name."

"So Sebastian came to live with you?"

"Aye. Father thought of finding a farm family to raise him, but I wouldn't hear of it. Because of my sorrow for Sebastian's loss and my remorse over it, I wanted to see that he got all the advantages in life I enjoyed. 'Twas the only compensation I knew how to give him. He accepted it readily enough, too, until he reached manhood. Then he went his own way, and now disdains anything I might offer him."

"How did his childhood go?"

"Poorly. At first he refused to speak much, and was solitary. But, in time, he became an utter terror to the household. He was never obvious with his tricks, but patient and clever, planning his schemes well. He rarely got caught at them."

"But when he did get caught, what did the marquess do?"

Christopher gave a strange, private smile. "Each time, I told Father I had put Sebastian up to the mischief. I took his canings myself." He looked up at the clouds. "'Twas a penance of sorts, I guess."

"You took his punishments yourself?" Lark exclaimed, appalled.

"When I could."

"And did Sebastian appreciate such a sacrifice?"

Christopher shrugged. "He expected it. You see, to his way of thinking my punishments were justified. And in my heart . . . I agreed with him. I had killed his mother, after all."

"You must have hated him at times."

Christopher sighed. "Nay. I always loved him, just as if he were my true brother."

Lark's understanding of the surgeon, of the Earl of Glassmeade, of the man she loved, was crystallizing, forming a cohesive whole at last. "Your becoming a surgeon had something to do with the death of Sebastian's mother, didn't it?"

"Aye."

"And Sebastian . . . did Sebastian love you?"

Christopher took a step forward. "He despised me. He despises me still."

When Lark remained silent, Christopher took her arm and began their stroll again, leading her down a gentle hill where their shoes sent stones trickling down the path ahead. Sorrow filled Lark's breast, and she began to wonder if the man beside her, the man born with title and substance, had ever been loved, truly loved, by another living soul.

All around them, made nervous by wind and the coming storm, birds cried wildly and circled above their heads. A pair of startled ducks rose up suddenly from the rustling, dry-smelling gorse, their wings madly aflutter, their protests raucous. In the distance, winter announced itself with a mournful tune played on eddying leaves and clattering boughs.

When a few fat drops of rain began to fall from the clouds, Lark tightened her hand in the crook of Christopher's strong arm and made him halt. Then she raised up her hands and drew down his head.

Her kiss was given in devotion, in empathy. And he seemed to accept it with knowledge of its meaning, for his response was not of a carnal nature, but gentle and full of gratitude.

She held him and let him hold her, listening to his breathing and hers mingle with the storm's gasps. Textures, smells, and sounds were heightened now in her blindness, and all at once Lark was roused by the feel of his form beneath her fingertips, by the taste of his mouth and the scent of his skin. She could have surrendered herself then, abandoned reason, become nature's creature and nothing more, lying down with him upon the cold, wet earth.

Sensing the change, he whispered her name, began to touch her in the tenderest acts of persuasion.

"Perhaps 'twill only lead me to a hell of my own making, Lark, but . . . let me. I need you."

So she allowed him to lower her to a bed of moss, she allowed him to take her face between his cool, gifted hands and kiss it. And she allowed him to put his hands beneath her cloak, touch the untouched flesh over her throbbing heart.

Christopher cradled her head in one hand, protected it from the moistness of the ground. Then he gazed upon the pearl of her throat, the shadowy hollow there, kissed with reverence the soft alabaster cleft between her breasts. Slowly he moved above her after that, put himself atop her soft, feminine form to shield it, to mold with it.

She was yielding totally, he realized, sacrificing her cherished, usually well-guarded scruples for his urgent need. Were he to ask now, he knew she would allow him, even implore him, to bind his physical self with hers. But he also knew she would do so mostly out of compassion, or out of a sorrowful kind of love, or even out of simple lust. She would not do so out of the joyful abandon, out of the commitment, that would give her no regrets tomorrow.

Somberly he put his hands on her shoulders and raised himself up, stopped what she would let him do.

With a bewildered frown, she reached to touch his brow, smoothed the damp, ruffled hair there, a question upon her lips. To silence her, he took her fingers and kissed them one by one. Then, in a gesture of finality, he drew away, extending a firm hand to pull at her cloak and cover her undraped, and still unenjoyed, charms.

The rain increased. She stood, slowly dragging the hood over her head while the clouds opened wide, poured their contents upon the turf.

For a few seconds Christopher continued to sit upon the ground, one knee upraised, an arm resting atop it, his head lowered. He watched drops of water run in rivulets from the ends of his hair and slither down the shoulders of his greatcoat to splat upon his boots. And he wondered at his own gallantry.

Then he stood and bent to retrieve from the mud the forgotten muff, its dark fur spiked and matted, ruined.

As the seconds passed he and the cotter's girl stood there in the deluge, facing each other, not even at odds, just sharing hopelessness. At last he took her hand, and together they trudged through the rain.

16

"Lark! Lark! *Can you hear me?*"

At first the furtive whispers only dimly penetrated Lark's consciousness. Afternoon waned as she had sat in the last of the sun's pale radiance, dozing beside the holy well, having spent a sleepless night after her heart-rending walk with Christopher.

"Lark! Answer me, confound it! I cannot come any closer without risking discovery!"

Startled awake, Lark stood up, tilting her head to determine the direction of the voice.

"Over here! Straight before you," the male voice instructed in an English tongue heavily accented with French. "There's an aperture in the garden wall—we can speak through it."

"Virgil?" Lark's heart leaped with joy. "Is it really you?"

"'Tis really me. How thankful I am to see you well!"

Hurriedly she made her way toward the garden

wall until she felt its rough, odd-shaped stones beneath her searching fingers. "Virgil? Where are you? Take my hand . . . I can't see."

"My arm is too large to get through the opening," he answered with impatience. "Isn't there a gate I can slip through without being seen?"

"There's a gate at the back, but I don't know how well concealed it is. You'll have to judge for yourself."

"Can you meet me there?"

"Aye, if I follow the wall around."

"Then hurry! I'm anxious to give you a crushing hug!"

Hurry she did, scraping her fingers upon mortar and stone, tripping repeatedly over obstacles in her eagerness to hold her brother close. It had been years since she had heard his voice, years since they had last embraced upon a crowded dock in France.

Finally she arrived at the gate and, flinging aside its canopy of vines, fumbled frantically with the stiff-handled lock. When it freed itself with a reluctant snap she threw it open and immediately found herself pulled into the arms of a more maturely built frame than memory recalled.

"Oh, Virgil!" she cried. "How happy I am to have you with me! Would that I could see your face again!"

"Are you well, *ma petite*? Do you suffer?" he asked anxiously. "The priest told me of your blindness. And Jamie, what of our dear little brother?"

"He's starting his first day at school soon, but I'll tell you about that later. For myself, I'm as well as can be," she assured him, drawing away. "But are we well hid here? Do the windows of the estate look down on this gate?"

"Nay, I think not. But I daren't tarry here long."

She agreed. "Though I yearn to have you with me, this house is a dangerous one to you. 'Tis Lord Glassmeade's property, and he—"

"You needn't tell me who he is. *Sacre Dieu!* You could not have chosen a more treacherous place. There are few in Ireland higher in the Loyalist ranks than he. I hope you've been careful of yourself."

She hesitated. It would hardly do for him to know the true state of affairs. "Very careful of myself," she murmured.

"Would to God I could spirit you and Jamie away to France, but I have no resources to keep you there. The country is still in a state of turmoil, and I live on the generosity of others at the moment, staying one night here, another there, beneath a friendly roof. But I yearn to get you away to France. Especially now, my poor darling," he said, smoothing her hair with a gentle hand. "And, anyway, since you must give up your part in our—"

"Nay!" she protested. "I'll not be giving up my work with the Cause. We're too close to the end, time is too critical. And I plan to stay where I am for the time being."

"But, Lark! You cannot continue to stay *here.*"

"On the contrary. I must. I—" She broke off, nearly having said her life was in jeopardy. There was no reason to cause Virgil concern. "Er . . . Lord Glassmeade has yet to complete my . . . treatments," she said, touching her still tender cheek.

Virgil's tone was one of serious concern. "Nevertheless, I think it quite unwise—" The rasping of a garden tool interrupted him, and he pulled Lark roughly into the prickly leaves of a yew bush.

"You must go!" she insisted, knowing a gardener

toiled nearby. "A Frenchman would be suspect here, and your accent is so thick you could never hide it if anyone questioned you. Besides, Lord Glassmeade knows in what direction my sympathies lie, and I would not like him to catch us together. Now, go!"

"Has he questioned you?" Virgil demanded sharply, ignoring her plea. "I know well your passionate nature, Lark. You have difficulty restraining your opinions. What have you divulged?"

"Don't upset yourself. I've not let slip any of our secrets." She patted his arm. "Come to me tonight—come precisely at eleven. There's a seldom used door on the mansion's east side—I'll be waiting there for you."

"And the earl? Will he be home, do you suppose?"

Lark recalled their walk together the day before, the delirious moments in his arms, then his abrupt constraint and, later, his detachment as he had left her at her chamber door. She sensed he would avoid coming to her now in the way he had done before. Their feelings for each other were too turbulent, their desires too insistent, to be easily contained. Likely wisdom and prudence would prevent him from making again his casual midnight stops into her room.

"Nay," she said, thinking of the powdered peeresses his father had commanded he court. "I daresay Lord Glassmeade has no dearth of diversions to occupy his nights."

"Remember when you pulled Mama into the lake the summer you were twelve, Virgil?" Lark laughed, putting a hand to her mouth to stifle the sound. "Remember when she rose up out of the water, scowling like a half-drowned cat with a lily pad draped square atop her head!"

"I recall better the whipping I received from Papa's hand," her brother replied.

They sat, heads close together, upon the floor beside the fire, using care to keep their voices low. Between them rested a pot of tea and a single cup for sharing. To avoid suspicion, Lark had declined to request a second one. Cushions were piled haphazardly around them for comfortable reclining, and Virgil kept the fire well nourished. At first glance an observer might have mistaken them for children, as they sat cross-legged, their faces fire-flushed and happy, their playful laughter barely muffled.

For the last hour they had enjoyed a spell of reminiscence, recollecting their most pleasant childhood experiences, avoiding mention of the more disturbing revolutionary years just prior to Lark's hasty exile to safety. Jerome's death they had quietly discussed and mourned together upon Virgil's arrival.

"Let me touch your face," she requested now as the hilarity died. "Let me touch you so I can imagine the changes time has wrought."

"And what if I say nay?" he teased.

"Then I'll grab you . . . like this. . . ." She took hold of his curly black head. "And hold you without mercy until you comply."

"In that case, I surrender. Here, explore this ugly chin, this protuberant nose, these hollow cheeks, with your curious little fingers. But I warn you, if you grimace and call me a scarecrow, I'll never speak to you again."

Without comment, but with a very concentrated expression, Lark let her fingers trail over the contours, finding them sharper, not as well fleshed as she imagined. He approached thirty years of age now, and maturity had left its lines of care, just as years of hard living during the bloody French revolution had left their stamp of gauntness.

"Well, how do you find me?"

"Are your eyes still brown—your hair black?"

"Last time I looked."

"Then you're quite unchanged."

"You are only being kind."

"*Me?*" she exclaimed in pretended horror. "Never!"

He poured another cup of tea and passed it to her hand, and they fell into a thoughtful silence.

"How go your efforts in France?" Lark asked quietly, turning the conversation at last toward the subject that begged to be discussed.

"Exceedingly well. Wolfe Tone has succeeded in securing a commitment from the Directory for the necessary men and arms to launch an attack here. General Hoche, the most experienced general in the field—save Bonaparte, of course—has been appointed commander-in-chief and will lead the expedition. And . . . a date and landing site will soon be selected—your agent must be advised."

"Really?" Lark cried in excitement. "When do you expect the fleet to sail?"

"Soon. Very soon. Indeed, though I would like to stay with you a while, I must return to France in only a few short days. Once there, I will do my best to send you some money." He touched her arm. "In the meantime, are you certain you and Jamie are safe in this house?"

"Aye. Certain."

She was despondent over his imminent departure but knew his political efforts called to him like a passionate mistress. No doubt his sparkling dark eyes blazed even now with thoughts of serving her. In childhood, that time just prior to the guillotine's heyday, both of them had been taught to serve ideals, much as other children were taught language or classic literature or the more mundane tasks of domestic life. During their impressionable years, they had had no shortage of revolutionary reading material and no lack of zealous dialogue while seated round the supper table.

How like Papa Virgil was, Lark thought, just as fervent, just as inspired to change the social order by the writings of Marat. But, as in the manner of his sire, she knew his beliefs would never take him to the slaughter of a battlefield. His was not the valiant character of a natural-born soldier, but the sensitive soul of a dreamy-eyed thinker.

"We must devise a new way for you to send the dispatches to me," she said after a moment.

"Now, Lark . . ." Virgil's tone was gentle with chastisement. "You know you cannot possibly continue—"

"I can and I shall," she said, protective of her position within the conspiracy. "I'm able to carry out my duties just as well as ever."

"How? Someone would have to lead you now to your meetings with the agent. You cannot—"

"I'll manage," she insisted, reaching to grip his arm, not daring to mention that Jamie had been her last escort. "You can accompany me this Sabbath when I go to tell the agent your latest news."

"Nay," her brother refused. " 'Twould be doubly difficult and dangerous for you now. I can find someone else to take your place—"

Her hand dropped from his sleeve, and she lowered her sightless eyes in dejection. "You only confirm

what I have been fearing since the fire. My blindness
has made me a useless creature, a creature to be pitied.
I'll be spending the rest of my wretched days sitting
stupidly in a chair, I daresay, and, if I'm fortunate,
some philanthropical society of old ladies will see
their way to feed me."

"Ahh, Lark." Her brother groaned beneath her
exaggerated self-pity. "You try me sorely. You were
ever one to worry me like a rat between your pretty
teeth until you had your way." He flopped back upon
his pillows as if in grudging submission to her will.
"Very well. Do you know the place they call the
Lottery Hall in Capel Street—and even more important, can you get there to receive my dispatches?"

"Uncle Jerome used to go there to buy tickets for the
lottery when he had a spare coin. Aye, I can get there."

"Then, if you're determined to continue, I'll
arrange to have the dispatches sent to a clerk there
who is with our cause. Go every week, ask for Peader,
tell him you need to buy a lottery ticket for a friend
from Bordeaux. That will be his signal."

"I'll remember," she promised. "And as for our
meeting with the agent, you'll need to join me here at
nine sharp upon the Sabbath. I'll wait for you downstairs again. Can you manage to find two horses for
the journey?"

"Do you doubt that I can?"

"Nay, I do not. But if you must steal them, pray do
so discreetly. I should not like to be hanged for such
an unromantic crime as horse thieving."

They laughed, the soft sound punctuated by a
sharp tap upon the paneled door. So unexpected was
the interruption, both brother and sister sat paralyzed
for several seconds.

"Sainted Mary! He has come! You must hide yourself, Virgil! Quickly! And whatever you do, don't let a single word slip from that French mouth of yours."

"Lark—"

"Swear to me! Swear you won't speak, no matter what is said."

"Very well. Where shall I hide?"

Another tap vibrated the door. Frantically Lark began to think. "Snuff the candles if there are any lit. Then go to the corner farthest from the fire—yonder—and get behind something. Stand there as still as a statue and I'll do what I can to discourage him from lingering."

"Lark!" Christopher called impatiently through the door.

Breathless, Lark heard him try the latch and, finding it bolted, rattle it as if he would force it free. After waiting until her brother whispered that he had concealed himself, she crossed the room and unfastened the catch.

Immediately Bacchus dashed through the door like a rompish colt, his huge paws thudding, his nails clicking like castanets upon the hardwood. He nearly knocked her down in his playful exuberance, and she stiffened, thinking of the hound's discerning nose and well-honed hunting instincts.

"B-Bacchus!" she called out frantically, leaning down and stretching out her hands. "Come here, lad!" She clapped. "Come and see me."

He galloped toward her and skidded to a halt in front of her legs. Anxiously she seized the creature's collar, securing him at her side and praying he would not strain to meet the stranger hiding behind her drape.

"I apologize for the brute's behavior," his master said, chuckling, strolling into the room. "But he's rather tipsy, I'm afraid. The old boy managed to get into the brandy again by nudging a decanter off the table downstairs. Lapped up every drop, he did." Christopher paused. "Haven't I told you about his habit? We discovered his passion for drink when he was just a pup—hence the name Bacchus." He laughed. "Have you ever heard of a drunken hound?"

Lark smiled nervously at the curious tale, murmuring some uncommunicative reply.

Eyeing her closely, thinking she must be mopish over the events of yesterday, Christopher spoke in a less convivial tone than before and murmured his partially contrived excuse for coming. "Er . . . my apprentice said you'd mentioned having trouble sleeping, said you'd gone without proper rest for days. You could have told me, you know. At any rate, I thought you might need a sedative—"

He trailed off as his attention was suddenly caught by the arresting scene just behind Lark's back.

With interest he perused the gloom, noting the fringed pillows strewn casually before the hearth, the pot of tea and the half-drunk cup beside them, and the two pairs of shoes kicked haphazardly beneath a spindle-legged chair. The entire scene was bathed in a romantic red fireglow, made cozier by the rumpled, fine-stitched quilt spread out upon the carpet.

With a frown, Christopher turned his keen eyes upon Lark.

She stood stock still in her nightdress and wrapper, holding the dog's collar so tightly that he could see the skin stretched ivory over the knuckles. Her expression was the epitome of apprehension.

Thoughtfully Christopher put a knuckle to his chin, regarding her for several seconds. "'Tis dark in here," he said finally. "Will you forgive me if I light a candle and thereby have the advantage of you, dearest Lark?"

"I can scarce prevent you," she snapped, and could have bitten her tongue, for her voice had been suspiciously sharp. But all her energies were required to curb the unhappily constrained, half-foxed dog.

She listened closely as the earl lit a candle, following with her ear his every move, suffering the utmost trepidation. She knew he stood beside the hearth, facing her, for the penetration of his stare upon her countenance was as tangible as the warmth of a light beam. She could picture his stance: legs slightly apart, one arm resting upon the mantelpiece, eyes searching her shadowed features. Was her face panic struck? Did he see the hem of her gown quivering?

"Er . . . thank you for bringing me the sedative," she said, knowing she had to make him leave. "But, I—I really don't think I'll be . . . needing it tonight."

"No doubt," he drawled, his intonation full of meaning. "Bacchus, you pie-eyed hound, what is that you've just unearthed from beneath Mistress Ballinter's bed? Show us."

With horror Lark felt something soft and weighty and damp with drool fall across her foot. When she did not immediately bend to retrieve it, but stood rooted in place like a pillar of stone, Christopher strolled forward to pick it up himself, then thrust the rumpled garment into her hand.

With a sickening lurch of her belly she realized it was Virgil's surtout.

"'Tis a gentleman's coat," Christopher said with mock perplexity, his low voice smooth. "Certainly not mine. And . . . 'tis still wet from rain. Feel? The owner must have only recently come in from the weather."

He put a hand to Lark's face and let his knuckles slide down the length of her jaw in a slow and exaggerated caress, his voice turning from silk to stone. "To whom does it belong, my sweet?"

Lark desperately searched her brain for answer but found none plausible, none that the sharp-witted surgeon would believe. To make matters worse, Bacchus had escaped her, and it was likely only a matter of time until the creature unearthed her brother in the same manner he had done the coat. Closing her eyes, she prayed to every saint she knew to bind Virgil's mouth, lest all be lost. Then she straightened herself and prepared to cross swords with her formidable host.

Christopher watched her. She faced him bravely, silently, her shoulders squared like those of a soldier making ready for a losing battle. He let his eyes wander the length of her slight feminine body, remembered the feel of its sweet and yielding form.

As he scrutinized her pale face, he knew without a doubt that he had disturbed her from the arms of another man.

His spirits plummeted with the knowledge, and rage assaulted him. The bitterness of betrayal tasted sour in his mouth. He renounced himself for a fool. He should have gone ahead and eased his lust when the opportunity was ripe, he told himself. Then he would have been done with her, instead of treating her as if she were any different from the painted whores or the bejeweled ladies he'd had before.

"Still no answer, madam?" he asked in a cruel tone. "Then, I'll address your gentleman, who listens so cowardly from between the drape and the clothes press. Sir, if you choose to be ferreted out of your hole like a damned rodent, I'll oblige—but be warned. If I must come after you, I'll send you away with a few well-earned bruises. Of course, you could step forward like a man and *speak*."

Slowly, then, very slowly, the drapery rings scraped across their rod, and the shadows relinquished their fugitive. In stockinged feet Virgil stepped a few paces forward and halted.

Christopher tensed and drew in a sharp breath. He had fully expected to see Sebastian O'Keefe creep out of the corner, but this was a man unknown to him, a dark, thin ascetic man. By his dress he was not a laborer, nor was he quality. Shabbily genteel, perhaps, with wary and intelligent eyes.

"This is rather novel, isn't it, now?" Lord Glassmeade snorted. "Hiding in a lady's boudoir from a man who isn't even her husband. Your name, sir?" he asked, making his tone a parody of politeness in order to hide the devastation he felt. "After all, you *are* a guest in my home. Surely I deserve an introduction, at the very least."

Again a hush fell. Only the thud of Bacchus's paws disturbed the lapse as he retired to the hearth.

Lark stood with her limbs frozen and her knuckles pressed against her mouth, listening, praying that Virgil would stay his tongue.

"Well, man!" Christopher demanded of the mute, red-faced visitor. "Ah, but it scarcely matters *who* the hell you are, does it, now?" In a violent movement he picked up the pair of well-worn masculine shoes, then yanked the surtout off the floor. "For I already know very well *what* the hell you are!"

"Christopher," Lark ventured fearfully. "I—"

"Quiet!" he ordered. "I'm speaking now to the

gentleman—if he may be so termed." He tossed the personal items out the door. "Take these and be gone with you, you cowering whoreson, before I change my mind and give you a good going over."

Nearly bursting with the need to respond, yet giving the tall, icy-eyed aristocrat a wide berth, Virgil stalked forward, hesitating when he reached his sister's side. "Lar—"

"*Go!*" she cried, fearing the worst should her brother talk. "Just go!"

A slight pause ensued. With her eyes pleading, she stared toward the spot where Virgil stood, begging him with a desperate look to cooperate. She heard his reluctant step after a second or two and, tugging on his arm, leaned forward to place a hasty kiss upon his brow before pushing him forcibly to exit.

Behind him, Christopher closed the door with such a force that a painting fell from the wall, its priceless frame splintering upon impact with the floor. Simultaneously Lark felt her arms seized, felt the earl's breath touch her cheek as he bent his face to within a hand's span of her own.

"Never, *never,* take a lover beneath my roof!" he shouted, his voice the cold, kingly one of his ancestors. "By God, you are bold, dallying not fifty paces from my door!"

His hands bit into her flesh so hard that she winced, yet the pain of it was nothing like the pain in her heart. He believed her faithless, traitorous. And, tragically, because the belief happened to be such an ironically convenient foil for the truth, Lark could not tell him otherwise. No matter that she yearned to exonerate herself, yearned to shake her head and cry out the truth—she could not, not even when she felt his own furious anguish, the anguish conveying itself through his hands, his gentle surgeon's hands. They clenched her flesh so brutally hard, she thought she might be crushed beneath them.

"I trusted you, Lark," he said simply but with emphasis, the words a slicing sword. "I nearly trusted you with my life."

For a few terrible moments he continued to restrain her, waiting for her defense, perhaps. But she could not give it and merely closed her eyes until he freed her from his hold.

When his hands fell away, she did not turn but remained facing him, refusing to bow her head, refusing to show him the shame he expected from her. After a moment, during which she thought he battled to master some reaction, she heard him call quietly to the wolfhound.

Lark tensed, wanting to say something, anything, to stop his going. After all, this was her great-hearted surgeon, the man who had cradled her in her most tragic hour of need, the man who had lent her strength so often and nearly become her lover only yesterday. Did he deserve such a brutal deceit?

He paused, suspended his steps as if yearning to hear a staying word from her just as desperately as she yearned to offer him one. She could feel his accusing eyes upon her and imagine his sharp and bewildered pain.

Yet, in the end, she only turned her back, dismissed him from her presence.

17

At dawn the next morning, bone-weary and heartsore, Lark eased out of bed, knowing that in spite of her despondency, she had a mission to accomplish before the day was over. As she brushed out her hair and braided it, she recalled the events of the previous evening.

It seemed the unlucky relationship she shared with Christopher had been severed once and for all, cleanly and swiftly, like a tender vine cleaved by a knife blade. There could be no chance of reconciliation now. But, perhaps, she thought, tying up the end of her braid with the worn green tassel, such a parting was easier to withstand than a more gentle, anguished tearing loose at the time of her departure.

Even so, she had never felt such sorrow. More than ever, a desperate need to leave Henrietta Street plagued her, a need to return to her old way of life, for being so near Christopher and yet so wrenchingly at odds with him was an excruciating sort of torture.

Yet Virgil's return to Ireland and the imminent approach of the French landing had complicated matters. She had to be able to function in her capacity as messenger. She had to concentrate on the important events at hand. She could not wander along the avenues, begging, putting herself at the mercy of not only the dangers of the streets, but that more malignant threat at which Christopher had hinted and from which he sought to keep her protected.

For the time being, she feared she had to remain where she was, as an unobtrusive guest, and endure as well as she could the anguish of Christopher's cold presence. She only hoped that, for a while longer, he would continue to allow her safe harbor.

The phantom agent posed a different problem. Today she had to use the token that would signal a meeting beneath the Faery Thorn this Sabbath. But how could she carry out such an errand? How could she, in her accursed darkness, locate a thorn tree, sever its branch, and then stumble through teeming avenues and alleyways in search of an apothecary named Alabar? Who could be trusted to aid her? Jamie was being outfitted today for his school wardrobe and would not be available, nor could Christopher's servants be asked to carry out the strange request lest they report it to their master. She would have entrusted Virgil with the mission had not tragedy interrupted their meeting last night.

Finally, after much thought, Lark hit upon a plan as she heard Grindle toddle in to tend the fire.

"Grindle," she murmured, holding her head between her hands as if in utter misery. "I must ask for your help in a private matter."

"What is it, mistress?" the old woman inquired, shuffling forth anxiously.

"Agh! I suffer from the most plaguesome headaches. I awoke with the fiercest pain and feel as if my head will explode with it. There's a cure, a tisane I know about. But . . ." Lark hesitated and managed a grimace of distress.

"But what? Is it a draught from the holy well ye're wanting now? I've already mixed ye a bottle—'tis corked and put amongst yer belongings should ye ever need it."

"Nay. 'Tis another cure Lord Glassmeade would not be liking. Indeed, I fear he would scorn it as much as he scorns your brews. 'Tis a very ancient country remedy, you see, one a man of science would ridicule."

"Shall I mix it for ye, mistress?" the maid offered.

"Nay, I should do it myself. But I need a few ingredients."

"I'd be pleased to get them for ye. Why, I suffer from headaches meself, and would be glad of a tisane if ye say it works."

"You'll not tell the surgeon? 'Twill put him terribly out of sorts with the both of us, you know."

"Oh, never, never, mistress," Grindle answered solemnly. "I swear on me mother's grave. But what ingredients do ye need?"

"There's an apothecary by the name of Alabar—do you know his shop in James Street?"

"Alabar . . . Alabar . . ." She tapped her teeth. "Aye! I know it."

"Then, will you take me there? I'd like to purchase the powders myself."

"Sure and I will. I'll just help get ye dressed. Then ye'll have your breakfast and we'll go out. But ye must bundle up, for the mornin' air is freezin'. The night has left us a heavy frost."

"Er . . . Grindle," Lark inquired as the servant brought her gown and cloak from the wardrobe, "is there . . . is there a thorn tree in the garden, perchance?"

"A thorn tree?" the maid repeated in a slow, wary echo.

"Aye. The tisane I need . . . it must be stirred with a forked twig from a thorn tree."

"Oh, nay, mistress, we daren't." The servant's dread was clear. "Thorn trees is sacred to the faeries, don't ye know? No mortal can steal even so much as a leaf without risking their mighty wrath. Why, me own uncle once knocked off a branch of a thorn tree—it were an accident, o' course—and that very night a most terrible sickness struck him down. Foamed at the mouth, and raved, and clawed the air like a mad cat." In a whispery croak she concluded, "Died, he did, afore mornin' came."

"Have no fear for yourself," Lark tried to reassure her. "I'll snap off the twig with my own hands. You need only lead me to the tree."

"Well . . ." Grindle paused, as if deciding whether or not her participation would attract the faeries' notice.

"Please?" Lark asked with a most heartfelt plea, for the good of Ireland depended upon this woman's aid. "My need is very great. God will bless you for your kindness."

With a resigned sigh, the servant grumbled a reluctant assent.

The weather proved unseasonably raw and bitter that morning. No breeze stirred, but it seemed as if ice crystals shivered in the air, sharpening it, chilling it so that breathing was almost painful. The earth beneath Lark's tread did not yield to her shoes, as it was rock hard, frozen with the night's black ice, and hoary with a frost coat.

"There be a thorn tree at the back of the garden," Grindle directed now, speaking low as if to conceal her voice from any miniature listening ears with unnatural points. "It be a poor specimen, half-dead and bent, with only a few green branches left. But the gardener's afeared to cut it down. Angered His Lordship, he did, by refusin' to take the ax to it. The master says he'll do the deed himself, come spring, and I say God protect him."

They walked a few paces more over the crackling ground before Grindle halted.

"Well, here it be. I daren't come no closer, mistress. But ye need only step forward a pace or two and reach up. And say a prayer for yerself when ye break the twig lose."

Lark attempted to quell the sudden rise of a superstitious fear. Was this wizened, declining tree before her a spawn of that supreme, prehistoric one beside the sea, a seed of its seed? Did she sever a part of the father by splintering a piece of the offspring?

Shuddering, she reached up, groped for a moment, then felt a dangling end, whose twig was splayed. Her fingers closed around it and she realized it was rigid from the cold. At first the stubborn bough would not yield, though she twisted and pulled, but at last she gave a mighty jerk of her wrist, and it cracked with a sharp snapping of sound as if making its dismemberment known to nature's ear.

Lark hurriedly shoved the twig inside her pocket and began trotting toward the gate.

"Here, mistress!" Grindle called. "Follow me! There's a path behind the garden that leads out to the road. Oh, God save us from the faeries' ire!"

Breathlessly Lark followed the strident voice, feeling at last Grindle's bony, ungentle fingers take her arm. Out into the road they scurried, blending with other pedestrians hurrying in the chill. Amongst the odors of fresh fish and rotting wharves, hooves clattered, wheels rumbled, and hawkers cried—frightening sounds all to one who had no vision and who without a guiding hand would be hopelessly lost amidst the turmoil of the streets.

"How much farther, Grindle?" Lark asked, tightening her grip upon the servant's sleeve.

"Two blocks. And step to your left, quickly! There be sewage in the road."

At last, after shaking off a beggar's hand and dodging the flying contents of a chamber pot, Lark's leader halted her hasty gait and with no uncertain relief announced that the apothecary's weathered sign swung directly above their heads.

"Thank you, Grindle. Now, I'll just go inside alone."

"But, mistress—"

"Wait out here for me. I'll not be too long. Is anyone inside the shop, or can you see?"

"A gentleman seems to be makin' a purchase. I can see no one else but a dark, slant-eyed fellow with a cloth wound about his head. He stands behind the counter, so perhaps he is Alabar."

"Open the door for me, then."

The servant reluctantly obeyed. A bell jangled, and immediately a cloud of warmth rushed forward, and with it strange odors, fragrances of exotic spice and incense, smells of unwashed flesh and burning wax. For a moment Lark stood back, listening to the crackle of paper and the exchange of coin. Then the shop's single customer prepared to leave and after bidding Lark good day departed through the creaking door.

"M-Mister Alabar?" Lark ventured. She took two steps forward, unsure of where the counter lay, and smelled a strong waft of pungent smoke.

"I am Alabar."

The voice was a reedy one and quite foreign to her, though Lark had met a lady once in France who spoke in an Eastern tongue. She sensed aloofness in his tone, as well as a degree of suspicion. Proceeding forward with her hands outstretched, she located the countertop and, fumbling about within her pocket, closed her fingers over the cloven twig. Feeling foolish and hardly knowing how to proceed with this strange communication, she placed it in a tentative manner atop the scarred counter surface, pushed it forward slightly, and then waited.

"You would like this delivered today?" Alabar asked tonelessly, taking the twig from her hand in a deft move, his dry fingers brushing hers only for an instant.

"Aye. I should like it delivered as soon as possible, sir."

"It shall be done."

Swallowing with unease, Lark wondered if this uncordial stranger so unsparing with words could be trusted with her dispatch.

She had little time to wonder. Suddenly the street door squeaked, the bell tinkled, and a footstep trod upon the floor, then halted just a pace behind her shoulder.

"Er . . . something for my headache, please," Lark requested hastily, the back of her neck tingling with disquiet.

A paper packet was duly placed inside her palm. Wanting only to escape this place of peculiar smells and muted footfalls, Lark searched her purse for its only penny, passed it to the apothecary's hand, and turned to go. Having no notion as to the whereabouts of the patron who had entered, she took what she hoped was a direct route to the door, praying all the while that the path was clear. Alas, it was not, and she collided head on with a solid presence.

She started. The paper of powders fell from her fingers. The stranger wordlessly retrieved it for her. She stammered an apology, did not wait for his reply, and scurried out through the open door to Grindle.

When they arrived at Henrietta Street the servant began to escort Lark up the stairs, but the younger woman declined her guidance and bade the poor shivering maid fetch herself a hot cup of tea in the kitchen. Fumbling along a corridor, Lark heard the high-pitched sound of a familiar irascible voice.

"Confound it! I've spilled the damned things. Where are those blasted servants? Never about when you need them, sneaking beneath your nose when you don't. . . ."

Realizing it was the marquess's voice, and noting the distress in his tones, Lark located the open doorway where he ranted and paused uncertainly. "Are you needing help, Your Lordship?"

"Eh? Who are you? Oh, my son's charity case, of course. Well, now you're here you can make use of that willowy form of yours, at least. I've spilt a bag of jade beads under the desk here, and cannot possibly crawl beneath it to retrieve them. Wouldn't want to lose them, quite valuable, they are. My brother brought them from the Orient."

Lark stepped forward, putting out her hands to avoid the obstacles of furniture. "Can you just direct me to the desk?" she asked, surprised at her own solicitousness toward this thoroughly unlikable man.

"I'd forgotten you were blind," the marquess said in a gruff, unsparing tone, but he took hold of her arm. "Don't know how much help you can be."

Ignoring him, Lark bent down to feel along the edge of the deeply carved desk, searching beneath its legs for the scattered treasures. She immediately discovered three or four smooth stones the size of robins' eggs.

"Can't trust half the blasted servants to do it," the marquess complained, perhaps warning her as well. "They'd hide them in their pockets and pawn them in a minute."

Just such a shameful idea had flitted across Lark's mind. The price of one bead would probably be enough to keep her fed and housed for a year.

"What room is this?" she asked in order to turn her attention from unscrupulous notions. Flattening herself upon the carpet and stretching her arms farther beneath the desk, she was able to gather a few more stray beads.

"The treasure room—or so I call it," he answered. "'Tis usually kept locked, for only I seem to enjoy its contents. On yonder wall is a pair of ivory tusks, and above it the mounted head of a lion. There's a sculpture from Greece behind you, and a rug made from zebra skins on the floor beside the hearth."

Lark made no comment, snatched another bead, then froze.

"Ah, Christopher!" the old man exclaimed as quiet footsteps joined them. "Come in. I wanted to speak with you. What in the devil's name are you staring at? 'Tis only that blind young woman of yours beneath my desk—she's searching for my spilt beads."

"Indeed?" came the chilly reply.

Lark's heart thumped over the sound of Lord Glassmeade's voice. Feeling wretched at having been caught in such an ignoble position, she made one last sweep with her hands, seized upon a single wayward bead, and rose.

When she handed the prize to the marquess, he declared it the twentieth and final gem, dropped it into its drawstring pouch with the others, and bade Christopher sit down. "You have the look of a sore-headed boar this morning, lad," he grunted. "Pour yourself a brandy, for God's sake, and make yourself more amiable. I have something to show you."

At the odd note in his father's tone, Christopher eyed him with speculation. There was a look of disturbance upon the noble, hawklike visage, an unusual brightness in the dark blue depths of the old man's eyes. He thought what a fitting setting was this room for the imperious aristocrat, what a complement were its eccentric treasures to his old but still regal aspect. By contrast, the plainly dressed Lark stood aside silently, blocked from the exit by Christopher's position so close to the door. She looked as if she wished herself far away. Not surprisingly, the marquess had forgotten her presence. It was often his habit to treat those beneath his class as nonentities.

Still feeling his pain from her betrayal like a raw wound, Christopher shifted his gaze away from her face.

"Have you been to the hospital already this morning?" the marquess asked him.

"Aye. I performed surgery two hours ago."

"What sort of surgery?"

"Removed a musket ball from a soldier's leg."

"Oh? And who put it there?"

"A United Irish who was a very good marksman, I believe."

The marquess grunted. "Damned revolutionaries. Anyway," he went on after Christopher had sat down on an ostrich-skin chair, "I've called you here to make an admission of sorts. 'Tis actually a secret I should have revealed long ago . . . but I thought to keep it hid in the hope of sparing pain to another. Sebastian . . . will he not come to see me here?"

Christopher hesitated, absently rubbing the taut nankeen fabric across his thigh with a thumb. "I think not, Father. He—"

"Do not excuse him!" A surge of mighty strength enervated the old man's frame, and he uttered the demand forcefully, half in ire, half in rebuke. "You have excused him too long already, Christopher . . . far too long."

The marquess paused to catch his breath after a sudden spasm of coughing seized him. Finally, clearing his throat, he issued a soft command. "Now, Chris, let us recall for a moment how Sebastian came to us, for necessity demands that I get the tale straight in order to relate my secret clearly. Think back to the day the boy arrived in Kildare. He was finely dressed, was he not?"

Christopher regarded his father with keen blue eyes, his curiosity whetted. "Aye," he answered slowly.

"And his mother was finely dressed as well, correct? She wore about her neck a ruby of considerable price, remember, and her horse was valuable, as was its saddlery. We all surmised that Sebastian was of some wealthy, perhaps even titled, background, a background just as lost to him as his own surname. He himself seized upon this notion and tormented you with it throughout your boyhood, until you were quite ridden with guilt. Indeed, I know you carry the remorse with you still."

The marquess stopped his speech here as if waiting for his son to admit to the charge. But no confession came, nor, however, any denial.

"Sebastian believes," the old man went on, "that through the death of his mother and the resulting loss of his identity, you cheated him out of some birthright, an inheritance of wealth and property which—somewhere—waits for his return. He hates you for it, for your act of carelessness involving the cursed snake. Of course, as far as I'm concerned, you were absolved from blame immediately by your tender age and lack of malicious intent."

Wheezing a bit, the marquess stood and stumped about his treasure room, halting here and there to touch first an amber paperweight, then a rare book.

"For your sake, I wanted to do my best for the boy," he said. "I spent many years searching for even one relation or solicitor or acquaintance who could give me his name and solve the riddle. At last I received a letter to satisfy my efforts. 'Tis nearly a decade old now." He jerked his head. "You will discover it folded in the top drawer of my desk."

Lark sensed the significance of this scene between

father and son, the impact of such a long concealed revelation upon Christopher's guilt.

His footsteps, measured but unhurried, crossed the room toward her, and she stepped back unobtrusively, hearing the scrape of well-waxed wood as a drawer was opened. The rustle of old, stiffened parchment followed, then a long silence, as the lines of the letter—surely time-faded—were carefully perused.

"Sebastian is the son of a Gypsy woman," Christopher said a moment later in near wonder. He read on. "His mother, it says, 'a woman of loose character and devoid of morals, was a seductress and a thief, who robbed me of money and jewels after I kindly offered her and her son respectable housing and employment. My horse she stole as well, and clothes from my family's wardrobe. It was my understanding that the boy's father was unknown, but 'tis my personal speculation he was the by-blow of some Gypsy camp.'"

The parchment crackled again as Christopher turned to another page and continued his reading. "'Apparently they are, and have ever been, little more than vagabonds, who wander about the countryside stealing what they can. I wish you good luck with the boy. As for his mother—I cannot lament her death.'"

The young earl refolded the missive and finished quietly, "The letter is signed by a Yorkshire squire."

"So, you see, Christopher," the marquess said, "Sebastian has falsely imagined himself some titled heir, allowed his entire life to be soured by this mythical loss. He did indeed lose his mother, whom he loved, but we gave him every privilege and every gesture of affection we had to give to try to make recompense."

A silence ensued between the two men, and Lark kept as still as stone, unwilling to break it, amazed at what she had learned.

"Christopher . . ." The marquess's voice came quieter suddenly, more enfeebled. "Let Sebastian go. Protect him no more, suffer no more for his errors. For too long you've indulged him." There was sorrow in his tone. "I overheard the argument you had with him the other day, the one that resulted in blows. Release Sebastian to the custody of his own character, allow him the consequences of his actions. Be done with him."

Christopher walked to the window, stared out at the shivering landscape, and thought about his sire's absolving words. "I cannot, Father," he said finally. "I suppose the sense of honor with which you raised me is too ingrained in my nature. I wronged Sebastian. Unwittingly or not, I killed his mother. 'Tis my burden to carry. Always."

Lark slipped out quietly then, distressed to have been privy to this most private conversation between Christopher and his father—though neither seemed to mind her presence, at first, and later took no notice of it. She thought what a tragic path the lives of the two boys—the two very different boys thrown together by a capricious fate—had taken.

In her distraction and hurry to leave, she made a wrong turn and for several minutes wandered around the corridor in confusion, too proud to call for assistance in case Christopher himself should come. She had just pivoted back in the opposite direction when a commotion in the vestibule arrested her.

Guests had arrived. She heard the murmur of masculine voices and the fuss of greatcoats and umbrellas being handed over to a footman. Then Christopher's footfalls crossed the marble tiles. In his resonant voice he greeted his visitors, addressing each by name.

Lark stilled, her limbs tingling as she heard their titles.

Just below her, all in a row, stood three of Ireland's most powerful rulers, a group of men dominating the Irish cabinet with such heavy hands that their detractors had begun to call them the "Junto." In theory, Ireland's executive power was wielded by the Viceroy, who was directly responsible to the British king, but these three guests had years of experience adroitly manipulating George's puppet.

"Shall we indulge in claret and billiards before luncheon is served, gentlemen?" Christopher asked after the usual pleasantries had been exchanged.

As swiftly as a mouse Lark stepped back, slipping into the nearest room and standing behind its door with her heart thumping. The billiards room she knew to be on this floor, in this wing, accessed by the set of stairs at whose foot the guests now stood. Uncertain what to do, hardly wanting to be caught wandering stupidly about the hallway, she stayed rooted in place as she heard the men ascend the stairs. They laughed at some witticism Christopher threw out, and she imagined the three infamous guests, imagined their finely made shoes as they tapped upon the steps together. She pictured embroidered waistcoats and satin breeches and dissipated demeanors. Finally she envisioned their host, younger, leaner, his beloved profile more handsome, but just as patrician as theirs.

For several minutes she pressed herself flat against the wall, waiting while the enemies to her class entered the chamber just across the corridor. She could hear their ribald jokes and chuckles, hear the clink of their glasses as refreshments were brought, make out the gist of their conversation as they spoke of women, horses, and . . . politics.

All at once it occurred to her that they might say something significant to the Cause, some morsel of importance that could be passed on to the phantom agent. Her heart beat faster with the notion. Eavesdropping suddenly took on the more noble name of espionage.

Hearing a strident crash, she knew the billiards had begun, and with the resulting rattle of balls her ability to catch dialogue became more difficult. Stealthily Lark moved nearer the open door of the room she occupied and crouched beside a table. After a while, with her ear pressed to the wall, and having distinguished the voices of each guest, pieces of meaningful conversation began to drift close.

"Is our militia up to form, do you think?" the elderly Lord Chancellor asked, his voice low and sober.

"Castlereah swears he is ready," Christopher replied. "And champing at the bit."

"Any idea how many Frenchies we're likely to face?"

Christopher's answer was nearly lost as a ball was struck and sent spinning about the table. "No idea at all. But I don't believe 'twill be a number of such magnitude that our troops can't manage it. Besides, 'tis still only rumor that the French are even interested in such a mad scheme."

"But we have to take it seriously. That damned Wolfe Tone!" cursed the Commissioner for Revenue.

"Wouldn't I relish his head upon a platter! We should have hanged him instead of exiling him. Who would have thought he could have gone so far in convincing France to listen to his plan for aiding his blasted 'Irish brotherhood.'"

"You know the French are interested in anything that will give grief to England," Christopher said. "I daresay Tone promised the Directory a complete Irish revolution for their trouble. 'Twould be quite a bright feather in their cap if they could see Ireland independent from the King."

"But Tone's aims are ridiculous," the Commissioner retorted. "As if Parliament could ever be opened to the Catholics. Why," he added with a snort, "beneath their ignorant hands the country would fall into the Dark Ages again all in the space of a fortnight."

A round of naughty witticisms ensued, and Lark shifted uncomfortably, her hatred for this callous group boiling strong.

"Of course," the Commissioner mused, changing the mood, "rule by the common man has already occurred in France and America, not to mention a few other European countries. We cannot treat the notion lightly, or with too little concern."

His statement seemed to dampen the conversation for a spell. Pipe smoke drifted out from beneath the door in thin clouds, pricking Lark's nostrils, and presently she heard the tinkle of glass again as their host refreshed the drinks. She imagined the three haughty men imbibing the expensive claret with surly mouths and drawn brows while they contemplated the position of the scattered billiard balls.

After another round of play, the Parliament Speaker said, "I fear 'twould not be impossible for the French to slip through our navy at present—with so many concerns elsewhere we cannot maintain a stalwart fleet in our own waters. I wonder which landing site the Frogs would choose—have you gotten hold of any information on that score, Lord Glassmeade?"

Lark held her breath, clenched her hands.

The clamor of billiard balls as they collided and thumped raucously against the table edges delayed Christopher's reply. Only after the orbs lay still upon the table again did he deign to speak, and his quiet, determined words caused Lark to feel as if the earth had just dissolved beneath her feet.

"Nay. But I have high hopes of getting it, my good friend . . . very high hopes indeed." The private humor in the earl's voice was strong and unmistakable, though only one who knew him well would have discerned it.

Lark put a hand to her throat. Perhaps this man, the man she loved so dearly, was more of a foe than she had ever feared.

Did he know what secret she was destined to carry?

18

"*By damn, Lark!* I've spent the past three days in a near panic wondering if you were safe, wondering what abuse you had suffered at the hands of the bloody insolent Irish swell!"

In high dudgeon Virgil uttered one furious complaint after another as his horse picked its way across a waterlogged terrain that was perilous even in daylight.

"It cost me dearly to stand still and say nothing," he continued. "To listen while he played his cat-and-mouse game with you, degraded us with his insults. How I yearned to put my fist to his nose! I swear, 'tis itching still to do damage!"

Tugging the reins, he slowed his piebald mount until his sister's steed trotted flank to flank. "But I am not entirely stupid," he added. "The bastard stands at least a full head taller than I, and has shoulders twice as wide."

"'Twould have been folly to have provoked him further," Lark agreed. "He's slow to anger, but once he's roused, his temper is black. You took the wisest course, if not the most satisfying one to your sense of honor. Besides, his assumption about our relationship couldn't have been a better cover for us. And he . . . did nothing to harm me after you departed."

She colored even in the darkness, recalling the episode that had left her spirits so drained and low. As for Christopher, his footfalls had not paused a single time upon her threshold since the dreadful scene.

"He certainly seems to have a proprietary air toward you," Virgil said, refusing to abandon the subject. "I didn't like it by half."

"'Tis the way of his class," she said, keeping her voice devoid of emotion, hoping the explanation would put an end to the topic.

Her horse balked suddenly, and with an impatient hand her brother yanked the leading rein, forcing the stubborn animal to cross the narrow, hump-backed bridge they had only half traversed.

"Sorry, *ma petite*. These rented nags are not well bred—indeed, they are the boniest, most spavined creatures I have ever seen saddled. But they will get us there eventually."

"And what sort of Sabbath is it?" Lark inquired, huddling more snugly within the depths of her cloak. "Besides a raw one with a very keen-edged wind."

"'Tis moonlit and black by intervals. The clouds are drifting high, in gray shreds, and at times they obscure the moon. Fortunately, I think we will not be drenched with any rain, although we may well freeze to death ere our mission is complete."

The old, unoiled leather of his saddle creaked as he pivoted about on his seat. "By the saints, 'tis a desolate track! I've scarce seen even a mud byre these last four miles. The path is so ill marked and soggy, I wouldn't be surprised if our clumsy ponies fell into a bog."

"I think I can hear the sea," Lark said, rising up in her stirrups and turning her head to listen.

"Not I," Virgil said. "But then, I've been told . . ."

"That blind persons develop keen ears?" she finished when he hesitated.

"Well, aye."

"'Tis true."

For two miles they rode in silence, paralleling the misty, undulating shore, drawing their flapping hoods more tightly as protection against the sea's damp and frigid blasts. The horses seemed to plod more slowly, lowering their thick-maned heads and flattening their shaggy ears as if battling the head-wind proved too much effort.

"Ah!" Virgil exclaimed. "The signpost you described looms yonder by the trail."

"Go beyond it," Lark directed, experiencing a shudder of excitement as her rendezvous with the agent neared. "Then you'll see our path dwindle to little more than a sheep track, narrow and deeply cut. If we follow it a quarter mile, 'twill put us near a grove of stunted, wind-bent sycamores. You may wait for me beneath their branches while I walk a little way to meet our cohort."

"'Tis a bleak and eerie place," Virgil said. "And, *Sacre Dieu,* I've never felt so blasted cold! The wind cuts me like a blade of ice." With an impatient flip of rein and a kick to his mount's sides, he urged their progress forward. "When Ireland's liberty is won and my job is over, I swear, 'tis to the south of France for me!"

A few minutes later he helped Lark down from her saddle, and as her frozen toes struck unyielding earth, she winced in pain, faltering a bit on unsteady legs.

"You must help me get my bearings, Virgil," she told him, shivering now without the horse's warmth beneath her. "I must stay to the path, climb the hill, and wait beneath the old Faery Thorn beside the sea cliff."

"Lark . . ." Her brother hesitated, obviously in dis-agreement with the plan. "You cannot do this thing. I don't mean to offend you, but, for God's sake, you could fall into the sea! How can you possibly know where you step?"

"Virgil, I'll not listen to your harping again. You fret like an old woman. I've walked this path in darkness a score of times and know its crooked turns by heart. The track is a deep furrow through the sand, edged by tufted grass on either side. 'Twill not be difficult to keep my feet upon it, and by judging the loudness of the sea, I'll know where to stand and wait."

"I don't like it. There is no good reason why I shouldn't go myself, or escort you down the path."

"There's a very good reason, one I've repeated a least a dozen times on this miserable trip. The agent won't appear if he believes anyone else awaits him, or if he sees I'm escorted. 'Twas a condition stipulated by his messenger before we ever met, made to protect his identity, no doubt."

"Oh, very well," Virgil said crossly, giving in at last. "I shall wait here if I must. But your passing of my dispatch should only take a few minutes, and if you fail to reappear in a reasonable time, I *shall* come and fetch you back."

"Agreed. Now set my feet upon the track."

He obeyed and after a moment released her arm with obvious reluctance. She set out alone then, passing first beneath the little band of sycamores, whose boughs cried piteously as the wind flayed their limbs. Shivering, nearly overcome with cold, she threaded her way through the trunks by keeping her shoes firmly to the hoof-etched path.

Even before her blindness, this had been an eerie place, a place deserted by men and haunted by spirits, as if it had been mislaid and then forgotten by all except those ghostly entities who claimed some purpose here. Now, she could see not even the vaguest gray outlines of its gashed and gouged land-scape, and it remained only a memory. But the roar of crashing breakers, the roll of timeless waves, and the sound of the whistling wind filled her senses instead, shaking her composure.

On she stepped, perhaps thirty paces in total. The spectral skeleton of the Faery Thorn should be near. Did *he* watch her from his vantage point beside it, follow with his hidden eyes the progress of her shuffling steps?

The sound of the sea grew deafening, and Lark's precarious sense of orientation began to fail, leaving her to wonder if she had wandered too near the cliff. She feared to go farther. Suddenly she could not dis-cern if she faced north or south, could not decide if the Faery Thorn rose to the left or right. Her heart began an increased beat. Dizziness plagued her, and she had to brace her legs to keep from swaying and falling down.

"Do not swoon and tumble into the sea ere ye have delivered yer message to me."

The voice came from blackness, barely distin-guishable amidst the clamor of the tide. But the hand that gripped Lark's arm was very perceptible, its clench so strong that it made her grimace. It directed her backward several paces, making her realize she must have stood dangerously near the precipice.

"I—I would not have fallen," she countered, pricked as always by his derisive tone.

Not deigning to argue, he said, "What do you have for me this eve?"

Lark took a deep, excited breath, the importance of her message sweeping away her irritation. "The time is near—very near. Wolfe Tone has done his work. Thirty-five French ships and twelve thousand troops are now assembling for the aid of the Cause. After they've helped us win our liberty, they'll march to London and defeat the king—take England for their prize. General Hoche will be the commander-in-chief of the expedition. My contact believes there's no better leader than he, save Bonaparte himself."

Even with the sound of the wind so strong in her ears, Lark thought she heard her companion suck in a breath of wonder.

The moment seemed a dramatic one, both conspirators realizing that history hovered upon the brink of change, a change the two of them had helped to engineer. Both realized, as well, that the most arduous, most costly work lay yet ahead. Lives would be lost changing Ireland's chronicles, and bloodshed had to occur before the taste of triumph could be fully savored.

"Has the date and a landing site been decided?" the phantom asked her sharply.

"It—" She halted, frowning. Something about his tone struck a disturbing but elusive chord. "What did you say?"

She heard him clear his throat before repeating the question in his low, coarse accent. "The date and landing site—do ye know them yet?"

She shook her head, still bothered by some nagging remembrance. "Nay . . . but, I will soon. Very soon. It will be my last dispatch for you."

A moment of silence from the agent followed, leaving Lark to wonder what thoughts occupied that shrewd and unreadable mind. Would he be as relieved as she to be done with these contentious meetings?

"Ye'll contact me through Alabar again?" he asked at last.

"Aye, of course." And having nothing else to say, vexed with his curtness, and so cold she had ceased to feel her toes, Lark added, "Now, I'll bid you good eve."

She waited for him to leave her. Only then would she turn around and attempt to find her ungraceful way back. But long seconds passed, and though she listened keenly for the sound of his departing footsteps upon the rock, he made no move to go.

Hardly knowing why he lingered without a word, she nervously turned around herself, praying her sense of direction would prove accurate enough to get her down the path. But she had no chance to test it, for her arm was seized immediately.

"I'll escort ye back to yer horse," her ill-tempered cohort said. His words were dim passengers on the tails of the wind, so low she could hardly hear them.

She stood still, resisting the force of his strong arm. "Nay. I'll make my own way back."

"Like hell ye will."

There was to be no further argument on the matter. Lark found herself towed along over the uneven ground like a rag doll, all the while wondering what her bullying guide would do when he discovered Virgil had accompanied her to the meeting here.

But the agent said nothing at all when they arrived at the place where Virgil waited. Without ceremony he lifted her upon her horse's back, put the reins in her hands, and bade her a gruff good night.

Then, just as he turned, a sharp report pierced the air.

Lark felt a stinging in her wrist, awareness of it only vague as she tried to make sense of the sudden chaos. Her horse reared and spun about while Virgil yelled words she could not distinguish, but she clearly heard the agent shouting a sharp command.

"Get her out of here! Ride for all you're worth!"

After that, as her horse lurched forward in terror, she heard shots ring out again and knew the phantom had fired his pistol . . . and had his shot returned.

By the time Virgil helped her squeeze through the gate behind Lord Glassmeade's house, Lark was so frozen that the slightest movement caused her pain. The injury to her wrist was even more painful, but it seemed only a minor graze from the pistol ball and was no longer bleeding, so she continued to conceal it from her brother. Virgil's physical state was hardly better than her own. Indeed, his had always been a rather delicate constitution, and as he paused to say farewell, his teeth chattered uncontrollably.

"Where will you stay tonight?" she asked him with concern. "Will there be a fire waiting for you?"

He ignored her questions. "Lark you cause me great anxiety living beneath this roof. Leave here soon. And those shots fired tonight—"

"Virgil, *go*. We're both frozen to the bone, and nothing you can say will persuade me from the course

I've set for myself. We've discussed this over and over again all the way here." She spoke brusquely to hide the quaver in her voice, for her brother was to leave for France tonight.

"When this is over," he said urgently, "when my revolutionary work is done, you and Jamie will come to France to live with me. For now, I'll send money when I can. Communicate with me through Peader at the Lottery Hall. And you said you had a friend to go to when you leave here—"

"*Virgil.*" Clasping him to her breast once more, Lark let her cheek rest against his neck for a brief, wrenching moment, then drew back firmly. "I'll be fine."

"Can you make it to the house?" he asked for the third time.

"I'll follow the wall around. Now go."

Moments later she wielded the stolen key in the lock of Lord Glassmeade's mansion and let herself inside. As she crept upstairs, she felt as if her spirits had never been lower. She was truly alone now. She wondered if even the phantom agent had been lost to her this night, felled by the ruthless assassin who had lurked beside their meeting place. Did he lie now on the eerie path to the Faery Thorn, his unnamed, mysterious form forever stilled?

She could not help but think the assassin had been her own nemesis, that golden-haired nobleman who had slain her uncle. She had kept the suspicion from Virgil, however, sparing him anxiety, insisting the shot had been fired at the agent. Yet, had the gunman's aim been only slightly better, her rebel activities would have troubled the merciless Loyalist no more.

And Christopher? Her feelings for him were such a confused jumble, she could no longer sort through them. Anger, suspicion, desire, gratitude, remorse, and even fear twisted together to make one big tangled skein, with love the strongest thread.

She sighed when at last she had arrived at her chamber. She went straight to the hearth, sank down upon the floor, and with a groan removed her shoes and stockings before stretching her toes toward the heat. Had she not been so preoccupied with her troubles, and less bone weary from her jarring ride, she might have wondered that the fire burned so well. Only a few hours remained until dawn, yet the flames hissed as if freshly fed.

"Your feet will likely be inflamed tomorrow."

Crying out, Lark gave a violent jerk and put a hand to her racing heart. "You have a nasty habit of announcing yourself unexpectedly," she snapped. "'Tis most ungentlemanly under any circumstances, and especially cruel to a sightless person."

Christopher stood at the threshold, bracing his tired frame against the doorjamb, and regarded his spirited guest with relief in his tired blue eyes.

Although he had discreetly followed Lark to Henrietta Street, and seen her safely to the gate—together with that cowardly bastard she had hidden in her chamber a few nights past—he had wanted to reassure himself that she was well. The sniper's shot tonight had been damnably close, and for one horrible moment Christopher had feared Lark struck. He still did not know if the ball had been meant for her or for himself. And perhaps he would never know, for the gunman had fled in the midst of Christopher's return fire.

But here Lark sat, safe and sound, leaning forward with her hands and legs stretched out to the fire while pretending to ignore him.

Christopher rubbed his eyes, and his face felt drawn by the stress. He was glad Lark could not see his despicable vulnerability for her. All the way home he had battled with conflicting choices in the matter of his relationship with this woman, his love clashing against reason, his passion against dispassion. This red-haired cotter's lass, who by her own choice was a member of the rebel underground, had only one more dispatch to give him—the most important one to his country. But could he let her continue her mad involvement, let her risk her life to help him win Ireland's freedom?

To his misfortune, she was not simply a cohort involved with him in deadly espionage. She was . . . what? Not his lover—would never be now. Yet he craved her still, so much that his belly tightened into a painful knot with need.

Looking at her small, almost childish posture by the fire, at the resolute profile he adored so much, he knew he could not allow his Faery Queen to continue with the plot. For at this moment he was neither a rebel crusader nor a staunch Loyalist. He was merely a man driven to protect the woman he loved.

And regardless of the cost to himself—or to their relationship—he would force her out of the game they both played so precariously in the moonlight.

"You look quite weatherworn, Mistress Ballinter," he said now, strolling forward, steeling himself against what must be done.

She sat upon the carpet, looking mutinous and yet not quite able to hide a quiver of apprehension at his approach. He could well imagine the wheels spinning madly in her head while she attempted to invent some excuse for her absence tonight.

After removing a decanter from the cabinet, he poured a drink and leaned to place it in her hand. "'Tis whiskey. Drink it."

She obeyed without hesitation, and he took up a comfortable stance beside the hearth, towering above her, scrutinizing her expression. "What pressing matter compelled you to trade the warmth of my house for the rawness of the night, milady?" he asked after she had swallowed and set the glass aside.

Lark shrugged and served up the thinnest lie. "Restlessness plagued me. I . . . went out into the garden for a while. To sit."

"Ah, but you have been gone hours . . . five, perhaps, or six."

"Time often escapes me."

"You don't say? Then I wonder, after you . . . er, *sat* in the garden, did you happen to go wading in the well?"

Flashing her sightless eyes at him, she modestly drew up her feet beneath her skirts. "Of course not."

"Nay? But the bottom half of your cloak is wet. Drenched, in fact."

Lark crossed her arms and silently cursed the blasted cloak. Upon her return, she had doffed the heavy garment and hooked it upon the edge of the mantelpiece, where it apparently still hung by its hood. She knew it was soaked from the splashing of her horse's hooves, since Virgil had led their mounts through a deep, fast-rushing stream in order to take them home more quickly. She could just imagine the insolent young earl lifting the hem of it between thumb and forefinger now, his discerning eyes examining it beneath raised brows.

"Perhaps 'tis wet from dew," she said, not to be without answer.

"Perhaps. . . .." Christopher's tone feigned perplexity before he went on to escalate the game. "But, how do you explain the horse hair that covers the underside of the cloak? You've had no occasion to ride, and only yesterday the laundress cleaned the garment—I saw her carry it up."

"Perhaps 'tis Bacchus' hair."

Christopher leaned down, took hold of her wrist, and turned it over, indicating with a gentle finger the raw red wound she nursed. "And this?"

When she opened her mouth to speak, he put his finger to her lips to cut her off. "I'm certain your reply is as creative as the others, Lark, but spare me this time."

He gathered soap and a wet square of linen from the washstand. Then, in the adroit way Lark knew so well, he cleaned the wound, his hands firm and personal, their familiarity making her tremble with remembrance of past caresses.

"Do you really think me such a fool?" he asked her quietly after a time.

She noted that his tone was candid now, inviting confidence and trust, almost imploring them. Unstrung by the old intimacy of his voice, she bent her head to conceal her face, refusing to allow him to scrutinize her expression. She realized the first phase of their duel was over at this point—or, at least, its verbal feints and parries were ended. Now he would be direct with her, demand answers she would not give.

When she remained silent, Christopher leaned forward from his kneeling position, and she felt both his hands clamp on her arms to draw her up with him. She cooperated, for a physical struggle with him would be pointless. But she did not let show on her face what his nearness cost her. Even though his hands were rough now and held her not in tenderness, but in anger, she relished the feel of them.

"What business did you conduct tonight?" he demanded, his silky breath touching her face, making her shiver.

She clamped her teeth together, refusing to waver. "My *own.*"

He snorted. "Wolfe Tone's, you mean! Don't think to lie to me, Lark. You did the business of the United Irish tonight, didn't you? *Didn't you?*" He shook her, his voice hardening, serious. "Even if I'd gotten no information of my own regarding your activities, you've made no secret of your sympathies for Tone's brotherhood."

"And what if I have!" she challenged, throwing off his hands, the strain on her composure finally giving way to temper.

"You're a traitor to your country, for God's sake, Lark. Do you know the penalty for that?"

"I know it very well, and is there a threat in your voice? Can I not trust you?" she asked in sudden disbelief. "I've lived beneath your roof during the lowest days of my life. I've been helpless here, despondent, lost . . . so *frightened.* While you held me in your arms like a babe, I cried out my fears to you, shed tears upon your shoulder—and, aye, I confided my politics as well. Should you have been surprised by them? 'Tis not as if a Catholic peasant would be supporting any other cause *but* the rebel one!"

She spoke hotly, but tears glimmered in her eyes as she thought of the fragile love they shared, felt it slowly breaking apart. Whatever thread had remained after the wrenching scene last eve was stretching now. She sensed the moment had come when the earl would use her politics against her, try to break her for his own shadowy purposes. The final parting between them approached, she was certain of it. Already she could feel the strings of her heart ripping asunder, and she cried out to him with the pain of it. "I believed you my friend, Christopher! I believed we shared a special bond. And for one reckless, foolish day, I would have let you *know* me, I would have been your *lover!* How could you even think of betraying me now?"

Christopher had to turn his head, look away from the sight of the tears trickling off her lashes. He focused his gaze upon the pattern in the carpet as he listened to the sound of her sniffling. When he could speak again in the terrible silence, he forced a toneless reply. "Perhaps you misjudged me, Lark. There's a dark side of me you do not know, a side I can neither reveal nor explain. But, even from the start, I have always been your friend . . . in more ways than you know."

He put his hands upon her shoulders. "Ireland is in perilous times, and I want you safe, out of the line of fire. I'll do whatever I have to do to stop you in your rebel work—*whatever*. I am ruthless when I set my will to a purpose. Do not think to cross swords with me, for I will win at any cost."

Even though she whirled away from him, he went on with his threat, staying back from her comely, tempting body as if distance could actually lessen his longing. "I can't think why a young girl like you would be so welcomed into the society of Wolfe Tone's radicals . . . unless, of course, you're privy to some sort of intelligence." He watched fear flicker across her face. "And intelligence, my love, makes you not only quite valuable to your own cause, but quite valuable to your opposition."

"Do you threaten me in another way now?" she asked, incredulous.

"I would rather not. I would rather persuade you to abandon your cause for the sake of your own skin. But being very well aware of your stubbornness on that score, I won't waste my time with it. I'll take another tack instead, impose upon our . . . friendship."

He paused, contemplated her hollow, sorrow-torn face with a countenance equally bleak, hating to harrow her this way but thinking this method less harsh than the alternative. Softening his voice, he asked, "Have you forgotten who I *am*, Lark? I'm your surgeon, aye. But, by my title, I represent everything you're attempting to throw down. I'm one of the very nobles your cohorts would delight in seeing dangle from a gibbet. You're operating from my *house*, for God's sake. Does that give you no qualms, no regrets?"

It was a question Christopher had pondered many times, and he waited for Lark's response with an intense, searching gaze. He could see the hazel eyes well up again, see her throat work convulsively, and knew she had agonized over the predicament before, as she did now. As he watched her, his hands twitched with the need to gather her in his arms, comfort her with his strength, find solace in her for himself, and toss politics to the wind. But he resisted the ill-advised impulse, knowing he must keep emotion at bay in order to see his objective finished.

"Have you no answer?" he asked.

She exploded then, swallowing her tears, battling to put up a spirited front. "What do you intend to do, *Lord Glassmeade?* Will you expose me to your high-nosed peers, see me interrogated, see me *hanged* for sedition?"

"Out of respect for my title, for my government," he shot back, "that's precisely what I should do."

"Then do it!"

"Perhaps I will."

"Decide quickly. I don't like suspense!"

For several seconds Christopher said nothing, then he took hold of her chin and lifted it until her neck strained beneath its tilt. Lark felt her pulse increase, as a reaction to his tantalizing proximity and a new-felt fear of him. In spite of the times she had been in his arms, she could not know the degree of loyalty the earl held for his government, the system that fostered his interests and those of his father. Did it surpass his bond of love for her? The history of a nation was at stake, after all. Many men had sacrificed stronger alliances, more delicate relationships, than this one in the name of patriotism.

Christopher no longer bothered to conceal the degree of his concern. Nor could he resist seizing her again, sliding his hands up and down the gentle curve of her spine, feeling the swell of her bosom where it pressed against his chest. "Swear to me you won't go out again, Lark," he breathed, clenching his teeth with the frustrating bliss of holding her, wishing he could simply retain her in his arms until danger threatened no more.

He closed his eyes even while he spoke a warning against her hair. "You're playing with a fire no less dangerous, no less deadly, than the one that burnt your cheek, my love. You are treading in deep and treacherous waters, and will find yourself drowning before long if you don't step ashore. Swear to me you'll stop your rebel dealings. If you persist, the time has come when I can guarantee your protection no more."

Lark stiffened. The words Lord Glassmeade had spoken to his powerful peers in the billiards room echoed in her brain. Was he telling her that he himself was the danger, that if he found her carrying the date of the French landing, he would show her no mercy in obtaining it?

How complicated was this web wove together, how complex this man! His arms tightened, and she shook her head vehemently to deny him. More than anything, hers was a refusal of his treacherous allure, for, given rein, it would lead her to a course of emotional surrender so strong, she would be tempted to spill all her secrets.

He kissed her then, put his lips upon hers in the most merciless brand of warfare, and she felt her defenses slowly, like melting iron, begin to weaken. His mouth invaded hers, and she welcomed its conquering. His hand encircled her breast, and she urged its advance. She allowed it all, responded with alacrity, until their fevered hands and straining bodies teetered on the brink of no return.

"Nay, Christopher!" Pulling back from him and pushing his arms away, Lark cried, "Do not think to sway me with seduction! Do not think to use your charm against me like a weapon! For tomorrow my beliefs would still be unchanged, regardless of the change you made in my body. Don't you see, I'm committed to what I do in a way I can never be committed to you. I *belong* with the rebels, they are of my kind. You are not . . . you can *never* be!"

Shaking her head, she struggled to find words, her voice breaking on them. "God knows I wish it were not so! I wish I could alter the circumstances of our births, I wish I had some divine power to turn back time. I would change everything so that we might belong together, be allowed simply to love. But the Almighty's design for us was set at the moment we were born, and we must live with that. Nay, I'll swear to nothing you ask me to do."

Christopher uttered an oath over his failed attempts to keep her safe. "Then, by God," he exploded in frustration, "I'll have you incarcerated this very day. Aye, milady! I'll haul you to Dublin Castle myself, toss you in a tower cell, and see to it you're kept there until this blasted revolution is done! Aye, since you want to make a sacrifice for your countrymen's cause, then you shall sacrifice well, with an army of pacing guards around your gaol. Perhaps then I'll get a few decent nights of sleep without worrying about your safety, without wondering where the hell you are!"

He did not wait for her answer but stalked to the door and delivered one last edict. "Pack what you'll be needing there."

With that he slammed the massive portal and inserted a key, making her a prisoner in his mother's bedroom.

Or so he believed. With a bitter and triumphant smile, Lark went to the clothes press, riffled beneath her linens, and removed the bunch of keys Jamie had stolen from the butler's pantry.

19

Lark groped about the room, gathering her belongings, stuffing them willy-nilly into her old tattered bag. She was so frantic that her hands shook, and thinking clearly was a difficult task. "Where should I go, where should I go?" she kept repeating beneath her breath.

But thoughts of that pressing concern were squeezed out by more agonizing thoughts of Christopher, and she crammed her extra pair of stockings into the bag with a vicious thrust. She was shocked at his threat to use her politics against her, have her imprisoned as his own personal captive. Could he possibly care for her at all and do such a merciless thing?

And what should she do now? Should she simply step outside and join the hundreds of beggars roaming the city in search of charity? Should she flee to Sebastian O'Keefe?

"Nay, nay," she whispered, absently dropping Grindle's vial of holy water in the bag. Sebastian was too intimately connected with the Cavanaughs. Even if she swore him to secrecy, begged him not to reveal her whereabouts to Christopher, could she trust his discretion? It seemed the hatred and jealousy the tinker bore the earl were too rabid, too volatile, for comfort. And her freedom was at stake now, not to be entrusted to careless hands.

With an aching sense of dashed hopes, she feared Sebastian had been right about Lord Glassmeade. In the end he was a true, callous son of his class, a hypocrite, a manipulator. The naive Lark Ballinter, it seemed, had indeed been no more than a temporary diversion for the worldly rake. Or had she . . . ?

She stilled, listening, hearing the first predawn stirring of sound upon the streets below. She would need to slip out quickly before full light, to blend in with the burgeoning traffic upon the avenue and hope no one would remember witnessing her stealthy flight. For when he awoke and found her escaped, the thwarted earl would surely send out a bellowing hue and cry.

Fumbling with the little collection of keys on their ring, Lark paused for a moment in the center of the room. Strangely, the chamber felt like an old friend to her now. She knew it so intimately, knew its smooth grained woods, the texture of its cozy tapestries. Even the sleek, glazed brush strokes of the paintings in their carved frames were tactile companions to her. Here she had discovered her blindness, learned to cope with it, wept over its tragedy in the hard, comforting arms of a beguiling stranger, a stranger whose face she had never even glimpsed but knew achingly well by touch.

She had fallen in love here, and she knew that by

simply vacating the room she would not leave behind that love as if it were nothing more than a piece of the sumptuous furnishings. She would carry it with her like a shadow always, its edges sharper during brighter memories, duller during darker ones.

All at once her fury diminished like a suddenly windless sail, and it seemed unfair not to say farewell, not to acknowledge the love she had for . . . whom? Not for the false-hearted aristocrat who had threatened her and certainly not even for the surgeon. But simply for the *man,* the man who, when he held her, was stripped of title and class and fashioned merely of flesh and bone. She believed that man had loved her.

Dropping her bag, Lark went to the desk and with both pain and painstaking care set down a letter.

Christopher slept not more than a couple of hours, and those were restless ones. Upon awakening, he groaned, still tired, and for a moment continued to lie abed, contemplating the single key resting upon the table beside him.

All at once, he threw off the twisted quilts and pulled on a pair of breeches, buttoning them hastily before walking barefoot to Lark's door. It was cold in the statue-lined corridor, and he rubbed his hands over his bare arms, wondering what in blazes he should say to the woman who, at sight of him, would probably lunge forward with her claws bared.

Yet surely she would be sobered this morning, rational, prepared to promise him she would bow out of secret societies and midnight trysts. He regretted that their late night argument had turned so bitter, regretted the threats he had had to deliver, but he well knew Lark's orneriness often warranted the taking of extreme measures. In this case the ends had justified the means, for she would be subdued now, reconciled to his guidance and sage judgment.

Running a hand through his thick, sleep-tousled hair, he decided crossly that he had to apologize for his abominable, though not unprovoked, temper of last eve. She would pout at first, of course, refuse to forgive him, but he would take her in his arms and tell her tenderly that he loved her. And this time, when she yielded to him, nothing would stop a culmination.

He inserted the key, turned it, depressed the latch. And found the chamber empty.

For a few seconds he stood scanning its furnishings, his eyes glittering, narrowing into slits with realization. Though he knew it a pointless effort, he strode across the room, flung open the clothes press, and with rough hands searched amongst the old silks from his mother's days, slapped aside the new, untouched gowns he had had made up for Lark, finding not a single scrap of her simple wardrobe.

Like a great incensed bear, he swung about then, his gaze flickering across the bed and its smooth untouched linens, the pillow left without indentation. But propped upon his mother's elegant desk, a rectangle of ivory begged attention.

In two strides he crossed the space, yanked the missive from its place behind the inkstand, and with fierce, devouring eyes, deciphered its scrambled, awkwardly penned lines. Twice he read them, and then his gaze shifted, and he stared unseeing out the window. A tremor ran through his body, and his

shoulders slumped, his features twisted. He closed
his eyes and laid back his head, until the strong column of throat was arched and vulnerable, exposed to
the red light of dawn.

"Laarrk," he breathed in anguish, the treasured
name a broken utterance.

From his dangling hand, the letter fell.

> *Dear Christopher,*
> *'Tis cruel to part this way, is it not? Would that*
> *it could be a more tender, a more kind, Farewell, if*
> *not an easier one. Would that I possessed a bit of*
> *the Faeries' Magic, for then I would reorder the*
> *Universe for us, meet you on a country road some-*
> *where plainly dressed like me, with the soil of the*
> *fields upon your hands. Thus, you would be my*
> *equal, and I would be yours.*
>
> *As it is, you must serve your Destiny and I must*
> *serve mine. I pray that yours keeps you safe and*
> *gives you joy.*
>
> *I loved you, Christopher. I love you still.*
>
> *Lark*

He turned the house upside down. Barking orders
like a tyrant gone mad, threatening positions at every
step, he assembled in the space of three minutes every
last one of the two dozen servants he employed.
Pacing up and down the length of the fire-warmed
drawing room, still unshaven, barefoot, his torso
naked, he brought to mind some barbarian of old,
and were the maids not so agog with their eyeful of
his virile handsomeness, they would have been shaking in their shoes with fear.

"Which one of you luckless fools unlocked Mis-

tress Ballinter's door and let her out last night?" he
demanded.

No one said a word. Twenty-four pairs of eyes slid
surreptitiously up and down the line, waiting for one
poor wretch to step forward and confess.

The master repeated his question, this time in a
lower, more ominous voice, and still no one uttered a
word. Nor did any of the apprentices from his medical
office have a helpful clue to offer, nor did any neighbors or their staffs.

Like a man possessed, Christopher threw on his
riding clothes and greatcoat, and without bothering to ply razor or brush, he mounted the gray and
sent it clattering out the gate. He searched every
teeming corner, every shadowed door, every glum
alleyway, his eyes alert, like those of a hunter after
prey. When his own fashionable neighborhood
relinquished no wayward form in faded green
petticoats, he went farther afield, entering the
meandering lanes of the poorer ends. But if the
secretive streets concealed his treasure, they
refused to give it up.

As the sun reached its zenith, and others stopped
to take a midday meal, Christopher gulped down a
mug of black coffee and went on. He put the gray on
the road leading to the cottage where Lark had lived,
thinking she might have caught a ride on some
farmer's cart and returned there, either to seek
shelter in the cottage or to beg room from a neigh-
boring cotter. With his bare hands he pried loose the
lumber boarding up the door but found nothing
inside save dank air and a family of mice.

He reached Dublin again at dinnertime but spared
no moments to take nourishment, instead proceeding

directly to Jamie's academy. The headmaster insisted the boy could not have seen his sister. The youngster had either been abed in his well-chaperoned dormitory or in classes since yesterday.

Darkness approached, creeping forward to apply its heavy sapphire brush over every gable and bridge. Christopher sat with his hands resting on the pommel of his saddle, regarding the city as it settled down for the night, cherishing little hope of locating Lark before the sun fell. But he did have one shred of optimism, one destination still left to search. Contrarily, he hoped Lark would not be found there.

Approaching Ormond quay, where on every corner footpads lurked amongst the scurrying rats, Christopher slowed his horse, growing more alert. The smell of rotting wood was strong—that, and the stench of sewage, fish, and whiskey. If Lark had come this way, he dreaded to imagine her fate.

His judgment of the place proved true, for in a flash three shadows detached themselves from a warehouse door and seized the gray's bridle, attempting to pull Christopher from the saddle. Wielding the butt of his pistol, he felled two would-be thieves, then dug his heels into the flagging horse's flanks, eluding the third clumsy-footed miscreant.

A half mile more and he found the address he sought. Without dismounting he leaned from the saddle, knocked thrice upon the faded door, and rattled it with a forceful fist until at last it opened slowly beneath a cautious hand.

A pair of unblinking black eyes met his, their pupils reflecting the fluttering candle held waist high in a dark hand. The expression in their obsidian depths hardened at the sight of the mounted figure looming just inches from the stoop.

"You look like hell," Sebastian O'Keefe said, perusing Christopher's dusty greatcoat, bare head, and fatigue-etched visage. Bracing his hands on either side of the door frame as if to bar entry, he added sarcastically, "What brings you to the low side of town, dear brother? Treating more ailing souls?"

"Is Lark Ballinter with you?" Christopher demanded, ignoring the mockery.

The surprise in Sebastian's gaze seemed genuine, and he straightened his wiry frame in order to eye Christopher with a keener regard. "What do you mean? Do you not know where she is?"

"She left my house this morning without a word."

Sebastian considered the announcement for a moment, then in a facetious manner lifted the candlestick much higher as if to illuminate the yard. An insolent smile lit his face. "Perhaps I'll go out and search myself, take *my* turn at keeping her."

Leveling his icy eyes at the person who had bedeviled him since childhood, Christopher replied, "I'll kill you if you do."

Sebastian barked a laugh. "Nay, brother. You will not. You haven't the stomach to take my soul."

"You are mistaken, Sebastian. Lay your hands upon Lark Ballinter and any regard I ever had for you will be exhausted. I have indulged you far too long."

Without waiting for answer, Christopher reined the gray about on its muscled haunches and spurred it across the patch of yard, its hooves flinging clods of turf at Sebastian's feet.

Behind him his foster brother's face creased into another ugly smile, and as the rider's swirling greatcoat disappeared, Sebastian wondered aloud, "Has she come to mean so much to you, then, Chris? Aye. I'm glad. 'Twill make her even more valuable to me. . . ."

On the fourteenth evening of Lark's disappearance, Christopher sat at his office desk, not too successfully penning a medical article for *The Gentleman's Magazine*. As he often did these days, he found concentration an arduous chore, with thoughts of Lark crowding his mind at every turn.

Over the last fortnight he had searched for her tirelessly, investigated hospitals, gaols, beggars' camps, charity institutions, and, with grimness, death carts, until there was scarcely a nook or cranny in Dublin left uncovered. He hunted for her still, taking circuitous routes on his way to calls, going out at all hours of the night, roaming alleyways like a restless, prowling cat.

But with every attempt to find her now exhausted, he had come to fear that Lark had fallen into the clutches of either the enemy or some unscrupulous villain on the streets. Or else she had flown to that man she had hidden in her chamber. The former fate chilled him; the latter gave him grief.

It seemed his only hope was to tarry, wait until he received a token from Alabar requesting that he meet his Faery Queen again beneath the tree. And when he did, there would come a reckoning between the red-haired rebel and the faceless agent.

Christopher hardly realized he had set down his pen and now absently fingered a square of linen. It was the piece Lark had tried so hard to embroider one day in the library, the only thing she had left behind of herself.

"Christopher?"

He glanced over his shoulder. "Helen! Come in."

Quietly his cousin crept toward him, her skirts barely swishing beneath her. He thought her manner even more annoyingly bashful than usual.

Rising, he pulled her forward and took her hand in his, bestowing upon it a gallant kiss. "Have you come to keep a lonely old bachelor company this dreary eve, my dear?" he asked, winking.

"Well, not exactly," she confessed, "though I'd be happy to do so. Mama sent me because I have a sore throat, have had since yesterday. She worries terribly about my little ailments, you know."

"Come here, closer to the light. That's good. Now, open your mouth."

He took her by the shoulders, positioning her so that candlelight fell full upon her face, and pulled her chin down lower. "Stick your tongue out at me—I know you've been wanting to for years."

He examined her and then moved to a shelf where vials and bottles were neatly aligned and took down a packet of lozenges. "These should help."

"What's this?" Helen asked, noticing the piece of embroidery lying upon his desk. Idly she picked it up and turned it over in her hands.

Christopher flushed and answered brusquely, "Just something Lar—Mistress Ballinter left behind. Here, give it to me."

He shoved it into his desk and closed the drawer. Then he noticed that Helen eyed him strangely, almost pityingly, before her fluttery gaze slid away to the floor.

"Y-you shouldn't worry about her, you know," she said. "I—I'll wager she's well enough . . . wherever she is."

With eyes as keen and surveillant as a hawk's, Christopher scrutinized his cousin's suddenly rosy cheeks, downcast lashes, and nervously twitching hands. "Helen?"

The ruffled lady turned upon a heel, speaking in a breathless, hurried voice. "Thank you very much for the lozenges, Chris. Mama will be grateful. I must go now or she'll fret—"

Christopher's hand shot out to capture her arm, and he spun her around to face him. "What do you know?" he demanded.

Her face screwed up as if with befuddlement. "Know?" she repeated faintly, her eyes refusing to meet her cousin's glare.

"Hel*ennn,*" he warned. "Don't make me lose my patience—which, I swear, is severely taxed already. If need be, I'll shake out of you what I want to know."

"Oh, Christopher . . ."

"You know where Lark Ballinter is, don't you? You do! By God, you do, and you're going to tell me!"

"But . . . she made me *swear.*"

"I don't care what she made you do. God knows she's made *me* do things I shouldn't have. Besides, knowing Lark as He does, I'm sure the Almighty will absolve you from your oath. Now, tell me where she is."

The girl's shoulders hunched obstinately.

"Helen, dammit! Tell me!"

Cringing at the force of his roar, she cried, "I told her not to go! I found her wandering about alone two blocks from here, attempting to beg a ride from passerby. I implored her to let me bring her back, told her you would be livid with anger!"

"Aye, and I am! Now, where is she?"

"It isn't right that I tell. She was so adamant that I keep her secret safe. I can't go back on my word."

"Oh?" Christopher intoned, merciless now. "When have you become so conscience-smitten over your promises? What about that letter you received yesterday from my apprentice—the good-looking fellow with the big brown eyes? Do you blush? Perhaps I should go and remind your papa about your promise not to see Master Ragland again. How many letters have I passed between you already?"

"You wouldn't dare tell!" she exclaimed.

"Wouldn't I?"

Wincing, eyeing her fearsome cousin like a dormouse eyeing an alley cat, Helen bit her lip. "House of Industry," she said in a rush. "Registered under the name of Helen . . . Helen Green."

20

The House of Industry earned its reputation for wretchedness. To Lark, a hopeless air hung in its gloomy communal rooms and sleeping wards, and tediousness and ennui were the pervasive companions of every inmate. Because she could not adroitly accomplish domestic chores or earn her keep performing any of the other work doled out to residents, Lark had been thrown in with the lot of females who were incapacitated in some way, whether lame, deformed, or mad. Many of these unfortunates had been brought in from the streets, captured by the wily beadle and transported to the house in his notorious black cart. The remaining paupers were constantly on the alert for the cart, for most preferred their impoverished freedom to the dubious comforts of the city poorhouse.

Since she was given no occupation, Lark was forced simply to sit most of the day, listening in her darkness to the screeches, moans, and blubberings of her fellow companions. By the end of the first week she feared she herself would go insane. Her only solace was the hope that her vision would soon return, for when she stared at the sky or a brightly lit taper, the shifting shapes of dark gray she had first distinguished at the holy well appeared again like tempting chimeras, only to vanish when the light source was removed.

At least the meals were adequate here, with meat served once a week, bread and potatoes every day. Though the diet was bland, Lark never suffered hunger. Moreover, most of the able residents were permitted to go out one day per week. Having met a friendly girl named Noreen, Lark begged her escort to the Lottery Hall on their days out. There, after the clerks had drawn winning tickets from two spinning wheels, Lark requested an interview with Peader, but unfortunately the young man had not yet received any word from Virgil.

Loneliness and isolation had put Lark in a near desperate state. She did not dare visit Jamie for fear Christopher had alerted the school officials and asked them to detain her if she appeared at the academy. Worst of all, she could see no hope of leaving the House—at least not until Virgil sent for her. Knowing all too well her brother's quixotic temperament and aversion to mundane employment, she wondered if he would ever settle long enough to make them a home. Perhaps this address would be hers for endless and woeful years. Ironically, she surmised it was an infinitely worse place than the cell Christopher had threatened to find for her in Dublin Castle.

She tried not to permit remembrance of the Earl of Glassmeade to intrude often upon her thoughts, but they did, haunting her most in the twilight time between wakefulness and slumber. Frequently she made a concerted effort to hate him, but malice proved slippery, ill thoughts fleeting, resentment nebulous. Love and yearning waxed so strong, in fact, that she could scarcely think of any subject save that of Christopher. There had even been frighteningly weak moments, when temptation had beckoned her to return to Henrietta Street, fly into his arms, and be held, if only for one brief moment. She could not help but believe that one ounce of joy there would be worth any cost.

On her fourteenth evening in the House she sat quietly chatting with the good-natured Noreen, who had been assigned the unsavory task of emptying slops in her ward.

"Listen! There's a commotion goin' on out in the corridor!" Noreen said excitedly. "Sounds like a set-to between a couple of gentlemen. Do you hear it?"

Lark cocked her head, irritated that the whines and babblings of her ward mates made listening to the distant, heated conversation difficult. She could hear clearly, however, the sudden sound of footsteps as they rang sharply, briskly down the hall toward the ward. She held her breath. Their tread possessed a certain cadence, a masterful determination. . . .

She stood. All the other surrounding sounds dimmed in her frantic effort to follow the *tap tap tap* of boot heels. Her heart began to race, and she found herself clutching her skirts with clenched fists while her breathing grew more laborious.

The footsteps slowed and then stopped.

"Bless me," Noreen said faintly, "and keep me from swoonin' dead away if I've ever seen such a splendid gentleman afore."

Lark could sense the presence of the man who had riveted the girl's attention, perceive it just as entirely as if she were witnessing it with sighted eyes. She could feel his gaze fastened upon her face, intense and probing, as she had felt it countless times before. She could envision his impressive form, his breadth of shoulder, his noble head.

Christopher had found her.

Again his boots rang, leisurely now but coming nearer, nearer . . .

When he stood before her there ensued a spell of silence. Even the poor, slowest-witted idiots seemed to sense the significance of the moment and grew still. The blood coursed so fiercely in Lark's ears, the sound was like a drumbeat. And then she felt a pair of arms go round her, enfold her like the warmest, safest cloak. They drew her close, closer, until the beat of her heart pulsed with another. He said no words. There was only the agonized tenderness of his embrace, the long exhaling of his relieved breath, the smothered groan. He held her tightly, as if she might escape, fly away again, and she pressed herself against his lean body, reassuring him she would not . . . indeed, she desired nothing but to stay just as she presently was forever.

After a moment he lifted her as easily as he would a child and made for the door, his step no less triumphant than some plunderer of old striding away with his spoils. The silence all around them was extraordinary, although Lark sensed that they passed scores of curious inmates, staring staff members, and, likely, frowning governors. With a brilliant smile for all their speechless faces, she gave an impish wave, then clung more tightly to her implacable rescuer.

Outside, with evening sounds clamoring in the frosty air, Christopher settled her in an open vehicle, likely his phaeton. With reckless flourish he draped a rug across her knees and threw a fur-lined cloak about her shoulders. Then, wasting not a moment, he leapt up and joined her on the seat, the length of his thigh riding close against hers.

When he urged the pair of horses into a speedy pace with a snap of the reins and a sharp command, Lark hung on to the edge of her seat lest she be thrown off balance. Shouting above the churn of the iron-rimmed wheels, she inquired, "Is His Lordship taking me to a cell in Dublin Castle, then?"

In the voice she knew so well, he gave a somewhat cryptic answer. "Nay, Mistress Ballinter. I'm taking you to another sort of prison . . . a much more confining one. And a more difficult one to escape, for the warden there is merciless in his attentions."

With the wind whipping past their faces, the captor and his captive spoke no more, both satisfied to press close in the crisp gloaming that reddened noses and piqued exhilaration. Delighting in Christopher's nearness, Lark was utterly content to bowl along at his breakneck speed with her destination a mystery, while the man beside her seemed content to keep that mystery guarded.

At last, hauling back upon the lines, he halted the laboring horses, and Lark realized they had entered rural climes. The peace of stretching, sleeping braes and valleys hung in the frosty evening air. The smells of the city were far away as well, with the perfume of sweet grass and autumn leaves replacing the stench of Dublin. There was no din of traffic, no late theatergoers clogging avenues with belligerent coachmen shouting from their boxes, only that soothing tranquillity particular to the country at nighttime.

Christopher lifted Lark down from the seat, and she felt her shoes crunch upon a pebbled path. Putting a hand to the small of her back, he guided her forward, then rapped peremptorily upon a door. When its hinges creaked cautiously open, he asked, "Is Reverend Kenny at home?"

"Why, certainly, Your Lordship," replied an elderly feminine voice, sounding surprised. "I'll just get him. Won't you come inside?"

Lark felt the welcome rush of warm air touch her frozen face and, with much bafflement, waited, concentrating on a dialogue in some distant part of the house. She felt the pressure of Christopher's hand around her waist increase, as if he tensed with expectation over what was to come.

Someone neared with a shuffling step, someone old, no longer lively, who issued a surprisingly hearty greeting. "Lord Glassmeade! It has been ages!"

"Reverend Kenny! You are in good health, I pray?"

"Excellent. But whom have you brought? And what can I do for you this night?"

"You can perform a marriage."

"A marriage?" the reverend repeated.

"Aye. Now. Tonight. As you can see, my bride accompanies me."

Lark almost gasped with astonishment. Christopher meant to *wed* her?

She could barely grasp the meaning of the earl's words, yet she could imagine too painfully the reverend's eyes now scanning her worn peasant attire and undressed hair in the ensuing hush. Her poor costume was surely a glaring contrast to Christopher's expensive garb, leaving the old man to likely wonder if the young earl had lost his reason and been overcome by some impulsive fit of passion. Truth to tell, Lark almost wondered the same.

"But, Lord Glassmeade," the clergyman said, "there are licenses and such—"

"Paperwork I'm certain you can manage to fix up later. If your influence proves insufficient in the legalities, I'll exert mine."

"She is Catholic?"

"Catholics have been permitted to marry Protestants since ninety-two," Christopher said impatiently.

After a pause the older man asked gravely, "Does your father know?"

"Nay." Christopher's voice was equally serious. "And it would not matter to me if he did."

After an astounding, dizzying hour of washing, taking tea, and exchanging wedding vows, Lord and Lady Glassmeade again spun down the lane at breakneck speed, to what ultimate destination Lark knew not. She could have asked, of course, yet in a perverse way she did not want to know. Her lover—nay, her husband—sat beside her and was bearing her away into a life with him. She almost feared to speak, feared superstitiously that the utterance of one prosaic word would cause the splendrous dream to shatter. So she simply leaned against the earl, buried her face in the fine wool of his greatcoat to protect her nose from the stinging cold, and let him carry her off to whatever place he would.

Finally he reined the horses onto what seemed to be a graveled drive. A moment later a bevy of servants offered deferential greetings, took charge of the horses, and ushered the lord and lady inside some great echoing hall.

"We are at Glassmeade," Christopher told her as the heavy door clanged shut behind them. "My country home in Kildare."

As he spoke, he removed her cloak deftly, then stepped aside to speak in low, unintelligible tones to a servant. Next, without preamble or further explanation, he drew Lark forward, and when they had reached a staircase, he lifted her in his arms as he had done earlier in the evening.

Upward they went, mounting many steps before turning into a chamber where a welcome fire burned. Christopher released her, let her body slide down his, then shut the outer door firmly. For a long moment he stood facing her, only bare inches away, and yet still he said no words, issued no further explanations. Instead he used his lips to communicate a quite different, though more effective, message.

The kiss was an urgent, scarcely contained caress that left Lark gasping. And he repeated it again and again, twisting his mouth roughly over hers and moving his hands with a fierce possessiveness over the ridges and dips of her arching back.

Knowing well what this marriage would cost him, wanting more than anything to insure that he would not regret a moment of it, Lark surrendered herself entirely, giving free rein to all the yearnings that had anguished her, all the dreams that had sustained her spirit. Throwing her arms around his neck with a need no less inflamed than his, she returned measure for measure the intimacy he bestowed. She touched his hair, his face, his throat, explored the rough male planes that were a counterpart to her softness. She felt his skillful fingers tug and loosen her hair from its neatly plaited braid.

Then, while he pressed his mouth upon the hollow below her ear, his hands worked insistently at her clothing—jacket, skirt, then blouse—yanking and tossing each garment with impatience to the floor. Lark followed his lead, sliding his redingote, vest, and finely ruffled shirt from the warm, wide span of masculine shoulders. She laid her head against his chest briefly, heard the loud thumping of his heart, inhaled sharply as he drew together for the first time, flesh to flesh, their undraped bodies.

A shared interim of fevered touching, exploring, and kissing followed before Christopher pulled away slightly, his breath uneven, to peruse her feminine charms. As if unable to be separated long, he took her against him again in a hard embrace and bound with her thusly, directed them across a short space of floor. Then he laid her upon a bed soft with down, eased himself atop her, and, as if beyond all restraint, freed himself from his breeches and groaned her name.

"I know not what folly I bring upon myself with this," he whispered hoarsely, panting, touching her face gently. "Or upon you, Lark. But I care not . . . I care not. I care only for this . . . for you."

In tumultuous, breathless ardor then, in a spinning passion that spared no time for further gentleness or wooing, the earl crossed a forbidden boundary and merged with the cotter's lass. He became a part of her, and she a part of him. And neither would ever be the same again.

*   *   *

A while later, the lord and his lady lay, passions relaxed, with legs and arms entangled. Lark leisurely stroked his chest, her fingers tracing languid circles, her breath wafting upon the rough flesh of his throat. In his hand he held a skein of her hair and twirled it idly, while with his other hand he outlined the curve of her naked hip.

Lark sensed he did not want to speak, did not want to verbalize thoughts about their lives tomorrow or speculate upon the future the two of them would have to face when they emerged as husband and wife from his ancestral home. Instead he seemed to yearn only for her nearness, for a constant touching, for the pleasure her womanly softness brought his male physique. He did murmur often his love, his completeness, and inquired gently if he had caused her pain. She reassured him, breathed her devotion, and respected his unspoken but obvious wish not to speak about any time beyond the present.

Serene, their bodies close, they listened to the rain tap upon the eaves, to a yowling dog, to the hissing fire. And then, as their heartbeats again increased and their breaths came in quicker rhythms, their hands began to move more purposefully. When their lips met once more, they met more lingeringly, with a more thorough searching, and this time the husband taught his wife the act of loving fully.

Lark's tactile sense was heightened as never before, taking her to soaring, spiraling levels, as if compensating for those candlelit glimpses of her lover that blindness had cruelly denied her. While Christopher gazed upon her trembling, eager form, she could not see his own, and this injustice tormented her. She longed suddenly, urgently, to observe his face, see the body that gave hers pleasure, look her fill at the man she had never seen, who was now her husband. The need burgeoned to such a magnitude, she could not suppress a sob. And even as Christopher rose to culminate their bliss, she buried her face into the curve of his neck and cried out, cried out not only with pleasure and with the shuddering desire his body moved to sate, but with frustration.

A time later, secure in his hard arms, which were relaxing into sleep, Lark murmured, "Christopher . . . ? My things, my bag of belongings . . . did you bring them when you fetched me from the House of Industry?"

"Umm . . . the servants have put everything outside our door." Nestling closer to her then, he pinned her with a strong, lean arm in a most possessive manner and promptly fell into a deep and tranquil slumber.

For a long while Lark lay beside him, her eyes turned in his direction, straining to perceive the man her fingers had so wondrously touched in love. She wanted to *see* him, peruse at leisure every plane of his countenance, every feature of his form. The unfairness of her blindness galled her more bitterly than ever before, and tears began to slide down her cheeks. After easing out from beneath his hold, she pulled a quilt from the foot of the bed and draped it around her shivering body, then began a long and tedious search for the door. The chamber was quite large, larger even than the one she had used in Henrietta Street, and by the furnishings she encountered in her clumsy meandering, she judged it filled with heirlooms.

At last she located the portal and stealthily, so as not to wake her husband, released the latch. Groping, bending low, and sweeping the air with her hands, she discovered two trunks, a valise, and her well-worn bag. After snatching it by its handle, she closed the door and retreated to the corner farthest from Christopher's slumbering form.

Carelessly, bent upon a goal, she began to toss out the contents of the bag—the extra set of underthings, her woolen stockings, an old nightdress—until, at last, her fingers closed about the smooth, rounded shape of glass.

For a lengthy spell she merely held it in the palm of her hand, weighed it, felt its coldness, tilted it this way and that to hear the liquid gurgle inside. For a long while she pondered Grindle's advice concerning the clear, sacred drops that had been blessed by a priest. The maid had assured—no, sworn—that whoever had faith that God's divine hand would heal affliction through the partaking of this angel's brew, would be cured.

Clutching the bottle, Lark listened to breathing of the being she loved most in the world and thirsted so to see. She sighed in anguish and bowed her head. Gently rocking back upon her heels, she closed her eyes and breathed deeply. Then, in a soft, reverent voice, she recited a Hail Mary, not once but many times, and afterward began to say a fervent prayer that her sight would be returned.

"I beseech thee for my sight, for a glimpse of my lover's dear and cherished face. . . ."

Deep in meditation, she uncorked the bottle and without hesitation upended the vessel, letting its crystalline contents splash between her parted lips. The sensation of fire and ice startled her, but she swallowed anyway, still rocking back and forth, crooning a feverish petition for sight. At last tranquillity crept through her quivering limbs, and, exhausted, with perspiration dripping from her brow, Lark rose. Almost fearfully, she blinked and opened her eyelids wide.

Her disappointment was keen. No glimpse of fire flames, no glimmer of candlelight, pierced the ebony curtain of her blindness.

Defeated and weak, she stumbled back to bed, desperate for the warmth of Christopher's arms. She chastised herself for begging God to give her another favor when she was so richly blessed already. Didn't she belong to Christopher now, wasn't she his wife for all time? He loved her, and there could be no greater gift than that.

Christopher stirred when she slipped beneath the sheets beside him and made a sleepy, though impudent remark concerning her freezing feet before tucking them solicitously between his warm, muscled calves. Then he pulled her close, so that her cheek rested against his chest, and tenderly he entwined his fingers in her tangled hair. His touch rendered solace to Lark's troubled spirit, and she moved her head a little so that her ear could count his heartbeats.

"Tell me a story," she whispered with a hint of anguish in her voice. "Tell me a tale about Kildare. 'Tis so loved by you and your father, the landscape must be beautiful. I'll never see it . . . paint a picture for me."

His hands tightened around her naked, shivering body, stroked it, and in his tender touching there was compassion for her suffering as well as adoration. When he spoke, it was with the natural warmth and poignancy of a man invited to speak about that which he loves.

"There once was a nun named Dara . . . a saintly nun who was blind," he began quietly, reflecting upon a story his nurse had told him long ago. "Her abbess prayed that Dara might be allowed to see the landscape of Kildare—even for an hour—because its beauty was so wondrous, it could not be adequately described by words. God granted the prayer, and for the first time Dara was allowed to behold the glory of a Kildare sunrise as it blazed behind the mountains."

Christopher paused and with a gentle hand caressed Lark's brow, pushing a long curling strand of hair away from her eyes. "What do you think happened, love? Do you think Dara was disappointed by her glimpse of beauty?"

"Few could be disappointed by a sunrise," Lark answered solemnly.

Christopher shook his head. "As a matter of fact, Dara asked that her blindness be returned. It seems the glory of Kildare was so great, it dimmed in her mind's eye the very image of God."

Lark remained quiet a moment, then asked in a voice tinged with frustration, "So, should I be grateful for my sightlessness, or grieve for the glimpse of beauty denied me?"

With his thumb, Christopher stroked the velvet flesh above her eyelids and said, "You must answer that for yourself, Lark."

"I suppose Father Peabody would say I lack godliness and obedience," she mused. "But when I search my heart, I find only bitterness over the tragedy of my lost sight. Sometimes, when I stare into the awful blackness before my eyes, I even question God's purpose. Then, quickly, I admonish myself, for surely such questioning is presumptuous and sinful."

"'Tis neither, but merely pointless." Christopher tilted her face upward and brushed her tears away with his thumb. "Don't you think I too have pondered the Almighty's reason when I see death take a good man or carry away a newborn babe? And when I look inside your lovely eyes, do you doubt that I ask why they can see the light no more? I have no answers for you, my love. I only know that you and I have a duty to persevere, to have faith that all will come right. If nothing more . . . you've a hand to hold along the way . . . a loving hand."

He squeezed her fingers hard, encouragingly, and slid an arm beneath her waist. "And if fate is kind," he murmured against her mouth, "you may yet regain your sight one day."

She sighed and nestled closer, reaching for him, his low spoken words lending her peace, even while his flesh roused again an excitement that could not be quenched during this too brief night . . . nor, perhaps, during a thousand nights to follow.

When he spoke again, his lips pressed warm against her throat, she scarcely heard him. "I only hope you won't rue your glimpse of beauty, Lark . . . as Dara did. . . ."

21

An hour before dawn's arrival, while night still cloaked the great chambers of Glassmeade, a hissing noise prompted Christopher to shift beside his wife and glance at the candle on the table beside the bed.

"'Tis sputtering in its wax," he said, leaning to blow out the flame. "The fire has died down, too. I expect the maid to be clattering up the stairs with her coal buckets soon."

Sleepily Lark opened her eyes. "Um . . . I hope she brings hot water for a bath as well. If not, I shall pull the bell cord and ask her to fetch buckets for Her *Ladyship.*" The words were uttered with an affected imperiousness, but as soon as she'd said them, Lark exclaimed, "Good heavens, Christopher! I'm not certain I like that title at all. Indeed, I'm sure I don't! It sounds positively traitorous, as if . . . as if I'm a *turncoat.*"

Although Christopher could have availed himself of the opportunity and goaded her without mercy, he did not. The time to speak seriously with Lark had arrived, though he did not relish the conversation at all. Admittedly, the decision to take her to wife had been a rather impulsive one, though truly desired, and he did not now regret it. Indeed, never had he felt so complete, never had he loved so fiercely or so well, nor had love been returned to him in such pure and selfless measures.

Yet this union could be his undoing if caution were not heeded. All during the journey to Kildare, and even as he held his eager wife in his arms, he had considered, calculated the best course for this marriage. Unhappily, he had concluded that artifice had to be relied upon to avert disaster.

Frowning, he rubbed his bristled jaw, conscious of Lark's slender fingers caressing the long line of his back, doubtful that the plan he was about to suggest would be at all well received. Regardless of her disgruntlement, however, the marriage had to be kept secret for a while. If the Earl of Glassmeade were to announce that he had wedded a blind Catholic peasant, what scandal would ensue! Behind every painted fan and every glass of claret, astonished mouths would whisper, ask why one of the most eligible nobles in Ireland, with scores of peeresses from which to choose, had attached himself to a common cotter's girl.

It would draw Christopher into a limelight he could ill afford to stand within at a time when his underground activities were drawing to a crucial end. Already his sympathies were suspect, and were it made public, this marriage would seem a blatant statement of lower-class sentiment. Moreover, Lark's life would be scrutinized, which could place her in more danger than ever.

Unfortunately Christopher could not explain to his wife the reasons for deceit without unmasking the identity of the Faery Thorn agent, and that he was not prepared to do. The less his spirited young wife knew about his other self, the less knowledge she would have to protect. As it was, he would need to take Lark back to Dublin within the next few days, for surely she had devised some way to communicate with her French contact, who might send the final dispatch at any time. Once the rebellion was finished and Ireland's freedom won, the need for concealment would be over. In the meantime, discretion was the watchword.

Christopher frowned, glanced down at Lark, and touched a lock of her hair. If the rebel fight to overthrow the government failed, leaving the *status quo* intact . . . well, he would have to cross that bridge when he came to it.

"Lark." He stroked her brow, suddenly needing reassurance. "You're happy with me, aren't you?"

She turned her head, puzzled by the very uncharacteristic lack of confidence in her husband's tone, and put her lips to his, kissing him with a new, experienced thoroughness. "Need you ask?"

"Nay. But—" He sighed, plunging into deep water with both feet. "I must talk to you about the . . . conditions of our marriage. I'm sure you realize we cannot return to Dublin and simply announce it to the world. We'll have to keep it between ourselves for a while. Reverend Kenny has already been taken into my confidence, and the servants here know only that you're my . . . guest."

His wife's reaction was more fiery than Christopher had anticipated. She rose up from her warm place at his side and sat stiffly with the sheet drawn to her breast, seemingly speechless for the moment. If there had been a candle lit, he was certain he would see her face growing pink with indignation.

"Keep secret our marriage? Whatever for? And you haven't announced to your servants who I am? Sainted Mary, they must surely be thinking me some—some roadside *whore* you fancied for the night."

"Lark . . ." Christopher began, propping himself on an elbow. He reached out a hand, only to find it slapped furiously away.

"Nay! Do not thing to start kissing me again." Lark yanked the sheet off his legs to hide her nakedness with it, then scrambled out of bed as if he were suddenly the most repugnant of bedfellows.

"Lark, the truth is, our marriage has rather complicated matters—"

"Are you having second thoughts, Your Lordship?" she interrupted. "Now that you've had your night of pleasure, are you wondering if 'twas worth the price? Perhaps 'tis not worth facing your father's scorn, facing questions from your high-nosed peers?"

"Do not make me lose my patience," he warned.

"Or perhaps," she continued, going straight to the point she feared most, "perhaps I am not worth the price of losing your inheritance—of losing Kildare?" She uttered the words with a taunting lilt in her tone.

Cursing roundly, Christopher vaulted across the bed naked, to seize her by the shoulders and pinion her in place. "Now, listen to me, dammit! My reasons are not selfish ones, and though I will likely pay a heavy price for this marriage, I am not having second thoughts about it. Moreover, I don't make decisions lightly, and this one was no exception. But for reasons I cannot now discuss with you, I have determined it prudent to temporarily keep the marriage secret. That does not make it any less valid."

Lark pulled away from his grip and stepped back to face him. "Oh, doesn't it, now? And how do I know 'tis valid? There was no license—your *Protestant* reverend said so. Perhaps the whole ceremony was nothing more than a ruse to provide Your Lordship with a tumble in bed—and with the only woman who has ever told him nay!"

Christopher gritted a response through his teeth. "We were wed in the eyes of God, and that wedding consummated—*well* consummated. 'Tis legal enough for me."

"Until you tire of me, you mean!" she shot back. "Then there shall likely be no documents anywhere in the whole of Ireland to prove it. You would have managed to have your paramour, after all, neatly tucked away in the country to serve you at your convenience. Well, unfortunately, Lord Glassmeade, your plan has gone awry."

"How can you attribute such motives to me after the night we've had together?" he demanded.

"Because I know well the nature of your breed! I understand how you and your kind lightly use those beneath your class, and discard them when usefulness is done. Your own sire starved my uncle, Jamie, and me, then evicted us from our home so he could graze his blasted cattle, with not a care that we would have to go a-begging!"

"And didn't I shelter you myself?" he countered. "But you couldn't possibly credit me for that, could you? Nay! You cannot see far enough beyond your own self-righteous nose, beyond your damned bitterness!"

"Bitter or not, any wife would have cause for suspicion when her husband announces that, for *reasons he cannot discuss,*" she mocked him, "the marriage must be kept secret. Ha! Surely a brilliant surgeon, a fancily educated *lord,* could invent a more clever excuse than that!"

"I need not invent excuses, and since you seem to like playing up our class disparity, I shall act the autocratic lord, and you the oppressed pauper." Putting his face within inches of hers, he raised his voice to a threatening roar. "You will keep this marriage secret until *I* say it can be announced. Furthermore, you will stay on this estate until *I* decide to take you off of it. The grounds will be guarded, so do not think to fly the coop again!"

Furiously, he bent to snatch his rumpled clothing from the carpet, pulled on his breeches and shirt, and stalked across the floor with his boots in hand. Seeing Lark's old patched clothes, he savagely wadded them into a bundle, which, in an ill-tempered bellow, he declared destined for the fire.

It was only at the door that he hesitated. With a hand upon the latch, he turned to look at Lark, at her small but rigid form ridiculously swathed in the long pale sheet. Remorse over their arguing rankled him, especially when he recalled the happiness so recently shared in their bed.

"I'll have a maid bring up some hot water for your bath in a while," he offered in a sullen, half-gracious attempt at reconciliation. He opened the door and pulled one of the trunks inside. "Here are some respectable clothes. The maid will help you dress."

Lark merely turned her back upon him in a pointed dismissal.

A minute later, at the sound of his retreat down

the stairs, her aching shoulders slumped and she sank upon the bed. For a moment she lay fuming anew over his arrogance, his magisterial treatment of her, marveling at how two such opposite beings could maintain an attraction that at times was utterly divine. How could a man and woman be so intimate one minute and so divided the next?

Recalling too clearly the warmth of Christopher's body as it had reclined so fittingly with hers only a quarter hour past, she experienced a sudden wretched loneliness. The place beside her seemed woefully empty and cold. She punched the pillow with her fists, buried her face in its soft folds, and wept until, exhausted, she fell into a doze.

At first, when she awoke, she thought she still dreamed. Often her dreams were filled with vivid color and light, so that she took refuge in them to escape her daytime darkness. But now, as she lay upon the pillow, she was certain her eyelids were opened wide, was certain that a circle of light shone in shifting rays before her eyes. Perhaps she had died, regained sight through the passage into eternity, and was now witnessing heaven's glow.

Closing her eyes, she moaned with the sudden ache in her head and put both hands to her temples. Then she blinked and reopened her lids, sure the vision of light would be gone.

But it was not.

Startled, she sat up, looking all about. Light streamed in from a circular window, a window glazed with myriad tints of rose and violet and gold. The hues spun round and round, blurring into fragmented flickers of light. She moved her head from side to side, looked down to stop the dizziness, and . . . saw her hands.

Gasping, she wiggled her fingers, watched their dim, fuzzy shapes straighten and flex. With frantic energy she thrashed her legs, watched the pale shape of the sheets writhe and curl. Then she tilted her head back. Above, a great wine-colored canopy soared, festooned with tasseled valances, embroidered scenes, and gold fringes. Beyond the bed, wainscoted walls stretched, silk-covered and hung with brightly hued paintings.

Not yet daring to believe what had occurred, she stumbled from the bed, putting out her hands to touch the shapes of furniture, drapes, and ornaments. Several times she fell, for her vision wavered, grew focused and unfocused, wreaking havoc upon her balance. Yet there was no doubt that her curtain of blackness had lifted. Though her eyes viewed the room as if through a gauze-draped looking glass, each object in it possessed a discernible outline.

With a shriek of joy, she raised her arms high and twirled round and round on unsteady legs, crying out exultantly over the glorious miracle, all the while blinking and laughing hysterically until tears streamed from her newly sighted eyes.

The ring upon her hand caught her attention then, the ring Christopher had slid upon her finger when he'd recited his vows. It was a magnificent *claddagh* ring, the symbol of love and friendship, fashioned with two gold hands clasping a heart-shaped emerald, which winked brilliantly as she moved her hand.

"Christopher!" she cried, wanting nothing more than to run, to tell him of the news. Their argument would be forgotten amidst an exchange of kisses, they would laugh and voice their love, and she would gaze her fill at the face she had never seen.

Throwing open the trunk lid and riffling through its contents, she pounced upon the brightest gown of all, crimson with ecru lace dripping from the sleeves. Hurriedly, still half-dazed, she struggled into it, fastening only half the tiny, countless buttons marching down the spine. Not bothering with shoes, she made for the door, only to stop abruptly as her reflection flashed upon the silver surface of a mirror.

Instinctively she clapped a hand to her cheek and with sudden trepidation stepped forward to peer at her image. Her sight was still blurred, yet she could see the oval outline of her face, the heavy mass of hair about it, the deep shadows above her eyes. She put a finger upon the soft furrow on her cheekbone, traced it, just perceiving its faint pink lines. Her complexion was indeed scarred—not as badly as she had feared— but more noticeably than she would have wished.

Nevertheless, joy quickly snuffed dismay, and eager to find Christopher, she abandoned the mirror and dashed out the door.

A neatly uniformed maid lugged two pails up the staircase, and Lark nearly collided with her. Breathless, she inquired where Lord Glassmeade might be found.

"Why, madam, he's out on the front lawn," the servant replied, trying to hide her astonishment at Lark's half-dressed state. "I believe he's preparing to ride. His horse has just been brought round."

Lark scampered down the stairs, only to stop suddenly midway, awed by the beauty all around her. She put a hand on her dizzy head and swayed, trying to keep her vision focused on the sight. How lovely was the rich dark wood of the curling bannister, how warm the mellow walls gilded by sun ribbons streaming from the clerestory. Rich, jewel-toned carpets covered the great hall below, and cheerful sprays of flowers graced the gleaming tables. Ancient-looking stag horns, shields, swords, and hunting horns were the only decor, and a pair of hounds dozed comfortably at the foot of the stair.

Lark thought there could be no greater place to pass one's life than there, and she yearned to see it all, to have Christopher guide her through every chamber. Feeling giddy with excitement, she descended the remainder of the steps as if gliding on air. She threw open the huge front door, stepped out, and halted in the shade of the portico.

At first the glaring radiance of the brilliant morning dazzled her still sensitive eyes and forced her to squint and raise a hand to shade her brow. For a moment she felt like a mole emerging from its tunnel. But at last the scene before her began to shimmer and clear like a rippled reflection in settling waters. She saw the sun rising over the purple peaks of the Wicklow Mountains, its rays like prongs over gentle braes. Two azure-colored lakes sparkled in the distance, connected by a rushing stream of silver.

Movement caught Lark's attention then, arrested her dazed eyes. She saw first a fine chestnut horse, then . . . a man. . . .

With his hands adjusting the stirrup straps, he stood facing the steed, giving Lark full view of his back. She had no doubt that this lean-hipped, well-knit creature was her husband. His very bearing suggested grace, vital health, and nobility, and his golden hair gleamed in the sun.

The sight of Christopher's physical self stirred her anew. In a moment, after she had feasted her eyes upon him in delicious stealth, she would call out, run into his arms, and shout her news. Her eyes burning with reflected light, she watched as he gathered the reins and prepared to mount the skittish horse. Before he had quite slid his boot into the iron to vault up, however, a small grizzled cur scampered from the hedge, causing the steed to sidestep. Pivoting to find the cause of the disruption, Christopher then gave Lark full view of that face she had prayed to see.

For a moment she could only stand immobile, staring at it, awestruck.

Never, not even in her most exaggerated imaginings, had she conjured up such a magnificent demeanor. Beyond handsomeness, his looks were a model of austere, masculine beauty. No fault did his face or form display, all features were starkly, purely male. Complementing each other were the strong line of jaw, the classic straight nose, the deep-set eyes, and the well-formed mouth that smiled brilliantly now as he knelt to pat the hound.

Lark found herself without breath. All at once she wanted to be held in his arms again, wanted their quarrel forgotten, wanted to watch his face light up as she cried out to him.

Smiling excitedly, she took one step forward . . . and hesitated. She examined once more the Earl of Glassmeade's face, every plane and line. Her memory suddenly aspin, she felt herself whirling back in time, standing at a window, looking in, frozen with terror. Crystalline clear, she could see again the prone body of her uncle, see strong hands upon his shrunken neck, see a gentleman, finely attired with striking looks, kneeling down. She recalled the color of his hair touched by candlelight, the shimmering beads of moisture on his dark cloak, the expensive, muddied boots. . . .

"God have mercy—" Clamping both hands to her mouth, she stifled a piercing scream of shock.

Her husband, her surgeon, her beloved Christopher . . . *he* was the man she had seen commit murder.

For several excruciating moments Lark did not move. She could not. As her mind grappled for understanding, her heart cried out that her memory held some mistaken image. But, nay, reason insisted, the image of the assassin was indelibly etched, too clear to be forgotten.

In her shock, Lark had failed to notice at first the line of horsemen cantering officiously down the drive. A billow of dust rose up from the churning hooves of their steeds, and each rider wore a scarlet coat with shiny brass buttons.

"Dragoons," Lark whispered through stiffened lips, fear of the government's militia instinctive in her rebel bones.

She saw Christopher stride across the lawn to stand before the approaching ranks, his stance casual, self-assured.

At the front of the line, an officer detached himself from the rest, reined his mount to within a few feet of the earl, and produced a parchment tied up with ribbon. "Lord Glassmeade!" he called. "Son of the Marquess of Winterwoode?"

"Aye," Christopher acknowledged.

"In the name of King George the Third, I've been charged to arrest you on suspicion of conspiracy against His Majesty's government."

"The hell you say." Glaring at the impassive dragoon, Christopher yanked the proffered document from his hand, unrolled it, and silently scanned its lines.

Even as he read, two other officers dismounted and walked round behind him, irons in hand. But when they reached to pinion his arms, Christopher shook them off violently and glanced over his shoulder toward the house.

In that instant he caught sight of his wife, and his eyes fastened upon hers like magnets.

Lark saw that they were fierce with rage over his threatened arrest and yet surprised at the sight of her. He seemed to understand that she could see him, for his gaze locked perfectly with hers across the distance, and a question briefly crossed his face.

"Lark?" he called, bewildered even as he struggled to throw off the men. "Lark!"

But she did not respond. She merely stood rooted to the ground, staring at him.

A cart trundled up from behind the ranks. Pulled by four sweating horses, it stood ready, its tiny window barred, its solid door wrenched open by a stern, musket-bearing dragoon. Though Christopher fought valiantly, landing blows on a pair of unwary jaws, he was summarily brought under control as six soldiers leaped from saddles to assist their fallen fellows. The earl cursed them all, battling to break free until at last his strong wrists were fettered.

Growling, one of the offended officers raised a muddy boot and, with a mighty kick to his back, knocked Christopher to his knees.

Lark watched the whole of the horrifying, confused scene as if detached from it. She was nearly insensible, her nerves stricken numb from her shocking discovery. A merciless part of her consciousness cried that the golden-haired assassin *should be* manacled and jailed so justice could at last be served.

And didn't her uncle's murderer deserve a double punishment as well, a punishment for making love with her last night after speaking vows that were never meant to be recorded?

"*Lark!* For God's sake!" Christopher shouted again in a hoarse voice. Struggling to stand up, he stared at her in desperation while sentries yanked him toward the waiting wagon.

But she neither answered nor moved a muscle in his direction, merely watched as he was shoved inside the dark confines of the portable prison and the door was slammed upon his handsome, rage-twisted face.

Slowly the frightened servants began to gather upon the lawn. Shading their eyes to watch their master driven away with his formidable escort of soldiers, they paid Lark scant heed. And even as the scarlet-clad lines disappeared, the servants' attention was claimed by a lone rider barreling down the drive.

"Lark! Lark!"

The shout dimly penetrated her awareness, and she stiffened, squinting against the blaze of the morning light to find Sebastian O'Keefe dismounting and striding quickly toward her in his rough black corduroys.

"Lark!" Taking her freezing hands in his, he put an arm around her and bade her come inside to warmth. "I've just ridden posthaste from Dublin! They found incriminating documents at the Henrietta Street address. I fear your esteemed surgeon—my dear brother—will shortly meet the hangman."

He had to catch her as she fell.

22

The following hours passed in nightmarish confusion. Benumbed, Lark listened to Sebastian's excited voice as he related the events leading up to the earl's arrest. She stood with the restlessly pacing tinker in the midst of the sun-drenched great hall, shivering and muddle-headed, catching only a part of his list of the damning documents found in Christopher's desk in Henrietta Street.

"Copies of the *Northern Star*—that seditious paper," he said, "correspondence signed by leaders of the United Irish, even a letter from Wolfe Tone himself." Sebastian snorted. "My incautious brother has dug his own grave, and dug it deep."

Lark merely nodded, too befuddled and strained to respond, her brain struggling to reconcile into one cohesive image both the golden-haired assassin and the man whose arms had held her in love last night. And now Christopher was being accused of some connection with the United Irish? Impossible!

Sebastian insisted she return immediately with him to the house in Dublin. In his brother's absence, O'Keefe officiously declared, he would need to see to things, especially since the marquess had lately grown so enfeebled. And surely, he added with thinly veiled censure, Lark would not want to stay in Kildare alone now that her . . . host was in jail.

Of course, Sebastian could not know—with or without proof—that Lark was the Countess of Glassmeade now. He would naturally assume she had fallen with brazen abandon into the role of the earl's trollop. Nevertheless, recalling all too well Christopher's vehemence regarding secrecy, Lark did not enlighten the unpredictable foster brother; her wariness of him had grown too strong. He wore a smugness on his long face that she found disquieting, and a fevered excitement danced in the depths of his bright black eyes. She knew there was no love lost between the orphaned Gypsy and Christopher Cavanaugh, but could his hatred be so poisonous that the young earl's trouble actually gave him pleasure?

To his credit, he was just as solicitous toward her as he had ever been, though he only belatedly noted her ability to see. She supposed in the trauma of learning Christopher's treachery, her gaze had been so stupidly fixed that her sight had not been obvious. He did indulge her distraction, however, and all in the space of a half hour had ordered the staff to ready a carriage and pack her things. Lark soon found herself dressed properly by a maid, bundled against the morning chill, and handed into the plush, high-wheeled vehicle, while Sebastian swung up upon his mount and cantered alongside.

By the time the driver had whipped the horses over the bumpy, pitted roads of the country, and then along the smoother avenues of Dublin, Lark's thoughts had begun to focus and assimilate more clearly. Yet when she entered again the house in Henrietta Street, her nerves were jangled anew. She could only stand riveted upon its threshold for a moment, agog at the high domed ceiling with its beautifully painted angels. Christopher's presence was strong here. She could not help but imagine him striding up the curving stair, walking purposefully toward her old chamber. She remembered with a sudden aching emptiness the sound of his steps and recalled his tender ministering hands.

She tried not to think of the savagery of those same hands . . . the deed they had done on a wild, rain-soaked night in a humble cottage. And she couldn't possibly fathom the strangest news of all: that he was a member of the United Irish!

As Sebastian strode to the library, she gathered her wits and bombarded him with questions, asking in what prison Christopher was incarcerated and if visitors were received there.

"He's a state prisoner in Kilmainham gaol," the young man replied over his shoulder as he walked to the earl's plundered desk in the library and eased down onto its leather chair. "But I wouldn't advise you to see him, if that's what you have in mind," he added, gazing at her shrewdly.

She did not waste a moment in argument with him. Instead, using exhaustion as an excuse, she stated her intention to retire for the evening and made her way, unerringly for once, to her old chamber. Once there she paced back and forth, her feet, in the first pair of elegant kid shoes they had ever worn, treading soundlessly upon the finely woven carpets. The room seemed to welcome her. She found that the tapestry chairs, the glowing fire, and the glossy paintings of spaniels and kerchiefed children lent her a sense of calm, that the closed drapes and turned-back bed offered security. Savoring the familiarity of her surroundings, she almost expected to hear confident footsteps approaching the threshold and for an aching moment wished more than anything that she would.

Again and again the anguished question came aloud to her lips. "What am I to do? What am I to do about Christopher?"

Finding no answer, she at last sat down upon the bed and rubbed her reddened, bleary eyes. Her brain ached with the swirling images of a gentle surgeon, an arrogant earl, a masterful lover . . . and a cold, merciless murderer.

Putting her head in her hands, she groaned, not knowing what course to take, what to *believe*. Over and over, marching across her memory and haunting her, came visions of Christopher's arrest and his questioning eyes, his desperate face. What was behind the charge of conspiracy? If the evidence were to be trusted, the Earl of Glassmeade had been plotting to overthrow the English-appointed government, his efforts in tune with those of the United Irishmen. Had his cause really been that of her own, then? Was his pretended high-hatted loyalty only a veneer to cover his clandestine treachery? She recalled the night of his injury, his orders to keep the servants away, his fevered insistence on secrecy. Even the surgeon MacTavish had kept hidden the truth.

"So much secrecy," she murmured aloud in frustration. "Secrecy at every turn!"

Grindle came with a tray of food, her old wrinkled face slyly smiling over Lark's returned sight. As Lark forced herself to take nourishment, she admitted to having drunk the little bottle of holy water just before her vision had cleared.

After enjoying a moment of smug satisfaction at this, the maid launched into an hour of indignant outrage over the arrest of Lord Glassmeade. It had thrown the household into an uproar, and long lines of poor ailing people were being turned away from the medical office door. Even the old marquess had taken to his bed, she said, nearly broken over the disgrace of his son's arrest as a traitor.

After the distressed maid had gathered the dishes and departed, Lark slipped into a nightdress and, pacing the floor once more, began to formulate a plan, staying up late into the night until the last detail was calculated. Then, knowing she required rest in order to carry out her efforts, she at last lay down to sleep.

She declined to blow out the candle. It would be a long while before she felt comfortable in darkness again.

At dawn she rose, washed, pulled back her hair in a smooth twist, and dressed herself in a blue robe-style gown with a dove gray petticoat-dress beneath. Decorated with ribbon knots, the décolletage dipped below a transparent neckerchief, and the tight-fitting sleeves ended in wrist-length frills. Stepping back from the looking glass and focusing her still unpredictable vision, Lark nearly gasped, scarcely recognizing the image.

The fashionable clothes and sophisticated chignon lent her an air of maturity and grace. No longer was she a simple cotter's girl in frayed woollens, but by all appearances an earl's wife indeed. She shook her head in disbelief. During her blindness she had traveled a long and remarkable road. But where exactly had it led her?

As she scrutinized her reflection one last time, she experienced an enormous feeling of guilt. She was a traitor to her cause, dressed in such costly finery, and yet she was young and feminine enough to have a healthy vanity. After a moment's hesitation she set the matching feathered hat atop her head to complete the ensemble.

Next, following the design of her plan, she retrieved a small silver-plated music box from the dressing table, listened once more to its melancholy, tinkling tune, and then slid it inside a satin purse. At last, without saying a word to anyone, she slipped outside.

Unlike the day she had stood blind and destitute upon this elegant street, she had no trouble hailing a coach. The driver, however, did give her an odd glance when she instructed him to proceed to the nearest reputable pawnshop. Obediently, though, he wended through rows of coffee shops, alehouses, brandy stores, milliners, and tailors, where upon every corner the strident calls of herring and turf vendors vied.

Near Fitzwilliam Street stood a gallows, and Lark caught a glimpse of the ominous hangman in his black garb. He appeared to be dreadfully hump-backed, but Lark knew men of his profession often placed a huge wooden bowl between their shoulder blades to deflect stones hurled by hostile crowds.

Shuddering as she thought of Christopher's fine strong neck, Lark tore her eyes away.

After she had pawned with considerable remorse the beautiful music box—an item likely once treasured by Christopher's mother—she clutched her purseful of coins to her breast and bade the coachman drive to Kilmainham gaol. When she stepped down before the formidable structure, however, and saw its fierce-eyed soldiers with their drawn bayonets, she knew a moment of panic. Several of her cohorts had passed through this very portal, only to reemerge as stiffening corpses.

Steeling herself, she entered, and after being detained two hours in a small stone anteroom, she was granted an interview with the gaoler of state prisoners.

"Nay, madam," said the corpulent, bewhiskered warden, shaking his head and pulling down the jacket of his soiled blue uniform. "The Deputy Governor says Lord Glassmeade is to have no visitors. Wouldn't want him to be passing on secrets to his rebel friends, ye know," he added, giving her a gap-toothed smile.

She said nothing in reply, merely stepped closer to the odoriferous presence, turning the bulging purse of coins between her palms. The fox-eyed warden licked his greasy lips, quick to sense the bribe—indeed, she guessed he and his family likely lived relatively well upon this type of windfall. She watched while he gave the offer greedy consideration. Then, with one stealthy move his hand darted out, dropped the purse inside his pocket, and closed the flap.

Removing a ring of keys from his waist, he bade her follow him down a maze of gloomy corridors, where the prisoners in huge cells grumbled, swore, coughed, or hurled obscenities in their direction. At last she was brought to a smaller, private cell, one with a tiny barred window and rough stone walls, incongruously furnished with a bed, chairs, table, and blazing fireplace. Standing at the window with his back to her stood the Earl of Glassmeade.

Outlined by the meager light of afternoon, his tall straight frame was still attired in the riding breeches and shirt he had been wearing at the time of his arrest, the backside much stained with dried mud from his violent struggle with the dragoons. His hair was disheveled, and one sleeve of his fine linen shirt was torn and bloodied. He had braced an arm upon the wall beside the window, and where the cuff fell away from his wrist a ring of raw flesh showed, chafed by the manacles he had worn. Hearing the key grate in the lock, he turned around with a cold, arrogant gaze, as if daring the jailer to harass him.

Lark nearly gasped when she saw his face. The left side of his jaw was cut and bruised, the eye split at the outer corner and much swollen. The front of his shirt, minus several buttons, was spattered with dried blood and rent in several places. Fatigue showed clearly in the set of his shoulders, in the thinned line of his mouth. She wondered how much abuse he had endured in these past grueling hours.

At sight of Lark his eyes narrowed with obvious surprise. Simultaneously his hands twitched and he started forward, as if he would cross the room and take her in his arms. But he seemed to check the impulse immediately, squelch emotion as if it were anathema, and in its place affect a dispassionate pose.

Folding his arms across his chest, he addressed her

coldly. "So, the countess has come to say a tender farewell to her husband—or perhaps," he amended, raising a brow, "she has only come to assure herself her marriage is legal, and will guarantee a handsome widow's income."

Taken aback by his animosity, Lark flushed. The very sight of him intimidated her. His was a powerful presence, preposessing even in these surroundings. Like a mesmerized fool, she simply stared at his face, at those perfect planes made even more elementally male by the bruises he wore from fighting.

His arms were still folded, and her gaze wandered to his strong, dexterous hands where they rested just above the bulge of each bicep. She remembered those hands touching her, tending her burns, loving her with gentleness and knowledgeable moves. For a moment she could not abide they were the same hands that had squeezed the life from her uncle's flesh.

Christopher watched her unwaveringly until her lashes lowered and she turned her head away in the direction of the table across the room. When her eyes flickered across the untouched, sumptuous meal of roasted capon, Dutch cheese, plum pudding, and wine, he twisted his lips in a wry smile. "I'm a privileged prisoner, you might say," he said, indicating the furnishings with a blasé sweep of one hand. "Money and title have their advantages wherever one goes—as I daresay you have already discovered for yourself."

Lark glanced down at her empty, gloved hands, bereft of the purse strings they had clutched so tightly only a short while ago. "He took the bribe willingly enough," she murmured, fixing her eyes again upon her husband's damaged face. "Did you have no bribe large enough to keep the brute's fists at bay?"

He lifted a shoulder unconcernedly. "There are some here more driven by brutality than greed. They would not forgo their perverse pleasures for any amount of coin."

"The gaoler in the blue uniform?"

"He was the last in a line of several. It amused him to try to extract 'secrets' from me." He eyed her closely. "You didn't, perchance, happen to honor my wishes and remain discreet about that particular ceremony we underwent the day before yesterday?"

Wounded by the insolence in his tone, she snapped a haughty answer. "Never fear, Your Lordship. I honored your wish for secrecy." Raising her chin a notch, she added, "Or shall we simply call it your reluctance to claim me?"

"I didn't see you jumping forward to claim me in front of His Majesty's venerable troops. You might at least have come close enough so that I could ask you to have my lawyers summoned."

She lowered her head. His condemnation of her disregard was justified, yet she was not willing to discuss the reason for her hesitation on the lawn at Glassmeade. That, she would save for later.

Christopher regarded her silently for a time, taking in the captivating transformation she had undergone, from a simple cotter's girl to a woman elegant enough to compete with any blooded countess. He wondered if her allegiance to the common cause had wavered any now that she was enjoying the benefits of his wealth. At any rate, he did not remark upon her charm. His anger was still too raw, and the picture of her unconcern at his arrest far too vivid.

At the same time, he was not so insensitive to realize that Lark might have been regaining her sight during those frenzied moments at Glassmeade and might have been dreadfully confused. Yet in the instant their eyes had locked across the lawn, she had stared at him with such malevolence that he had been stunned. He could not fathom the look, the repugnance, the utter refusal even to reach out a hand toward him. Neither had a cry of despair issued from her lips, nor any show of distress over his violent apprehension.

They had quarreled a few hours earlier, granted, but they had also loved with intimate abandon through the night, as close in flesh and spirit as any man and wife could be. So what had plagued her? He knew she was no coward, would not have shrunk in fear of the dragoons. He had wondered over her behavior during his long journey to Dublin, and later, in the dark of night upon his prison bed, he had nursed his hurt in quiet and terrible solitude.

Yet he spoke to her softly now, knowing there was no time for bitterness. "I'm pleased for you that your sight has returned. Is it a full recovery?"

"Nay. That is, my vision is blurred most of the time." Lark moved forward, conscious of the fleeing minutes. Unable to help herself, she put a hand upon his arm, feeling the warmth of his flesh through the tear in his sleeve. "Your arrest, Christopher—are you justly charged of conspiracy?"

The muscles of his forearm tensed beneath her fingers, and she feared he would shrug off her hand, incensed at the question. Unexpectedly, she saw a brief look of humor brighten his eyes, and a thin smile flitted across his mouth before disappearing as quickly as it had come.

"I can assure you," he said, tilting her hat back slightly with a forefinger so he could better view her face, "I left no seditious papers in my desk drawer, or anywhere else in the house, for that matter. After all, what self-respecting traitor to His Majesty's government would be so careless, I ask you?"

His implication of her own traitorous activity caused color to rise in her cheeks. Yet she regained enough self-possession to realize he had not answered her question. "Are you saying the papers were planted there?"

"That's precisely what I'm saying."

"But, by whom?"

"I have my suspicions." Christopher moved away, for his wife's touch unnerved him, made him want to hold her and spend these precious minutes in other pastimes. But Lark was keeping something back from him, something that stemmed from the arrest, he was certain. Her manner was still reticent, almost wary, and he surmised she would not welcome his husbandly attentions.

Following him as he strolled to the table, and looking with concern at the wound oozing blood at the corner of his eye, Lark asked anxiously, "What will happen next?"

He snorted. "Quite an impressive show at Dublin Castle, no doubt."

"What do you mean?" She watched him refill the wineglass before forcing her eyes away from his skillful fingers.

"Care to share a drink with me?" he asked casually. "Nay? I've considered bribing the warden for some arsenic and aquafortis, you know. If I were to drop a little in my glass, 'twould save the hangman his trouble."

Lark gasped, the mention of his death too wrenching to contemplate. Yet it brought home to her the direness of his situation, the imminent approach of a reckoning with the law. How confused were her feelings! He was a murderer, deserved the harshest judgment, and yet . . .

He smiled crookedly and touched her quivering chin. "I'd not cheat Dublin of such a sensational hanging as mine shall likely prove to be. Besides, I wouldn't dream of disgracing you by taking the coward's way out, Countess. And by the way, once I'm safely tucked in my satin-lined box, you can announce the news of our marriage with my blessing. Reverend Kenny will give you the papers, which will prove that I legally"—he made a mock toast—"and with a sane mind, wed you."

Lark twisted the folds of her skirts with agitated hands. She yearned to touch him again and beg him to be serious. But she suppressed the need and clutched the fabric more tightly. A moment later her voice came breathless, husky. "They won't really . . . hang you, will they?"

He took a swallow of the wine. "Oh, I assure you, milady, they will most definitely hang me. And relieve me of my head, I daresay, for good measure."

His words caused her a jolt of utter horror. "But you haven't been tried yet!"

He shrugged. "May as well have been. I spent three hours with the Lord Lieutenant and the Chief Secretary last night in the Castle, attempting to convince them that the documents were planted in my desk by someone wishing to incriminate me. But to no avail. I should have expected it, I suppose. 'Tis no secret I've been rather brashly"—he gave her a rueful glance—"mingling with the lower classes. No doubt the government intends to make an example of me. Indeed, my trial will be day after tomorrow. They waste no time these days with rebel sympathizers.

"And that brings me to a point." He looked at her squarely, his sarcasm put aside. "The Lord Lieutenant has issued a proclamation offering five hundred pounds to anyone with information leading to the arrest of a rebel. Be careful of yourself, Lark. Especially careful."

She looked up, searching his eyes. They were so fine and keen, made grave with the understanding of his probable end, but calm with acceptance of those things he could no longer fight or change. In that moment her love for him spilled over in a rush.

She saw a like emotion flicker clearly in his own steady regard, but after a moment of heartrending anticipation, during which she expected him to take her in his arms, he only lowered his lashes and looked away. He poured another glass of wine and sipped it with an aspect of a man considering his own mortality.

Lark despaired. There would be only a few more moments left to them. The turnkey would arrive at any second. Yet a grievous matter still hovered unspoken in the dank air of Lord Glassmeade's prison, one she knew she must address, must force him to discuss for her own peace, if nothing else.

"Christopher," she began with the most burdensome dread. The dove gray feathers upon her hat nodded gracefully as she lifted her face to his. "I must tell you why I stood by so unresponsively at your arrest. You have a right to know."

He glanced at her over the rim of his glass, examining her expression with curiosity.

She took a breath. "I recognized you—I'd seen your face before."

"Go on," he prompted her.

She steeled herself for his reaction, attempted to muster the long-held but waning hatred for the golden-haired assassin who had taken a precious life from her. "You murdered my uncle," she said with soft, stunning censure, her eyes never leaving his. "I saw you. I saw your hands upon his neck."

Myriad expressions crossed her husband's face in the next seconds. Astonishment was the first, then incredulity, and finally a smoldering anger. He seemed to struggle with all three in turn, his eyes glittering with the effort to master some retaliation. She thought for one anxious moment that he might even raise a hand to strike her.

Then his visage grew shuttered, blank. Setting down his glass, he went back to the window and braced an arm against the frame, idly watching the activity in the courtyard below. She saw him rest his brow upon the iron bars after a moment, as if he were suddenly too weary to hold up his head.

Lark stared at him, waiting, perusing his long, well-muscled legs in their muddied breeches, the beleaguered line of his bent head, his strong neck with its spatters of dried blood. But though the seconds passed, he said nothing, made no defense, no denial, no confession of his crime.

Suddenly heavy footsteps pounded the corridor, and through the grate in the wooden cell door the turnkey announced, "Ye've got five minutes more in there!" Then he stumped away.

Lark felt the strain of the fast-approaching, grievous separation, and she trembled with the tragic turns her life and Christopher's had taken. Watching her husband's rigid spine, she finally, in anguish, came to the conclusion that he had done with her. She didn't know what she had expected him to say after her accusation. After all, she had seen him kill her uncle with her own eyes. She had only hoped he would vehemently deny her charge and offer some glib, plausible excuse to free her from her torment.

Just when she was about to turn her back on him and wait alone for the return of the gaoler, Christopher turned around. For a long moment he said nothing, only contemplated her with those expressive eyes of his, their blue depths aglimmer with an emotion too deep to hide.

Then she saw his chest heave. His face was stark, the cheeks taut and pale. After hesitating for a heartbeat, he rushed forward, crossing the room in three long steps. She saw his arms lift, reach out for her, and with a tortured cry she fell into his embrace and clutched him.

"We won't be able to see each other again, Lark," he whispered urgently, his lips pressed against her ear. "Pray God, just let me hold you these last minutes, will you? With no words, no condemnation, no thoughts of tomorrow."

She shook her head and cried, "Nay! I'll come tomorrow. No matter what the bribe costs, I'll come—"

"He won't take it tomorrow. 'Twould cost him his own neck." Taking her face in his palms, he looked deep into her eyes, which swam now with gathering tears. "Why is it we are fated to such an end?" he whispered in desolation. "Why could we not have been granted even a bare week together at Kildare, time to hold each other and love, walk the fields at sunset, speak tranquilly beside the fire? 'Tis what I planned for us, you know. I wanted to indulge you, I wanted to forget the schemes of armies and the injustices of governments for a few days . . . and make you forget them, too. Forget them in my arms."

His honest words of dashed hopes caused Lark to sob and cling more tightly to his shoulders.

"Don't come to the hanging," he ordered fiercely, taking her face in his hands again. "Swear to me you won't."

"Nay," she wailed, "do not speak of it, I beg you!"

The ring of footsteps sounded then, distant and ominous.

Christopher buried his face against the soft curve of her neck, breathing raggedly. "There are many things you do not know about me," he said. "Things I wish to tell you but cannot, things which should go with me to the grave. But, if you knew all . . ." He frowned in frustration at inadequate words. "If you knew all, it would please you. I know it would."

With frantic eyes she searched his battered face, dimly lit by the lantern on the wall, and wondered at his meaning. Only a moment was left, only a moment more to look at him, touch him, tell him of her love. It seemed bitterly unfair that he was to be taken from her now in this way, without a resolution between them, but he was right . . . their relationship had been doomed to disaster from the start.

"Oh, Christopher!" she cried in despair, flinging her arms around his rumpled collar, breathing in his scent, relishing the feel of him, all with the knowledge that these sensations would be the last. "I can't bear it!" she sobbed with her face buried against his chest, her tears dampening the linen of his shirtfront.

"I've borne many tragedies—hardships and death have been a part of my life. But this—*this,* I cannot bear . . . I can't! Why must God ask it of me? Why must He ask it of you?"

He embraced her with hard arms and bent his head to kiss her warm, swollen mouth, his every movement frantic and rough with the knowledge of their impending parting. "I love you, Lark," he breathed, putting his cheek against her own. "Remember that. No matter who you believe I am, or what you may discover about me in days to come, know that I've always loved you."

She raised upon her toes to kiss him feverishly then, uncaring of his crimes, his politics, his class, wanting only to be close, to hold on to his solid, beloved flesh. With no less desolation and urgency than she displayed, Christopher ran his hands over Lark's slender body as if to remember its essence. Backing her to the stained plaster wall, he pressed himself more determinedly against her, intent, she was certain, upon their enjoying one last time the full pleasure of their marriage. He began to touch her with possessive male purpose, pushing aside her clothing with rough, frantic hands.

But the sound of a key scraping the lock told them their time had flown.

"Step out, please, madam," the gaoler commanded, watching their farewell with a lewd, slowly spreading smile.

Weeping, pushing down her skirts, Lark made to draw away, but Christopher held on to her, speaking low. "Have you returned to Henrietta Street?"

She nodded, white-faced, on the verge of hysteria.

"Do you know where Sebastian is?"

"H-he's moved into the house—"

"My God, he has not!"

The gaoler raised his voice. "Out with ye, madam. Now!"

She stood frozen, torn.

The warden made a threatening move with his club. "For every minute ye delay, lass, His Lordship here will pay with more of them red badges upon his hide."

With a sob, her swimming eyes affixed in anguish to her husband, Lark moved numbly to obey.

But Christopher caught her sleeve, jerked her back. "Swear to me you'll stay away from my brother. Sebastian O'Keefe is a British agent. He'll do anything to get the date—*the date*, Lark," he emphasized through his teeth, putting his back to the turnkey. Do you understand what I'm saying?"

She had no time to reply. With one quick swing of his club, the burly warden struck Christopher a blow to the head.

As the devil yanked Lark out the door, she caught only one last, harrowing glimpse of her husband's form, slumped over the cold stone floor. To her ears, the snap of the twisting key in the cell door echoed the twisting of her own heart. She shrieked Christopher's name.

But the sound went unanswered, reverberating like a ghostly wail through a multitude of moldering, forgotten corridors before being lost as a sigh.

23

Shuffling into the house on numb legs, Lark was barely conscious of the mute servant who obediently glided out of some corner to take her cloak; she wanted only to seek solitude in her chamber.

"Why, Lark! You look nearly on the verge of collapse."

She almost started out of her skin at the low, smooth voice. Turning round, she found Sebastian standing behind her, his obsidian eyes taking in every aspect of her bedraggled appearance.

"Kilmainham is a ghastly place, isn't it?" he asked knowingly. "Sobering."

She nodded, tiredly dragging the hat from her head, its now limp feathers reminding her morbidly of the bird made to sacrifice its life for a frippery. Her eyes ached from weeping, and she was still so distraught that they threatened at any moment to start afresh with their endless supply of tears.

"Come," Sebastian said in a sympathetic tone,

touching her elbow with a cool hand. "Take some sherry and then dine with me."

"Nay," she said, shaking her head and turning to the stairs. She could scarcely abide Sebastian's touch now that she knew who and what he really was, could hardly believe she had let him deceive her. To think she had actually contemplated marriage to the imposter!

She remembered Christopher's warning words. Had Sebastian ever cared for her at all, or had he merely hung around her simply because he suspected her involvement with the underground and wanted to use her? Obviously his jaunts around the cotters' cabins in his tinker's costume had been no more than a piece of cunning dupery. He was a British agent! To her mind, such an occupation put him barely above the status of a snake, and she despised him.

But she would respect him just as she would any reptile, by giving him a wide berth and being on her guard. As soon as Christopher's trial was over, she would slip away from O'Keefe's treacherous fangs and find safer lodging elsewhere.

Sebastian reached out to capture her arm and stroked it, seeming not to notice that she shuddered beneath the touch. "Of course you must continue to stay on here, Lark," he said as if reading her thoughts. "I shall be in residence myself for a time, trying to tie up loose ends. I've at least managed to banish that wretched lot of ragged people from queuing up for my brother's medical charity." He snorted. "I fear his days of wielding a scalpel are over."

Sickened by his pronouncement of doom, and with the picture of Christopher's slumped figure on his cell floor still unbearably vivid, Lark started up the stairs. Determinedly she pulled away from O'Keefe's persistent hold, not bothering to hide a sneer of utter distaste.

"They'll hang him, you know!" he called after her, his anger obviously piqued over her rebuff. "They'll hang him within the week."

After enduring a dreadful night of anxiety, during which she slept only one hour, and that hour fraught with gruesome nightmares of dangling ropes and rough-hewn gibbets, Lark dressed herself at dawn. Refusing breakfast, she concealed in a silken bag yet another of the elegant chamber's treasures—this time the silver thimble collection—then bit color into her pale lips and hurried down the stairs.

Her thoughts were so fixed upon arranging another visit to Christopher that she scarcely heard the sound of quarreling voices emanating faintly from the drawing room. But as their tones grew particularly contentious, grating upon her stretched nerves, she slowed her step with sudden indecision. She had learned that eavesdropping could provide useful information if one were patient and clever enough at it. Wanting very much to know Sebastian's plans, she hovered near the closed doors for a moment, pretending to have dropped a glove should anyone notice her loitering.

The conversation within grew sporadic, punctuated with long silences, and for a spell she could glean not a syllable of dialogue. Finally, from an unknown voice she caught a few harshly spoken snatches: "I'm growing impatient . . . the time is near at hand." But she could make no particular sense of them.

Just then Sebastian's voice bellowed, its angry tones clearly penetrating the thick mahogany panel, "I got *him* out of the way, didn't I? One of the biggest catches in the whole damned organization! That should be worth something!"

The words were accompanied by the hard rap of heels, and though Lark scurried out of the way, she barely avoided a collision with the door as it was shoved open violently.

His face livid, Sebastian barreled through, catching sight of Lark just as she bent to retrieve her artfully dropped glove. He leaned to snatch it up ahead of her, his flashing eyes pinned suspiciously to her face.

"On your way out?" he inquired.

She noted he had abandoned his rough corduroys for more flamboyant attire. In a gold, close-fitting spencer coat with a stand-fall collar, high white stock, and pantaloon-style breeches, he was the image of a dandy. Even his unruly hair was tied back in a queue, and the scent of expensive soap wafted from his person.

Surreptitiously Lark glanced behind him, noting that the other occupant of the drawing room showed no signs of emerging. All she could see of him was a garish, bejeweled walking stick of the type Dublin bucks often brandished, lying upon an empty chair in clear view.

"On your way to gaol again?" Sebastian asked when she ignored his first question.

Lifting her chin, she replied in the affirmative, trying to hide her fear of him. He seemed to be commandeering the house, crowding out Christopher's lingering presence. What did the exchange between

the two men in the drawing room signify? She began
to suspect that Sebastian himself had placed the
incriminating documents in his brother's desk, that
he had deliberately sent Christopher to prison and
put him at the mercy of the hangman.

"There's no need for you to hire a coach," he was
saying now, searching her pale face. "My brother's
carriage is at your disposal. Indeed, I anticipated your
going out this morning and have ordered it ready.
You'll find it waiting."

She managed a murmur of gratitude and hastened
out the door, wanting only to escape the tinker's
sharp gaze.

Though the servants in Christopher's employ were
too well trained to utter a skeptical word or even to
give her a questioning glance, she sensed the driver's
chagrin when she announced her unusual destination.
Later, while she was inside a musty-smelling shop
haggling with the pawnbroker, she noticed one of the
postilions lounging near the dingy bow window, slyly
watching her exchange with the proprietor. With sudden suspicion, she wondered if every move she made,
every place she visited today, would be duly noted
and, for a discreet reward, reported later to the tinker-
turned-gentleman in Henrietta Street.

Hastily completing her business at the pawnshop,
she returned to the carriage and gave the wolf-faced
postilion a hard glance as he lowered the step, leaving
him no doubt that his indiscretion had been noticed.
As the coach plunged forward, she clutched her purse
of coins even more uneasily than she had the previous
day, beset by sudden misgivings.

Her disquiet proved well founded a few minutes later
at Kilmainham, when she discovered Christopher's

prediction woefully true. No amount of money, no amount of pleading or tears, could induce the gaoler to permit another visit. She even demanded an interview with the Deputy Governor, stamping an emphatic foot and shouting so defiantly that her voice echoed through the cold dark corridors. But that haughty personage refused outright to hear her anguished appeal.

Two guards escorted her outside, entrusting her with stern words to the postilion waiting smugly beside the carriage. Disdaining the fellow's aid, Lark gathered her skirts and stumbled inside the vehicle, nearly crazed with her need to see Christopher again before his trial. She gazed up at the impervious facade of the jail, at its rows of little barred windows, wondering if her husband could see her and understand that she had tried her best to arrange a visit.

Feeling forlorn and in need of comforting arms, Lark ordered the driver to take her directly to her brother's academy, where she implored the priggish headmaster to allow Jamie a few hours out.

Her brother's unrestrained flight into her arms and his cheerful greeting did much to raise her spirits. She was relieved to hear him express happiness with the school, whose discipline and routine had already changed his manner. He was more dignified and proud in his somber academy attire, she noted, and more mature in his conversation. But his red hair still stood on end as in the cottage days, at least, and the freckles across his nose had not vanished in the long hours of indoor study.

The two of them strolled in the vapid winter light of Phoenix Park, and then with a wicked smile Lark sent the hovering, sharp-eyed postilion to fetch them a luncheon of cheese and bread.

Though she tried to be attentive, thoughts of Christopher crowded her mind, and Lark listened with only half an ear to Jamie's chatter about life at school, about his studies and his new friends. When lunch arrived she ate silently while he went on about his Latin classes and a garrulous pal named Edward.

"I've been wondering," Jamie began between mouthfuls. Huddling down into his new tweed coat, he crumbled a piece of his bread and tossed it out to the gathering birds.

"What is it, pet?"

A dry tuft of grass sprouted beneath the bench, and he swung his short legs, kicking at it with the toe of his shoe. "The other boys have been talking," he imparted a bit reluctantly. "Whispering together, saying things about Lord Glassmeade—dreadful things."

Lark tensed, struggling to keep her tone calm. "What sorts of dreadful things?"

He looked up at her with anxious green eyes. "They say he's going to be hanged by his neck for being a traitor to Ireland. I said it was a cockeyed lie. I'm right, aren't I?" he added, his bravado turning quickly to uncertainty.

Taking a ragged breath, Lark glanced away, staring at the trees over her head, whose leafless branches clacked like brittle bones with each tiny puff of wind. Winter had crept forward to breathe its frosty breath, but she had hardly realized it until now. In the last days she had forgotten the seasons, the signals and changing of nature she had once so closely marked and enjoyed.

"I don't believe Lord Glassmeade is a traitor to his country, Jamie. I'm certain he only wants what's best for Ireland. But . . ." She faltered, her face twisting with the pangs of heartache. "But, about the . . . sentence. I fear it might indeed come to pass." She almost whispered the words, as if saying them too loudly would somehow seal Christopher's terrible fate.

The horror of his benefactor's hanging seemed to dawn fully upon Jamie, for his face paled in dread. He curled his small gloved fists so forcefully that an impassioned glow began to suffuse his cheeks, hiding the freckles. "It isn't fair!" he blurted with a vehement cry. "They should hang the tinker instead!"

"Jamie!" Lark exclaimed, appalled by his outburst. "What in heaven's name are you saying?"

"I'm sayin' Mister O'Keefe should be hanged for what he did to Uncle Jerome. After all, that's a great deal worse than bein' a traitor, isn't it?"

Lark took his small chin between her fingers and stared intently into her brother's tearful eyes. "What did Mister O'Keefe do to Uncle Jerome?"

Though the lad clenched his jaw, his lower lip began to quiver, and he looked at her imploringly. "I don't know why I haven't told you before," he said in a small, miserable voice. "I—it's been . . . locked up, I think. Locked up inside my head."

"What, Jamie? *What?*"

"Just that I saw Mister O'Keefe in our cabin . . . that night. I was in the loft, supposed to be asleep— you remember, don't you? I had a cough and you gave me a dose of something. But I never swallowed it. When you turned your back, I spat it out."

She nodded impatiently. "Aye, aye?"

"Well, I heard Mister O'Keefe shouting at Uncle, asking him questions. I—I peeked down, watched them start to fight. They circled each other like the fighters at Donnybrook Fair. Once or twice they landed punches. Then . . . then Mister O'Keefe put his hands about Uncle's neck and held on and held on until he couldn't breathe anymore. You know," he quavered, "like some of the cotters do to kittens they don't want."

"Mother of God." Lark barely mouthed the words, horrified at this sudden, devastating revelation. Her eyes remained affixed to her brother's chalk white face, as if to verify the truth of what he had said.

"When Uncle fell to the floor," Jamie went on, "Mister O'Keefe ran out of the cabin. But a few minutes later Lord Glassmeade came burstin' in. 'Course, I didn't *know* it was Lord Glassmeade, then. But I saw him kneel down and shake Uncle, to see if he was still alive. But he wasn't." Jamie shook his head mournfully. "Mister O'Keefe had killed him too good."

Lark wept bitterly that night. By dawn she was exhausted, nearly prostrate with heartsickness. Her head ached with churning thoughts of her own betrayal. What a faithless wretch she was! Like some self-appointed judge, she had stood in Christopher's prison cell and accused *him,* the compassionate surgeon, her beloved husband, of murder. How could she not have sensed the truth? How could she have believed those fine, sensitive hands capable of mercilessly squeezing life out of an innocent man, when they had ministered to so many others and loved her own flesh so well?

Not even the ready excuses of the earl's habitual secrecy could soothe her or make her unrelenting self-condemnation any less harsh. Most grievous of all, in a few hours Christopher would be tried and sentenced in Dublin Castle, and by all accounts, if one could believe the papers, hanging was indeed to be his fate.

And what of the real murderer . . . what of Sebastian O'Keefe?

Throughout the night Lark had kept her door bolted securely, fearful of his intrusion, his ruthless purpose. She wondered if he meant to kill her, had been stalking her all along.

At dawn she dressed herself mechanically, declining the aid of Grindle's bony hands, choosing a gown of brightest emerald—emerald for Ireland's hope. She prayed Christopher would see her wearing it at the trial. Since he was to die for Ireland, this would be her meager tribute to him, the only signal she could devise to show support.

She could scarcely grasp the concept of his death, its finality, or the emptiness that would mark her world once he had departed it. She was only now beginning to realize just how much he had risked to take her into his home, tend her, protect her so vigilantly . . . love her. And he had risked even more to make her his countess.

What had she done for him?

She stared at her elegantly garbed image in the mirror, seeing in the silver reflection the rich furnishings behind her. In the most astounding irony, she had become a part of this setting through legal entitlement. Through her marriage to the Earl of Glassmeade, she now belonged here in the sumptuous house on Henrietta Street—in one sense, at least. And she was strangely proud—not smug over the gaining of a title or wealth, but proud to have had

Christopher's love. Was that pride unconscionable? Had she betrayed herself by it, or Virgil, or her Catholic countrymen?

She did not know. But in spite of her marriage to an aristocrat and the acquiring of her new identity, she was still a cotter's girl at heart and always would be. She had not forgotten the people of her past, or the gathering French forces . . . or the agent beneath the Faery Thorn. They had never been far from her thoughts, and countess or not, she would not abandon their ranks.

When she ascended the magnificent staircase a moment later, a servant moved to open the enameled front door on its well-oiled hinges. Even in her grief she almost smiled, wondering what thoughts tumbled about in the mind of the man wearing his ornate gold-braided uniform and powdered wig.

There goes Lord Glassmeade's peasant whore, all trussed up in her finery, brazenly making use of the house with the master in gaol, just as if she had a right to it.

What would he think if he really knew?

Outside, much to her dismay, the carriage awaited as it had done the day previous. Sebastian was nowhere to be seen on this morning of his brother's trial, but she was certain that her movements were being monitored.

She could not allow the watching eyes of these men to follow her today, however, not under any circumstances. But what could she do? She could hardly dismiss them and then hail a hired coach without rousing considerable suspicion. Likely one of them would only trail behind her anyway, then report his findings to Sebastian for a handsome token later.

Barely missing a beat, she proceeded forward and settled herself in the carriage with a queenly air, as if enjoying the accommodation. She ordered the straight-faced coachman to take her to Capel Street, giving him the name of a stationer's shop there that she knew to be a block or so from Lottery Hall.

When she entered the small, stuffy establishment with its fawning clerk, she inquired discreetly if there was a back entrance, explaining in hushed tones that an obnoxious gentleman whom she wished to escape was pestering her on the street.

With a gallant bow, the little clerk spirited her out the rear, promising heroically to deter the trouble-some fellow should he dare to enter the shop.

Then she made her way slowly through the impor-tunate, suffocating crowd straining into Lottery Hall, Lark at last pushed through to the garish green-and-gold building with its shimmering chandeliers. She was nearly bowled over in the press, as scores of wagerers vied for space, shoving and cursing, some clutching tickets bought with their last coin, others gambling sportively as a balm for boredom.

Using her shoulder to make a path through the boisterous wagerers, Lark struggled to the rear office, where, with a sigh of thankfulness, she found Peader sitting behind his desk. When he glanced up and saw her, his harried young face expressed both profound relief and considerable agitation. Quickly, putting a finger to his lips to indicate silence, he came around behind her and shut the door.

"Thank God you have come!" he said in a shrill whisper. Taking her by the arm, he steered her out of sight of the two vertical windows on either side of the office door. His voice was charged with excitement. "I have news. The French forces have slipped past the British naval blockade at the port of Brest!"

Lark gasped and clutched his hands.

"Aye," Peader went on, his round gray eyes intent. "They should land at Bantry Bay the day after tomorrow—thirty-five ships carrying twelve thousand troops with General Hoche at the helm, and Tone himself on board the flagship."

"My heavens, Peader," Lark said, momentarily awestruck by the glorious information. Her elation was tempered only by the knowledge that bloodshed and turmoil would precede victory. "Revolution is really at hand, then."

"Very close at hand. Virgil says you are to inform your agent as soon as possible. He, in turn, will report directly to Harvey so that his command can be mobilized according to plan. There are others in our brotherhood who have also received this news, but only a few. As you would imagine, notice of the landing is being channeled very carefully. We cannot have word leak out. Surprising the British troops is paramount to our success."

"I understand," Lark replied solemnly. "Is there anything else?"

"Nay. Except you should take particular care of yourself." Cocking his head to the side, he hesitated. "And, your eyes?"

Lark smiled, though the corners of her mouth felt strained with both the ever-present worry over Christopher's fate and, now, the weight of the knowledge she carried. "You may tell Virgil I can't wait to see him again."

When she reemerged onto Capel Street a moment later, Lark took care to keep herself hidden, crouching with thumping heart behind two hatted men when she glimpsed the Cavanaugh carriage crawling along the avenue. Obviously, her absence from the stationer's had been noted, and the driver had begun to search for her along the street.

Trying not to call attention to herself, she moved along beside a group of half-drunk sailors, then sped across the street in the wake of a coach and six. When she had traveled two blocks, dodging squatting bootblacks and bickering shoppers, she halted, scanning the corners for transportation to hire. She could have stopped any number of sedan chairs or noddies, but she needed a closed vehicle to provide concealment, so she stepped back in the shade of a building and waited until a coach lumbered down the street. Then she dashed out and hailed the master, ignoring his speculative glance when he realized his lady passenger was to travel unchaperoned.

"Take me to James Street!" Lark ordered breathlessly.

As soon as the driver had closed the battered door, she settled herself in a corner, pulled down the water-stained shade, and retrieved a scented sachet from the lining of her bodice. After ripping the stitching down one side, she shook a coin from the perfumed folds and clutched it tightly in her fingers. It was gold, antique and imprinted with a snarling lion. She recalled clearly the dark hand that had passed it to her, and restlessly rubbed a thumb across its worn, tarnished face, realizing she would likely never again see the mysterious Faery Thorn agent after their rendezvous tonight.

The team of horses must have been an ancient pair, for they seemed to progress at a crawl, picking their way through traffic and balking at every intersection. Lark fretted, acutely aware of the passage of time and knowing that less than an hour remained before Christopher's trial. She yearned to take charge of the plodding horses herself and whip the poor beasts into a faster pace.

At last the coach drew up before Alabar's establishment, an unobtrusive structure, and she climbed out. When she neared the small arched doorway, the pungent scent of smoke pricked her nostrils, the same exotic odor that brought vividly to mind her last visit there.

After making certain no polished black carriage sporting the Cavanaugh insignia was around, Lark slipped inside. Adjusting her still unpredictable vision in the pervading, hazy gloom, she could just make out a scarred counter of umber wood flanked by dusky shelves arrayed with colored bottles. For a moment she could see no sign of life in the cramped space, and she nearly panicked, fearful that the phantom agent's liaison would not appear to take her urgent message.

But at last, from behind a tapestry curtain, a shadowy figure emerged. He was turbaned and dark of skin.

Although Alabar offered no greeting, Lark approached the counter, where she discreetly slid a gloved hand over the worn, darkly varnished wood. The coin she kept concealed in the cradle of her palm.

When the inscrutable Alabar stepped forward out of the dimness, she noticed that a small tattoo of indeterminate inscription marked his forehead. Slowly Lark drew back her hand, leaving the coin on the oily, fingerprinted surface of the counter.

The sight of it caused not even a muscle to twitch upon Alabar's impassive face as he picked it up. She thought he must have concealed it in his coat with some sleight of hand, for when he folded his fingers together upon the counter a second later, there was no sign of it.

"You have a message?" he inquired. His voice was as toneless as she recalled.

She glanced over her shoulder to reassure herself no one else lurked in the shadows, and then met the eyes of the foreigner and nodded. "The coin is his signal to meet me posthaste. Tell him to meet me tonight . . . without fail."

At her request, some distinct reaction caused Alabar's eyes to flicker strangely, as if with unease or even alarm. Yet whatever emotion affected him, he chose not to reveal it to Lark, but merely bowed deferentially in dismissal of her.

Vaguely disquieted, Lark left the shop and promised the indolent driver of the coach double his fare if he would deliver her to Dublin Castle before the striking of the hour. He earned it, or rather the poor beasts harnessed between the shafts did. But little good did it do Lark in the end.

The cruel-eyed guards patrolling the formidable stone fortress where the Earl of Glassmeade was shortly to learn his fate flatly refused to grant her entry to the trial.

24

"Your Lordship! Your Lordship!" Frantically Lark shook the frail, velvet-clad shoulders slumped on the leather wing chair.

His sparse gray lashes fluttered, revealing his red-rimmed eyes. Above them, the old one's high forehead looked as pale and fragile as eggshell, but hardly lined.

Straightening abruptly, the marquess cleared his throat, his withered Adam's apple bobbing up and down above his loosened white stock. "Hem . . . what is it? What is it, for heaven's sake?"

His gaze focused upon Lark's face, and she knelt down at his side, impulsively grasping his knotted fingers and squeezing them. "Your son is to be tried in a quarter hour!" she said urgently. "Had you forgotten? You must go, he will be watching for you, he will need to see you there. And, please, take me with you! The guards won't even let me through the gates on my own!"

For a moment, the marquess regarded her curiously. He frowned, appearing bemused. "Do you believe there is a hell?" he asked abruptly, shocking her with the question. "I was just dreaming about such a place . . . most unpleasant, most unpleasant."

Taken aback, Lark stared at him, praying he was not suffering from one of his abstracted spells. "I—I don't know, but—"

"But what do you *believe?*" he demanded cantankerously.

If she could not convince the marquess to depart with her in the next few minutes, she would miss the trial. And Christopher had to see her there, to know that she would support him through her presence.

"I believe the soul is a constant thing," she answered hastily, searching for simple words to explain a most complex notion. "Eternal, forever enduring."

"That does not answer my question," he announced with a testy scowl. "Do you believe that those men whose deeds are found by some higher being to be unworthy—even wicked—suffer forever in some underworld, some Hades furnished with fire and brimstone?"

"I believe in Paradise, Your Lordship," Lark replied directly. "And it seems to me that everything has an opposite."

He sat back and contemplated her as one would a conundrum, his ample brows drawing together as if her identity were just occurring to him.

"Please, Your Lordship!" Lark entreated again. "Christopher should not be facing his judgment alone, without his own sire near. 'Tis cruel."

"Of course 'tis cruel. But I warned him, didn't I? And still he disgraced me, put a stain upon our family name that will never be lived down." He shook his head and fell back into the depths of the chair. "I can do nothing to help him now. 'Twould do no good for me to go. He's got himself into this sorry state of affairs by being undutiful to all I hold dear."

"He's still a son to be proud of!" Lark countered, uncaring that she overstepped bounds. "Regardless of his politics, he's deserving of his father's support."

"You dare to reprimand me, young woman?"

"He is of your flesh," Lark continued. "You cannot abandon him. His mother would never countenance it. Were she alive, she would be at Dublin Castle with him now, I am sure!"

This last persuasion had come to her impulsively, as if that dead presence from the chamber upstairs had suddenly materialized at her side and whispered the sentiment.

It hit its mark.

The marquess's hands clenched upon the chair arms. For a moment he closed his translucent eyelids, muttering, "A man should not have to witness his son's disgrace. . . ."

"A son should not have to endure alone a judgment upon his life."

A spell of silence followed her remark, and Lark held her breath.

At last the marquess grumbled, "Well, then, dammit, why do you dally? Get me my walking stick."

She scrambled to her feet and snatched a cane that was propped beside the hearth.

"Not *that* one!" He rose out of the chair as if some surge of strength had suddenly energized him. "The gold-headed one by the door—there. I swear I don't know what the world is coming to," he complained, stumping crookedly across the threshold with Lark trotting at his elbow. "A peasant lass dressed up in a lady's garb, daring to tell *me* what I ought to do with myself!"

Lord Glassmeade was to be tried by his peers. However, due to the publicity of his case and the large number of lords and ladies clamoring to attend, the trial was scheduled for hearing not in the House of Lords, but in the more commodious House of Commons. Lark entered the imposing structure at the marquess's side, immediately awed by the sight of such palatial splendor. But even more amazing was the crowd of hundreds of venerable spectators, seated in order according to social position. Lining the galleries were the commons and their families, while the first rows were occupied by fashionable ladies of rank, with a special compartment festooned in red drapery designated for peeresses and their daughters.

"I'll not sit in that suffocating hole," the marquess said as a sentry attempted to escort him forward into a special box. Belabored from the climb up, the old man seemed alarmingly pale and winded. "Fetch me a chair! I shall sit here near the passageway where there's a breath of air."

The sentry obliged and afterward would have directed Lark into the commons seating, had not the marquess stayed him with a barked command. "She shall remain beside me."

Giving Lark an appraising glance, and obviously assuming her the old lord's mistress, the young guard nodded and stepped aside.

With her stomach churning in dread of the ordeal that she knew could lead to the end of Christopher's life, she strained forward, craning her neck to see

over the elaborately coiffed heads. She yearned for
sight of him, for just one opportunity to make her
presence known, for it was vital to her that her husband realize he was not alone.

Overwhelmed with apprehension, Lark scanned
the scene, wide-eyed. The entire house was richly car-
peted, and below, she saw the Speaker's chair elaborately adorned to receive the esteemed backside of
the Lord Chancellor.

There came a murmur of voices all at once, and col-
lectively the spectators leaned forward to view the
unfolding drama. In a stately procession, the Peers
filed in according to their rank, each bewigged and
draped in full ceremonial dress, their rich robes
rustling. Frantically Lark studied each of the lordly
miens—the ruddy, heavily jowled ones, those thinly
fleshed, and those florid with dissipation. These men
were to judge the life of her beloved, decide if he
should lose his head for acts against their government.
With dismay, she realized none of them appeared to
have the soft mark of mercy upon their faces.

Fear squeezed her chest as each in turn took his seat
in the most grave ceremony. The Chancellor carried a
white wand, wielding it majestically as a king would
flaunt a jeweled scepter. The next character to enter
was the king at arms, carrying the armorial bearing of
the accused nobleman emblazoned upon a gleaming
shield. At long last, then, the accused was called to
come forth. A weighty silence followed. Lark put a
hand to her throat, her lungs suddenly devoid of air.

He was dressed in most sombrous black, the dark
attire setting off his golden good looks to great effect,
emphasizing the muscular neatness of his physique,
the leanness and height of his elegant frame. Though

the strain of adversity had etched lines about his mouth and eyes, his countenance still maintained its stamp of unvanquished dignity. Even the purpling bruises on his jaw failed to dim the lure of his handsomeness. He stood head and shoulders above all others, and every female in the gallery seemed to release a wistful sigh at once. Some dabbed at dewy eyes, as if the tragedy of such a dazzling man's fall from grace touched them with more than a little force.

Icarus, Lark thought . . . the god in Jamie's borrowed picture book. She remembered well the faded etching of the hero tumbling helplessly from the azure heavens, his glorious wings melting from his bold venture too near the sun. . . .

With calm arrogance, his eyes cold with challenge, the Earl of Glassmeade took his place beside the king at arms. And then, in an appalling moment Lark would never be able to erase from memory, an executioner entered the arena with a monstrous hatchet, its broad blade painted black, all except for a two-inch strip along the wicked edge. Light glanced off its polished steel and winked sharply at the mesmerized spectators.

The terrifying headman positioned himself at the bar, on the right of the prisoner, and in a ghastly show of ceremony, he lifted the blade to the level of Christopher's neck, making a show of aiming the awful blade edge away from the prisoner.

The marquess leaned close to Lark and said, "If my son is found guilty, the blade will be turned toward him . . . as a symbol of his imminent execution."

Lark froze, horrified. This spine-chilling spectacle, blended with the odors of countless sweating bodies and cloying perfumes, nearly overcame her. "Christopher," she breathed, rising to her feet in an unconscious gesture of desperation.

Although she was far in the back, nearly concealed by curled wigs and colored hat feathers, her movement caught Christopher's attention, and his gaze fastened upon her face. For an incalculable time their eyes communicated, and she had to check a violent impulse to run forward and cry out his name. During those few, aching seconds, she fervently wished them both far away, out of the realm of politics and armies, out of the reach of judges, safe from the waiting scimitar of death poised at his neck. At the same time she attempted to convey her love to him, her sorrow and regret.

She did not know if he understood, for although his eyes were bright and penetrating, she found not a flicker of readable emotion in them.

As their gazes broke, Lark spotted Sebastian O'Keefe sliding onto a seat in the crowded gallery. His black eyes immediately located her stricken face, and a slow, spiteful smile crossed his face. She turned away in disgust, but his laughter seemed to float upon the stifling air to find her ears.

The legal proceedings commenced, with the charge against the young earl read aloud in stentorian tones. Witnesses were called up. The first one, Lark noticed with dismay, was Christopher's own valet, O'Neal. His testimony proved damning.

"My son," the marquess breathed beside her in a quavery voice. He shook his head. "Those bastards . . . they have stacked the deck against him." He gripped Lark's wrist, his touch conveying his despair.

She stared at his sorrow-glazed eyes and grew more benumbed than ever with increasing fear. Only his tenacious grip upon her arm, his brittle nails biting into the tender flesh beneath her cuff, kept her conscious.

Again she fixed her gaze upon the stalwart figure of her husband. The blade still threatened his head, but he stood expressionless before his peers, before the hundreds of other Dubliners watching like eager vultures. Lark suspected many of them claimed to be his friends, and she wondered how true they would be at the close of the day.

"They will surely execute him," the marquess said, closing his eyes briefly. "They will make an example of him."

At his repeated prediction of doom, the blood began to pound in Lark's ears, creating such a dull roar that she put her hands to her temples in anguish. She wondered if she would be permitted to see her husband before he was marched to the gallows, wondered if the two of them would be permitted even a few brief moments alone. Perhaps not. Perhaps these distant, inadequate glimpses across a sea of powdered heads would be the last ones granted.

In that moment, while the voices of his prosecutors droned on, condemning him, Lark was struck by a swift impulse to dash toward the gallery rail in her bright emerald gown, raise up her arms, and in a loud shout proclaim herself a traitor to Ireland's government, no less guilty in her deeds than the charged prisoner. Gladly would she have traded places with him, been hanged and beheaded in Christopher's stead, rather than leave him to endure the ordeal alone . . . rather than be the one left behind.

She despaired that these pompous figureheads could be allowed to decide her lover's fate, that they had the right to strip his life from him. Who were they to decide? Wasn't his spirit of far greater value than any set of rules men created? Generals and kings spent their lives plotting and killing to preserve governments that would simply pass from the earth in time, end up no more than words in history annals. How much more significant was a life—a son's life, a husband's life. Was it not sacred to God and angels, far above the foolish dictates of man?

She glanced again at Christopher's golden head, agleam with a single shaft of light, the same light that sparked off the blade poised above it. And in that moment an idea began to take shape in her brain.

Indeed, she grew so dizzy with the sudden shattering thought that the vast rotunda seemed to spin around her. In that whirling moment, she realized that the power to save her lover's life rested in her own small hands. That power was in a simple piece of knowledge, a few words needing only to be spoken aloud to an eager ear. A brief exchange, no more. To share it was to spare Christopher's life; to keep it silent was to risk his death.

She never stopped to consider that the one she would save would never condone the price of his rescue. She never stopped to allow the terrible consequences to sway her purpose, and consequences there would be, indeed. She would suffer them later—perhaps with her life.

After laying a quivering hand upon the marquess's shoulder, she moved into the passageway and leaned to speak a few low words in the sentry's ear. Nodding expressionlessly, he left her and returned a few moments later to bid her accompany him.

Before long, following his uniformed back, she found herself in a courtyard, standing alone upon moss-edged cobbles, surrounded by the stone walls of Dublin Castle. The bleak enclosure stood mute and empty, a place of many ghosts, while the wind eddied at her feet, creating a miniature maelstrom of swirling dust and leaves until she had to put an arm to her eyes to shield them.

"Quite a ghoulish picture in there, eh?" a familiar voice asked. "An ax threatening the poor sod's head."

Lowering her arm, Lark stared with hatred at the dark, cunning face of Sebastian O'Keefe. Though she was about to commit an act that would affect countless lives and brand her with infamy— or even demand a greater sacrifice—she stood straight and resolute. The frigid wind whipped her skirts, penetrating the green velvet gown, but she neither shivered nor cringed. Without preamble she said to him, "I am prepared to give you the information you have so mercilessly sought to obtain from me."

O'Keefe raised an interested brow, then smiled with satisfaction. "I thought you might."

"You'll get it for nothing less than Christopher's life."

Sebastian shrugged. "A small price, really."

"Do you have the influence to arrange it?"

He regarded her speculatively for a moment, as if assessing her sincerity. "That depends. Do you have both the date and the landing site?"

She nodded.

He laughed then, threw back his head and crowed with triumph, the sound reverberating off the hoary fortress walls. "My God! This has worked out well for me—your infatuation with my dear brother, I mean. It could not have evolved more perfectly had I designed it this way from the start. I had planned to wed you so I could better monitor your activities, or persuade you to trust me with your secrets. But this was far more satisfying than the alternative."

Lark spoke curtly, wanting to hear no more of his gloating. "Christopher must not be executed, no matter the outcome of the trial. I will require a letter from the Viceroy himself, with his seal upon it. He must guarantee my own immunity from prosecution as well. Once I've the document in hand . . ." She paused and gritted her teeth as she uttered the critical words. "I will tell you what you want to know."

Sebastian cocked his head to one side. "I believe the Viceroy will agree to those terms. But you must understand my own terms as well. If your information proves false, if you make a fool of me . . . you will not live to see out the day."

"The information will not prove false."

"Well, we shall see, shan't we?" He motioned her inside.

Nauseated by the entire exchange and by Sebastian's smug presence, Lark swept past him and followed the sentry back to her place beside the marquess. Every nerve in her body quivered over the significance of what she had just accomplished, and she prayed she could reach her seat before her legs gave way beneath her, before the pounding in her temples made her scream. Once there, she eased down, her hands shaking so violently that she had to clasp them tightly in her lap. Closing her eyes in anguish, she breathed deeply to keep herself from swaying on the chair.

In exchange for my husband's life I have jeopardized the cause of the Irish brotherhood. I have sold their secret.

The words echoed in her brain like the damning voices of a thousand Irishmen. She was a traitor twice over. Initially she had betrayed the English government with her rebel involvement; now she had imperiled the carefully laid plans of many shrewd minds in both Ireland and France. She had disgraced the Cause, sacrificed her integrity, and failed her brother . . . and the agent beneath the trysting moon.

Desperately she turned her eyes to Christopher.

He sat impassively, listening to the mounting evidence against him with an air of near unconcern, his face showing neither chagrin nor rebuke toward those once trusted friends who now condemned his actions.

The hours dragged on, tormentingly, exhaustingly. No one abandoned the airless gallery, but waited with wide eyes and bated breath for the final verdict. Next to Lark, the marquess remained mute, holding his old, lionlike head with pride, even when surreptitious eyes turned his way to gloat over the piece of dirty laundry being aired in such a public fashion. Finally, as early eve tinted the windows gray, the testimonies ended and the Chancellor solemnly requested a decision from the Peers.

The hush around the rotunda was profound, with every ear attuned to the dramatic moment. Lark's heart thumped so hard, she feared she would collapse. Instinctively she reached out icy fingers to find the marquess's clenched hand. Cool and dry, it returned her desperate grasp unsteadily.

Below them, according to rank, every Peer rose from his seat. The first stepped before the Chancellor, placed a hand solemnly over his heart, and proclaimed, "Not guilty, upon my honor!"

Gasps could be heard all around. Lark put a hand

to her throat, thinking she had misunderstood the proclamation. Yet a buzz of whispering voices circled the gallery, confirming her own surprise, then quieted abruptly as the second Peer approached the Chancellor.

"Not guilty, upon my honor!"

Lark rose, triumph and disbelief flooding her senses. She strained over the bobbing heads of the stunned audience, searching for a glimpse of Christopher's face in the scene. At last she was able to sight him, expecting to see his face flushed with surprise, and saw instead that it was as calmly inscrutable as it had been throughout the trial.

After the fourth Peer had echoed the decision of his predecessors, Lark sank back onto her seat, giddy with relief yet bewildered by the unexpected turn of events. How had Sebastian been able to arrange the innocent verdict so expediently? She had expected a guilty sentence today and a stay of execution tomorrow. . . .

Amidst the excited hum, she only dimly heard the marquess's incredulous voice. "'Tis not possible! 'Tis glorious, but impossible. . . ."

After the last Peer had declared the innocence of the Earl of Glassmeade, the Chancellor rose and in a resounding voice proclaimed, "It is the opinion of the Peers of Ireland that Christopher Cavanaugh, Earl of Glassmeade, is *not guilty* of the charge made against him!"

He broke the white wand in half with one swift snap and then descended from his dais and sailed out of the rotunda.

Every spectator surged to his feet. The hubbub of clamorous voices grew almost deafening. Lark struggled to see Christopher, but just before she could press forward against the crowd, her arms were seized, and the sentry who had hovered near her side throughout the trial dragged her backward.

Without uttering a word he hauled her away from the marquess, propelling her briskly down the passageway until she pleaded with him to ease his crushing grip upon her arms. Ignoring her, he shoved her into a small anteroom, where she stumbled forward and found Sebastian O'Keefe lounging placidly beside a fireplace.

Upon seeing her, his face lit up, and he ordered the sentry to wait in the passageway. He strolled close to her, assessing her flushed face and disheveled hair and smiling with mock politeness. "So . . . are you satisfied that your lover is to keep his head, after all?"

She returned his stare steadily. "Do you have the paper from the Viceroy?"

With a negligent flip of his hand, he indicated a desk beside the wall, upon which rested a curled parchment.

Lark scanned its contents and, satisfied, carefully rolled up the document and slid it into her skirt pocket.

With the black fire in his eyes burning bright, Sebastian reached out a hand and caressed the slim line of Lark's jaw. "And now, my little rebel colleen . . . I believe you have something for me."

For a moment the ability to speak seemed to abandon Lark, so that the treacherous words dooming the efforts of an army, the dream of a nation, could not be formed upon her lips.

Fiercely Sebastian grasped her by the neck, throttling her, and then produced a knife from his waistcoat and poised it under her chin. "Tell me, damn you! Tell me where and when the French are going to land! If you do not, I swear I'll slice your throat in half. And your *lover*," he went on, cruelly drawing a drop of blood with the tip of his weapon, "he is not yet out of the Castle, you know. He can and *will* be detained here if you choose not to meet your obligation to me."

Lark swallowed and felt the knife blade prick again, causing a trail of blood to flow down to soak her velvet collar. The pain of it was not so great, really, she reasoned. Much more could be endured. Indeed, if only Christopher were safe and away, his life secure, she would allow the tinker to move his ruthless hand and spill her blood before she would speak the words of betrayal against the United Irish.

She closed her eyes and prayed for forgiveness. "Bantry Bay . . . day after tomorrow." The words were nothing more than a few scant, strangled breaths.

O'Keefe released her. Then he shouted out a victory cry, raising a fist and shaking it several times. He laughed as well. "I shall tell that bastard, that debauched whoreson Buck Infamy, of the news before I tell anyone else! I shall cram the information down his bloody, despicable throat and hope he chokes to death upon it!"

Her nerves stretched to the breaking point, Lark yearned to flee this gloating madman and find Christopher before he departed the Castle. Drawing herself up, she said, "Now that our business is conducted, I shall bid you good-bye."

At once Sebastian turned upon her, his flushed face breaking into another sly grin. "Oh, nay, nay, my naive colleen. You shall not go on your merry way— at least, not yet."

"What do you mean?" she demanded.

He raised his brows. "I do not yet know whether or not you have played me false. After all, I have gone to a great deal of trouble to meet my end of our arrangement. Surely you don't believe I'd simply allow you to walk away from me now. Besides, you would only run to your agent and tell him the plot was spoiled, and the rebels would abort it. I would be made the fool either way."

Staring at his glittering eyes and realizing his relentlessness, Lark lunged for the door, but before she had managed two steps he seized her hair. Twisting it around his hand, he jerked her backward against his chest.

"You will be taken to Kilmainham, my love, and detained there until what you have told me has come to pass," he told her, smiling grimly.

He opened the door and barked orders to the sentry, releasing Lark only when the other man had her arms firmly pinioned. She was summarily pushed into another room, and though she struggled to free herself, the sentry could not be evaded. He pushed her to the floor and clapped manacles upon her wrists, and when she spat at him, he slapped her mouth. Dazed, she felt herself propelled out the door and into a small, dark courtyard, where a soldier astride a caparisoned horse awaited them. In his hands he held the reins of two other mounts.

With no gentleness, Lark found herself tossed atop the saddle of one, and she cried out in pain when the heavy iron bands of the fetters bit into her flesh. Her lip throbbed where the sentry had struck her, and the bitter cold of winter whipped her body until she shivered. Adding to the general misery, a gray drizzle began to fall.

"Giddap!"

Her horse's bridle was jerked forward as the sentry towed it from the courtyard. In a flurry of flashing hooves Lark and her wardens departed the looming Castle. She nearly lost her seat as they wheeled sharply to the right, for the unwieldiness of the manacle chains disturbed her balance and the stirrup straps were too long for her feet to reach.

The sentries proceeded at a fast clip, wending their way among countless elegant carriages leaving the trial, some of them stalled in tangled traffic. All around them coachmen exchanged curses, lashed their whips across stubborn haunches, and bawled out commands. The lanterns posted on the equipages created a jagged line of amber light down the narrow avenue, and Lark searched in vain for the marquess's coach, thinking to scream out a plea to him. She wondered if Christopher would even be informed of her whereabouts. How easily she could be incarcerated in Kilmainham and then forgotten, one of many nameless souls squatting upon filthy straw in that place of terrible gloom.

Forcing down panic, she attempted to get her bearings in the lamplit avenues; she saw St. Catherine's Church just ahead, which told her they had turned into Thomas Street.

On either side of her horse, the sentries were chuckling, sharing some ribald joke. A group of pedestrians, shadowy forms in the night, were exchanging boisterous jests as well, and somewhere near, a young man drunkenly sang a naughty tune. In desperation, Lark opened her mouth to call out for help. Before she could take a breath, however, a sudden, forceful explosion ripped the air.

She screamed in fright. The horses were no less startled and, in a flash, shied in three different directions. Another explosion followed, and another, each popping like intermittent musket fire down the street, further terrorizing the half-crazed horses. Glass flew everywhere, and Lark felt slivers of it pelt her face and hands. Attempting to protect herself, she leaned over the neck of her fleeing steed, clutched its mane with her fettered hands, and squeezed her knees tightly about its sides, knowing a tumble to the glass-strewn cobbles would be disastrous.

Somewhere she heard the sentries shouting, but amidst the darkness and bedlam she could see no sign of them. Wild and unguided, her horse went of its own accord, the bridle reins trailing, nearly tripping the rangy bay in its mad, undisciplined gallop.

Hardly believing her good fortune, but fully aware of how precarious was its continuance, Lark struggled to master the steed. Jostled and off balance, keeping her seat only by dint of will, she managed to bend down and slide both bound hands over the straining, sweating hide of the horse's shoulder. Then, though half-blinded by the wind-whipped mane, she managed to capture a dangling rein. She twisted it through her fingers and forcibly turned the horse down the nearest shadowy alleyway. As she rode helter-skelter through a maze of secretive streets, guiding her horse through their darkest portions, she smiled.

Then, silently, she blessed every last one of the pranksters of Trinity University, who seemed to have a penchant for blowing up street lamps and throwing Dublin into cloaking darkness.

25

Finally managing to bring the hard-mouthed nag under control, Lark kept to the darkest, most convoluted streets, pulling the horse into alleyways or courtyards whenever she heard approaching hooves. Once, too close for safety, she heard the furious voice of one of the sentries as he questioned a late night stroller. She guided her horse beneath a bridge and crouched low over its neck, praying the beast would not snuffle or paw and attract the soldier's ear.

At last, secure in the knowledge that she had managed to slip from the sentries' grasp, Lark quickened her pace and, avoiding the main roads, made for the obscure country lanes beyond the boundaries of Dublin. Over miles of rain-soaked earth and rippling puddles she went, pushing the tiring horse with relentless heels. The bands of her manacles cut viciously into her wrists as she employed the reins, and the bitter wind nearly flayed her alive with its damp, whistling gusts. But she had a mission to accomplish, and nothing would deter her from its completion.

Hours had slipped away. By now, she despaired, Sebastian O'Keefe would have done his damage and doomed the rebel plan to ruin. All she could do was admit her folly and hope the Faery Thorn agent could salvage the situation from disaster. Through his aid and judgment, perhaps the doomful course she had set in motion could be halted somehow.

She only prayed he would be there.

The flagging horse stumbled upon the muddy ground, hardly able to see its way even when the moon flirted coyly with the clouds and scattered its pale glitter across the road. In spite of the eerie surroundings, the night noises of the remote countryside were comfortingly familiar to her ear, and when she heard the rollicking crash of the sea, she knew her destination loomed near.

At last, in the distance, she discerned the shape of an ancient tree, its boughs creating silver zigzags against the brooding, starlit sky. Beyond, the cliff face jutted out over the sea like the rough-hewn chin of a giant, fiercely overlooking the black horizon.

Pray God, let him be there.

She pushed her laboring mount onward over the moss-slick terrain, then drew it up beneath the grove of stunted sycamores. Dismounting proved awkward with her bound hands, and she could only tumble from the saddle and fall hard upon the ground. She struggled to stand and ran toward the meeting place, desperate to relay her catastrophe. Looking up through the strands of damp hair plastered to her face, she saw the Faery Thorn's rigid outline and beneath its branches . . . a familiar dark figure.

He seemed to tower above the earth, more than

ever a part of the wild face of nature, but, oh . . . how
welcome he was tonight! Beyond dignity, she tripped
toward him, breathless, her shoes slipping in the mud.

He stood waiting, unmoving, his stalwart frame
defying the riotous wind, his cape whirling around his
faceless form. As always, he inspired a respectful
fear, and Lark faltered a bit. Tremulous and discomposed, she stared at him a few seconds and then,
mustering courage, stepped forward to meet him.

"The French are sailing toward Bantry Bay . . .
twelve thousand of them, transported in thirty-five
ships! They'll be landing day after tomorrow. . . ." Her
voice came so breathless, the words were barely more
than a series of gulps, and she had to swallow once or
twice in order to continue. "But I've betrayed us all!
Several hours past, to save another's life, I repeated the
dispatch to a man named Sebastian O'Keefe, a British
spy." Brashly she stepped closer and spoke with agonizing honesty. "Deliver me to the rebel leaders, if you
will, let them judge me as they may, but you must go
now and warn them that the plan is in jeopardy."

For several seconds the agent neither spoke nor
moved. Around him the wind howled like a banshee,
and the moon lent an icy silver sheen to the landscape, yet Lark could still not see the eyes that
regarded her so fiercely. She could only feel them like
sword points upon her face.

Then, in an extraordinary gesture, the agent raised
his hands and put them upon his hood. In that second
Lark realized they were not gloved, but devoid of
their usual black leather. She watched them move
slowly and deliberately to draw back the covering
from his head. The moon's rays fell fully upon his
hair, his brow, his nose, his mouth. . . .

The world spun, came loose from its axis, and Lark swayed with it, falling back.

Her companion reached out and drew her toward him with a strong hand. "Do not swoon at my boots, Faery Queen. I'm no apparition, only the usual cohort you meet beneath this tree—though tonight I nearly missed you. Damned inconvenient time for a trial, eh?"

Too stunned to speak, Lark merely gaped at him for a few seconds more. Then, reassured by his tender smile, she threw herself against his chest and held him tightly, delirious with relief. She wondered how she could not have known, not have sensed his identity long ago. Then she wondered if, in some obscure part of her consciousness, she always had.

"Oh, Christopher! I've ruined us!"

He grasped her arm and drew her back, his voice urgent. "What have you done? Tell me exactly."

She gazed up into the face she loved so well, drawing courage. "I received the dispatch earlier today from my brother Virgil—the man you found hiding in my chamber—"

"Indeed?" Christopher's voice held mild chagrin. "In that case, I don't feel so bad having let him off with his nose intact." He removed his cloak and threw it over Lark's shivering shoulders. "Go on."

"I was certain you were going to be convicted and hanged," she continued, feverishly attempting to make him understand. "You expressed such pessimism yourself when I visited you in gaol. And the newspapers were full of the talk of hanging. Even your father thought they would pass a guilty verdict. I grew desperate. And then it suddenly occurred to me that I possessed considerable bargaining power. Even while the trial was in progress I met with Sebastian, knowing how vital my information would be to the scoundrel. When he assured me the Viceroy would be willing to trade my dispatch for your life, I—"

She lowered her head, then raised it again with sudden defiance. "I traded the date and landing site of the French troops to save you. In exchange, Sebastian gave me a document from the Viceroy, guaranteeing the staying of your execution. When you were found innocent I knew he hadn't played me false."

She paused to take a breath. "He planned to keep me detained at Kilmainham until the French troops landed. Fortunately, I escaped the sentries *en route*."

"Lark," Christopher said quietly, "the Viceroy is not presently in Dublin. He left yesterday for the country."

Her jaw sagged. "But your verdict . . ."

"I spoke briefly last eve with the Lord Chancellor, and reminded him that I've been loyally providing the government with information on the rebel activities for months."

At her gasp of surprise, he explained, "All with the knowledge of Beauchamp Harvey, of course. We fed the Chancellor valid but inconsequential tidbits when it suited our purpose. In spite of my rather unconventional charitable work, he assumed I was true to the government by virtue of my title and my father's good name. In the end, with a bit of cajoling, he decided I was more valuable alive than dead." He smiled ruefully. "Poor judge of character, wouldn't you say?"

Christopher took her chin in his hand. "I fear you got nothing for your bargain, my love," he said soberly. "Nothing at all."

Lark lowered her eyes, utterly ashamed, able to think of no words to express the depth of her remorse.

"I appreciate your sacrifice, Lark. But I would

never have agreed to it, even were my neck circled by the hangman's noose and threatened with the blade. You know that, don't you?"

She nodded.

Running a hand through his hair, Christopher pondered their predicament. "I wonder what Sebastian has done with the information. Perhaps—" Breaking off, he quickly drew a pistol from his belt.

Alarmed, Lark followed the direction of his gaze, scanning the eerie landscape. Upon the ridge a solitary figure strolled toward them, his dark shape blending so entirely into the darkness that only the most vigilant eye would have noticed it. Frightened, she glanced at Christopher, but he stood almost relaxed as he waited for the visitor to join them.

"I thought I might find the two of you here," O'Keefe said when he had come within speaking distance. "You've made it convenient for me, at least."

"I do what I can to oblige you, Sebastian," Christopher said sarcastically as he lowered his pistol.

"Your efforts at obliging me have always cost you little. A bit of money and influence thrown here and there to ease a guilty conscience . . . bah! What are those things compared to that which you robbed me of?"

Glancing from one fierce face to the other, Lark wondered if Christopher would now reveal the truth to the bitter, deluded young man, inform him that he was a bastard, an heir to nothing.

He did not but inquired instead, "Whom have you told of the French landing, Sebastian?"

"Since you ask, I wasted no time informing a certain gentleman who is closely connected with the Viceroy," O'Keefe boasted before glancing at Lark. "Unluckily, my little red-haired rebel managed to escape her guards. I had no doubt she would run here. I've known of these meetings for some time—you'd be astounded to learn the number of informants within your own precious brotherhood. Of course, I could have saved myself a deal of trouble had my aim been sharper during your last meeting. But as ever, dear brother, I found you a difficult bane to remove."

"Perhaps you haven't applied yourself sufficiently."

This insolently delivered charge seemed to pique Sebastian's temper. Slowly, with his eye on Christopher's lowered pistol, he slid a hand inside his cloak and withdrew a weapon of his own. With trepidation, Lark stepped back out of the line of fire, watching in horror as Sebastian raised his gun and targeted Christopher's chest.

"You realize that I can allow neither you nor Mistress Ballinter to leave here tonight," he said. "Before morning you would have spread the word, and the rebel plan would be scrapped while some alternate scheme was speedily devised. I stand to gain much by the uncovering of this invasion. Indeed, 'twill earn me my fortune. And I shall not see it spoiled . . . not at any cost."

"You and I have a private score to settle, Sebastian," Christopher stated. "It seems the time has come to see it out."

"Indeed it does. And I shall enjoy it, for I've always despised you. Despised you for what you were, what you had, what you stole from me."

"Perhaps I should be flattered by your intensity of feeling," Christopher said. Then, in an attempt at level-headedness, he added, "Your unforgiveness has lasted a lifetime, Sebastian. Perhaps 'tis time to set it aside before disaster falls."

"Nay, I've grown too accustomed to it. But, perhaps

I shall leave you puzzling over a possibility ere we begin to settle the score." His voice held a lazy taunt. "The gentleman I informed of the French landing was far into his cups tonight. Frankly, I've been wondering if the bastard was lucid enough to comprehend what I told him and pass it on. Perhaps your secret only fell upon deaf ears, and still rests here"—he brandished the pistol—"between the three of us. If 'tis true, then you would have to kill me, dear brother, to insure the success of your cause. Who will die here tonight?"

Sebastian swung his pistol with deadly intent in Lark's direction. "How would it feel, do you think, Chris, if I took from you a woman you value, just as you took my mother from me?"

As Sebastian sighted Lark at the end of his gun barrel, so did Christopher target O'Keefe, pointing the weapon squarely at his brother's heart.

The dark one laughed again. "Nay, Chris, as I said ere now, you do not have the stomach to take my life. That soft regard you have for me would stay your finger upon the trigger."

"Don't misjudge me, Sebastian. I've called you my brother just as if you'd been born such, and my forbearance of your bitterness has endured from boyhood to manhood. But you've exhausted it tonight."

"Then it appears we have reached the end of a relationship that has done little more than try us both. We've competed on every sort of field together over the years, haven't we? And you've always been the winner. But we have not yet enjoyed a contest of nerve. Shall we indulge ourselves?"

"Don't do this, Sebastian!" Christopher commanded, his pistol no less steady, no less determinedly aimed. "For God's sake, do not!"

In that paralyzing second, Lark viewed the scene as if detached. The ghostly landscape, the groaning Faery Thorn, and the two fierce men were surely of some terrible dream from which she would awaken before long. But, too clearly, she saw the silver light glinting off the pistol aimed at her and glinting off the metal in Christopher's hand.

Spurred by instinct, she lunged for the ground, throwing her body across the cold, soggy earth. Her fall lasted aeons, it seemed, suspended within time's hold. Simultaneously, out of the corner of her eye, she saw two flashes, one a mere split second behind the next. The resounding cracks that accompanied them were enough to make her scream.

When she dared look up, she saw one man felled, sprawled flat upon the earth.

Across from him, the wind whisked away the curl of smoke from Christopher's pistol, and he stood frozen for a moment, no less still than some ancient stone warrior carved from the cliff. At last, his eyes never straying from the body, he lowered his arm so that the pistol pointed at the serpentine roots of the Faery Thorn.

Quivering with shock, Lark watched him walk to his brother's side, kneel down, and reach to touch Sebastian's neck. He uttered some word she could not catch and looked up toward the sky, the handsome features twisted with sorrow. Then he bowed his head and put one hand over his eyes.

Around him the frigid wind quieted from howl to whimper, while the moon covered her nudity with cloud shreds again. And surely, Lark thought, the Irish faeries, if they gazed down from their frosted boughs, shook their heads at human folly.

26

They traveled through the wild and bitter night, Christopher leading the horse bearing the body of his brother. He spoke not at all. Following behind him, Lark watched the implacable outline of his shoulders, which, since he had given her his cloak, were bereft of outerwear in the cold drizzle. She knew he must be half-frozen, and earlier she had made a gesture to remove Sebastian's surtout so that he might have the warmth but found herself stayed with one curt word.

Afterward she made no effort to speak to her husband at all, leaving him alone to suffer his grief.

"I'm taking you to Reverend Kenny's," he informed her a while later as the horses tentatively picked their way along the dark paths. "I'd rather not leave you to the estate or anywhere else you might be found. If Sebastian's contact was sober enough to have his wits about him, his men may be searching for you even now. As soon as we arrive, I'll send

Reverend Kenny's servant with a message for Beauchamp Harvey, explaining all that has happened tonight."

And then he was quiet again, never pausing once in their trek across the boggy, treacherous ground.

When they arrived at the modest stone house of Reverend Kenny, Christopher found a tool to cut loose Lark's manacles and quickly cleaned her wounds and disinfected them, all with a detached solemnity. The housekeeper kindly offered to lay out Sebastian's body, but Christopher refused, requesting only that she bring him a few necessary items so that he might do it himself.

For a while Lark hovered in the doorway of the little sitting room, watching mutely, uncertain what to do or say, declining the housekeeper's offer of escort to the guest bedchamber. Christopher said nothing to her, nor made any sign to acknowledge her presence. With forlorn eyes she watched his dutiful hands pull the blood-soaked shirt from Sebastian's torso and replace it with one of Reverend Kenny's clean ones.

When he and the clergyman spoke in low tones, making arrangements for the burial, she went to the tiny bedchamber alone, the hem of her mud-stained skirts dragging like a beleaguered emerald flag tattered from battle. Too exhausted to do more than pull off her shoes, she lay down on the bed, not bothering to turn back the white coverlet, scarcely feeling the discomfort of her damp stockings and hair.

Staring up at the low-beamed ceiling where the fire in the grate created designs of shadow and light, she sighed, the burden of regret no less weighty than a stone in her breast. What catastrophe she had wreaked upon all she held dear! None had been spared—not Christopher, not Virgil or Jerome. Even Sebastian, who had deceived her to the end, lay dead. Of the French forces sailing purposefully toward Bantry Bay, she could not bear to think, fearing that Sebastian's contact had already begun to deploy British troops to the landing site. How many would be slain as a result of her act of treachery?

And would Christopher forgive her?

The door latch opened and closed so quietly that Lark hardly heard it click. Her husband walked in, his heels muffled on the carpet, his movements noiseless as he crossed the room. She followed his every gesture with full, despairing eyes, watching as he removed the pistol from his belt and dropped it on a chair.

Because of me, he had to use that deadly tool tonight . . . slay his brother. . . .

Lark sat up slowly. The modest chamber seemed to have shrunk with her husband's presence, accentuating the silence between them, a silence that had somehow seemed less tense in the spacious outdoors. Shrugging out of the black jacket and waistcoat he had worn at the trial, the earl walked to the washstand and bent to splash his face. Lark noticed the smears of red brown staining his sleeves and cuffs. Sebastian's blood.

She slid her legs over the side of the bed and stood up, yearning to say something, anything, to break the terrible hush but finding no words to express the depth of her sorrow.

After sluicing water onto his face once more, then rolling up his cuffs and washing his hands thoroughly, Christopher took a clean linen towel and dried, though his fair hair was still damp at the temples.

When he was done, he went to secure the window sash, which was slightly cracked and permitting whistling drafts to blow inside the room. The candles that had been fluttering in their holders stilled, their tranquil flames pointing upward.

"There's only a hour or so until dawn," Christopher commented, staring out the window, the weight of his troubles evident in his tone. "I must leave then, see what damage has been done, if any, by Sebastian's treachery. If the secret is out, British forces will be converging upon Cork and Bantry Bay within hours. Reverend Kenny's servant is already on his way with a message to Harvey. I will likely have to take command of my regiment as soon as I arrive in Dublin."

He grew quiet again, his expression pensive as he gazed toward a horizon that would soon be tinged with red. Lark had little doubt as to the thoughts occupying his mind. By his clamped jaw and the bleak lines etching his face, she knew he agonized not only over the fate of the rebel plan, but over his brother's death, over the fact that he had slain him with his own hand. The justifications for the deed would not matter to him. Regardless of their differences, regardless of the bitterness stemming from one innocent act of childhood, Christopher had loved the Gypsy lad, and his loss would be difficult to bear.

Unable to abide the strain of their distance any longer, she pattered in her damp stockings across the space dividing them. Halting a pace away, she opened her mouth to speak, then closed it, for words refused to come. She realized she was afraid, afraid that the tenacious but often battered love she shared with Christopher had been another victim of tonight's tragedy, slain by her mistakes.

Unable to hesitate a second longer, but too tormented with love and grief to speak reasonably, she reached out instead and encircled her husband's waist from behind with shivering, needful arms. With a desperate frown she leaned her head against the smooth curve of his back and whispered, "Whatever remorse you suffer tonight, Christopher, it can be no greater than mine. . . ."

For a moment he responded not at all, but she felt his chest heave and the muscles of his belly constrict. Then he took her fingers and entwined them in his, and they shared thoughts that, because they were so obviously in tune, did not need to be spoken aloud.

While they watched dawn brighten the faraway point where sea met firmament, even while the rest of the earth remained wrapped in its night quilts, Christopher's hands tightened on Lark's. And then he turned about to face her. For a long while he looked intently into her eyes and she into his. His arms around her hips, he drew her near, holding her tightly to him. Then he bent his head and found her lips.

He kissed her with hunger, twisting his mouth upon hers, his breaths short and hard. His hands moved to her hair and loosened it before moving over her body from shoulders to hips in long, reckless strokes. Pressing the small of her back, he arched her frame to fit his, pulled their hips flush, trailed his warm lips along the length of her throat until she quivered with equal need. In frantic haste she responded, returning his kisses in full proportion, her hands ranging feverishly, with remembered knowledge, over his firm male body.

There was to be no languor, no patience, in their coming together again. His lovemaking was needfully bold, elemental. Lowering her to the floor, one arm braced, the other supporting her back, he bothered not with a thorough undressing. He had immediate need of her, of the solace she could give him, of the bliss of forgetfulness her body could provide against the sharpness of his pain this night.

He wanted her to know that her selfless but misjudged act, and his brother's death, did not diminish what he felt for her. Quickly, undeniably, he would heal the sorrow between them, show her he absolved her of any blame, for he knew how destructive guilt could be. He had lived with it long, and he would do all he could to save Lark from its gnawing hold.

After releasing his breeches, he fastened his mouth upon hers with loving purpose, murmuring her name again and yet again, avowing his love. Fierce but silent, his consummation rocked her, rocked them both, so that in the aftermath of tumult, peace came more sublimely.

A while later Christopher leaned his back against a chair, then drew Lark between his raised knees, her spine supported by his solid chest. He put her hand atop the hard apex of his knee and with his own hand tenderly rubbed her knuckles.

"There are things we should speak about," he said quietly. "Things I probably should have told you long ago, but . . ." He shook his head and leaned back against the chair. "I felt I had a duty to Sebastian, I've always felt I did. 'Twas difficult to abandon it even for wisdom's sake."

"Christopher—"

But he interrupted her protest by squeezing her hand. "Nay, Lark. Let me speak of this. I shall start by telling you of Sebastian's motives. He suspected your uncle of conspiracy, assumed it was he delivering the rebel dispatches. It was his initial intent, I think, to befriend you both and insinuate himself into your confidence by posing as a harmless, sentimental countryman. I got wind of his plan only through a slip he made in one of our more . . . heated conversations. Unfortunately, the significance of it struck me too late, and though I rode hell-bent to your cottage the night of Jerome's death, I found Sebastian had been there before me. Obviously having failed to get the information he sought from Jerome, he had lost his temper and killed him in a struggle."

He paused. "When I found your uncle dead, I could have accused Sebastian, of course, had him hauled before a magistrate and tried for murder. But I feared questions would arise that would lead to suspicions of my—and your—connections with the United Irish."

He idly touched the *claddagh* ring he had placed upon Lark's finger on their marriage day and smoothed the gem with his thumb. "But, most of all, I found I could not condemn my brother to hanging." He swallowed. "And yet, tonight . . ."

His words ceased as he struggled with emotion, with remembrance of the tragedy beneath the Faery Thorn. Lark gently pulled his head to hers in understanding of the pain, in acknowledgment of the sacrifice he had had to make for her and for the cause they both believed greater than themselves.

"As for the fire," he continued a moment later, "'tis my guess he started it simply to remove you from the cottage long enough to search for any documents you may have hidden."

"'Twas you who rescued me," she whispered, clenching his forearm with her fingers as if to hold him with her forever. "Always my rescuer. . . ."

In answer he bent his head to hers and rested his cheek against the smoothness of her hair. "You have rescued me as well . . . though from different demons."

As they sat on, both thinking of the impending, wrenching separation but loath to speak of it, Christopher said, "Though I sought to keep you safe from his impredictable temper, and from his more . . . personal attentions, I don't believe Sebastian ever intended to harm you, now I reflect upon it. You were too important a link to the information he needed. And . . . I believe he cared for you genuinely. Quite a great deal more than he ever cared for anyone else."

With sadness, Lark remembered the tinker's desperate words. *I'm mad for you, Lark . . . I've never wanted to offer my name, my life, to a woman ere now. . . . Truthfully, I've never had anyone to love before.*

"It was I he wanted out of the way," Christopher continued. "For I stood between him and what he wanted—" He smiled grimly. "Or what he thought he wanted."

"And yet you never told him what you'd learned about his true beginnings from the squire's letter. . . ."

"Tell him he was some Gypsy's bastard? He would have despised me more. Besides . . . maybe he needed something to believe in . . . all of us do, don't we?"

They fell into a ruminative silence for a while, and Lark put her hand upon his thigh, rubbing it in an absent but intimate fashion. Then, with bowed head, she murmured, "I don't know quite how to say this . . . how—how to tell you of my regret. That I could have accused you of my uncle's death—"

He put his fingers over her lips, staying further words. "Don't speak of it more. You had my forgiveness the moment the accusation was made." Then he glanced up at the window. "We've only a little time left together before I must go."

Leaning back once more against his chest, Lark tilted her head and looked into the sober depths of her husband's eyes, prompting him to lower his lips to meet hers again, kiss her with the all the anguished thoroughness of a man departing for war.

"I'm fearful for you, Christopher," she said a moment later against his mouth. "If the French land, fierce fighting will begin. 'Twill be the start of a long and bloody revolution in which many will die. And if the French don't land . . . what then? What will our lives be?"

"As long as we're together, does it matter, my sweet?" he asked softly. "You surely know that regardless of the outcome of this rebellion, I'll move heaven and earth to keep Kildare for us. I'd like to see its old halls filled with children. Would you protest too much if I asked you to oblige me?" He spoke suggestively against her ear, then caressed her arms reassuringly. "Even if worse comes to worst, your French is excellent and mine is passable. I believe we could manage to be tolerably happy exiles in Paris, don't you? France can always use another surgeon, and Virgil will be glad to have you near. If you asked him nicely, perhaps he'd even manage to overcome his dislike of your arrogant husband."

Despite his attempt to ease her fears, Lark clasped

desperate hands around Christopher's neck, knowing that in a moment more he would stand, put on his redingote, take up his pistol, and stroll out the door. "I feel as if we're standing upon a precipice," she whispered with a dry and tightened throat. "I feel as if we're staring out at a vast, unknown darkness, a future of which we cannot be certain. I'm frightened, my darling, so frightened. . . ."

He laid his fine, strong hands upon her shoulders and squeezed them as if to restore her courage, then moved his arms down and embraced her fiercely. "'Tis true that the future is unsettled—our own and Ireland's. But if we *are* standing upon a precipice, my love, we stand upon it together. And no matter which course history takes, I shall be at your side."

He put his lips to her ear and closed his eyes. His whispering voice held vehement conviction. "I won't let you fall. . . ."

Afterword

On December 22, 1796, the last great French invasionary force ever to set sail for the British Isles lay off the coast of Ireland, eager to land. But beneath strong winds and squalls of snow, over half the fleet departed from the flagship *Indomptable,* upon whose deck Wolfe Tone himself paced. By the following day the storm had grown so mighty that the admiral ordered the *Indomptable* to cut her cables and flee, leaving behind fourteen ships, the French staff, and Tone, still with desperate hopes of landing.

Their hopes were not to be realized, however, for on December 27 the storm became a hurricane.

Thwarted, the dwindling fleet turned back for France, her expectations for victory defeated not by human blunder, but by Nature herself.

AVAILABLE NOW

ORCHIDS IN MOONLIGHT by Patricia Hagan

Bestselling author Patricia Hagan weaves a mesmerizing tale set in the untamed West. Determined to leave Kansas and join her father in San Francisco, vivacious Jaime Chandler stowed away on the wagon train led by handsome Cord Austin—a man who didn't want any company. Cord was furious when he discovered her, but by then it was too late to turn back. It was also too late to turn back the passion between them.

TEARS OF JADE by Leigh Riker

Twenty years after Jay Barron was classified as MIA in Vietnam, Quinn Tyler is still haunted by the feeling that he is still alive. When a twist of fate brings her face-to-face with businessman Welles Blackburn, a man who looks like Jay, Quinn is consumed by her need for answers that could put her life back together again, or tear it apart forever.

FIREBRAND by Kathy Lynn Emerson

Her power to see into the past could have cost Ellen Allyn her life if she had not fled London and its superstitious inhabitants in 1632. Only handsome Jamie Mainwaring accepted Ellen's strange ability and appreciated her for herself. But was his love true, or did he simply intend to use her powers to help him find fortune in the New World?

CHARADE by Christina Hamlett

Obsessed with her father's mysterious death, Maggie Price investigates her father's last employer, Derek Channing. From the first day she arrives at Derek's private island fortress in the Puget Sound, Maggie can't deny her powerful attraction to the handsome millionaire. But she is troubled by questions he won't answer, and fears that he has buried something more sinister than she can imagine.

THE TRYSTING MOON by Deborah Satinwood

She was an Irish patriot whose heart beat for justice during the reign of George III. Never did Lark Ballinter dream that it would beat even faster for an enemy to her cause—the golden-haired aristocratic Lord Glassmeade. A powerfully moving tale of love and loyalty.

CONQUERED BY HIS KISS by Donna Valentino

Norman Lady Maria de Courson had to strike a bargain with Saxon warrior Rothgar of Langwald in order to save her brother's newly granted manor from the rebellious villagers. But when their agreement was sweetened by their firelit passion in the frozen forest, they faced a love that held danger for them both.